Zein:
The Homecoming

A Novel by
Graham J Wood

███ Clink
███ Street

Published by Clink Street Publishing 2015

Copyright © Graham Wood 2015

First edition.

ISBN: 978-1-910782-01-9
Ebook: 978-1-910782-02-6

In loving memory of George Rodney Birchall, a great man who brought much joy and richness to many lives and will be sorely missed by his family and friends.

Contents

Prologue

Kabel watched the sea crash onto the rocks of the picturesque Cornish retreat. Gemma snuggled into him on the coastal bench they had stumbled upon during their visit to this famous beauty spot. *Lands' End. Only the humans could give such a finite name to such a wild and majestic place,* he thought.

He saw Tyson and Amelia laughing as they messed around in the cool autumn breeze, each trying to be the last one to touch the other in a never ending game. It was good to see Tyson with a smile on his face, not the wild, hooded-eyed angry man who threatened unimaginable acts of wanton violence on Zylar; the man who was responsible for taking his mother when he was defeated at the Battle of the Southern Palace.

As for Kabel, his thoughts were on the delicate features of his adopted sister Delilah...he missed her deeply. He hid his true feelings from the majority of people; as the newly adorned Lord Chancellor of the Earth Zein Colony he could not afford to display his wrath in the eyes of the human public and unremitting intrusion of their press hounds. No, his role was to influence, cajole and lead his people if they were ever to return home. His attention was diverted to a huge wave that built and built as it approached the razor sharp rocks with their jewelled brooches of many limpets adorning the blackness of the ancient boulders. The wave reached a crescendo as its foaming mouth roared in and broke against the unmovable barrier, sending a fine spray high into the air. He felt Gemma cuddle into him more as the biting wind cut into them, quiet, unobtrusive, happy to have calmness and love in her life.

Amelia was venting her frustration as she attempted to catch Tyson and touch his shoulder to pass the game back to him and Tyson, using his magics, jumped up in the air and did a forward roll over her head to land behind her, wearing a wide grin on his face. Amelia spun round and stamped her foot in disapproval but she could never stay angry at her beloved for long and soon they were hugging each other, before Amelia, using her female wiles, touched his shoulder shouting 'You're it', at the top of her voice before running away. Tyson chased after her, still grinning.

Kabel stared into the sky, the clouds were low and it was likely to rain but that was not what was on his mind. He ached to see Zein, endless questions always in his thoughts, how many Zeinonians still lived, how did they survive the impact of reducing stocks of zinithium and the brutal attacks of the Pod, did they still dream of the Expeditionary Force's return after so many years? All this and more tortured his mind, day and night. He knew the burden of his role and wondered who carried that same weight of responsibility on Zein? How did he survive the endless pressure of knowing that if you made the wrong judgement call your friends, family and many lives would be at risk?

Whoever you are, I will find you and we will be one nation again, that I promise you, Kabel vowed, aware his half-brother would pick up his thought. Tyson, who had in the meantime caught

Amelia and was playfully struggling with the protesting girl, peered over her shoulder and his eyes found Kabel's. His eyes conveyed his agreement to Kabel but then they grew to a brilliant blue and his face twisted, only briefly, with a violence of retribution making Kabel catch his breath. In an instant it was gone, his blue eyes back to their normal hue and he continued with his game.

Kabel shuddered; his office carried many burdens but only one he could not control. Still shaken by what he had seen in Tyson he let his body and mind enjoy the experience of the scenic beauty in front of him. Zein, would have to wait for another day but soon, very soon it would be at the forefront of the life of every man, woman and child on this beautiful planet.

Chapter 1: Aeria Cavern

The shrill klaxon sounded, breaking the silence of the early morning. Tate Malacca groaned as the noise pulled him from his restless sleep.

Not again.

This was the third breach in the last week of the outer defences that protected the delicate zinithium powered Inner Perimeter Barrier. The Pod were not letting up. Rising from his makeshift, lumpy and inhospitable bunk, he rubbed his sleep filled eyes as he peered around him.

He pulled his worn boots on and picked up his two seckles which lay beside his temporary sleeping area, strapping his beloved long sword to his back and his photon blaster around his waist, both of which were well used with much action in their history. His bunk was in the main guard post that covered the entrance to the South Gate and around him others were tumbling out of their light or heavy sleeps, dependent on what nightmares they were experiencing. For the inhabitants of the Aeria Cavern, the last village city of Zein, nightmares were a common occurrence.

The door burst open, 'Lord Malacca, there is a breach near to the North Gate,' said the young soldier panting heavily. Tate looked at the tall freckle-faced teenager. He couldn't remember his name. *The soldiers were becoming younger and younger,* Tate thought. How many more men and women would they lose before there was no hope?

'Keep calm soldier, how many Pod?' asked Tate, keeping his voice low and even. He could not afford panic to entrench itself into his troops.

'Lots Sir, they just said lots,' replied the young soldier, screwing his eyes up in concentration as he tried to remember the message relayed via the antiquated intercom system.

Once they commanded the foremost technology, now they simply managed with what still worked. Their depleted mineral reserves struggled to maintain the Inner Perimeter Barrier and even their weapons had mainly regressed to seckles, old photon rifles and swords. Gone were the powerful photon shotguns and levitation tanks, the latter now standing, rusting on the surface of the planet.

Tate thought through the implications of the brief report. None of his options filled him with confidence. He knew the North Gate was not the most heavily guarded section as most of the troops were situated to the South and West Gates. It was there the community needed the greater protection due to their proximity to the larger and more accessible entrances to the Aeria Cavern.

The Aeria Cavern was the principal Zein mining settlement, which rested above the once richest seam of zinithium on the planet. In the days when the village cities on the surface prospered this was the largest permanent underground settlement that remained untouched by the winter and reflection periods. The city village was deep into the earth and four great ramp-ways were used to transport the massive mining trucks loaded with the precious ore out to the waiting villages on the surface. Each ramp-way was historically protected by four steel outer gates, North,

South, East and West, which through the decades closed during the brutal weather the winter and reflection periods brought. The Zeinonians sought the protection of this massive underground city village during these periods after collapsing the top storeys of their own city village buildings, intending them to be built back up to their previous glory at the start of the summer. Today the impressive outer steel gates were all but destroyed by neglect and carelessness, exposing the Inner Perimeter Barrier and huge internal gates to not just the remnants of the weather but also to attack. The gates were only at the four intersections to the ramp-ways as the rest of the city's perimeter was encased in rock and an inner lining of zinithium steel.

The weak Inner Perimeter Barrier was a sporadic shield that could not be relied upon and this only covered the actual entrances and barricades. Yes, the weakness was the entrances. Lose those and the city would fall. The Aeria Cavern was their last safe haven, the difference between survival and extinction.

'What's your name, soldier?'

'Bertrand Mallory, Sir, of the Blackstone clan,' said Bertrand proudly.

I should have guessed, Tate thought, noticing the tallness of the young man. *Is this all the once famed Blackstone clan can provide to support the perimeter; children!* He fumed silently.

The Blackstone clan kept very much to themselves now, not lifting a finger to help the other clans. They still formed the largest army after the Malacca clan but chose to remain behind their walls, mumbling their dissent. Not far behind them for intransience was the Changelings community. Always whispering, plotting and looking after their interests only.

'Who do we have stationed there?' said Tate, brushing away his irritation and knowing he should be able to answer this himself. Heck he was tired. Constant fighting and lack of sleep were having a major impact on his health. He pushed this all to one side and he dragged his bruised and battered youthful body out of the guard room closely followed by the young soldier.

'Prince Southgate, Sir,' answered the young soldier. Tate groaned. Of course, just what he needed, that fiery fool crowing about how brave he was. He had purposely placed the remnants of the Southgate forces to the North and East Gates to keep them out of his way.

Prince Southgate was the remaining hope for the Southgate clan. After his marriage to the young Cadence Fathom, Tate had hoped that supporting dependents would curb the prince's more excitable ways. It hadn't. If anything, it had triggered more irrational and impulsive behaviour which his young bride still struggled with.

Cadence was the oldest surviving Fathom. Her family had been nearly wiped out during one of the first Pod attacks and just Cadence, her younger feisty sister Eva, and youngest sister, Mia, had survived. Cadence had grown up with such responsibility, looking after Eva and Mia, coupled with her sadness at the loss of her parents, that her spirit was broken and when Taio Southgate began to show interest in her, it was not long before she fell under his spell.

Tate shook his head. Cadence put up with so much from the weak and bullying attitude of the vain prince that sometimes he had to hold his own tongue for fear that he would cause a split in the Inner Council. Any split in this most important civic body and the Aeria Cavern may fall due to the warring factions not working together. He could not let that happen, his own burden resting heavily on his shoulders. Fleetingly he felt the weight of his office and then he remembered Eva and Mia, and he

felt re-energised. Cadence's spirit might be broken, but in
Eva and Mia they carried the spirit of the entire Fathom
clan. The young sisters were irrepressible. No one could
tame or control them, not even him. In his heart he didn't
want to, they were what Zein needed. Spirit. Fight. If
Cadence represented the past horrors, it was Eva and Mia
who stood for the promise in the future.

As his thoughts drifted, around him the squads on
guard were rushing to the barricades. He caught some of
the soldiers' looks as they pulled on their red tunics and
slung photon rifles onto their weary shoulders – women,
men and children – pressganged onto the front line. Their
eyes displayed the fear and resignation they felt.

For a moment despair washed over him. His mind was
racked with guilt and his body ached from recent battles
and old injuries.

*Pull yourself together Malacca. If you let fear take over, the Zeinonians
would not last a week.*

'Sir, what are your orders?' The calm request came from
his right. It was Kron, the Captain of the Malacca clan,
who had fought with his father and now his allegiance
transferred to the youngest surviving male heir. The one
person he could rely upon in this madness. Tate took in
the eye patch on his left eye gouged out by one of the Pod
and the stump of half a left arm swinging casually at his
side. No, if he was the leader then Kron was the enforcer.
His eyes traversed to the gleaming machete that Kron
held loosely in his one good hand. How many hours did
he clean and sharpen the blade each night? Tate shivered,
probably too many to count. He never wanted to be on
the wrong side of Kron.

Tate turned his mind to the task at hand. He could not
leave the South Gate unguarded due to the risk that the
Pod usually attacked this entrance as it enabled them to

5

mass their numbers in the large access tunnel. There were five thousand men and women guarding the South Gate with the bulk of them resting in the barracks behind the barricades that were at each side of the enormous gates, ready to support any attack or breach, the remainder walking the numerous ramparts that sat above and around the gate, enabling the defenders to shoot into any advancing enemy.

The shift change happened over a week to ensure numbers were maintained. The number guarding never fell below five thousand; they could not take the risk of a successful attack by the Pod on their main entrance.

'Pull together five hundred of your best men Kron and some of the Tyther engineers,' said Tate. 'We are off to see if Prince Southgate needs reinforcements at the North Gate barricades.'

'Prince Southgate…' Kron spat out the name in disgust but then held his retort back after Tate gave him a warning look. He may agree with Kron in private but he couldn't let the young soldiers around them see the disrespect. Kron, with a grimace, hurried off to pull together the force. Everything was on a knife edge of uncertainty – food, raw materials, weapons and bravery.

Within a short period of time Kron's assembled force, climbed into a number of the gliders which connected each of the main sentry points. The doors shut with a barely perceptible whoosh and the zinithium propelled vehicles sped away clockwise, hovering over the steel encased tunnel. The journey was not a long one but sufficient for Kron to relax and remove the protective guard on his shortened arm. He flexed the muscles on his stump of an arm, sometimes he still thought he felt his non-existent fingers but then looked down at what was left of his arm below the elbow, a victim of the fangs of a fateful bite from an enraged Pod; he survived but the Pod's life ended shortly after. Kron looked around the glider's cabin reviewing the team he had pulled together. The team consisted of some of the most experienced fighters, but it was becoming harder and harder as the toll of the attacks reduced their ranks. For his part he didn't fear the Pod just saw them as the basis for his life. No Pod. No need for Kron. He had turned killing the Pod into an art form. Kron saw it as a battle of steel and guts against wild animals; to him peace was an uncertain world as he revelled in the violence and backs against the wall mentality.

The fierce looking warrior glanced across at Tate, and although his duty led him to follow the Malacca prince, what confused him was how much respect he held for the young royal. They had nothing in common; Kron's was brought up by uncaring sadistic parents in a small outlying cottage on the extremes of civilisation, and Tate enjoyed the splendour of the Malacca Royal Palace. He shook his head as he already knew the answer to his own question… it was simple, when they found their backs to the wall, there was only one leader who stepped forward to face the threat. Tate. He could see the worries the man carried and though Kron had sympathy for this crushing responsibility on such a young man, he knew without it there would be no Zeinonians left standing. Time and time again, Tate had saved them with his calmness and leadership.

The glider began to slow down from its tremendous speed as it passed one of the key gates. Kron pushed all thoughts to the back of his mind, placed his armour back onto his stub, with the spikes that he had himself driven into the material, dully shining in the lights of the tunnel, making his apparent handicap into a fearsome weapon.

The gliders swept past the East Gate, which bristled with men and weapons from the Tyther clan. The barricades and ramparts looked bleak and old. Tate shook his head slightly. It was just sheer guts keeping the Pod at bay.

They continued on their journey until they came to a halt at the North Gate barricades where the men climbed out. It was eerily silent outside the gate where hundreds of soldiers should have been patrolling.

What is going on!

Where were the Southgates? Tate screamed in his head, although his face remained emotionless.

'Sir,' said Kron pointing to a frightened young face, barely in his teens who stood trembling in a corner near the open door of the large steel encased sentry pill-box that housed the powerful photon machine guns; each main entrance had at least two of the remaining temperamental machine guns; sometimes they worked and sometimes they jammed. It was pot luck.

'Bloody ridiculous,' muttered Tate as he walked purposely across to the lad. He took in the old photon rifle he held in his hands and glanced into the pill-box and saw a mixture of women and similarly aged teenage lads behind the photon machine guns which poked out of their pre-ordained slits. He then looked behind the steel barricades that rose up behind the pill-box that covered the large expanse around the gates and he saw a few hundred soldiers, but they were dwarfed by the number of teenagers and women nervously holding makeshift old blasters and shotguns.

He surmised there were five hundred soldiers in total, when the barricades and barracks should be manned by over three thousand.

Women and kids! The stupid idiot has left women and children to guard one of the main gates. If the Pod had attacked here then…he tried to remain calm…as calm as he could. 'Okay soldier what is the status?' said Tate deciding that authority and leadership were required.

'T-h-h-e Pod have a-a-ttacked the corridor between the North and West Gate b-b-barricades Sir,' said the teenager, shaking with fear. Tate smiled warmly and placed a hand onto the boy's shoulders.

'You are doing an excellent job young man,' said Tate smiling encouragingly, 'Where did Prince Southgate go?'

'He took the main force in the gliders to see what has happened,' said the teenager.

Leaving one of the principal gates practically unguarded! Tate ground his teeth together in anger.

'Kron, leave a hundred of the regiment here to support these brave soldiers.' Kron pointed to a number of his group and they peeled off to support the gate and pill-box. The defenders smiled in relief. 'Let's go,' said Tate and the remainder of the force re-entered the gliders and set off down the tunnel.

The journey took more time than Tate remembered. The north to west part of the tunnel covered one of the largest lengths of corridor between the main gates. The tunnel was purposely engineered to be wide, enabling the Zeinonians to bring down the collapsed elements of the buildings prior to the winter and reception periods and the raw material from their mining operations up to the surface.

How could they break through the steel covered tunnel wall? he thought worriedly. It was the toughest metal known to Zein – made from iron ore and zinithium. The Blackstones' made the composite and the Tyther clan welded the steel sheets together – they had never been breached…until now it seems.

Flashes ahead signified that they had reached the battle and Tate ordered the driver to stop the leading glider, causing the other vehicles to stop, as they took their lead from the first glider. He turned to his second-in-command, who waited patiently; he had no doubts that the young royal would not be found wanting. Many battles fighting shoulder to shoulder had reinforced the gnarled soldier's expectations.

'Kron, form the soldiers into four columns. Tell them to hold their fire until I give the command. We don't want to be killing our fellow soldiers,' said Tate, his face tight with anticipation. Kron went to execute his Lord's orders.

The men formed the columns and Tate drew his seckles and flexed his muscles, his muscles rippling against the tight, red, battered body armour. He took a quick glance behind him and saw the experienced grim determination of his elite guard focused ahead. He started jogging towards the flashes ahead, his men following, their feet rhythmically thumping onto the steel floor as they ran after Lord Chancellor Tate Malacca.

The flashes began to grow in intensity and the noise of battle cascaded down the steel encased corridors. They turned a corner and were faced with an unbelievable sight. The bulk of the Southgate army were in hand-to-hand combat across the huge tunnel with many of the Pod, the seven foot creatures with shaggy dark blue hair and razor sharp claws that could scythe through body armour as it was paper, were pressing the soldiers back by their ferocity. At their feet were large numbers of lifeless bodies from the Southgate clan, whose spilt blood pooled into newly running mini tributaries throughout the tunnel.

Where had they all come from? Then he saw the answer to his question. In one of the sides of the tunnel there was a massive hole with steel curled up on the inside, where the Pod must have created the breech. Streaming through the hole was more and more of their hated enemy. Tate knew he had to seal the hole or the Pod would gain a foothold which would first threaten the North Gate and then the other gates, leaving the city protected only by the flimsy zinithium run Inner Perimeter Barrier and inadequate Inner Defence Wall.

'Kron, take one hundred men and the engineers and secure that hole,' he ordered the one man who could do such a thing. Kron didn't hesitate. He fired out orders and the battle hardened men selected moved within firing distance of the hole. The Pod hadn't noticed them, concentrating on the fierce combat with the Southgate soldiers. Kron lined up his men and they pulled out their photon rifles. Kron shouted an order.

One of the Pod, who was still some distance away, heard the shout over the noise of the battle and turned to look at the new arrivals. His face turned into a roar and his two sabre incisor teeth that jutted from the menacing mouth rose as he shouted a warning to his brethren. The Pod near him turned to see what the warning was about.

Kron wasted no time and organised the men into two rows of twenty-five and the rest in two columns behind them. On his order the men reached into their backpacks and pulled out a powerful zinithium powered rocket each, which they then fixed to the barrels of the rifles like a bayonet. He didn't want to use these precious remnants of their arsenal but he had no choice. On his command the first row dropped to their knees and the second row aimed high in the direction of the breech. The Pod saw the danger and charged the men.

The second row of soldiers fired and an arc of rocket propelled weapons sped towards the hole. When they hit, the multiple explosions threw the charging Pod off their feet, many dying. Arms and limbs were torn off the crazed beasts by the devastating explosives. The tunnel became full of smoke, like a thick London pea soup fog rolling in from the River Thames. Even with this killing field in front of him, Kron knew that the battle was only half won.

Tate led the rest of the soldiers in a charge against the melee in the tunnel. He assessed that there were around two thousand Pod covering the wide tunnel floor.

In advance of Kron, Tate and his men tore into the left flank of the Pod as they reeled from the first photon grenade strikes. Tate skilfully wielded the seckles that seemed to be glued to his hands. He evaded the vicious sweep of the clawed hands of his attackers by levitating slightly at key moments to alter his position. His red force-field pulsated from his body. Surrounding him were his troops, relying on the accuracy of their long swords or seckle and blaster to compensate for their weaker force-fields.

A shout from one of his men drew his attention to a Pod who had approached him from behind. Tate spun round to face the beast, raising his seckles in defence.

What he saw surprised him. The tall Pod was injured, the rage, so present on the Pods' faces absent. There was sadness in his eyes and his clawed hand reached out as if asking for mercy. The mouth drooped and the sabre-teeth rested unthreateningly out of the corners of his mouth. His bare chest heaved with exertion. Tate saw the wound in his side from the shrapnel caused by the grenades and the resultant free flowing green blood of the animal.

Tate dropped his seckles to his side in astonishment. The Pod began to make hand signals. 'What are you trying to tell me?' said Tate, blocking out the fighting around him. The Pod stamped his foot in frustration as he made the sign again, a circle and a finger gesture to firstly to Tate and then pointing to his chest. Suddenly, a shot whistled past Tate's ear and the creature's head was flung back and a mighty roar issued from his mouth. A new green gushing hole appeared in the Pod's shoulder and with one last desperate look at Tate, the Pod male lurched off back to the hole.

Kron shouted his next command. The soldiers in the front row stood and they replicated the firing sequence. The explosions ripped through the tunnel. The smoke billowed out further into the main fighting.

Tate looked around as the second blast of grenades decimated the Pod's ranks and the hole in the tunnel was nearly closed, the explosions bringing stone and rubble crashing down from the Pod-made opening. The Pod began to retreat.

He saw the manic grin of Taio Southgate, the twenty-five year old senior prince of the Southgate bloodline. Taio was chasing the fleeing Pod brethren and killing them where they stood with powerful cuts of his gold plated extra-long seckle – one of the heirlooms of the Southgates.

What was she doing here! Beside Taio was Jaida Blackstone. Ruthless, cold and killing with precision. She was also beautiful, tall and had a grace about her that would make a ballroom sway to her dancing. Why was a Blackstone with the Southgates? Had they reformed their alliance? He spotted members of the Blackstone Royal Guard supporting her and Myolon, the alpha male of the Changelings with his personal guard consisting of twenty. The Changelings were fighting as Roths and gouging the Pod with their horns, without holding back.

He made his way to them as he battled his attackers.

'Hi Tate, nice to see you joining in the fun,' said the grinning Taio, skilfully disembowelling one of the Pod who was covering the retreat.

'Why did you leave the North Gate post so lightly guarded?' said Tate, panting with the exertion of the violence, as he ducked a claw and then parried another with his seckle.

'Heck, they will be fine…the attack is here not there.' Annoyance crept into Taio's voice as he brought his wicked looking seckle crashing into an outstretched arm. Pod blood spurted from the separated limb, adding to the slick wetness of the gore of the slain.

Tate decided not to push it. He was conscious that Taio still had his main guard close by and he only had a small force and there would be a time to debate this properly at the next Inner Council meeting. He deactivated one seckle and thrust it into his body armour and with one fluid movement pulled the ancient sword from the scabbard on his back.

Two Pod launched their huge bodies at Tate; he leapt away from the vicious trajectory of their swinging claws and then skipped past both his attackers' now unbalanced position to dispatch them with two swings of the razor sharp sword, sending them to whatever afterlife they went to. He leaned on his sword to catch his breath.

'Tate! Behind you!' shouted Jaida. He pushed any thought of tiredness to the back of his mind and dropping into a crouch he swung his sword in a lethal arc into the side of a Pod who was attacking his seemingly unprotected back. The Pod let out an agonised scream and then Jaida, with relish, plunged her seckle through his heart. The Pod toppled over and lay still on the steel floor, resting on the bodies of his brethren, his face twisted in the pain of death.

Jaida offered Tate her hand, which, with a wry grin, he took and as he stood up, Jaida pushed her body against his and he could feel her hot breath on his face. Tate cursed as he felt his heart race and Jaida, as she apparently guessed what he was thinking, allowed a mocking smile to spread over her face. She cheekily pecked him on the cheek and then moved away.

Damn that woman.

A cheer rose from the defenders. The final remnants of the Pod had disappeared back through the reduced hole. Tate looked at the carnage in the tunnel. The Pod lay two and sometimes even three deep on the brushed steel floor. They had no weapons except their claws and ferocity. *Why were they so hell bent on killing them?* He wished he knew.

'Hello, Tate, my darling, were you missing me and wondering where I was?' Jaida again. His eyes rested on the most beautiful face you could ever hope to see. Younger than both Taio and himself, Jaida was a force of nature.

Both had courted her, where she teased, pulled them along until they couldn't resist and then casually cast them aside when she was done. Tate had moved on but the scars still scoured his heart, there was no one else he had connected to or wanted to Join with and now he had settled in his own mind that he may be alone for ever.

'Not exactly. What brings you down here, morning walk, sabbatical?' he asked, the sarcasm, hiding his true feelings, or so he thought.

'My dear Lord Malacca, sarcasm does not suit your usual dark brooding look,' she teased, wiping a non-existent piece of dirt off his cheek, knowing full well what buttons to press. 'Can't a girl go out for an early morning stroll with a friend?' indicating Taio, who smirked. Jaida then linked her arm around the tall figure of the most senior Changeling, Myolon, now transformed into his Zeinonian shape, the only outward sign that he was not all he seemed to be were the animalistic amber flecked, multi-coloured eyes that looked impassively at Tate.

Tate didn't react. There were tasks to do and he didn't want to antagonise the Blackstones or indeed the leader of the Changelings. He called out to the Southgate troops to start stacking up the bodies of the Pod so they could burn them. Taio's lips tightened. Tate knew it irritated him that he was in charge – the Inner Council was still his to command. The Southgate soldiers did not wait for their own royal bloodline to issue orders but began to stack the bodies. Lord Malacca had demonstrated to them many times his bravery and there was grudging respect in acknowledging that they and the Aeria Cavern would have fallen in the last few years if it hadn't been for this young lord.

Annoyed that his soldiers were following Tate's orders, Taio swaggered up to him until his face was within touching distance. Tate didn't move but his hand rested on one of his now deactivated seckles within his tunic, He saw the blood lust in Taio's eyes. Mentally Taio was still in the battle so Tate kept his body relaxed but ready for any challenge. Tate had seen and accomplished so much, that a spoilt prince was not a major issue for him.

Taio's face was full of rage. 'You think you are just the best don't you,' Taio spat out, spittle spraying out, some onto Tate's face, but Tate didn't move and stayed silent, enraging Taio even more. His vindictive eyes, burning still with the triumph of the battle, flashed, 'One day my dear Malacca, I will be ordering you around.'

'Sir, anything wrong?' It was Kron. Taio took a pace back. If there was one man he feared it was this man. Kron just looked through him as if he didn't exist.

'Nothing wrong Kron, just a friendly chat between royals,' said Tate, 'Well Taio, if that day arrives, I will let you know,' he concluded sarcastically. He wished for a time when he didn't need to handle Taio's tantrums.

'Have the engineers close that hole up, fast,' Tate directed his trusted captain who saluted and moved off to carry out the orders.

16

The engineers had taken their large backpacks off and each removed a set of steel sheets from each one. The soldiers had cleared away the bodies around the hole and most of the debris. The engineers then cut away any remnants of steel that jutted out and removed any remaining rubble. Then at a mesmerising speed the Tyther men in a coordinated display of team work joined each of the steel oblongs together one by one with their powerful operated drill packs. Within a short space of time the hole was covered with a patchwork quilt of steel joined with rivets. Tate surveyed the work in admiration.

They hadn't finished. The chief engineer, with goggles over his eyes, pulled out a small device, similar to a blaster. The other engineers stepped back and placed goggles over their eyes. He switched the tool on and even Tate, who was standing a safe distance away, had to turn his head away from the brightness of the light.

The experienced engineer traced the edges first, the steel melting to become one with the rest of the tunnel steel. Once done he switched to any rivets or inconsistences where the other oblongs met. When he had finished he switched off the beam and took off his goggles to survey his work. Except for some red glowing areas where the heat had last been focused it was hard to see where the hole had been. Tate shook his head in amazement. He knew that the Oneerions were the number one builders and skilled craftsmen in the Universe yet you just knew the Tyther clan would challenge such a statement.

The survivors climbed onto the gliders to make their way back to their respective posts. The fire took hold of the piles of stacked bodies as numerous bonfires were lit. Tate tracked the thin tendrils of smoke climb to the roof of the tunnel where it was whisked away by the venting system. He had two questions crashing around his head.

How had the Pod penetrated the steel walls? The weaknesses had always been the gates and barricades.

But the most disturbing question that challenged him was his encounter with that particular male Pod. *What had he been trying to say?* Why communicate at all? Were they not both committed to destroying each other? He was confused, not helped by the weariness he felt from the endless fighting. As they climbed back onto the gliders Tate's mind drifted to the history of the Expeditionary Force and wondered whether they would ever come back. What he didn't know was that he would find out the answer to his questions sooner than he thought.

Chapter 2:
Friends and Enemies

'What were you thinking of, Taio?' said an exasperated Tate, banging his fist down on the dark mahogany throne where many figures, both animal and Zeinonian, were carved into the impressive decorative back that swept up the wall like ivy. The room they were in was relatively small, as space in the packed city was at a premium, and Tate missed the grand throne hall where his father once ruled after the death of Lord Ricken Blackstone. That now seemed so long ago with the throne hall now split into many temporary sleeping dormitories.

Taio didn't reply. He just looked everywhere except at the Chancellor, his face a deep crimson as he held back his anger at such a public dressing down. Tate had no choice but to call an emergency Inner Council meeting to discuss the recent attack which had altered the status quo of the settlement.

In the meeting were the senior representatives from each of the clans and also from the enigmatic Changeling community, the latter silent, watching. They were all seated in a semi-circle facing Tate. Behind each of the clans were two soldiers from their personal bodyguards and situated at the locked main doors was an armed guard drawn from the Malacca clan. Beside Tate was the reassuring figure of Kron, who stood directly to his left.

'Now, Tate, leave Taio alone,' said the calming voice of Eben Southgate, the oldest person in the room and Taio's grandfather. 'Did he not take on the Pod and beat them? We should be congratulating him not castigating him.' Tate turned his attention to the old man. He needed to be careful here, the old man's voice carried weight with the Blackstones. He was also as wily as a fox and Tate never underestimated him.

'Lord Southgate, you know and I know leaving the North Gate fortification unguarded would have been catastrophic if the Pod had attacked. It leads directly into the city and with the limited inner defences the settlement has, the Pod would have annihilated us.'

'But they didn't, did they?' Tate turned to face the mocking face of Jaida. He kept his temper under control as Jaida sauntered seductively across the council room floor until she was facing Tate. 'Now, dear, beloved, Tate.' She reached out with her hand and stroked his clenched fist; Tate couldn't help but think of more pleasant times he and Jaida had once had.

'We had no choice really did we? There was a significant breach and if we waited behind our barricades like scared children, we wouldn't now be having this discussion,' she said silkily.

Tate saw the nodding heads of the bulk of the Inner Council. He was losing the argument. *Damn Jaida.* He decided to push on another front instead.

'I hear what you and my learned friends say,' he started smoothly, sitting down and unclenching his fists. Jaida gave him a wink and then slowly went back to her seat with the majority of the male eyes upon her. 'What we must agree to is a more appropriate distribution of our forces.'

Around the room the Tyther and Southgate Elders were not disputing this request so Tate went in for the kill.

'Lady Blackstone, you have the second largest army in Aeria but you only have less than ten per cent on the fortifications?' Tate addressed Jaida's haughty and regal mother, Safah, who was now the most senior Blackstone in the city.

'I have, young man as I need to ensure the safety of my people,' she retorted, not pleased at the attention moving to her. Safah had retreated behind her walls after the death of her husband, the then Lord Chancellor, some four years previously. He had been a good man but his wife had proved, in her grief, to be manipulative, greedy and above all arrogant.

'Lord Chancellor is his title Lady Blackstone in this chamber,' said an angry Kingsley Tyther, his youth clouding his judgment as he jumped to remonstrate against the lack of respect. His father, Quinlan Tyther, urged him to sit down.

'Quinlan why do you bring a child to such an important meeting?' said Safah with a disdainful look at the hot headed prince. Quinlan stood up with one hand on his young son's shoulder, his weight concentrated on his hand to keep his son seated and thereby making sure he didn't rise to the bait. Lady Blackstone was one royal you did not want to cross.

'Lady Blackstone, he has reached the age of majority and you know I am not one for these meetings, preferring to focus on the practical work which is needed and I hope my son will take my place here in time.' He broke off as he gave a regretful smile, 'Of course, he is young and speaks before he has thought things through.' The last words were said pointedly to his son as a warning. Kingsley glowered back but no one challenged the tall, muscular Tyther lord. Safah accepted the apology gracefully.

'Lady Blackstone,' said Tate, deciding he needed to leverage his authority as Chancellor, 'I recognise your need to protect your clan, just like I recognise the need for each of us to protect our own clans. However, together we are stronger and our first line of defence needs bolstering.' Tate paused for effect, 'What I ask is that you provide another thirty percent of your forces to the North and East Gates. That still leaves you over ten thousand to protect the Blackstone enclave.'

Safah was just going to retort when Tate asked for a show of hands to support the motion. Each of the clans had two votes compared with the Changelings' one. The hands went up into the air and predictably Safah kept her hands down, as did both the Southgates, along with the Changelings as they sided with the Blackstones. No surprises there then.

Four votes lost.

Tate was not able to vote due to his position; however, his mother Darya could and her hand was up high. The Tythers joined her.

Three votes!

Beaten…usual situation! Tate suppressed his annoyance. The Fathoms had no vote as the only survivor of the royal bloodline was the troublesome young princess Eva Fathom who at the age of thirteen was too young to vote. Eva was looked after by Cadence, her sister, but since she had married into the Southgates, in accordance with Inner Council guidelines, her Fathom vote was lost.

He may be the Lord Chancellor, but Tate's power was limited as long as the Southgates, Blackstones and Changelings voted together. He was just going to concede defeat when the unexpected happened, Jaida put her hand up, much to her mother's shock and disgust. *A tie!* Her face held an amused look, as if she found the whole situation a little bit of fun.

Tate cleared his throat. 'A tie and therefore my vote can be cast as a decider and I vote the motion in.' Kingsley whooped with delight under the disapproving eye of his father.

Safah looked like she was going to hit Jaida, who didn't seem perturbed in the slightest.

Why did Jaida help me? Tate thought.

'We have one more agenda item,' Tate carried on hurriedly, 'from the Changelings' enclave.' He raised a questioning eye towards the Changelings.

Myolon rose. He was in the principal form of the Changeling's when they were not "transforming". He was relatively tall, with the usual Zeinonian features. You could tell that he was a Changeling only by the animalistic eyes, amber with black flecks and a whirl of different colours that echoed around the iris, looking out from the heavy lids. Tate knew he was old, probably over three hundred years, remembering the stories about his role in the second Xonian War and that he was one of the Changelings who brought the magics to the clans.

The Changelings lived long and when one of their numbers bore a child, it was feted by the entire colony as a miracle; however, the last child was born over twenty years ago and was already fully grown, causing the clans to grow concerned about the longevity of the race. The Changelings were ruled by ancient folklore and Heathlon, the High Priestess, Myolon's mother, was the Law. Heathlon was not present, sending her son in her place.

Tate monitored them carefully knowing that if they chose to do so, the Changelings were a powder keg within the Aeria Cavern that he couldn't take the risk of setting off.

'Greetings, Lord Chancellor, worshipful Elder and head of all our illustrious clans,' Myolon's rasping voice ground across the council room. 'We all know that our time on this planet is under the darkest threat and that we cannot hope to keep the Pod at bay forever,' he continued. There was a murmur of agreement and a little fear around the room.

Tate's expression did not alter. *Where was he going with this?*

'We can no longer rely on the Expeditionary Force returning and a solution is required to free us from this infernal prison once and for all,' said Myolon, his deeply flecked amber eyes circling the room.

This was a day that he had waited for; today was the day that the Changelings would create history. He felt the spark of the magics within his body stir. It always started in his hands and then enveloped him internally, majority in the room oblivious to what was happening. Changelings could suppress outward displays of the magic.

Not like these puny Zeinonians who have to glimmer and glow with their magics, they have no idea of the damage they are doing to themselves, Myolon inwardly sneered.

Everyone in the room leaned forward; even the usually cool and disinterested Jaida's attention was on the tall Changeling royal prince. Tate watched, waited. His magics, the ability to taste a change in the environment and strength of the magics, felt the pulse of the magic that was pumping around in the Changeling's blood.

'Lord Chancellor, we are concerned at this latest breach,' Myolon began, 'to be able to break through our strongest steel means that the Pod are developing their own magic. Can you imagine the risk to the settlement if they develop that magic further?'

Tate was worried about the direction this was taking the Council. He was still confused as to why that male Pod had been trying to communicate with him earlier. *What was that all about?*

'I have a solution to all our concerns,' Myolon paused for effect; he was enjoying this. 'You will agree that our problem is the Pod?' he asked. There was no disputing response. 'We have developed a serum that will eradicate the entire Pod from this planet within the next three termins.'

There were gasps of shock and then excited whispers.

Myolon knew he had them. 'We propose to the Chair that this serum is placed in the main reservoir of the Pod enclave deep in the planet,' he concluded with a flourish. There was uproar. Everyone was whooping with delight, even the normally hesitant Quinlan Tyther was all smiles.

A solution at last! everyone thought.

The only person unmoved was the Lord Chancellor. Tate sat back in his chair with a thoughtful look, casting his eye over the delight of the other members of the Council but was drawn to the contingent from the Changelings, whose facial expressions were frozen, impassive. *Why speak up now?* Tate thought, trying to see behind the motion.

Myolon ignored the bedlam around him. For such a decision Myolon knew that he would need the Lord Chancellor's agreement irrespective of the vote. Anything which impacted the planet of Zein and way of life was the sole responsibility of the Lord Chancellor.

Tate observed the behaviour of his fellow Council members with concern. They all were shouting their agreement to the plan. Kingsley and Taio, who usually hated each other, were clasping hands and shaking with excitement, and Jaida's eyes were wide expressing her astonishment. *This is news to Jaida. Odd,* he mused.

All this time Myolon waited patiently, not taking his eyes off the Lord Chancellor. Tate guessed that the move to add the serum to the underground reservoir stemmed from the lessons learnt after the first attempt to wipe out the Pod. They had survived deep in the bowels of the planet with the Queen reproducing and creating new brethren who in turn were nourished by the underground water and food. Attacking this food source would permanently wipe out the Pod, something not lost on the people in the Inner Council.

Tate held up a hand. The noise continued until Kron slammed down his fist on the table in front of him for order. The noise subsided and reluctantly the Inner Council members reclaimed their seats. Tate stood tiredly, his body complaining with every move he made, to face Myolon. 'What you are proposing is genocide is it not?' he asked. Myolon confirmed that this was the case. Tate looked around him and realised that he stood alone. He saw the excited and flushed faces around him and could not blame them for their joy. They had all lost loved ones to the Pod, including him, and this was coupled with the life they led in the Aeria Cavern not being the life that any Zeinonian would choose. He felt his own unease begin to disappear and then he remembered his history lessons.

He had to try. 'Myolon, did we not try this before, yet the Pod grew back more powerful and their hatred for us immeasurably greater?'

Myolon hesitated, choosing his words carefully. 'I do acknowledge, Lord Chancellor, this has been tried before but this serum is stronger and now we know that rather than dispersing it in the atmosphere, if we place it in the main reservoir deep in the planet, where their queen resides, we will be able to wipe out all the Pod.'

Tate's breathing became more forced as panic rose within him. He deployed every fibre of his body to suppress the fear he felt. He knew he was losing the argument.

'Yes, that is what we need!' Quinlan shouted, He had lost his wife, Aaila, six manos ago in a foraging expedition on the surface and his hatred of the Pod was all consuming. Tate fully understood that with the Tythers backing this approach there was only one way to go or he stood the chance of being deposed which would provide Safah with the chance to step in to become Lady Chancellor. *Then all hell would break loose,* he thought morosely.

One last try. 'That would mean killing all their women and children and how can we be sure there will be no impact on us?' he challenged.

'They kill our women and children!' said Eben angrily. He had lost many of his kin when defending the barricades.

Myolon did not waver. 'The question you need to ask yourself Lord Chancellor is, will the savagery and hatred likely decrease or increase in the Pod and if that answer is increase, then the whole blood line needs to be cleansed.' Cheering for his words echoed around the chamber but he wasn't finished, realising he still needed to answer Tate's other question; 'We have already tested this serum with the Blackstones.' Tate looked across at the smug Safah, who inclined her head to confirm the statement. Jaida whipped around to look at her mother, her face registering shock and Safah returned the look without flinching. 'There were no side effects.'

'But…' Tate started to say in rebuttal but it was now Myolon who went for the jugular.

'Lord Chancellor, the Pod are savage beasts with no empathy to us. They want to remove us from Zein and they are happy to kill our women and children. Why are you defending them? Your father would not hesitate to back this plan.' Tate felt hostile eyes on him. He was angry that Myolon had brought his late father, Lord Lambert Malacca, into the discussion. That was a low blow.

Irrespective of how he felt, the challenge brought the desired effect in the room. He had no remaining allegiances in the Inner Council on this issue and knew he had lost. Tate stood and with a heavy heart, and after clearing his throat, stated, 'I, as Lord Chancellor, accept and uphold your proposal. Proposal to be carried out within the next two termins.' The chamber went wild, Myolon bowed to Tate and with a satisfied smile sat down and surveyed the impact of his proposal impassively as the excitement rose in the room.

Tate caught Jaida's eyes and saw her sympathy for his position. He slumped back down on his throne, knowing he had just signed the death warrant for over five million souls. There could be no joy in that.

Chapter 3: Journey Home

His mother was running towards him, hands outstretched, glancing back behind her fearfully. The dark brooding figure in red and black was gaining, his hand reaching out and grabbing hold of her shoulder. Photon shots pinged past them indiscriminately from the raging battle around them seeking targets. The disdain on Zylar's face drove Tyson against the brick wall of the stony faced Ilsid in front of him, his seckle slashing through the air in its lethal arc of death.

Tyson heard her screaming in his head, his magics out of control as he tried to reach his mother. Zylar's hand held her back as he pushed the device on his wrist and vanished into thin air. Leila screamed one last time as she disappeared from Tyson's view, leaving him shouting at the top of his lungs, 'Leave her alone!'

Then he became aware of a growing light and felt a hand on his chest gently shaking him as his nightmare rescuer forced him to open his tired eyes and the face of an angel came into the line of his vision. A loving smile played sensually on her lips. His shout must have been confined to his own dream as there was no worry on his girlfriend's face.

His eyes flickered awake, forcing the glue like sleep apart. He saw her eyes. Those eyes, those brown soulful eyes, you could dive into them and swim all day as they lured you in. He blinked, the light dazzling him and his confused brain struggling to understand where he was? 'Take your time champ,' said Amelia. 'Takes a little time to come around.'

Tyson blinked again and the face above him became clearer as the nightmare receded. Amelia leaned forward and kissed him passionately, the warm brush of her lips awakening his memories of the times they had enjoyed before the start of the journey. He smiled. What a few months that had been.

He groaned and sat up feeling a little woozy but began to regain his concentration. Bailey, who was situated next to his capsule, turned to him and rubbed his stomach. *I am starving.* Tyson picked up Baileys silent cry for food and couldn't help but laugh. There was only one Bailey, thank God!

His friend had not taken long to regain his humour once he and Gemma had been informed by the United States authorities that their parents had been found safe and well. On that fateful day, when the two nuclear weapons had fallen, their parents had decided to take a trip out to Long Island away from New York, but not before they had pushed back their flight home a few days. Through the ensuing firestorm they were rescued and luckily not hurt. When they safely arrived home everyone was overjoyed and the reunion was emotional. They listened incredulously to both their children's exploits and pride replaced their initial horror.

Tyson hauled his body from the capsule. All around him others on the third deck were awakening from their slumber. The bulk of the crew, soldiers and technical staff had all been asleep for three months which enabled the resources on the *Elanda* to be rationed during their long thirty trillion light year journey from Earth to the Capulus Novus System.

It was in this galaxy that they hoped to find Zein and its surrounding planets. The three months' duration was a significant change from the horrific two year journey that the Zeinonians took to travel to Earth. The copious amount of zinithium that the authorities on Earth had mined made it possible for the new Expeditionary Force to concertina time and space more effectively.

Tyson let his eyes wander around the bustling deck, following the wide range of people stirring from their enforced deep sleep. There were soldiers from both the Zein Colony and Earth but the third deck also consisted of a large number of civilians and, of course, his friends.

Before they had embarked on their epic journey, it had been an eventful six months since the fall of Zylar's rule. Earth and Zein had built a formidable new governing body, simply called The Council, which had taken complementary objectives and rules from both the United Nations charter and Zein Council Law.

The Council was made up of an Inner Council, which included representatives of the Zein five clans and members of the UN Security Council and the Outer Council which had a rotating membership policy of ten countries from Earth that were randomly selected for twelve month advisory roles. Once the countries had served they would not be selected for the following three years. Once this period was over they would again be placed into the random selection process.

All other Earth and Zein institutions still existed; however, the mandate for The Council covered all space and Earth Zein Colony business.

The dual Chairs of The Council were decided on a yearly basis and selected from the Inner Council members. The first year was in the hands of the United States President and Lord Southgate and the second year would be in the hands of the new United Kingdom Prime Minister, Charles Hamilton, and Lord Fathom.

At the first meeting of The Council it was unanimously agreed that all focus would be on refitting the powerful and enormous *Elanda* battleship and building two smaller destroyers to act as convoy protection. The Tyther clan, now released from the tyrannical Zylar, applied their ancestors' knowledge stored in the archives to build the two destroyers. The manufacture of the impressive ships was also supported by the full array of raw materials and skilled tradesmen on Earth. Knowledge and skills were shared to create a formidable team.

The principal objective of the refitting of the *Elanda* and the building of the two destroyers was to free Zein. On Earth "Free Zein" badges were all the rage and people started to wear the different clan coloured tunics. The Blackstone clan blue tunics were, of course, the most favoured due to their place in the stories now circling the world. The tunics of the Fathom clan were not far behind with the Battle for the Core entering folklore for its ferocity and ingenuity. For your children you could even buy plastic seckles to pretend you were a Zein warrior; a favourite at Christmas time for both girls and boys – dolls and swords fading into the past.

Initially the inclusion of the Zeinonians into Earth's population was welcome, though there remained voices against relaxing immigration rules too far, especially around business and social benefits. It was now common for the strangely attired Zeinonians to be seen walking the streets of the Earth's tourist sites. They had built up a solid fan base around social media sites and Zeinonian themed parties were all the rage. In return the Zein Inner Council opened up their quadrants to the humans and people flocked to their villages and environmental coded countryside.

Approaching the launch of the Expeditionary Force in full pomp and ceremony, the initial euphoria felt, began to fade on both sides, with the humans the worst. Envy of the aliens' greater technology and the resulting fear of hidden agendas, created an uneasy alliance.

In relation to the quadrants, you could still look into the sky and see no alien world, as they still kept the Outer Perimeter Walls active, as not to do so would cause issues for the airline businesses and also act as a block to the sun.

The Council passed laws enabling greater mining of zinithium and new mines were opened in Europe and in the Antarctic. The Core settlement was expanded and now was covering nearly double the area for mining that it had before.

In political circles, Victoria Kirk was the surprise winner as she was appointed Head of Zeinonian Support, or as she was quirkily dubbed "Kirk HaZs arrived". Victoria was the principal contact with the clans, overseeing their integration into the Earth population. She had her work cut out. Charles Hamilton, the British Prime Minister, knew that her family's long military history including the adversity they had faced in the World Wars and before gave her the natural organising and never-say-die attitude needed. It was an easy appointment, one which Victoria accepted with much humility. She was everywhere, attending memorials for the fallen in the Battle for the Core or the Southern Palace triumph, handing out blankets to the survivors of the New York nuclear blast, meeting and greeting Zeinonians in the different quadrants. She had her own issues to deal with though, the murder of Michael Dunstable; the last British Prime Minister at the hands of Zylar, still haunted her. The Zeinonians took to her forthright and easy manner and she was instrumental in supporting them in the increase in mining substantial amounts of zinithium.

In the United Kingdom and the Ruhr Valley in Germany old mining collieries were reopened, drained and repaired after Tyther and Fathom scientists pointed out, that under the coal, some of which had once driven the Industrial Revolution and two World Wars, was an enormous tonnage of zinithium. Using new techniques and the greater technology of the Zeinonians they had bored new mine shafts and were now bringing up significant tonnage of zinithium, quantities that would have only ever been dreamed about when the coal industry was in its heyday. Everyone was growing rich.

This never ending supply of the powerful raw material brought about a considerable leap in the Earth's technology – previous deserts were dusted with the zinithium and within weeks flowing grasslands appeared. The Sahara became a rich land for farming and Africa was one part of the world that saw an immediate impact on its quality of life due to food shortages becoming a thing of the past. Plentiful food was not the only success as medical enhancements leapt forward. It was a unique moment in Earth history when cancer was eradicated, as a new X-ray like scanner pumped zinithium into the body killing the diseased cells with very few side effects. On the days leading to the launch of the Expeditionary Task Force the Zeinonians had started on enhancing humans' ability to travel by teleporting. This was not a straightforward task with the huge volumes of people – they had started with small groups and hoped to increase numbers with time.

Tyson looked at the still half a sleep and slightly stunned faces of some of the previously sedated civilians, who had been nominated for the journey. Some of the greatest minds from all fields were on this ship. There were biologists, civil engineers, physicists and geologists to name but a few of the professions supporting the quest.

Chosen from a wish list of the Inner Council the majority had put away their fear of the unknown to have a chance to see a new galaxy and alter mankind's destiny.

Someone slapped Tyson on the back. 'Hey, dreamer how are you?' It was Hechkle and beside him was a grinning Bronstorm. Tyson's face lit up and he gave them both a firm handshake and a manly clasp around their shoulders.

'See you have put a bit of weight on, big fella,' said Bailey to Hechkle.

The giant of a man leaned forward as if to hit him and Bailey briefly flinched, at which point Hechkle roared with laughter and good naturedly rubbed his still very firm stomach and said, 'Well Bailey, I am like you, I needs my food, boy.'

'Look at that?' said Gemma, pointing out into space, 'Hi Tyson,' she added with a long appraising look at him. Amelia saw the look and hooked her arm protectively around his as they joined her. Gemma just shrugged her shoulders and turned her attention back to what had caught her attention. Separating them from space was the floor to ceiling of specially toughened glass. The vision gave them a wonderful, clear view of their surroundings outside the ship.

They stared out in amazement at one of the ships providing escort duties, which since they had entered their cubicles prior to launch, they hadn't seen in all its glory. The ship was a quarter the size of the *Elanda*, with its beautiful sleek hull making its serene way though the cloak of blackness that surrounded it. The ship name, *Manhattan*, glistened in black italics on the side of the silver hulk named in honour of the New Yorkers who had lost their lives. They could only guess how impressive the much larger *Elanda* looked to those on the *Manhattan*. The other ship which flanked them on the other side and was hidden from their view was named *Brooklyn*.

Behind the ship the depths of space stared back at them, deep, never ending and mysterious. The friends looked out in awe, slightly intimidated by what they saw. None of them could have expected to experience what they were seeing now with their own eyes. The noise around them grew as more of the third deck personnel sleepily awoke from their slumber. On the third deck there were more civilians than soldiers, the expedition's army resources mainly on the lower floors.

Tyson saw the expedition's leading scientist, Dr Walter Moore stretch and fumble around for his glasses, which were resting on the bedside cabinet next to his cubicle, before clumsily climbing from his capsule. Walter had spent many hours with the small group of companions prior to the journey as he pieced together the cultural and scientific differences of the two species. He saw Tyson and waved. Tyson, who had taken an instinctive liking to the clumsy, spaced out but highly intelligent scientist, waved back.

Walter's gaze rested on the famed scientists and experts he had helped handpick as they pulled their protesting bodies from the capsules. He saw the nervous glances of his fellow colleagues towards the Zeinonians, adding to his discomfort. Before they had entered the hyper-sleep he had detected the distrust, envy and downright dislike towards the aliens from some of the greatest minds on Earth. Walter had gone out of his way to convince them that the Zeinonians would share their knowledge and he thought judging by the medical and farming advances they had demonstrated that this had largely been done. He was wrong. The memory of the destruction of New York still rested in the minds of even the most advanced minds. Walter sighed as he flexed his limbs, helping the circulation in his legs. He had much work to do to make the different species work effectively together.

Kabel and the rest of the group had nicknamed him Boff, short for boffin. Walter, who rarely had been part of any group, even at school, took it all in his stride. He was one human who welcomed the friendship of the Zeinonians; they made him feel special and part of their world.

On each of the decks, they had not used the full capacity of sleeping capsules. On the third deck, over two thousand people were just coming out of their hyper-sleep. On the other dormitory floors, where the bulk of the forces rested, there were between one thousand and three thousand people per deck. The other floors carried the bulk of the Expeditionary Task Force with a mixture of Zeinonian warriors from each clan and a multi-national force gleaned from around the world, although the bulk of the soldiers came from the United States and Russia.

In total, including the support ships the Expeditionary Force numbered an impressive eighty thousand people, consisting of mainly troops, tradesmen, a variety of scientists and supporting crew. With over six billion people on Earth it was relatively easy to make the decision that if the human race was to step into the wider Universe it wanted a substantial armed capability coupled with some of their best brains across a whole range of specialties and industry sectors. A large proportion of the main crew provided the catering, cleaning and general administration required for such a large expeditionary force.

'How long is it until we reach Zein, Boff?' Gemma asked.

'We have just travelled nearly thirty trillion light years in three months,' said a disbelieving Walter shaking his head in wonder. 'We should be very close to the Capulus Novus System and then a matter of days to Zein,' he concluded.

'You said during our training that the atmosphere on Zein is fine for us. How do you know for sure?' said Tyson, as he hugged Amelia close to him. Gemma monitored the display of affection with a pang of jealousy; she was missing Kabel. Tyson picked up the strength of feeling and a thrill went through him before guilt took over. He stopped his probing of her mind.

Behave yourself Tyson.

Walter was running the modifier instrument over his body scanning his vital organs for any areas for concern to check that he was fully fit for duty. His mother always said he was a hypochondriac. He looked up at Tyson's question.

'The tests we ran on the biological differences between both races,' he gestured to those listening, 'confirmed that we are ninety-nine per cent similar in our DNA.'

'That's good isn't it,' said Tyson.

'It is not as simple as that,' replied Walter, who was now in his element as he talked to the eagerly listening group. Other scientists also joined the group, interested in his view. 'If you take the difference between a chimpanzee and man, most biochemists feel there is only one per cent difference, and I am guessing that you don't feel like a monkey?' he pointed to Bailey.

'To be fair Boff, not the best example, Bailey acts like a monkey most of the time,' said Tyson sardonically and then moved hastily as Bailey aimed a playful punch at him.

Walter joined in the laughter and then continued, 'In that one per cent we found major differences. Our body mass is denser which makes us stronger but our internal functions act much less efficiently then the Zeinonians.' He saw the expectant faces and knew that he had started so had to finish his explanation. 'There seems to be something impacting the Zeinonians' key organs, they are very resistant to viruses and illnesses. It seems they have an internal medicine that drives away things that we as humans come to expect, like colds.'

'Is it due to our magics?' asked Bronstorm. Walter saw the unease spread across some of the scientists.

Why does everyone fear what is new? We really haven't changed since we found that the Earth was round and not flat! He shook his head in despair.

'Yes, I think it is. You have these wonderful capabilities and they benefit you broadly, but push these capabilities too much and I worry that it has a destabilising impact on your chemical balance,' said Walter, Bailey saw Tyson frown and swap glances with Amelia. 'Now when we arrive at Zein, I expect that the mixture of air to favour the Zeinonians and that additional strength we humans experience will not be such a factor during any fighting.'

'Hey, Boff, look, these beauties are always going to show up those weak aliens,' said Bailey as he flexed both his arms, showing off his large biceps.

'Oh my hero,' said Kabel's sister, Belina, jokingly, as she joined the group. Everyone again broke into laughter. Since Belina had been rescued from the Eastern Quadrant by her brother, the change in her morose attitude was remarkable. Now with freedom to travel and make friends her cheerful demeanour made her popular amongst all those that met her.

Amelia happily joined in with the merriment pleased that the group were all together again. Except Kabel. Where was he?

Chapter 4: Deep Space

Kabel watched the stars go by. He marvelled at their brilliance against the black landscape, their number seeming to stretch to infinity and beyond. Was this how his grandfather had felt?

Excitement? Dazzling stars and endless space, with the anticipation of seeing a new galaxy or planet? He wished he could have been part of the Zein Expeditionary Force that found Earth. That day must have captured a truly memorable occasion with the Zeinonians desperate for a new start and a renewed hope of returning to Zein and rescuing loved ones left behind.

The piloting crew, handpicked to support the humans and Zeinonians fast asleep in their individual hyper-sleep cocoons, busily went about their everyday tasks. The crew were mainly Zeinonians but there was a strong human military presence supporting them. When the orders were sanctioned by the Joint Earth and Zein Council, trust was there but also nervousness. The humans wanted control of the military aspects of the expedition and the Zeinonians, who had retained autonomy through many conflicts and enjoyed their independence, required input into key decisions. The humans would only support the recently named Expeditionary Force of the United League of

Planets if military control was placed into their hands. Reluctantly, the Zeinonians agreed. They needed the humans to support the long journey to their homeland. The whole process left grumbling on both sides.

He smiled at the elaborate title of the expeditionary force. The title was grand, the Earthlings liked their organisations; The United League of Planets, consisting of the populated Earth, Zein, Oneerio, Skegus and five other inhabited planets in the Zein galaxy, was the title given to a vision. The vision objective was not just to free worlds but to free the Capulus Novus Sector from tyranny.

Kabel remembered the bold speech he had given at his inauguration and as he did, he couldn't prevent his smile growing wider. He never knew he could speak like that. At the United Nations in Washington, everyone stood to applaud; he was initially shocked, but then proud when he caught his adoptive mother, Maggia, in the crowd, cheering him on. He ached to see Delilah and missed his late adopted brother Drogan. Even though he had lived with Drogan all his life, after being rescued as a baby from the Southern Quadrant of the Earth Colony, his relationship with him had been distant until, in those final weeks before the quadrant was invaded, they had grown close. Real brothers.

The loss of Drogan tugged at his emotions and he had initially looked to Tyson to replace him. But Tyson was distant, almost cold or indifferent to Kabel, and even though he knew the magics Tyson had inherited were impacting his half-blood brother, the rejection still hurt.

For company, on the first phase of the journey, he had Zebulon, the Changeling, who kept to his wolf shape nearly all the time, in an attempt not to freak out any of the ship's crew. Kabel found his presence and insight comforting and he reflected on how far their relationship had progressed since he had rescued the enslaved creature at the Federation Fair in the Western Quadrant. Kabel sighed, that seemed so long ago, before all this madness started. They had fought many pitched battles and hopeless situations together. The ability for this creature from Zein to change its shape into any animal it had seen proved extremely useful and had pulled the group from some pretty tough scrapes. Zebulon had wondered off to meet up with the other companions and Kabel found that he missed the creature's reassuring company.

'Chancellor Lord Blackstone, General Corder wants to speak with you,' said Lieutenant Anton Morrison, jolting him from his thoughts. It still took him by surprise to be called "Lord" let alone "Chancellor". Once the clans had come together in peace it had been unanimous that the next Chancellor would be him. He had rebuffed the initial attempt saying that it should be Lord Fathom or Lord Southgate but they wouldn't have it. He was the Chancellor. The Blackstone clan were the principal clan by Zein Law and nothing he could say or do could change their minds.

He had surprised them immediately by, for the first time in history, appointing a non-royal as his Vice-Chancellor. It was Cronje. Everyone had been taken back, including Cronje, until his initial surprise was replaced by his pragmatic old self.

It was a smart move, Cronje had the backing of the still powerful Malacca army and by tying him into the Inner Council, Kabel had strengthened his political base by just one appointment. Though, to be honest, Kabel enjoyed the matter-of-fact advice he received from the taciturn Easterner. He had left Cronje with Remo as his captain to support Lords Southgate and Fathom as they assimilated the two cultures and environments. Kabel felt uneasy not having this pair with him but he needed to provide much needed protection and experience to the vulnerable Zein population, shorn of their technological protections.

Kabel walked behind the muscled back of Lieutenant Morrison into the Command and Control Centre. He had rarely seen a black man and the imposing statue-like bear of a man brought out the strong, almost regal bearing of the African-American race. Lieutenant Morrison was General Corder's right hand man and Kabel had immediately established a friendship, learning about each other's race. Morrison pointed to the figure staring at the wall to ceiling viewing screen which showed the way ahead.

Standing in front of Kabel was another imposing man. General Prescott Corder was a soldier through and through with many years of experience mapped into the lines on the craggy face. No one was under the illusion that there was not a hard, tough core behind the amenable manner of the American. Even though Kabel towered over him, the presence General Corder exuded, dominated the room. With him was the equally tough and older Admiral Nikolai Koshkov from the Russian Federation Forces, who commanded the second largest force on the ship with the United Kingdom and China the next two largest contingents.

Admiral Koshkov was an argumentative in your-face man. This was a far cry from his command of the Black Sea Fleet and with General Corder out ranking him as military leader of the Expeditionary Force, he focused on ensuring his forces, numbering some twenty thousand soldiers from air, sea and land forces, delivered their side of the duties.

'Lord Blackstone, glad you could join me,' said General Corder, the welcoming smile lighting up his square jaw. 'We have picked up a cluster of signals approaching us fast.'

'Asteroids?'

'Could be, travelling fast. We should know shortly when they pass in range of the afibilator,' said General Corder, his smile now replaced with a studious look. The afibilator was an ultra-sensitive radar system that was augmented by zinithium. In fact once the Zeinonians had shared the secret of zinithium, the technology of Earth had not just leapt forward but moved into a whole new stratosphere.

This was a subject which worried Kabel. The humans liked to be the aggressor rather than the follower and that was what he saw in the meetings he attended with his fellow Elders. If the humans disagreed with a point their initial reaction was to reject the position put forward rather than talk; eventually they came around to compromise but the whole experience was destabilising the Elders' way of politicking.

They went across to the young radar operator, Corporal Mike Batten, a soldier from the US Army, until they hovered over the four dimensional radar screens that could see some five light years away. The zinithium-powered radar was extraordinarily detailed and just as magnificent to watch.

'What are we looking at soldier,' commanded General Corder.

The unflappable young man did not bat an eyelid, Batten pointed to some small flecks that were on the outskirts of the second layer of the afibilator, at four light years away. 'These are the unidentified masses,' he said, 'Once they pass into the second perimeter we will receive considerable more information on their size, shape and speed.'

'What is the likelihood of them not being an asteroid belt?' asked Kabel. He was concerned that they had started waking up those in hyper-sleep only in the last hour. They bristled with weapons on every floor but had insufficient forces to fire them.

'Well we have run into five asteroid belts and due to our technology were able to change course or use our deflection shields. It is likely to be another asteroid field, Sir,' replied Corporal Batten.

Kabel was relieved. His main fear was to enter into a fight too early, harbouring doubts that they just did not know whether the joint force would work effectively together. The relief didn't last long. The blips on the screen suddenly changed into a recognisable battle formation as they entered into the second perimeter unlike the chaos of an asteroid belt.

'Sir, I count thirty ships,' the young radar engineer calmly stated. *Good, some action*, thought Admiral Koshkov. He itched for a battle. He was bored with the waiting around and endless drills.

'Sound battle stations!' General Corder was now all business. The communications officer, a Fathom soldier, set off the noisy klaxon throughout the ship. Admiral Koshkov departed to organise the Russian forces.

On the third deck Hechkle was the first to react, picking up his cap, thrusting it onto his head and walking towards the nearest entrance. He brushed past two American soldiers who were patrolling the deck, his large shoulders unbalancing both of them. Hechkle didn't break stride and it was the following Bronstorm who saw the dark looks the two soldiers gave the disappearing back of the tall Fathom warrior. They then turned their hostile glances towards Bronstorm, who blanked them, before walking past.

'Follow me,' Hechkle shouted to the group over his shoulder. The rest of the companions pushed their way through the still groggy civilians and made their way to the main corridor looking around for what to do next when a familiar voice called out.

'Greetings, my friends, you are all looking rested, it is amazing what three months can do for your complexion!'

Kabel, Gemma's heart raced and she ran to him and gave him a big hug which he returned, realising how much he had missed her these last three months. The others promptly surrounded him and once pleasantries had been exchanged he beckoned them to gather closely around him.

'Look, we have many photon anti-ship guns on this ship but we do not have enough trained soldiers to fire them. The others are awakening from hyper-sleep but it will take too much time before they are combat ready. I need volunteers.'

'We trained on the guns before we left, though I admit I will be a little rusty,' said Bailey. The others nodded their heads as they all had previously volunteered to train on the weapons defence.

'That's what I wanted to hear. Go to the first deck and grab yourself a position – we have only a few minutes before the enemy are upon us,' Kabel stressed, 'I will join the aviators in the Cobras.' He was referring to the reconditioned double manned sleek aircraft that used to protect *Elanda* all those years ago. Now in full working order, they were aptly renamed after the venomous snake, and how the neck of the plane coiled before spitting out the deadly pulses of zinithium photon torpedoes.

'Good luck,' said Gemma, a lump in her throat. In answer he kissed her and then ran up the corridor. Gemma swallowed hard. It had been long time since she had seen him, and for him then to go was hard.

The others made their way to the first deck, fighting through the bedlam around them. Tyson felt the tightness of the excitement gripping him as he followed the others. He like all the others had practised on the huge anti-ship photon guns with his natural hand to eye coordination proving an instant hit, leading him to record the highest number of "kills" in the training programme; nearly twenty-five percent higher than the previous record, held by Kabel. When he had finished the exercise and the other companions were congratulating their friend, he held back on what he had experienced, the connection with the gun that transcended pure metal and ammunition. He saw Zylar in his sights and every virtual ship he transformed into the hulking presence of his nemesis. The outside world faded from his consciousness – all he wanted to do was kill.

'Tyson, Tyson?' He shook out of his trance and turned to look at the worried face of Amelia. Amelia had grown used to the faraway looks of her boyfriend. She knew that he thought of Evelyn often and her death had changed him – possibly forever. Sometimes it took her minutes to wrestle him away from whatever place he tucked his mind into. What she knew for certain by the look on his face, it was rarely a pleasant journey.

'You with us now, honey?'

'Sure I am.' Tyson flashed an indulgent smile and entered one of the anti-ship photon gun booths. The booths were positioned strategically down the spine of the ship with a one hundred and eighty degree angle of engagement. Due to this there were many booths on the first deck and these were supplemented by numerous others on each side of each of the other decks. The *Elanda* effectively bristled with protection, but the overriding problem was there were too few trained gunners awakened from hyper-sleep to arm every one.

Tyson settled into his seat with the command hologram immediately sensing him and surrounding his head with a series of monitors. The electronic pulses took a matter of nano seconds to align with his brainwaves, the guns fitting comfortably into his dry hands. He was ready. The guns just needed to be directed and then his mind would direct the firing. Zebulon had quietly observed the companions awake from their hyper-sleep and sensing the stirring of the magics within the young human he decided to stay with Tyson. He could easily fit in the booth in his wolf form and sat patiently beside Tyson.

'Hi buddy, looks like I will need to wait for my breakfast,' said Bailey, into the communication link, laughing. Tyson wasn't listening; his mind was in a different zone waiting for someone or something he could destroy.

'You just have a one track mind dear brother,' Gemma retorted.

'Well I do have other vices, don't I, Belina,' smirked Bailey. Belina, who was hooked up like the others to the communication network, blushed.

'Soldiers, can I just remind you to keep your eyes on what is in front of you and cut unnecessary chatter,' said the powerful voice of General Corder, cutting across the banal discussion.

Kabel smiled at the banter and joined in the fun with his co-pilot in the cockpit of the impressive Cobra. The co-pilot was Sean Lambert who was providing the support on manning the aft weapons console, which like the anti-ship guns on the *Elanda* was operated by thoughts. Sean was one of the humans who had supported Kabel during the last three months, refusing to accept the hyper-sleep option. He and Kabel had grown to respect and enjoy each other's company and Kabel welcomed the light relief that broke the monotony of the journey.

'Cobra Ten can you read me,' said Kabel, searching through the hundred Cobra fix wing strike aircraft.

The unhurried and calm voice of Hechkle, who was supported by Bronstorm, came back in acknowledgment, 'Kabel, I mean Lord Blackstone, we are ready, as you humans say it, to kick ass,' in a monotone flat response.

'Just make sure you look after my back, you Fathom reprobates and no shirking off for some sightseeing,' said Kabel, jokingly.

'Ready to launch Sir,' said Lieutenant Michaels to General Corder.

'Launch in squads of ten, Lieutenant.' The soldier acknowledged the order and his hands ran over the array of lights in front of him. General Corder was tense but knew that this was what he had been trained for.

As the Cobras were catapulted out from their launch bays into the blackness he felt a surge of pride. *The first human to command a battle in space,* he thought. His chest poked out with pride before he admonished himself. *Focus, man, focus.* 'Sir, there they are…,' said Lieutenant Michaels, his voice petering out, as he and everyone else on the ship followed the approach of the marauding ships towards the flotilla at incredible speed. The ships were considerably smaller than the two escorting destroyers but the Cobras were dwarfed by their size.

'Xonian scum,' said one of the Zeinonian navigators. The puzzled General Corder asked how he knew they were Xonian ships. 'You see the four wings each with four torpedo launchers.' General Corder looked harder at the fancy "X" shape of the ships which attached to a black, gnarled and ribbed main body. He picked up the menacing torpedo launchers. He nodded his head. 'Well, in our training they went through the ships in our databases that held records of all known space fighters and this type of ship was included in the lists and it is an Xonian ship called a Vening,' said the experienced Zeinonian, Zachary

Harris of the Blackstone clan, recalled General Corder. 'In Xonian language it means "Spitting Death", nice hey?' Those in the Command and Control Centre looked round at the frowning, tall Blackstone man.

'Good job we named our fighters Cobras then; let's get into a spitting contest,' General Corder retorted. Suddenly, the nearest Vening opened fire on the destroyer to the port side with two torpedoes launched from each of the four wings. The eight missiles within a blink of a second crashed into the side of the destroyer. The Vening pulled away from its attack and was immediately replaced by a second enemy ship, which did the same. The flashes made those following the action flinch.

Kabel, tracked the explosions as he sped towards the ship. He knew that the plentiful stores they had of the precious ore, that fed the protective shield around all the ships, and extended more weakly to the Cobras, should protect them, but the extent of the firepower of these ships still caused him concern. If they were not careful they would rapidly exhaust the current zinithium loaded into the cell batteries, which would mean they would need to be replenished from reserves, an activity they could not afford at such an early stage in their quest. Who knew what faced them when they reached Zein?

'Cobra ten and two, are you with me?' Kabel queried. 'Always,' was the succinct reply from Hechkle; the other pilot a soldier from the British Royal Air Force also acknowledged. 'Let's get stuck in,' said Kabel.

Kabel rocked the Cobra to the left as he followed the departing Vening. In the virtual controls wrapped round his head, his thought pulses picked out the homing beacon mark, which sent a powerful laser ray to track the exhaust pipe of the enemy ship. The tracking device locked onto the power source and he gave the silent order to fire the pulse expulsion in the cone of the ship to release the deadly torpedo.

These were no ordinary torpedoes. Inside with the nuclear device there was a powerful zinithium core that on detonation would quadruple the already significant payload. In Earth it would be the equivalent of five times the power of "Little Boy", the name of the bomb dropped on Hiroshima. This was just one torpedo. He had some pity for the enemy.

The torpedoes sped towards their destination. They smashed into the back of the ship and Kabel let out a small cheer. There was no explosion. *What the hell...*

The torpedo just thumped into the ship and fell away. All around him the same thing was happening to the other fighters; something was deactivating the bombs before they hit, nullifying them. 'Bogie on my tail can't shake him, Mayday, Mayday.' The cries came from one of the Russian pilots; Kabel saw that it was Cobra seventy-nine. Firing with increasing accuracy a Vening was on his tail keeping up with the frantic movements of the smaller aircraft. The shield could only protect the ships so far, with a sustained assault the Cobras were vulnerable.

'Don't panic, Cobra seventy-nine,' said Kabel, momentarily turning to Sean after switching off his communications link. 'Who is flying seventy-nine?' Belenov, was the response. Kabel reconnected to the pilot and told him to go high as he moved in with a burst of concentrated firing to support the under-pressure Cobra fighter. It was too late for Cobra seventy-nine. The plane exploded.

Kabel heard anguished screams over his communication link as other pilots' shared the same fate as Belenov. The Vening ships had turned on the offensive and although slower than the Cobras, their greater experience and the shock to the Cobra fighters that their weapons were useless saw six Cobras blown apart within seconds. Others relied on their photon machine guns rather than their torpedoes to provide some element of protection.

'Kabel, watch out,' shouted Sean. The Vening in front of them had gone into a steep climb and now was coming in range to return fire. Two torpedoes were launched at them. Kabel flung the Cobra to the right and released photon flares to pull the torpedoes away from the ship. The manoeuvre worked. The weapons exploded away from the ship, which rocked with the sonic blasts. Sean turned his photon machine gun on the Vening and poured round after round into the ship. Kabel just focused on evading the gun sights of the intimidating enemy ship. Perspiration dripped from his brow.

On the *Elanda* they watched the dogfight with bated breath. Gemma's stomach lurched left and right with worry as she saw the distinctive command Cobra fighter with its red tip cone come under increasing fire. The other Cobras were using their greater speed to stay out of the fatal grip of their attackers. Survival was now the overriding objective.

'We're next,' said Tyson, as he sensed fierceness and hate emitting from the ships arrayed in front of them. Sure enough, four ships peeled off heading directly for the *Elanda* with the deadly torpedo launchers on each ship facing the defenders.

Ready. He sent the command into all the minds of those controlling the anti-ship guns and opened fire. Bailey and Gemma followed him. Soon the air was crisscrossed with blue energy pulsating from the bores of the weapons with the fire pouring into the ships approaching them. Their ammunition was making little impact and the ships kept coming. The Venings launched four torpedoes each and they streaked across space smashing into the ship in an instant. The flash made all the gunners flinch and made the ship shake with the impact.

'What's the damage?' General Corder asked, worriedly. He felt tense. *This was not going to plan.*

'There is no damage, Sir, but we will need to replenish the Protective Barrier if they continue with this barrage,' said the tall Blackstone operator.

The attacks on the *Elanda* increased. Kabel was confused why the powerful battleship's weapons were having no effect. They had lost another couple of Cobras as the pilots lost confidence in their ability to hit back. They were flinging their ships all around space as they desperately tried to prevent the Venings obtaining a fix on them.

Tyson heard Kabel's and the other pilots' doubts. He focused his attention on the incoming spaceship, which was trying to get in as close as possible to launch its power draining load. He focused on the turret which stuck out from the body of the ship and then cautiously reached out, immersing his thoughts into the minds of the enemy. There were ten warriors to each ship, he counted. They were laughing and discussing the attack but he didn't understand the language. He decided that he needed help so redirected and projected the thoughts to Zebulon, who still sat patiently in his wolf shape watching Tyson with growing unease.

What are they saying?

They are pointing out that they can destroy us at their leisure as our useless weapons have no impact, Zebulon replied.

Any weaknesses you can identify?

They keep mentioning the "transmitter", which I think is disarming the explosive devices before they hit.

Tyson searched the exterior of the spaceship and he couldn't see anything. Four more torpedoes were launched from two other Venings and the *Elanda* rocked again, causing, for the first time, sparks from the Protective

Barrier, which could be seen glinting in the starlight. The barrier was weakening. The Venings turned away readying for another attack.

'There!' he shouted aloud to no one in particular. As the enemy ships turned away he saw a red pulsing light on the underbelly of the ship which was relatively small but noticeable. Tyson instinctively knew that this was the disabling transmitter. 'Patch me into all communications, I have a solution,' he ordered. In the Command and Control Centre, General Corder frowned. He was not used to receiving orders, but they needed help so reluctantly he gave the requested direction to patch Tyson in to the communications.

'Attention everybody, there is a red light on the underbelly of the ships. It is a very small target but direct all your fire on to that area,' said Tyson.

'On it,' said Kabel, pulling his Cobra into a vertical climb and looping behind the previously attacking Vening. He dropped the Cobra at an angle so he could see the red light. Yes he saw it and set his guns onto the belly of the Vening firing off streams of powerful pulses from the Cobra's' photon machine guns. The Vening began to manoeuvre itself violently to escape the intensive firing. Sean joined his co-pilot in firing at the underbelly. There was a force-field but the concentrated fire power eventually told and blasted the light to pieces; immediately Kabel ordered the Cobra's torpedoes loose. The torpedoes sped upward into the desperately manoeuvring ship and on impact they tore the ship apart.

Tyson heard the panic stricken alien guttural voices in the ship and the scream of death and his lips curled up in satisfaction. He sensed panic begin to ripple through the enemy and could not stop licking his lips in delight, as if he tasted the fear. Zebulon looked up at him, keeping his thoughts hidden. If Tyson had seen that look he would be concerned; it was not a look of admiration but of fear.

Tyson turned his guns onto the incoming enemy ship, aiming for the underbelly, swiftly joined by Gemma, Belina and Bailey. The light went out and a Cobra following the ship let loose its pay load and the enemy ship exploded. Tyson felt the buzz of the battle and the magic inside him feed off the adrenalin.

Zebulon made sure his thoughts were protected by his deep magics before he allowed his concerns to surface. *The magics are turning the boy into a rogue warrior,* Zebulon thought, sensing that the human's body could or would not control the magic within the vibrant body. *If he goes too far, it is not Zylar we should fear. I will need to watch him closely.*

Tyson was now in the zone and deadly. He was relentless and once he had blown the transmitter of two enemy ships he let his agile mind send photon blast after photon blast to blow each of the ships to smithereens. Within minutes the enemy were on the run. The Cobras followed until Kabel gave the order to desist and keep within the protection of the *Elanda*. He was concerned that the crews needed more training and he didn't want them to overstretch their luck. Only two of the Venings survived and they retreated away from the flotilla until they disappeared off the radar.

Cheers rang out across the decks. Tyson stared glumly at the enemy-free space. He felt cheated, he had felt the huge spike in his power coursing through his body as the adrenalin from the fight and the anguished screams of the defeated echoed through him. He uncoupled from the turret and exited, followed by a thoughtful Zebulon who padded along behind him. Along the deck the other gunners were congratulating each other and their spirits were high. Bailey hugged his sister and then caught Tyson emerging from his turret. He began to smile a greeting to his friend and then it froze on his face as he saw the Changeling's demeanour behind him. Zebulon was walking slowly behind Tyson with his tail between his legs and his ears pinned back to his head. Bailey was aware that Zebulon exhibited the mannerisms of the animal he was transformed to and these mannerisms pointed to a high level of stress. His alarm bells were ringing and his eyes drifted to Tyson's and what he saw chilled him to the bone.

So much anger and scorn.

At this point he was happy that he had the training sessions with Kabel to work on blocking his mind to Tyson's incursions. Fortunately, Tyson was looking for Amelia and didn't see Bailey's expression. Zebulon looked at Bailey and the message was loud and clear…they needed to keep an eye on Tyson.

Amelia emerged from her photon gun booth and saw the glint in Tyson's eye and chose to ignore it, just pleased that they had fought off the deadly attack. She went to hug him and did not see the resentment directed at her by Gemma who had no Kabel to turn to as he was still sweeping the perimeter. Gemma stood with her arms folded taking in the picture of Tyson and Amelia greeting each other with hugs and kisses. Tyson seemed to access her thoughts as he looked past the relieved Amelia's shoulders and his eyes twinkled as he smiled at her. Gemma stubbornly refused to smile back.

There were no cheers from General Corder. The direction the Venings had taken was the exact coordinates of the planetary cluster where Zein resided. This was far from over.

Chapter 5: Coliseum

Belina laid her head on Bailey's bare chest, which heaved with the recent exertion of their love making. Bailey stared at the smooth steel ceiling in deep thought. Belina ran her fingertips over his chest tracing the outline of his pectoral muscle. She looked up at his vacant expression and was immediately concerned. Their love making had been as passionate as ever but now he seemed distracted, worried about something.

Belina remembered a phrase she had heard the humans use and thought it was perfect for this very moment. 'Penny for your thoughts?' she said warmly.

Bailey turned to her and kissed the top of her head. He was torn between the loyalty to his friend and his feelings for Belina. It didn't take him long to make a decision, his uncertainty was cancelled out by the concern he felt. He needed to talk to someone about Tyson. Bailey told her of his concerns and then went on to describe his feelings towards his friend and what had happened yesterday. Belina listened with her head resting on her hand staring up at him. When he had lapsed into silence Belina raised herself until she was the same height as Bailey and face to face. The warmth of her body pressed against her boyfriend.

'I think we are all intimidated a little bit by Tyson. He is very powerful but his heart is in the right place and you have to agree he loves Amelia?' She kissed him sensually on the lips, leaving her lips barely touching but lingering.

'Hmmm, you may be right. I just have never seen Zebulon so subdued,' Bailey pressed. Belina kissed him repeatedly, slowly, softly. Bailey felt his worries begin to fall away from him under the caresses of this beautiful woman.

Belina's hand drifted to his chest. 'I think I can take all your worries away,' she teased. It wasn't long before Bailey was in total agreement.

□□□

Kabel was faced by four of the Malacca clan. They flanked him from each corner of the room, each carrying a weapon in front of their bodies. Kabel tossed his seckle up into the air with his left hand, catching it smoothly with his right.

'Come on, do your worst,' said Kabel beckoning them forward. One of the men ran at him. He was a tough looking soldier with huge broad shoulders, knotted with substantial muscle, the same muscle that was behind the hand sweeping upwards to Kabel's gut. Kabel sidestepped bringing the back of his hand down on the attacker's arm and using the momentum of the run to fling the man into the side wall. Before he had completed the move two of the other men attacked. Kabel used the movement of the throw of the first man to carry him into his next offensive move.

His seckle clashed with the second man's weapon and he used the body of the second man as a launch pad into the third man with a two footed kick to his chest, sending the man crashing into a number of boxes stacked at the side.

Kabel jumped to his feet as the first man came for him again. The fourth man just hung back, waiting for his moment. The first man was more cautious this time and moved in slowly looking for an opening and Kabel intentionally let his eyes wander to the second man, struggling to climb back onto his feet.

The third man took this as his opportunity and moved fast to close the distance between him and Kabel. Too late, the man saw the error of his assumptions as Kabel whipped round, blocking the incoming blow and punching with his left hand into the solar plexus of the third man, who collapsed to the ground. Engrossed with this move he didn't see the copper pipe come spinning through the air, thrown by the second man and though Kabel just activated his personal shield in time, the force knocked him off his feet.

The fourth man saw his opportunity and he raced in with the second man and they both brought their seckles up to strike the telling last blow when, with a heavy grunt from Kabel, a spinning seckle traversed in a split second hitting and removing both seckles and spinning the two men around. Kabel followed up with two kicks to both the men's chests to send them toppling backwards.

Clapping broke out breaking Kabel's concentration as Amelia and Gemma whooped their support from the side-lines of the training mat. Kabel wiped the sweat from his forehead and provided a flourishing bow. He then made his way across to the fourth man and offered a hand up.

'Good move, Linus, using that intelligence well, you nearly had me,' said Kabel.

'Lord Blackstone, I think you give me too much credit,' said the huge soldier rubbing his bruised chest gingerly. The other soldiers stood up, each with a rueful smile.

Under strict instructions not too hold back they still came second best in the training sessions. They all saluted the Chancellor, respect clearly seen in their demeanour, and traipsed off to the showers.

'Well done, bro, now are you going to stop playing with the hired help and have a real fight?' said Tyson, with a sardonic tone whilst slowly clapping the spectacle in derision. He had entered the gymnasium just in time to see the sparring.

'Tyson! There is no need for that,' admonished Amelia as Gemma passed a towel for Kabel to dry his sweat covered upper body. Gemma handed him a drink of ice cold water from one of the many drinking fountains in the training arena.

The training arena was a massive room covering half of the forty-eighth deck with only the main aircraft and shuttle decks below it. It had a training capacity for a thousand soldiers at a time, with state of the art technology that worked on every muscular element of the body and included a hologram simulation area, now renamed the Coliseum, after the famous Roman monument, enabling whole platoons to practice battle movements and tactics across all manner of terrains.

The Coliseum was placed at the far end of the arena and was shielded off from the main arena by massive sliding doors. Behind the doors, members of the Tyther clan had spruced up the original environmental programmes, providing experience across desert, sea, fields and urban areas. If in single combat you were killed a bleep would trigger in an ear device and the training session would end. If a group exercise, then the programme would calculate the algorithms of the tipping point where the battle was won or lost either based on numbers slain or terrain taken. The area was amplified by the written code, which meant that once you entered it could feel like it was a particular city, country, ocean or continent and already during the last six months one exercise had gone on for days, until a senior officer called an end to the exercise.

'Amelia, I am only pointing out that fighting with those foot soldiers is hardly going to improve his skills to match Zylar's.' His statement earned a glare from Linus as he made his way to the showers.

'So what do you suggest dear brother?' Adrenalin causing Kabel to rise to the challenge. Amelia shook her head at Tyson sensing the wildness in her partner.

Tyson ignored her. 'Why don't we have a go in the Coliseum and fight the Ilsid?'

'Sounds good, which programme?' said Kabel, not backing down.

'How about one of the urban ones?' Tyson retorted and Kabel accepted without reservation.

'Kabel, there is no need to do this,' said Amelia, exasperated. She knew that nothing good would come from this bravado.

Men and their egos.

Amelia realised that nothing she could say or do would change their minds. People had been hurt in these realistic programmes and Amelia did not want either of her friends injured. The blades or guns wielded by the opponents had no impact when they hit a person, though the code registered a "hit" but soldiers could be thrown around and impact on the sets had left men and women bloodied and with a few broken bones. 'Look, if you want to do this hair-brained stunt then I am not watching,' said Amelia, stamping her foot in frustration.

Tyson laughed and placed an arm round her as Kabel tugged on a top. 'Don't worry we will look after each other, won't we, Kabel?'

'Of course dear brother, of course,' Kabel answered. Amelia didn't like the rising tension between them. She had spent many hours teaching Tyson how to calm his mind and anger and now just as she thought she was winning, they have to resort to this macho challenge.

'Gemma you coming?' she turned for support from her friend, only to find Gemma was engrossed in the battle of wits between the boys and therefore declining Amelia's request. Gemma's heart was beating fast caught up with the excitement of the situation.

'I would like to see how this plays out,' she said, running a hand across Kabel's back. Amelia just stared at her friend and seeing that she had no intention to either say anything to stop this stupidity or storm off like *she* had every intention of doing, vented an annoyed grunt and left the arena in disgust.

Tyson's eyes followed his girlfriend's ramrod retreating back with a hint of regret. Then shrugging his shoulders in resignation he raised his hand gesturing to the Coliseum, 'Now, shall we go and have some fun?' he said. They both walked to the console outside the Coliseum and Kabel opened the panel and reviewed the different programmes. He selected one of the urban ones and punched in the details, setting the number of opponents at twenty. Tyson playfully asked for more by holding his palm out and bouncing it up and down. Kabel doubled it to forty and as Kabel rested his hand on the panel, Tyson nudged Kabel's hand and it increased to four hundred.

'Four hundred Ilsid!' said a shocked Gemma, now wishing she had supported her friend to stop this nonsense. 'No one has faced four hundred Ilsid in the Coliseum, ever.'

'We are not just anybody, are we, Chancellor?' Gemma detected the resentment in Tyson's voice and for the first time felt a level of uncertainty. If Kabel had noted the change of tone he did a convincing act of ignoring it and turned to Gemma and took her hands in his.

'We will be fine, don't worry,' he said, his blue eyes twinkling. 'Remember we have our shields,' he reminded her. Gemma understood he was trying to alleviate the tension, it didn't help, and her heart was still racing. She gave him a quick peck on the cheek.

He dropped her hands and pulled from his jacket one of his real seckles to replace the wooden one he had used during the earlier training session. Tyson pulled out his own weapon; he now had his own seckles, handcrafted by skilful Tyther hands from the finest zinithium. Each picked up a photon shotgun from the rack of weapons outside the Coliseum.

'Shall we go, your Excellency,' said a smiling Tyson, cocking his shotgun and then holding his hand out directing Kabel to the doors, bowing with a mischievous look on his face. Kabel, following his gesture, laughed and took him up on his invite. The doors opened and on entering Tyson was surprised to find they were on Tower Bridge in London.

'Good choice brother,' said Tyson, 'A little history whilst we fight.'

'Thought you may like the setting as you are always going on about London,' replied Kabel, looking carefully around them. They were on the middle of the famous bridge which was built in the late 1900s and is a combined bascule and suspension bridge crossing the River Thames. The bridge itself consisted of two towers joined together at the upper level by means of two horizontal walkways, designed to withstand the forces of gravity exerted by the suspended sections of the bridge on the land facing sides of the towers. The vertical component of the forces in the suspended sections and the presence of the two walkways are supported by two robust towers. The bascule pivots and operating machinery, housed in the base of each tower, providing the mechanism that drove one of the most impressive sights in this large city allowing the bridge to part to allow large sailing ships or other large vessels through. All this above the dirty, murky, battling currents of the River Thames which flowed under the bridge, caressing its supporting foundations.

At this precise moment Kabel wasn't dwelling on the history lessons he used to enjoy with Malkin, his teacher for many years before he was killed in the attack on the mast in the Eastern Quadrant, more on what was happening on the opposite side of the river to the Tower of London where a charging mass of Ilsid were running to the bridge. He paled what had he signed up for!

'Come on let's go brother,' Kabel began to run towards the empty side of the bridge where the imposing silhouette of the Tower of London rose up from the ground. He stopped. Tyson wasn't moving but waiting for the hordes to reach them. 'Tyson, enough of your insane posturing, move,' shouted Kabel. Tyson looked with regret across the bridge and then reluctantly turned and ran with Kabel back towards the start of the bridge.

The Ilsid poured onto the historic bridge and without any hesitation stormed across it holding a collection of photon shotguns and seckles.

Tyson turned to face them when he reached the end of the bridge and let go a couple of shots at the advancing Ilsid. Two men fell. Kabel joined Tyson and sent a couple of rocket grenades from his all-purpose pump action photon shotgun. The grenades soared and then dropped into the mass of soldiers. The explosives exploded, killing many and sending a number of the Ilsid reeling, but still they came.

Kabel swore, and Tyson smiling at the apparent discomfort of his sibling and couldn't resist a quick quip, 'Now this is what you call a fight, Kabel.' His half-brother ignored the jibe. They ran down the steps and under Tower Bridge, followed by the rampaging Ilsid, their faces frozen in time.

Kabel went through the deserted gates until he was in front of the infamous Traitors Gate of the Tower of London. Above Traitors' Gate, set back was the Wakefield Tower and next to that was the Bloody Tower. The Tower of London, the building of which began in 1078 as part of the Norman Conquest of England by William the Conqueror, was a magnificent sight. Tyson always had a thrill when he saw it, yes, Kabel had chosen well. They turned to face their pursuers.

The Ilsid came at them five a breast, forcing the pair to fire a barrage of shots into the front line, but there were too many. Soon the Ilsid were close enough to use their seckles. Kabel's hands were moving so fast he made no attempt to follow their movement; he just relied on his extensive training. He knew he could not be terminally hurt, except if he fell over his own two feet, but the press of the bodies was intimidating.

Tyson was slashing and parrying with ease, Ilsid after Ilsid warrior falling dead before him, but still they came. The brothers were pushed back to the edge of the railings outside Traitors' Gate.

'Tyson, this is madness, we can't fight this many,' yelled Kabel. In answer, Tyson turned to face Traitors' Gate, using his shield to ward of the blows, and hooked one of his arms around Kabel's waist.

'Hold on tight, bro,' said Tyson with a manic look on his face. 'What the...,' Kabel spluttered, before Tyson leapt over Traitors Gate taking Tyson to the top of the Bloody Tower. Before Kabel could say another word, Tyson released him and set off across the battlements towards the steps down to Tower Green, a patch of grass beside the imposing White Tower, which stretched high into the sky. Kabel looked across and could see the Ilsid making their way to the main entrance below Tower Hill. It wouldn't be long before they were flooding into the fortress. He chased after the energised Tyson.

Outside following the fight on the big screen, Gemma felt her heart racing as the action unfolded, the excitement initially causing her body to shake with anticipation but quickly turning to dread when she realised Tyson was out of control, acting as if he had drunk four Red Bull cans in quick succession. She heard footsteps behind her and was pleased to see Amelia half running, half walking and following behind her were Hechkle and Bronstorm.

'How are they doing?' said Amelia, gasping for breath. When she had stormed off it wasn't long before she had sought her friends out and after explaining what had happened they all agreed they needed to see if Tyson and Kabel needed help.

'What the heck are they doing?' said the disbelieving Hechkle as he saw the Ilsid burst into the Tower of London fortress. Tyson and Kabel stood back to back on Tower Green fighting wave after wave of attacks. 'Can we not stop the programme?' asked Gemma.

'No, once started, the algorithms kick in and the only one who can override proceedings is the senior officer who set the scenario in motion,' Hechkle said, looking thoughtful.

'I am scared,' said Amelia, staring at the screen worriedly. 'I don't think Kabel will back down and I think Tyson will not be able to hold back any longer, look!' The companions all focused on Tyson. His face had lost the carefree wide-eyed look and the tension and fury were building within his face. Kabel was unable to see what was happening as his back was turned but

Tyson was now using one of his hands to spurt power directly into the midst of his attackers, reducing their numbers drastically. His force-field was building in strength and he seemed to be growing in height.

'If he allows his magics to explode he could kill Kabel,' said Amelia, noting the temper and lack of control in her partner, which she had spent hours managing.

Gemma began to panic and her heart rate was going off the scale. 'We have to do something,' she said pleading to her friends.

'I have an idea,' said Hechkle. He grabbed four bracelets and handed them to the worried friends. They didn't hesitate, trusting the big Fathom warrior immediately, all snapping the bracelets on. 'Grab a weapon,' he ordered, pulling his seckle from his tunic. Bronstorm, following the instruction, did the same. The girls grabbed a photon shotgun each. Hechkle punched in some details then turned to the waiting companions.

'Place your bracelet into the hologram and hold on as we enter the game.' They all nodded. 'Amelia you need to get to Tyson and calm him down and we will form a perimeter around you.' Amelia confirmed she would. With dry mouths they each thrust their arms with the bracelets on into the hologram and to their shock they were pulled into the programme by a powerful force. Amelia felt a sickness to her stomach as her centre of gravity shifted and she felt herself catapulted to another dimension.

Kabel had felt the increase in Tyson's power. It was so strong he could not fight back-to-back with his brother as Tyson's force-field pushed him away. He heard a loud pop and his face betrayed the surprise he felt when he saw Amelia, Gemma, Bronstorm and Hechkle in front of him.

'Help Tyson,' screamed Gemma to Kabel, laying down a concentrated blast of gunfire. Kabel turned and had to raise his hand to partially cover his eyes as the brightness emitting from Tyson was blinding.

Tyson hardly noticed the arrival of his friends. Inside him the magic was twisting this way and that, he felt it grow and consume his every movement, sound diminished. He didn't use either of his seckles but power was cascading from his fingers. The same thought came to him over and over again. *Kill, Kill, Kill.* Just like an Ilsid warrior.

Amelia fought against the force-field, using techniques taught by Lord Southgate to position her body to circumvent the powerful magic. There were three rules. Get close. Move slowly. Establish contact. Tyson felt soft arms wrap around him, a voice murmuring in his ear. The warm words began to seep through him. An Ilsid warrior launched himself at Amelia who was now at one with Tyson. He stretched out a hand and pure energy streamed from his outstretched fingers, tearing apart the programmed initiated attacker. Tyson felt calm return as the soothing words, like tendrils of smoke, curled around his thoughts and the tension eased from his body.

Amelia, it was Amelia.

Suddenly the Tower of London and the attackers disappeared. The battle was won, the algorithms calculating that the tipping point had been reached and switching off the game. The group stood gasping for air in the centre of the Coliseum, which was now just an empty box, the environmental programme no longer active.

Tyson felt Amelia's body against his and snapping out of his adrenalin fuelled battle state he looked down at her gentle brown eyes that shone with concern and love and he pulled her to him in an all-consuming embrace.

'What is going on here?' The sliding doors to the Coliseum had opened and in stalked General Corder, anger spilling out from his broad frame. Flanking him were twenty of his personal guard of US Marines. 'Who gave you permission outside prescribed hours to use the training programme? You know this is against regulations, don't you?' he snapped.

Tyson, who had felt the anger subside, now felt it surge forward, much to Amelia's and his other friends' alarm. He pushed Amelia away from him and before General Corder could react he had taken a few steps forward and placed his hand round his throat. The general's personal guard reacted swiftly with all the soldiers' weapons raised and pointing at Tyson's head. Not that this bothered the focus of their attention. 'Don't tell me what to do, Grandpa, you got that?' Tyson hissed.

'Let him go Tyson,' said Kabel, shocked, hastily stepping forward and placing a hand on the hand gripping Corder's throat, Tyson ignored him.

'Tyson, we should not have been in the game, please let the General go,' said Amelia, softly, her words enveloping him in that sweet manner that soothed his soul and the anger left him as abruptly as it had fired up. Tyson's shoulders slumped and he let go of Corder. The soldiers moved in but General Corder put a hand up to halt them as he clutched his throat, trying to catch his breath. It was Kabel who took charge.

'Stand down, let him go, put your weapons up,' said Kabel. The soldiers glanced across General Corder but he could not speak as he still had trouble breathing. They hesitantly and reluctantly dropped their weapons to point to the floor. Tyson flung a furious look at Kabel and then marched out of the arena, closely followed by Amelia. The rest watched them go with a sense of foreboding.

Chapter 6: Undercurrent

Prime Minister Charles Hamilton settled back in his chair, his hands creating a steeple for his chin to rest upon.

'Good move Charles,' Lord Southgate said, reaching forward and moving his bishop to build his attack on the expensive looking chess set. He then reached for another sip of the incredibly smooth and strong Mee wine that had now taken the unsuspecting palates of the Earth's wine drinkers by storm. The Zeinonians could not produce enough to meet the growing demand. The wine was now a must at every civilised dining table.

'You are not going to sucker me with faint praise Edgar,' said Charles, as he moved his queen to threaten his opponent's rook and knight at the same time.

'Hmmm, I don't think I am over doing the praise,' said Edgar. He shook his head and moved his rook. Charles immediately took his knight.

'Check,' he said. Lord Southgate laughed.

'And it is checkmate in two moves.' With that he toppled his king and stood up from the chess set. 'You beat me again Charles. Don't you find it uncomfortable carrying such a large brain on those shoulders?' he asked jovially.

Charles gave a wry grin and joined his friend at the drinks cabinet. They were in No. 10 Downing Street, the residence of the British Prime Minister, his family and the epicentre of the United Kingdom government. It had been a nailed on certainty that Charles would be made Prime Minister after the demise of Michael Dunstable at Zylar's hands. Charles missed the younger man greatly. The funeral was a day he would wish to forget, memories of Michael's tearful wife and distraught children hard to accept. He had also been struck by the sadness within Victoria Kirk. He knew that Michael was influential in her rise to prominence but the devotion she showed stripped away her political façade and showed how much he meant to her. Charles made a shrewd guess that the professional feelings were mixed with a deeper, personal connection.

On the day of his appointment the party members backed him nearly unanimously as the natural successor, a title he took with much regret. Since then he had worked non-stop to integrate the Zeinonians within Earth's population, though he owed a lot to the man opposite him. Lord Southgate had kept up an incredible workload within the Inner Council. He had made many friends and the relationships Charles had seen him nurture made him realise he was working with a consummate political animal; even the tough, no nonsense, Victoria, had taken to him. After a busy day, Lord Southgate and Charles had decided on a quiet game of chess in his private residence which he shared with his wife, Patricia, who had built up a strong bond with Lady Lucinda Southgate. Holding similar values both Charles and Edgar loved their wives deeply and the friendship had flourished.

Tonight a doubt was nagging Charles. A growing concern he had but kept to himself. Lord Southgate saw the dilemma in his friend's eyes and enquired as to what was troubling his chess companion.

Charles didn't reply initially, he leant forward and poured a generous portion of Mee wine into his goblet. They both followed the deep red wine flow from the bottle into the crystal glass. Standing up from his chair next to the stylish chessboard with his glass in his hand, he pondered the question his colleague had asked. 'The attacks by the Cabal are increasing all around the world,' he said, lifting his full glass to take a sip of the wine. The Cabal was the name, derived from the graffiti littered around the capital cities of the world, of the mysterious organisation that appeared to be behind the anti-Zeinonian movement, driven by their mistrust fed from the devastation wrought on New York, the thousands of deaths in Manchester, England and the promise of destruction from Zylar's own lips. Social media was riddled with scare stories like the one that rumoured the aliens would kidnap Earth's children and turn them into zombie-like soldiers. Decent people ignored the most outrageous claims but New York, Manchester, Zylar had all happened and Charles knew that an argument based on a solid foundation was a compelling one.

He sauntered over to one of the comfortable chairs in front of the roaring fire; it was a cold early spring night outside. Victoria had briefed Charles earlier that day on this very subject, concerned that the overall media coverage was working against the Zeinonians. The reporters almost seemed envious or suspicious of the Zeinonian achievements – that it was all too good to be true.

Lord Southgate joined Charles in front of the fire. 'I know but surely it is just misguided fools?'

'Edgar, I am not so sure,' said Charles, 'today there were six demonstrations in the capitals of Germany, France, Spain, Italy, Brazil and India. It was said that the totals across all demonstrations amounted to a million people. That's a worry.'

'They are just peddling uneducated fears surely,' said Lord Southgate, as he stretched out his legs to take in the heat from the fire.

'Yes, in some ways they are, but I can see people are fearful that what happened at Old Trafford or New York could happen in their countries and through history the fear of the unknown has always resulted in kneejerk reactions,' answered Charles.

'But surely we have shown that it was Zylar who was the threat.' Lord Southgate took a sip of his drink, 'We have turned most of your deserts into flourishing grasslands and eradicated cancer and HIV,' he espoused, drawing on the incredible progress made in the farming and medical worlds.

'I know, I know,' said Charles, struggling to hide the frustration he was feeling towards the negative elements within the political community, 'but they continue to complain that we should not trust you and that you're the aggressor.'

Lord Southgate gently placed his glass down on the table, noticing Charles's dilemma and concerned by the inflection in his friend's voice. A coldness swept through his body not related to the chill outside. 'Charles *you* don't think we have ulterior motives do you?'

Charles hesitated, only momentarily, but that was enough for Edgar's anger to spill over, his force-field sparking out of his body making his fireside companion inadvertently shrink back into his chair. 'You do, don't you? You believe this drivel?'

'Edgar, I don't, it's just…'

'What, just what?' said Lord Southgate, angrily, standing up.

'Zylar is still alive and he could return,' said Charles defensively.

'Zylar! All I hear is Zylar this, Zylar that, on your communication channels. If you peddle that he is what Zein stands for, you and your kind are very mistaken.' Lord Southgate's face had turned an unhealthy puce colour. Charles stood up, so he could be face to face with a man he had just, some few minutes before, been playing a splendid game of chess in a socially relaxed environment, which had just exploded as if a hand grenade had been lobbed into the room.

'I am sorry, Edgar I didn't mean to upset you. I am just worried.' He hadn't expected the conversation to deteriorate so rapidly.

'Charles if you don't believe in us then the Cabal have won, do you not see that?' said Lord Southgate, picking up his thick cloak and attempting to calm his anger, fearing to unleash his magics. His face displayed the sadness he felt at the turn of events, regretting that his concern was now manifesting into an attack on his friend. It all stemmed from the frequent reports he was receiving of the intimidation his people were facing from a sometimes sceptical human race. 'Charles, please don't lose faith in us,' was all he could muster before leaving the room. He left his friend cursing his own uncertainty.

Charles sat back down in the comfortable armchair and picked up the wine remembering the last debrief from Victoria. The most distressing element of the report was that the protests were turning violent with the demonstrators battling with the different police forces across the world. They had targeted Zein store owners and market stores where the previously popular clothes and goods of Zein folklore could be bought. The demonstrators' banners called on all Zeinonians to be given a distinguishing mark on their clothing so no interbreeding could happen and to limit their business expansion. They were the least aggressive suggestions. Others called for them to be locked up, moved into designated areas in the cities and segregated from the human population.

One particular distasteful episode was when a family of four from the Fathom clan, visiting Rome, had been cornered by the mob and the woman and daughter partially stripped and sexually assaulted, making the youngest child, a boy, watch. The father initially tried to stop the attack and was beaten to a pulp for his efforts and by the time the authorities were able to rescue them, it was too late for the man. The rest of the family were now in hospital with an armed guard.

In other cities stories of stalls being ripped down, physical intimidation and mob behaviour were more frequent but what happened in Rome ratcheted up the violence. In retaliation a platoon of Malacca troops had turned on a couple of hitchhiking students in the Eastern Quadrant and beaten them to within an inch of their lives. The two men were now both in a coma with their families angrily denouncing the "alien scum" across the media.

He slammed his fist down on the arm of the chair. As a historian he knew that he was facing a wind of change. Did they not see that over the centuries this had happened before, whether it was the Crusades, Spanish Inquisition, Nazi Germany or Apartheid and segregation in South Africa...that no good would come of this hatred or distrust?

Charles's gaze rested on the burning embers of the fire. He had to find a solution and promised that he wouldn't let all the good work go up in smoke. He didn't rest that night as he pondered his options. Tomorrow was going to be a big day.

□□□

The focus of his worry, the men and women of the Cabal, were on a video conference call, at the same time of the fiery meeting between Charles and Edgar. Their faces shrouded in darkness as they hid their identities from each other, a pre-requisite of their leader, the Speaker. They were listening to the update and pleased to hear it was all going to plan. The Speaker, the only one who knew each of the identities of those on the call, finished the events that had occurred that day and sat down.

One of the faceless members, with a strong accent that placed him in Asia, spoke. 'How are we going to secure the flow of zinithium?'

'Over the next few weeks we will be moving our assets around to each and every site where the raw material is mined. Before the end of the month all supplies of zinithium will be under our control,' said the Speaker.

'How about the remaining Zein forces, the Malacca clan army is still strong?' an American voice asked.

'They will be compromised and too busy protecting their own quadrant to be an issue,' the Speaker answered assuredly.

'The protests are going well but there are still many supporters of the aliens,' a strong guttural Germanic voice uttered.

The Speaker rose and leaned against the desk. 'Ladies and gentlemen, all will be taken care off. I have to ask, are you all still behind the vision?'

One by one they all confirmed their allegiance and when the last agreement was received, the Speaker raised hands to the ceiling triumphantly. 'The Cabal has spoken. Soon we will become the most powerful force not just on Earth but in the Universe,' the Speaker concluded, envisaging that the silhouettes of the twenty or so people from the most influential families, organisations and military in the world wore smug and satisfied smiles.

The Speaker closed the call on the powerful laptop and settled back in the chair at the solid Regency table. All was going to plan, control of the zinithium mining was nearly complete, and manipulation of public perception, even on the Zeinonian achievements was inflaming feelings towards the aliens. The Speaker smirked. The Cabal could only see the riches available; however, for the Speaker this was personal, with hatred for the Zeinonians running deep. Satisfied by progress the Speaker was ready to twist the knife and the most critical part of the plan would be set in motion. Soon the alien race will be under the Cabal's full control with nowhere to run.

Chapter 7: Zein

The companions decided to split up to search the vast ship for Tyson. When he left the fitness arena he seemingly disappeared with no one able to confirm where he may have gone. It was now almost three hours since the confrontation and his friends concern for their friend was growing. Kabel, Bronstorm and Hechkle took the stern, spreading out across the multiple corridors. The rest moved to the bow. They all worked from top to bottom, except Gemma, who decided to travel down in the sleek lift to the Embankment Floor.

Gemma's intuition told her that Tyson may have been drawn to the levitation tanks lined up side by side on this floor. The deck that contained the Embankment Floor was impressive, spanning the whole ship and included not just tanks but every other type of vehicle that any self-respecting expeditionary force would die for. Now the attraction of this impressive array of vehicles had brought her here. The floor, above the hangars that contained the fixed wing fighters, was an enormous space. She cast her eyes down the ranks of tanks and armoured vehicles and only saw a few token sentries. There was no one else down here so if he wanted to hide finding him could take some time.

'Hi, Gemma.' The greeting, though whispered quietly carried clearly in the large hangar.

Or not so long! Gemma turned to where the sound generated from and there he stood; her doubts of being able to find him evaporating quickly, a mixture of anger and concern overtaking her worry. He was leaning against one of the levitation tanks, staring into the distance, as if he carried the troubles of the world on his shoulders.

'Come to give me a lecture?' His voice was bitter and she realised that she needed to tone down her anger knowing he would be able to sense it.

'No, we are all worried about you,' said Gemma, approaching him slowly, unsure whether his anger was under control. Tyson turned to stare at her. His eyes were a dull blue and she noticed that his face looked a little grey as if he had aged a couple of years in the space of a few hours. 'You okay?' she asked.

'If you mean feeling like my body is not my own and endangering my friends, probably not?' said Tyson. Gemma reached up and held her hand against his face: it was cold She was concerned.

Where was the Tyson who used to have so much energy irritating the hell out of me?

Tyson turned his cheek against her warm hand, nuzzling in. Gemma moved closer. The physical attraction was immense. She was close to Kabel but Tyson was… dangerous. She ran her other hand down his right arm feeling the muscular outline. Tyson didn't say anything but kept his eyes in contact with hers. *Amelia.* His mind screamed at him. He was confused and felt his grip on reality slipping away from him as the magics inside him twisted this way and that, gnawing at his very soul.

The touch of Gemma caressing his arm and his cheek both inflamed him and soothed his turbulent internal thoughts. His whole body began to shake with wanting. The thoughts of Amelia were pushed to the side. Gemma felt Tyson's body shake as she pressed her body to his. The heat of his body radiated off him as the temperature around them soared. Her head was level with his neck and chin. She tilted her head back and Tyson felt the warm delicacy of her breath. His lips moved to meet hers and when they touched it was like a reverse electric shock. It didn't throw them apart but acted like a magnet as their bodies moulded to each other.

Sensual. Exciting. Dangerous.

They kissed hard and violently. No caressing now, their bodies on fire. Gemma felt herself lifted off the ground as Tyson wrapped his arms around her.

Amelia, Amelia…the voice in his head said her name over and over again pushing him back from the brink. Tyson relaxed his grip on Gemma, returning her feet to the ground and pushed her gently away from him. They could hear voices coming from the main lift as they stared at each other. Both panting, breathless, unsure what the last minute meant.

'Hey there they are guys,' said Bailey, spying the two across the hangar as he ran forward and then slowing down when he saw his sister and Tyson standing there silently with their chests heaving with the intensity of the kiss. Thinking quickly he turned round as Amelia and Kabel approached the pair. 'It's all right, Gemma has found him. He is fine,' said Bailey, shielding them from their approaching partners.

Pull yourself together, he thought so Tyson could pick up the warning.

Tyson gulped and dropped his gaze from Gemma's who snapped out of the dreamlike state she was in. Amelia ran past Bailey, ignoring Gemma and wrapped her arms around Tyson. He hesitantly did the same to her and she then surprised him by pushing him away and hit his arm with a clenched fist. 'Don't run off like that again,' said Amelia, angrily and then hugged him again. The others, even Gemma, smiled and Tyson couldn't suppress a small smile either. Bailey gave a sideways glance at his sister and she dropped her head to avoid his accusing stare.

The companions made their way to the Command and Control Centre via the main lift, where an uneasy silence descended with all thoughts focusing on Tyson, for different reasons. Tyson ignored the thoughts that swirled round his consciousness and cleared his mind, resting the back of his head on the cold steel of the lift. When they stepped out of the lift, Bailey pulled Gemma back. The others made their way to the nerve centre of the ship.

'What do you think you are doing? Don't you think this is screwed up as it is without you making a play for Tyson?' said Bailey, angry at his sister.

'I can't help it,' mumbled Gemma. Bailey could not hold back the dislike for his sister he was feeling.

'For years you knew Tyson liked you, yet you ignored him, leaving me to pick up the pieces. Then he finds someone as lovely as Amelia, your best friend, and you want to mess it all up!' Gemma blushed, the shame she was feeling reflecting the trueness of what her brother was saying.

'Amelia always gets the attention,' she said, feeling sorry for herself, a few tears rolling down her cheeks. Bailey eased off realising that this was a combination of long term issues and picking up that Gemma was truly regretting her actions.

'Gemma, I understand how you feel, I have seen Amelia sway even the most hard-hearted of boys but you can see, can't you, that she is the only one who can control Tyson?' His sister agreed knowing this was true.

'She loves him terribly,' said Gemma, quietly. 'I suppose I am still uncertain about Kabel and it is messing with my mind.' Bailey wrapped his arms around her and kissed her forehead.

'I know, give it time, a lot has happened and Kabel is a good man.' Gemma gently pushed her brother away and wiped away the tears and gazed respectfully up at him.

'Wow, look at my sensible brother, looking after his emotional sister, who would have thought?'

Bailey laughed. 'Hey, I am all grown up now, have a proper girlfriend and a gun.' Gemma laughed along with him and they hooked arms and went in search of their companions.

In the Command and Control Centre, General Corder was absently feeling his neck where the bruising was now apparent from Tyson's previous grip when they walked into the room. He was studiously reviewing the latest charts, ignoring the group, when Tyson approached him.

'Sir, please accept my apologies for my actions. It will not happen again,' said Tyson, formally. General Corder slowly put down the charts and turned to face Tyson.

'Accepted, young man. Any other action like that and I will have you confined to the Brig. Understand?' the army man replied standing straight and using all his military bearing to reinforce the words.

Tyson accepted the admonishment. Sometimes he felt lost, looking in on someone who was him, but not him. There were times he wished he could return to the old Tyson, playing sport and drinking beer. He just knew that he was never going back to those carefree days with his body and mind firmly pushing him into a strange world that he was struggling to keep pace with.

'Good. Lord Blackstone, can I ask you to look at these charts and to help us understand where we are on our journey?' said General Corder, dismissing Tyson from his concern. Kabel joined him and they began to review the charts. They had a pre-set course programmed into the ship's computer, similar to how they teleported. The difficulty they were facing was the lack of understanding of the impact related to the more aggressive bending of space and time on the accuracy of the coordinates that the Zein Inner Council had provided to the Expeditionary Force. The others retreated from the Command and Control Centre glad to leave the strategy decision makers to their own, egotistical world.

They all decided that they needed food and went to the canteen which was packed. This was no dreary metal room with stodgy food. The first thing which hit you on entering was the huge atrium housing full grown trees centred in a room that spanned a quarter of the top deck at the back of the ship. The glass roof could be covered with sliding steel shutters in the event of approaching asteroid belts or in the time of battle it would close like large all weather stadiums.

Looking up at the reinforced fused silica heavy duty glass you were able to look out on the twinkling stars of wherever in the galaxy you were travelling through. There was every cuisine known to man and Zeinonian on offer, all beautifully cooked by the extensive catering staff complement. You could eat at formal tables or take a stroll under the trees and have a picnic. This was a place you came not just to eat but to relax.

After selecting a range of meals from their daily allowances they sat down at one of the large oblong tables, similar to those used at the Federation Fair. Hechkle and Bronstorm sat opposite each other as they tucked into their food. Bailey, sitting next to Bronstorm, glanced across at the big warrior and then at his other companions. He saw the strain of the last few days clear on their faces and it was then Bailey decided it was time for some light relief. He grinned inwardly; it was time to bring the big man down. He cleared his throat and roughly pushed away his empty plate so that it clanged against Hechkle's plate and stood up, leaning his fists on the table facing his hulking companion. Hechkle initially went still and then continued eating his food as if nothing was happening.

'Hechkle, I bet my evening meal against yours that I could eat ten doughnuts quicker than you,' said Bailey, with his stance wide and moving his hands onto his hips, trying to intimidate the six foot four inch muscle man. Hechkle still didn't look up at him but simply finished his food, placed his knife and fork in the middle of his empty plate and then wiped his lips with his napkin.

'Scared are you, Mr Muscle man?' Bailey goaded him with a big smile creasing his face, taking away the menace in the aggressive statement. Tyson laughed as did Amelia. Gemma's mind was still on what had happened on the lower deck and was quietly eating her chicken salad. Then Hechkle slowly stood up. On the table they were seated at and on other tables around them, those who had heard the challenge exited their seats and formed a circle around the two men. Hechkle dropped his napkin onto the plate.

'Is that your white flag of surrender?' Bailey prodded at the great man's pride. Hechkle, with a twinkle in his eye, eventually raised his bushy eyebrows and emerald eyes to stare at his tormenter. He stood up and leaned on the table, mirroring Bailey's initial stance. Even though it was a playful challenge, Bailey couldn't help but swallow nervously when faced with the man mountain just a few feet away from him.

I never want to cross this guy for real.

'Bring it on, puny human,' Hechkle growled. As soon as he accepted the challenge, Bronstorm as quick as lightning fetched twenty doughnuts from the plentiful desert table and plonked them on the table. Hechkle gave his fighting partner a look that would curdle milk. Bronstorm just raised both his eyebrows in complete innocence.

'Just helping,' he said, sweetly as if butter wouldn't melt in his mouth.

Hechkle gestured Bailey to the seat opposite to him vacated by Bronstorm and they both took their places.

'Now big man, the rules are you must eat all the doughnuts and have nothing left in your mouth to win, have you got that or do I draw you a picture?' said Bailey, cheekily. Hechkle gave no smile. It was as if he was facing a squad of Ilsid and not a light-hearted eating contest.

'Zeinonian versus Human,' said Hechkle, adding to the laughter around the table and more raucous name calling from the watchers.

Amelia stepped forward and gave the count down. When she reached one the two men grabbed two doughnuts each. They alternately took a bite out of each doughnut, and then stared at each other as they swallowed the first mouthful before cramming the next huge bite into their mouths. Within the first minute they demolished the first two before moving onto the next two. Both wouldn't avert their gaze from each other, making it a very comical picture.

The shouting of their supporters became louder and louder, clearly split between human and Zeinonian. Tyson, who up to this point had been joining in the fun, began to pick up abundant random thoughts from the supporters.

Show him that we are better.
Humans have no guts.
Muscle freak is going to lose.
How dare he challenge one of us!

Tyson opened his mind to more thoughts. He was shocked. The enmity between the opposing camps was clear to see. He felt uneasy. This did not bode well for the expedition. Bailey was ahead and had two doughnuts left and Hechkle had three. The crowd grew closer and the shouting of encouragement louder. Both Hechkle and Bailey, fixated on each other, did not pick up the building atmosphere around them but Amelia and Gemma did. They had both been laughing with Gemma breaking out of her quiet state, now they began to pick up the vibes, as did Bronstorm whose stance changed from relaxed to anticipating trouble. Bailey stuffed the last doughnut in his mouth and chewed vigorously. Hechkle looked beat but continued as best as he could. Bailey finished his last doughnut and stood up triumphantly, his arms out wide accepting the cheering from the human contingent. Hechkle groaned. It was then that Bailey realised that the activity he had thought of to lighten the day had backfired. The resentment emanating from the Zeinonians and the aggression of the humans made for a volatile mix.

One of the Malacca soldiers standing behind Bailey pushed him. Bailey pushed him back. Another Malacca soldier stepped aggressively towards Bailey and Hechkle leapt across the table to stand in front of Bailey, protecting him. The Malacca soldiers backed off a little faced with the intimidating presence of the Fathom warrior. Bronstorm turned to face the human wall of the crowd behind him. The soldiers pushed forward. Bronstorm automatically crouched waiting for the attack from the jeering onlookers. No weapons were allowed on the ship, with all of them locked away unless given dispensation by either General Corder or Lord Blackstone; this would be a fist fight.

Two US Marines attacked Bronstorm. He blocked the first punch thrown and ducked the other man's fist, he then pushed the second man into the first and they both went tumbling down. Hechkle took his eye off the Malacca soldier in front of him to see if Bronstorm was all right. The man used this diversion to deliver a punch to the tall man's stomach. His fist met stone-like muscle and he let out a yelp. Hechkle just grinned evilly and grabbed him by his shirt and then by his trousers and picked him up and threw him at the man's advancing friends. They all went down in a heap of legs, arms and torsos. Then it was a free for all as the canteen erupted into a mass fight.

Hechkle made his way to the side of Bronstorm who, without catching breath, saluted his fellow companion who grinned back with a reckless smile as he flung a heavyset, crew cut US Marine across one of the tables, the man rolled off the table and crashed into the chairs beside it. The partners of many a fight relished the support of each other as they fought off the hordes of attackers and for a few minutes their Fathom battle cries rang over the melee in the canteen. Tyson gleefully joined in, revelling in the physical confrontation, less so Amelia and Gemma who had to defend themselves not just against some of the Malacca clan female soldiers but also their male counterparts. It was complete anarchy and then Bailey became isolated with a group of ten Malacca soldiers who had armed themselves with chairs and cutlery. Bailey had blocked a couple of the attacks but the chair he was holding to defend his body was shattered. He fell to the floor and caught his breath when he saw the madness in the eyes of the Malacca men converging on him. Hechkle was fending off an attack by four humans and couldn't reach him, and then the cavalry arrived for Bailey.

Tyson leapt in front of the attackers with his blue force-field activated and he grew before their very eyes with the power radiating from him. This time he was in complete control of his magics and the attackers backed off. Fear flashed across their faces. He projected his thoughts throughout all those fighting. *You will all calm down now or I will need to take action,* Tyson articulated the words in the others minds, pronouncing each telepathic syllable carefully. Those fighting shook their heads to remove the voice but they couldn't; even those trained to prevent incursions had no defence against such power channelled through Tyson.

The fights dwindled and then stopped, many just stood panting with the exertion and a few nursing minor injuries and nose bleeds. All had a certain level of residual resentment. However, the temperature in the room cooled as tempers were controlled. Then the ship alarm began to echo around the room and all in the canteen pushed the recent altercation to the back of their minds and picked up their jackets and rushed out of the room.

'Are we under attack again?' Bailey asked, confused. Tyson cleared his mind and sought out the mind of the young radar engineer in the Command and Control Centre.

'Bronstorm, let's go straight to the Cobra,' said Hechkle, pulling his colleague towards the entrance.

'That will not be necessary, Hechkle, we are here,' said Tyson, quietly amidst the commotion all around them. Amelia went to his side.

'You mean…' said Gemma.

'Yes.' Tyson looked at the faces of his friends, excitement breaking across his face. 'We have reached your home planet my Fathom friends.' Both Bronstorm and Hechkle faces became flushed with a building expectation. 'Zein is in our sights.'

Chapter 8: Master Race

Leila wiped the perspiration off the young girl's face. 'Push, Megan, push,' she instructed the young woman who was on her back with her knees up. She mustn't be any more than twenty years old, yet here she was delivering her first baby.

Delilah wiped the forehead of the girl, who was yelling out in pain.

'Push, Megan, push,' said Leila, as she saw the baby's head. The baby came with a rush and the scream of the new arrival could be heard throughout the medical bay. Leila checked the baby, drawing on her past history of midwifery, and then, after cutting the umbilical cord, wrapped the baby up and presented her back to the young mother. The girl turned her head away from the baby.

'Take it away,' she said, her eyes dead. No love. No warmth.

'Megan, it is a beautiful baby girl,' said Leila, trying to convince the poor girl.

'It's a monster from a monster,' Megan retorted. Leila had half expected that this may be her reaction and she motioned to Delilah to take the baby away. She would give Megan time, like the others, in the hope she would eventually come around. This was the third baby born since they had been kidnapped onto the ship, the second girl.

'You rest honey, we will bring her back later,' said Leila, lightly with a hint of sadness in her voice. She turned to one of the guards at the door; a dour mercenary from the Malacca clan.

'Can you please let Zylar know that it is a girl and that the mother is very weak and needs plenty of rest and medical attention.' The guard scowled, lazy and not wanting to do any tasks, then he saw the determination on Leila's face and reluctantly left the room to deliver the message. Leila had played this game before. She did what she could do to protect the twenty human women from the breeding programme that Zylar had set out for them. Zylar, after experiencing first-hand the exploits of Tyson had realised that if he could sire enough half-breeds then he could create an army of Tyson's. A kind of master race, a clan of no equals. When Zylar was a child he loved to listen about all the battles that Earth's chequered path had brought. It was from one of these brutal warrior civilisations that he took the name for his master race. The Sparta clan now numbered three.

While plotting his now doomed conquering of Earth, he had set the late General Chad the task of capturing young women over eighteen but under twenty-five years old for the sole purpose of breeding. The women, selected by a range of tests which were administered to them unwittingly, including tests on intelligence genes, looks and level of fertility, undertaken while they were sleeping after a strong knock out gas had been injected into their own bedrooms, came from all corners of the world. When a girl passed the fertility tests they would be "harvested" and transported to Zylar's battleship *Discovery*. He had targeted a hundred women but the defeat at the Southern Quadrant Palace meant that his plan was curtailed.

Once he had recovered from his injuries he frequently selected one of the young women to be brought to his quarters. The scared women had no choice but to comply. One girl fought back, trying to stab him. She was a student from Oxford, England and quite beautiful. He brought her in front of the remaining girls and had her flogged. When her sobbing, bloody body was lying on the floor, he had commanded his troops to treat her wounds and bring her to his quarters when her wounds healed. From that point all the women did exactly what he wanted them to do. The girl with the bloody back was taken to the medical centre, where she was treated. Since that fateful day Megan had not uttered a word until now.

Leila asked the physician to administer a sleeping drug and left the medical centre with Delilah. The two had grown extremely close and Leila had pleaded with Zylar not to hurt Delilah but she didn't need to worry, there was no interest in the girl. She was Zeinonian and therefore her worth to him was in her link with Kabel. It was Zylar's hope that Kabel will rashly pursue him to free his step-sister.

'He has asked for Joanna tonight,' said Delilah. Leila groaned. Zylar had taken a distinct liking to a small number of the girls; although he bedded them all, some had more attention than others, making the last ten months a difficult situation. Joanna was South African and only nineteen and fragile. She was a petite, black, mousy brown haired girl and somehow Zylar had felt a connection. As his ardour increased, Joanna went further into herself. Leila knew she was protecting herself in the only way possible, by building up mental walls to separate the abuse.

'Enough is enough,' said Leila, disgust spreading through her. She had thought about trying to stab him when he was engrossed in something else, but he seemed to have a sixth sense or knew what she was going to do. There was no way to surprise him, leaving her no choice but to support the girls and help them through the nightmare.

'What are you going to do,' said Delilah, not liking the look on Leila's face.

'Give him what he wants.'

'No, you can't do that,' Delilah protested. Leila, leant over and kissed Delilah lightly on the forehead.

'Go and look after Joanna for me,' she pleaded.

'But...' Delilah started saying. Leila placed a finger against the young women's lips.

'I am a big girl Delilah, I can deal with Zylar.' With that she left a worried Delilah and went to her own room to change and then went through the quiet corridors to Zylar's quarters. Outside his doors stood two Ilsid, they stepped to one side and she entered the room with a shudder, the silent soldiers gave her the creeps.

Soft music was playing and Zylar was staring out of the window at the beautiful array of constellations. He was in a good mood; it was the end of a very successful day meeting the emissary of Prince Jernli of Xonia, a repulsive reptilian like humanoid, called Yisli. When the Xonian patrol had shown up on their radar, before they could attack, Zylar had used his magics to reach out to the aliens. The picture he painted of Earth and their inhabitants had intrigued the commander and the request for an audience conveyed back to Skegus. Zylar originally planned to go to Zein, crush any resistance and take control of the planet, that decision taken away from him with the loss of the core of his troops. He needed to rebuild his army and the Xonians he had studied from the histories collated from the original Zein Inter-Galactic Expeditionary Force databanks made the Xonians the logical choice...the main issue he now faced was that he could not trust them. He would need to watch them closely.

The meeting with Yisli started badly with threats to blow his ship out of the sky. It was only when Yisli was shown the recordings of Earth and a glimpse of the kidnapped human girls, via the CCTV in their quarters that the discussions became more amicable.

Agreement was reached with the Xonians pledging to support him in building his new Ilsid army in return for the coordinates of Earth and the rights to the planet. He had no issues with this request; lose Earth in the short term but these fools didn't realise the power of the army he was going to build and before they knew it he would conquer their empire from within…they wouldn't know that they were helping build an army designed to defeat them… yes a very good day as he scanned the two ships flanking his ship, *Discovery*, left by Yisli, to guide him to the conquered planet of Skegus.

I have the beautiful Joanna tonight, he thought. *So quiet and submissive, should be fun.* He heard the door open and shut and turned round to meet his guest; his face registering surprise at seeing Leila.

Leila let her eyes take in the music, soft lighting and the robed commanding figure of Zylar. She was going to dishonour the memory of Tyson's father tonight but it was a price worth paying - if she could take this monster's mind off the breeding programme, there might be a respite for the girls. Zylar had tried to win her over constantly and wanted her to accept him without force. Well, he had won. Zylar's face was confused. 'Where is Joanna?' he asked.

'Resting,' was the quick response.

'I am sure she is but I asked her to be here tonight. Do I need to provide another lesson?' he threatened.

'No, I just thought I could make you an offer you could not refuse.'

His face still retained that confused look. He had enjoyed the last few months. Travelling more slowly than he wanted to the Capulus Novus System so as not to deplete his limited zinithium stores, he had made sure that there was plenty of fun in the long nights.

Now what was this irritating human doing to disturb his pleasure?

Seemingly in perfect timing, as if she were reading his mind, Leila undid the belt of her kimono and let it slide to the floor, exposing her naked body. Her heart in her mouth, she walked up to him as his mouth fell open and his hungry eyes took in the beautiful, womanly, hourglass figure. He took note of the swell of her breasts and the sexual sway of her hips.

'Instead of girls, how about a real woman?' she said seductively. She kissed him, her neck straining to reach his lips. She fought the revulsion of the touch as his cold hands touched her skin as she untied his robe and slipped it off his shoulders. He broke off the kiss.

'Well, well, I knew you could not resist for ever.' His arrogant tone cut her to the bone but it didn't stop her as she kissed his face, chest and lips. His excitement rose and he lowered her onto the bed before joining her on the large round mattress. Leila let herself experience the moment, pushing her real thoughts deep inside her. He was only a man and one day she would repay him for this. For now she had to satisfy his desires to pull him into her web of deceit.

Chapter 9: Promised Land

The high level of excitement and anticipation was palpable around the ship. When everyone realised that their long journey was ending, all who could jostled for space at the many windows to look at the fast approaching new world. What they saw took their breath away. For the Earthlings it was the experience of a new star system and for the Zeinonians it was home. For the latter all they had ever known was what was taught in the classroom and the detailed environmental programmes they had grown up with, now they could see where their very existence emanated from.

They saw a smallish planet, when compared with Earth, flanked by two suns. The two suns were roughly forty-five degrees apart and both considerably smaller than the Earth's sun. If you made use of the numerous telescopes placed strategically on each floor of the ship you could make out two further planets, mere specks in the distance supported by their own sun.

'That there is Oneerio and its sister planet Skegus, take a look,' said Kabel, gesturing to Gemma to look through the telescope. Gemma pressed her eye to the device and could see a colourful planet and a more barren one. She looked up questioningly at Kabel.

'They share the same sun but look considerably different, why's that?' she asked.

'Oneerio is closer to the sun and the temperatures are higher and therefore the land has little moisture. The Oneerions first populated Oneerio, hence their name they inherited, due to the incredible range of raw materials below ground. To ensure their survival they intelligently populated the sister planet when they came to this system some four thousand years ago.' He paused as Amelia, who was standing cuddling into Tyson, gave a surprised gasp.

'Amelia, you are right their civilisation is much older than ours. They are the most skilled craftsmen in the known Universe with the ability to use any substance in the creation of their cities.' His mind drifted back to Malkin, his teacher in Earth's Zein Western Quadrant, and the many lessons he taught on this subject. He remembered one particularly point. 'Skegus gives them what they do not have on Oneerio, water and a more comfortable place to live. Oneerio is more of a mining planet where they work,' said Kabel, relishing the passing on of his previous schooling to the onlookers.

The group found this all very interesting but their attention inevitably switched back to the rapidly advancing planet of Zein and Kabel realising he had lost their attention, lapsed into a disgruntled silence. They could make out vast lakes and mountain ranges, grasslands and a few desert regions. Kabel and Tyson made their excuses and strolled up to the Command and Control Centre.

General Corder and Admiral Koshkov were in deep conversation with Walter Moore. As they approached, Walter, with a large welcoming smile on his face pulled out of the conversation and came to meet them.

'What's happening?' Kabel enquired, to be told by the likeable scientist that agreement was under discussion on how to set out the security perimeter when they landed.

'So we are going to land all three ships?' Tyson enquired. There had been discussions that they should leave at least one if not two destroyers in orbit for defence. The debate had raged for many hours at a number of the key strategy meetings, with General Corder wanting to conserve zinithium by landing all three ships and Admiral Koshkov, supported by Kabel, vouching for a more defensive approach by retaining at least one destroyer in orbit.

'I have completed my calculations on how much zinithium we would consume if we leave *Brooklyn* or *Manhattan* in orbit.' Walter abruptly stopped talking, as he saw over Kabel's shoulder, Admiral Koshkov angrily walk away from General Corder. 'And the base fact is that we would burn up too much of our stores,' he said, his attention still slightly diverted by the commotion across the room.

'Fair enough, but I don't remember anyone consulting me,' said Kabel, a little angry that the decision had been taken without Zeinonian, and specifically, his agreement. He decided he needed a talk with General Corder and marched across to the officer.

'I believe we are landing all three ships, General,' Kabel asked, pulling Corder's attention from the orders he was relaying to his command, a young female officer from the Russian Federation. She could see that to stay was to upset an increasingly frustrated Lord Blackstone and made a hasty retreat.

'Yes, not an easy one and I apologise that I did not confirm with you but you were nowhere to be found,' said General Corder, as he smoothed his pristine uniform with his hands.

'These decisions affect my people as well as yours,' Kabel said angrily. 'I feel we are leaving ourselves open to attack from the Xonians and Zylar.'

Their raised voices had caught the attention of the crew in the room. The mixture of humans and Zeinonians watched apprehensively the spat between their leaders. Tyson, as he had in the canteen, picked up the unhealthy vibes from all the parties viewing the spectacle, split evenly between the races. Walter Moore nervously licked his lips. Not one for confrontations he monitored the battle of wits between Kabel and the General. He was still concerned about the negativity within the human population he witnessed first-hand every day, which was only supported by what had happened in the canteen…news about the fight having filtered up to him…the ship was a powder keg of racial division. Since he was, he would like to think, a reasonably intelligent and learned man, he knew all about the history of such antagonism.

In the meantime, General Corder, who had brushed aside the canteen fracas as "high spirits" and not an issue, was not going to be dictated to by Kabel. 'I was placed in overall charge of the military operations of this expeditionary force and I made the decision based on the data from the head of the science team, Dr Moore, and so the decision stands.' The force of the last words hit Tyson hard and he felt the temper within him rising which he desperately tried to control.

Kabel stood his ground. 'I am warning you, Corder, don't overstep yourself.' A number of the US Marines stationed in the Command and Control Centre and who had sanction to carry weapons lifted their guns menacing at Kabel's change in tone.

'Any problems, bro?' Tyson edged forward to stand close behind Kabel, in control of his anger bubbling away inside him…*for the moment*, he thought wryly. General Corder's eyes immediately flicked to him, as did the soldiers. There were no armed Zeinonians in the room but everyone knew what Tyson was capable of. A couple of the soldiers licked their dry lips in concern.

Walter Moore had seen enough. 'Kabel, until we find what raw materials are remaining on Zein we need to be careful not to unduly deplete our store of zinithium.'

Kabel tore his gaze from the US General and stared at Walter, torn between his respect for the scientist and keen not to give in to the human in front of him. The likeable Walter seized his opportunity to calm the situation down further. 'I have devised, with members of the Tyther clan, a couple of probes that we can launch into the atmosphere before we land. These probes will beam signals to *Elanda* as an early warning of any ship coming within any threatening distance of Zein.'

Kabel glanced at the soldiers on the deck, nervously holding their weapons ready, and then asked Walter, 'Will we have time to launch the destroyers?'

'The early warning should provide sufficient time to send at least one of the destroyers into orbit,' replied Walter.

Kabel pulled his gaze back to General Corder. 'General, I accept your decision this time but please do not make the mistake of not involving me in a key order again.'

Tyson, fired up with the aggression in the room, was disappointed that nothing had escalated. He decided to have a little fun anyway, pushing his head forward aggressively and snarling at the US Marines, who held their weapons even more tightly. Tensions were running high and Tyson was in no mood to lower the friction, the magics licked at his senses feeding on the aggression and need for a challenge. The tension was only lightened when Kabel, pulled him away to prepare for the landing.

Nikolai saw the conflicts happening within the team and caught the eye of Tyson when he and Kabel were strapping themselves in, as *Elanda* prepared to enter the

Zein atmosphere. Tyson saw that the Zeinonians had a supporter in the experienced Russian officer. Nikolai had no love for the Americans, especially since he was responsible for the twenty thousand Russian soldiers making up a sizable proportion of the military force. He remembered the time prior to the launch when he was selected. He said no, his mistrust of the Western political apparatus running deep within his veins. He remembered the Cold War and the underhand tricks the Western intelligence agencies employed one which caused the death of his father, during an extraction of a scientist from Minsk by the CIA. He knew he was selected not for his ability to work effectively with the Allies but for his stubborn, almost protective manner for his country. The Russian senior command rationalised that it was this that would protect their interests during the quest coupled with his vast experience gained in Chechen and as a young soldier in Afghanistan.

Useful to know, Tyson thought. He touched his forehead in acknowledgment, which generated a curt nod back from Nikolai, before turning his attention to the approaching planet.

'General, the two probes are ready to launch,' said Walter, in a business-like tone. General Corder pulled his attention away from Kabel and issued the order to launch. The two probes shot from the *Elanda* and went spinning away in opposite directions until they settled in their pre-programmed orbit. Walter checked the tracking figures and then straightened from the console. 'The probes are fully operational.' General Corder switched on the Expeditionary Force intercom that connected all three ships. His voice boomed out across all decks.

'We will be landing all three ships on the surface of Zein shortly. Our target is the capital city, Reinan, where the last messages were sent from some twenty years ago.' General Corder motioned to Kabel to address the communication link. 'I would like to pass this moment to Lord Blackstone on what is a historic date for all of us but especially for every Zeinonian.'

Kabel accepted the offer, clearing his throat, unexpectedly feeling the pressure of the occasion and wishing Malkin were here with him on this historic day. 'Colleagues of this First Joint Expeditionary Force, this is a momentous occasion. We do not know what we will find. There could be tremendous danger in store. All I would ask is for your commitment and strength of character and as one of Earth's heroic figures once said "One small step for man" when stepping onto Earth's moon, I say now that this is a great leap of faith and achievement for both human and Zeinonian alike.' The speech went down well with cheering breaking out in the Command and Control Centre and echoing throughout the ship.

General Corder gave an impressed look to Kabel and then he commanded the pilots of the three ships to take them in.

The ships headed towards the planet. They broke through into the Zein atmosphere with the zinithium acting as the thermal protection system, keeping the hull of the ships cool on re-entry. The planet in front of them grew larger until they could make out numerous settlements. Kabel, held his breath trying to quell the excitement and anticipation rising within him; a feeling many on the ship were experiencing. Travelling closer to the settlements that sprawled the valleys, he now could make out individual buildings as they roared over the villages on the way to the capital, Reinan. His excitement changed to horror. Every village they flew over was wrecked. Buildings with walls and roofs partially demolished, empty streets strewn with rubbish, no sign of life, wild animals wandering through the once beautiful and mosaic streets with the bright white stone of the villages dirty and dishevelled. The villages were surrounded by plush gardens and acres of grass fields, blue in colour to the Zeinonians and green to the humans. They could see many strange and beautiful animals running away from the new noise, some galloping away with great speed. You could make out a waterfall on the outskirts of each village, contained within the once perfectly sculptured gardens.

Kabel surveyed the wreckage silently, his disquiet increasing as the destruction grew. The ships flew over a mountain range and then ducked down to the wide plain where the capital of Zein was situated. They approached the outskirts of the city. Reinan was sprawled over many acres and there was no sign of life, with buildings covered in vines and vegetation. You could make out the now common wheel structure of the city with the spokes of the streets leading to the central main buildings hub. They followed the spokes of the wheel for some distance until they hovered over the huge central circle that housed the Grand Zein Central Transportation hub next to the regal and intricately designed Royal Council. Both buildings showing considerable signs of distress but they still carried an awe-inspiring hold on human and Zeinonian alike.

The ships hovered for a moment taking the spectacle in and then all sped away until they reached the outskirts of the city that once held five hundred thousand Zeinonians. The ships landed in a wide valley near a fresh water river. Near to them was a vast ornamental park which was a huge version of the Falls in Livescale, the principle city village in the Zein Earth Colony Western Quadrant, where Kabel had grown up. The destroyers settled down on either side of the *Elanda* with their hulls to the river.

They were positioned a reasonable distance away so they could provide adequate cover for the enormous ship.

'Lord Blackstone, I will need your assistance to set up the defences,' said General Corder. Both left the Command and Control Centre, leaving Admiral Koshkov in charge.

The setting up of the outer defences took the rest of the day. Beacons were hammered into the ground around the three ships forming a temporary Outer Perimeter Barrier powered by zinithium, the beacons passing the beams between each other preventing any animal or person from breaching the defence. The force-field was projected to a beacon on the top of each ship, which meant that no attack from land or air could be made and the crew could walk within the perimeter freely without fear of attack. They offloaded a number of the levitation tanks and armoured cars, placing the tanks at strategic positions near the Outer Perimeter Barrier. Enjoying the exercise, Hechkle and Bronstorm busily moved crates from the ramp to the tented areas set up for training and research.

Gemma was taking in the fresh air after the staleness of the recycled oxygen that was pumped round on-board the ship. She saw Bronstorm and Hechkle exchange jibes at each other and marvelled at how they got on when Hechkle was some number of years older than the youthful Bronstorm. She had witnessed the closeness of the two over their many adventures and was intrigued to hear more about how they met.

Bronstorm took a breather, sipping some water as Hechkle continued, his strength undiminished by the demanding work. Gemma saw her chance and casually went to stand next to him. They exchanged warm greetings. Bronstorm wiped a bead of sweat off his brow and took another swig of his water.

'I see the big man is still going?' said Gemma, as Hechkle launched a huge crate at three of the US Army men to catch and they struggled to hold it, cursing the big Fathom man in the process.

'Yep, nothing tires out old Hechkle.' Bronstorm's pride in his voice was clearly noticeable.

'You think highly of him, he is special to you, isn't he?' Bronstorm nodded and took another swig. 'Don't get me wrong, I think Hechkle is brilliant and we are all very fond of him, but what is your story, how did you meet? You have never said.'

Bronstorm, at first, flashed a look at Gemma and she saw protectiveness in his eyes. He then let his eyes fall to the ground as he scuffed the ground with his boots. Gemma waited patiently. Seemingly to make a decision, Bronstorm replaced the cap onto the water bottle with a loud click.

'I was an eight year old kid and my family were travellers, not wanting to be cooped up in the Core.' Gemma held her breath, seeing the deep feelings this story was already dragging from the young soldier's memories. 'There was my Mama and Pa and my older brother, Jeb, and we were close you know, really close,' said Bronstorm, with a faraway look. Gemma let out her breath slowly not wanting to disrupt the story. 'We sold fine clothes, beads and the like and we were in the Eastern Quadrant visiting this pretty large settlement when it was attacked by the Ilsid.' Bronstorm's voice carried pain and Gemma began to regret bringing the story up. 'When they attacked we were near a well in the main plaza and Jeb told me to climb into the bucket and then he and my Pa lowered me down, before wedging the handle to keep me from going into the water.'

Gemma, seeing the tears in his eyes and now feeling guilty, placed her hand into his. Bronstorm squeezed her hand in thanks. 'I heard the screams of not just my family but the hundred or so other inhabitants as they were tortured, then killed,' said Bronstorm, his voice low and pained. 'They killed every man, woman and child in the settlement and no one died easily. They coldly wounded the men and tied them up and systematically made them watch their wives and children be cut up in every imaginable way before killing them all.' Gemma felt sick and it was Bronstorm who squeezed her hand, realising he had gone into too much detail.

'I must have been in the well for over two days, too petrified to move and then I heard angry voices and soon someone decided they needed some water,' said Bronstorm. His voice grew lighter. 'The person who winched me up was Hechkle, his face was like thunder and if I was an Ilsid warrior then I would have run away and not stopped,' said Bronstorm, with a glimmer of a smile. 'They wanted to give me to a family in the Core but he wouldn't let them, he took me in, taught me how to defend myself and the big lug has been there ever since,' said Bronstorm with much affection.

'He is a special guy, Bronny,' said Gemma, using her pet name for him.

'Aye and I best get back to helping him before he kills any of these soft humans for not working hard enough,' he said, with a snigger. Gemma smiled and gave him a quick hug before he sauntered across to work with his comrade, surrogate father.

Gemma, touched by the story, left them to it. She passed other soldiers as she walked up the ramp into the bowels of the *Elanda* who were setting out to take up their sentry duties. Bronstorm's story had affected her in more ways than one. She had regretted her kiss with Tyson almost immediately and had only started to realise that he was not the same Tyson she had grown up with. Something was wrong inside him and she felt that she was taking advantage of his confusion. Bronstorm's story of loyalty and friendship had rocked her and for the first time she began to see her folly. If the friends were to retain that same loyalty she knew it was time to back off.

Chastened, Gemma sought out her quarters and waited for Kabel. When he arrived tired and spent from the day's activities, climbing wearily into the bed, Gemma hugged him hard, taking him by surprise. Touched, he hugged her back and they drifted off to sleep holding each other tightly.

As night closed in all activity ceased and the Joint Expeditionary Force slept safe in the knowledge of the ring of steel around them. In the deep gloom they did not see the bright eyes of the watchers. The eyes flickered over the three ships, marvelling at the size and boldness of the newcomers. They saw the aliens and the returning Zeinonians. The scouts of the Pod made their mental notes and fled back to the safety of the breeding ground with a full report.

Chapter 10: Reinan

The morning came slowly for those waiting for the first exploration of this new and enticing planet. The Zein suns rose early in a splendid dawn, their pleasant glow bathing the planet in warm sunlight. Inside *Elanda* the team chosen to explore the empty city were completing their final preparations. The plan was to travel into the centre of Reinan to the principal community buildings and establish control of the area and seek information to assist the search for any survivors.

'Sleep okay, Bronstorm?' Amelia asked the Fathom warrior, while arranging her figure hugging Blackstone armour.

'Not really, too excited,' he said as he sharpened his dagger on a hand held tool.

'What's this, you don't sleep anyway,' said Hechkle, listening in. Bronstorm shrugged aside his friend's snide remark.

'I know you were sleeping, your snores could be heard across the barracks,' Bronstorm retorted, good-naturedly. Heckle grunted, not rising to the bait, and disappeared to search for other weapons to take on the expedition.

Amelia turned away from Bronstorm and sought out Tyson. She found him sitting pensively on one of the stools beside the armoured truck they would be driving into the city, seemingly lost within another dimension well away from where they were. She slipped an arm round his broad shoulders and rested her chin on one of them. 'You were very restless last night honey?' said Amelia, softly. She had not slept well, kept awake by Tyson's tossing and turning. Amelia did what she could only do; she wrapped her body around him providing comfort trying to calm down his internal demons.

'Not the best of nights,' he replied.

'Was it your mum again?' Tyson didn't answer, not wanting to talk about it. The vision had grown. He saw crying young women and his mother comforting them. He had seen a baby surrounded in darkness and the worry and despair on his mother's face

'Team, we need to go over our plans for the expedition,' said Kabel, rescuing Tyson from more difficult questions. Kabel went through the approach and plan which they had already heard a dozen times. The size of the expedition was impressive.

They would be escorted by two, M1117 Armoured Security Vehicles or the ASV as popularly known. Each ASV carried an Mk Grenade launcher and M2HB Browning machine gun mounted in the turret. The ASVs were flanked by four levitation tanks, two at each end of the column. In between all this protection were the main Armoured Personnel Carriers or APCs, which were over thirty tons and could carry up to fifteen individuals each in addition to the crew. In the five APCs there would be a mixture of soldiers and civilians.

Kabel and his companions were in the first APC supported by Sean Lambert and some of Remo's newly trained Blackstone clan troops. More Blackstone troops were in the second APC. Walter would also be accompanying them, but Zebulon had decided to stay on-board *Elanda*. Kabel didn't ask why. The Changeling had become withdrawn and frequently disappeared for long periods. They didn't need him anyway, he reasoned, as the firepower the expedition had at their disposal was immense.

It was already late morning when the brief was concluded and they all piled into their respective vehicles, eager to enter the city village. The expedition waited patiently for the security perimeter to be switched off briefly at the part of the shield facing the capital. The order was given and the convoy headed out towards Reinan.

Kabel looked around him in the APC, sensing the nervousness of the group. It was not hard to notice, their faces displayed the conflict of emotions, fluctuating from fear to excitement.

General Corder had tried to block Amelia and Gemma's involvement and neither Kabel nor Tyson could change the man's viewpoint. Help had come from an unexpected source in the shape of Walter Moore. He had taken the general to one side and explained that Amelia was the one who could calm Tyson down if matters became out of hand and that Gemma had shown tremendous fighting qualities in the destruction of the mast in the Eastern Quadrant. General Corder had eventually relented and the two women now sat next to their respective boyfriends suited in the figure hugging blue armour of the Blackstone clan. They still smarted from the indignity of having to prove their ability to handle themselves in a fight again.

As the expedition entered the outskirts of Reinan, they peered through the slits in the APC. They passed rows and rows of white painted houses that were in complete disarray. They took in the personal possessions left lying around in the rubble and now covered by layers of dust; part of a settee teetered over the edge of a collapsed wall ready to plunge to the street below; a child's stuffed toy sat forlornly on a dusty kitchen table, waiting patiently for its previous exuberant owner to come skipping past and to pick it up...years had passed, yet the toy waited expectantly.

'Whatever happened here, the population left in a hurry some time ago,' said Kabel, to no one in particular. Tyson turned briefly to look at him and marvelled at how much the responsibility of his position had aged him, maybe not so much in looks but in weariness and worry. He shrugged his shoulders, he had his own problems, and his brother would just need to deal with his issues.

There was little noise. Outside the rumble of the vehicles and the hiss of the levitation tanks an eerie silence was loud in its pervading voice. The expedition continued on its steady but slow journey into the centre of the city.

Tyson reached out with his mind. He could not hear any thoughts outside the increasing concerns of his companions leading him to supportively squeeze Amelia's hand, when he detected rising fear within her. She appreciated the support. The APC rocked back and forward as it chicaned between the rubble and debris strewn mosaic roads.

The roads were made of crisscross brightly coloured bricks which in their heyday would have provided a startling, inviting pathway for the citizens of the city. They could see that this had once been a tremendous city village, with plenty of colour and life which made it so sad to see it in this state.

'Because they didn't collapse the top half of the buildings the damage you see is probably from the winter and reflection periods. Over time this would have made all these houses uninhabitable,' said Kabel.

'But I thought you always collapsed the top half of the buildings before winter sets in?' said Gemma.

'Didn't have time,' said a grim looking Kabel, 'they didn't know what hit them.'

Eventually they turned into the central circle of the city. It was similar in size, if not shape, to China's vast Tiananmen Square, with the central circle stretching out far and wide. Overturned carts, vehicles and stalls littered the impressive space. You could see the imposing Grand Zein Central Transportation hub and the equally impressive Royal Council standing side by side.

None of the buildings stood over two storeys high; they were, though, wide and each covered a significant acreage. They, like the surrounding residential buildings were damaged. Whatever happened meant that the buildings had also not been formally collapsed and the considerable damage displayed was wrought by the winter and reflection seasons. Parts of the roofs were ripped off, as were doors, and window shutters hung loosely, partially ripped off their hinges.

The expedition moved closer to the two principal buildings and then formed a circle, in a good old fashioned Wild West wagon defence. The soldiers in the levitation tanks and the ASVs stayed on guard; all the personnel, outside of the three soldiers driving and manning the communications in the APCs, clambered out.

It was a sizable force; a mixture of civilians, US Marines and Fathom, Malacca or Blackstone troops. They created four parties. In Kabel's APC Group One, in addition to the usual suspects, Walter Moore and three Blackstone troopers joined them, making twelve in total. Joining them was Group Two, which contained environmental and senior scientists in a range of fields plus a further four Blackstone troops and two US Marines. They had thought to split up and enter both the buildings individually; however, Kabel decided strength in numbers made more sense.

The Royal Council was an especially impressive building, the centre piece of the community. Even in its dilapidated state it spoke of past greatness with its gold leaf intricate façade still glistening in the afternoon rays. Stone statues, of what must have been past historic figures of Zein, were situated at the corners of the imposing property, moulded into the fabric of the building. The spectacularly arched windows across both the floors held the remnants of exotic stained glass and the carved window shutters hung listlessly half off their hinges.

Kabel gulped nervously, overwhelmed by the history in front of him and his place in that story. Here was where his forefathers had agreed new laws and provided guidance to the populace across not just Reinan, but the planet. For the first time he felt the intimidating pressure of his office and the expectation of his role in the future of Zein. His nervousness subsided fast; pushing the negative thoughts to the back of his consciousness, now was not the time to have a crisis of confidence. As he issued orders, he saw Tyson watching him solemnly.

You heard every thought I just had, didn't you? Kabel asked, silently.

It wasn't hard brother; just remember none of us would have come this far without your leadership. Stop doubting yourself. Kabel welcomed the calming words. Protecting his thoughts this time, there was another first; he felt a growing closeness to his hybrid brother…maybe, just maybe there was a future in their relationship. He shook himself out of his personal thoughts and addressed the planning of the expedition conscious that the soldiers were waiting for their orders.

They would enter the Royal Council first and then the Grand Zein Central Transportation hub. The other three groups would strike out to other areas off the circle to scan and analyse the buildings for any sign of life.

Kabel sent the Blackstone troopers ahead with the two US Marines. They had their photon automatic rifles armed and aimed as they leapfrogged each other's position seeking to establish a perimeter, with the rest of the two groups following. The troopers and marines entered the Royal Council to establish a secure forward position once the safety recon was complete; the rest of the group was called forward.

Kabel stepped through the large, thick, mahogany doors that carried significant decay, into the Royal Council and found his breath taken away. In front of him was a large room divided into different sections. At the far end was the usual council seat configuration with numerous seats facing a raised platform with a throne-like ornate chair standing tall as if it was in command of the more junior seats. The seat was adorned with beautiful carvings of Zein historical figures and wildlife.

To his left was a large office-like environment with many desks arranged in circles around a master desk. The desks still had the computerised equipment built in with piles of loose paper scattered about. To the right was what must have been a communal area where people must have eaten and conversed as they relaxed at break times or in the evening; the soft furnishings, now broken and tarnished, spread into the corners of the large building.

He saw the curved stairs to the second level and motioned for the troops to proceed up the stairs to increase the safety perimeter. He saw Walter Moore and a couple of his colleagues talk excitedly, looking at the murals on the walls and the other decorations on the ceilings.

'Wow, look at that,' said Gemma, her head tilted back. He followed her gaze. On the ceiling was an intricate painted ceiling that would have challenged the Sistine Chapel for its elegance. The mural depicted the history of

Zein, from the first settlements, to the Xonian Wars and latterly the conflicts with the Pod. It was breath-taking. Walter had one of his colleagues take numerous pictures of the historic developments.

They moved deeper into the building. Tyson, with Hechkle and Bronstorm made their way up one of the curved stairs. Kabel remained on the first floor. He saw great holes in the floor everywhere as if someone had ripped back the floor to get in.

Walter saw Kabel's look, 'Something was attempting to get in by the look of how the floor is jagged upwards. If it had been the other way around of course, then those jagged edges would be below the floor,' said Walter, peering into one of the holes, saying what Kabel was thinking. 'Interestingly, if you look at the steel shutters and the additional iron bars across the door,' he pointed to the now ripped away shutters and the broken iron bars near the door, 'here is where they were making a stand, probably the last stand, looking at the dry and dusty bloodstains,' Walter surmised. Kabel took in the many blotches of dried blood scattered across the floor.

'Hey, look at this.' The shout came from Tyson who had followed the soldiers to the second level. Leaving the US Marines on guard near the door they all raced up the curved grand stairs. In front of them was a vast library, but not a library in the usual sense. There were row upon row of holograms of Zein figures, teachers, under different headings, including *Animals of Zein, Reflection, Awakening, The One Way, The Pod* and many more. The holograms stretched back far into the depths of the building. Excited, the group explored the different sections of the library.

Walter Moore settled in front of the *Reflection* hologram and the Zeinonian was speaking but he could not hear. Frustrated, he looked for a button.

'You have to press your palm on this,' said Kabel, pointing to a panel that stuck out with a hand print throbbing in red. 'Once you press this you will be the only one to hear the hologram talk as your DNA is recorded.' He looked around and addressed a few of the other scientists. 'And if you want to hear at the same time you can touch the device here as well.'

'How can it still have power after all these years?' asked Walter, as he observed his fellow scientists trying other holograms. He tried to ignore the hostile looks they gave Kabel as he helped them connect. *Can't they grow up, all he is doing is showing them how to use the damn machines.*

'The holograms will be connected to an underground cable that is built into the rock foundations below the museum,' said Kabel, remembering a particular lesson given by Malkin, with his teaching hat on. 'The cable is very sensitive and picks up the atmospheric power of even the slightest amount of zinithium. It would take hundreds of years to run out.'

Walter reached out and spread his hand to cover the handprint. It immediately changed to blue and Walter could hear the hologram talk. He let out a delighted gasp and motioned for some of his fellow scientists to touch the handprint. They all did. Kabel left them engrossed in the story of Zein's reflection period. He moved deeper into the library. He saw everyone participating with the hologram that stimulated their interest and saw Tyson was listening to *The Changelings*. Kabel was attracted to the *Blackstones – Early Years*, which was in a corridor with programmes on all the other clans. He placed his hand on the handprint, sat down and waited.

The voice of the woman in front of him was soft and gentle, her blue eyes twinkled. She took him through the years when magics did not exist and it was a hard but simple life. They had originally come from a small insignificant planet where they were enslaved by the Xonians, who had ruled vast swathes of the Universe with an iron fist. It was a woman who had led the uprising of the technically advanced race, outwitting their masters, who had grown sloppy. They had stolen two ships, one the impressive *Elanda*, which they had helped to build for the Xonians for the purpose of future conquests. In an incredible and daring plan, the whole race had escaped and they had searched for a planet that could become their home. It was nearly three years in space when they discovered Zein and settled their population on the planet. The hell of winter and reflection had caused many deaths until they mastered the ability to collapse the buildings and seek shelter in the newly built underground city, the Aeria Cavern. They had even fought off the inevitable Xonian attack in the First Xonian War, albeit with a heavy cost in lives.

The name of their leader was Cilan Blackstone, her name sent a shiver of excitement down Kabel's spine; the name was not new to him, Cilan's role in the development of Zein was taught to him by Malkin but he never took him through the deep history, preferring to focus on history that would impact Kabel on Earth. Now he was finding out about a whole period of history that he had no previous knowledge of. He listened closely to the light tones of the presenter.

He was told that the Blackstone clan were strong, ambitious and keen to develop Zein. They had encountered the Changelings prior to the Second Xonian War and had struck up a partnership, in which for promises and land they would be taught how to harness the magics of Zein.

At the Inner Council the other clans demanded the same treatment and the Changelings taught each clan different magics with understanding that the full extent of the magics was too powerful for any one Zeinonian. It was explained that the magics came with a warning. Misuse of the magics twisted an unsuspecting body in ways that are initially latent but then become a living nightmare with madness the result. The Changelings demanded that the Zeinonians agree to the limitations set. Keen to have abilities that they could use to defend against the violent and deadly Xonian hordes, they readily agreed.

There was always a suspicion that the Blackstone clan were granted more of the magics for their support of the cleansing of the Pod from the planet, the Changelings' main enemy. Kabel frowned, struggling to take in the warlike nature of the Changelings with his experience of Zebulon and he decided when he was back on the ship he would seek out the Changeling. The hologram figure pointed out that this was never proved, though rumours persisted through the years.

The party were all engrossed in the history of their choice and once they had finished with the hologram they were viewing, they swapped to another hologram. Time ticked on.

Tyson was engulfed in the history of the mysterious Changelings and the facts didn't stack up. Where did they come from? Why exterminate the Pod? The history lesson seemed one-sided and key facts were left out. He, like Kabel would seek out Zebulon when they returned to the *Elanda*.

Kabel was enjoying a tutorial on the Pod, and he was at a particular part of their history which showed that in the early years on the planet they kept to themselves, mainly around their breeding grounds in the south, when his headset sparked into life; it was Sean Lambert, who had remained in the first APC, the strong Scottish accent unmistakable. He was checking in with the five groups worried that time was passing and no one wanted to be in the silent city when night fell. They knew that night came quickly on this planet. Each of the teams rattled off their call sign as did Kabel; the title "Hybrid" was their call sign, much to Tyson's amusement. Kabel broke off from the hologram he was on and signalled to the others to wrap up and make their way to the front entrance.

For Tyson, the most interesting discussion was on the Changelings, which had proved more complex then he thought. It was clear that no one knew where the Changelings came from but common thinking was that they had travelled with another race and had been stranded on Zein with the Pod. He pushed the thoughts to one side and speedily ran down the stairs.

Soon they were out of the Royal Council and into the Reinan Circle, where a beautiful site met them. The suns were beginning to drop further in the sky, creating a kaleidoscope of colour, cascading over the landscape, reflecting an orangey glow to the rooftops of the desolate city. The team could not enjoy the picture for long, with the fear of the unknown beginning to grip them.

Kabel hesitated, balancing the need to leave for the safety of the *Elanda* with exploring further. He made the call and decided he needed to see the Grand Zein Central Transportation hub before travelling back. He flagged the retreating personnel and troops to move with urgency to the buckled doors of the building, which reluctantly they did. Cautiously they entered, with the US Marines flanking the team.

As they moved into the murky building they could make out the extraordinary height of the transportation field with its massive four towers pointing at each other across the divide. They identified the scorch marks where photon shots had burned the steel walls. There were also many ruptures in the floor, indicating breeches into the room from below the ground. The team moved deeper into the room.

Suddenly, Tyson saw a face across the transportation field. He made out the shock registering on the handsome face and the body encased in red armour. His mind flashed back to his fight with Manek Malacca in the Core. *Malacca clan*, he thought, taking in the colour of the armour and the swarthy nature of the skin. With him was an intimidating figure with half an arm and a group of four or five troopers all carrying what seemed to be old photon rifles retreating through a hole in the ground. They had also frozen in shock at the sight of Tyson and the soldiers around him.

'Hey, you?' he shouted. The strangers snapped out of their shock and without further delay disappeared down one of the main holes in the floor.

Kabel, who had swivelled round at Tyson's urgent call but only glimpsed the intruders as they disappeared down the hole, due to an obstruction in front of him, was just going to shout to go after them when his communication link sparked into life again. 'Team Leader One this is Team Leader Four we are under attack,' reported the calm voice of one of the US Marines leading Group Four. Photon shots could be heard across the Reinan Circle. 'Team Leader One, this is Team Leader Five, they are everywhere.' With that followed a scream and the line went dead.

Kabel acted. 'Quickly, to the vehicles.' He glanced across the room and saw Tyson move towards the hole the men had disappeared into. 'Tyson, leave it, we need to get back to the vehicles, now!' he commanded. Tyson hesitated and in that moment Pod appeared from a number of other holes within the building, pouring out from the ripped and jagged holes, converging on Tyson and fellow members of the team. The soldiers laid down defensive fire and in that moment the scientists and companions retreated to the outside, straight into a horrific scene.

The other three groups were running as fast as they could back to the vehicles. The last flickers of sunlight were gobbled up by the encroaching tendrils of night. The security detail protecting the other three groups, consisting mainly of US Marines and troops from the Malacca clan, had created a defensive line, firing into the mass of bodies that were jumping from roof to roof, exiting damaged buildings, swinging from exposed pipework as they attacked the convoy, to give the civilians a chance to make it to the vehicles.

Too many, thought Kabel.

I agree with you, bro, replied Tyson, as he fired his photon shotgun through the broken window at one of the massive forms rising from the holes in the floor at the Grand Zein Central Transportation hub. The soldiers supporting the other fleeing groups were now grappling with the attackers no match for the brute animal strength. The civilians had managed to climb into their respective APCs but the troops supporting them were losing their battles.

Amelia, alarmed, screamed a warning to Tyson when she saw a seven foot, dark blue furred, giant ape-like creature jump off the top of the Grand Zein Central Transportation hub and land behind Tyson with his frightening incisor teeth bared. As he brought his wicked looking claw down onto Tyson's unsuspecting back, Tyson's force-field flared up. He activated one of his seckles and whipped round severing both the lower part of the arms of the creature. The creature roared with pain, blood spurting from the stumps and then one of the troopers finished the creature off.

More and more of the creatures were racing to the centre of the city, drawn like moths to a light on a dark night, fixated on the convoy. A number of the troops exposed in the circle supporting the other three groups died where they stood, their limbs ripped from their sockets by the enraged beasts, who didn't break stride in their attack. Groups One and Two had not reached the vehicles yet and more and more of the vicious animals were launching themselves like maddened beasts at the frantically defending Blackstone troopers. Tyson heard and felt their fear. They were still untried even with all Remo's training behind them and were panicking at the unfolding nightmare. Then the levitation tanks and ASV weapons opened up and the barrage tore the front line of the attackers to pieces, momentarily halting the advance.

'Quick, get to the trucks, now,' yelled Kabel as he fired into the massed ranks. Some of the scientists were too slow and perished at the hands of the attackers. Walter Moore ducked as one animal launched a swinging arm at his head. Walter fell over, losing his glasses, and it looked like he was lost. Then Bronstorm and Hechkle went to his aid, dispatching the main attacker by simultaneously swinging and embedding their seckles deep into the creature's stomach and ripping out his intestines. They stood over Walter, protecting him as he found his glasses, placed them on his face and then continued his sprint to the APC.

The others fell behind him creating a meaningful barricade. Bailey was firing with unerring accuracy at the nearest Pod and Amelia kept pulling at his shoulder telling him to get into the APC. Eventually all the survivors managed to climb aboard and for the next two minutes the powerful guns halted the attack. Kabel could see that the halt in the attack would only last for a moment; the creatures appeared crazed, throwing their bodies at the vehicles even though their numbers were taking massive casualties.

'This is Group One Leader. Let's move. Don't stop until we are safely behind the barrier,' Kabel ordered all the drivers. 'Sean, contact the ship and ask them to send air cover, there are too many, we don't stand a chance without help.' The experienced Scottish man patched into the communication link with *Elanda* as the driver next to him followed the back of the ASV in front of them as the convoy snaked out of the large central circle. On the ship, General Corder received the request but delayed the order. At the back of his mind was the opportunity to be rid of Tyson.

The expedition, led by the two levitation tanks at the front, fought through the debris and the growing number of attackers. The tanks cleared the street before them before advancing back towards the ship, all the while with the creatures jumping on the tanks trying to find a way in and wrestle control away from the intruders.

On the ASV behind the fifth APC the troopers manning the Browning and grenade launcher were using them to good effect, until, one of the Pod managed to land on the top of the vehicle and tear the head of one of the troopers clean off and then slashed the throat of the man firing the Browning machine gun. Another joined him and they used their claws to rip the door of the ASV door off. They then swung in. The ASV careered off the street into one of the buildings.

Kabel heard the scream of the driver through his headset. *Where is the air support!*

The expedition was making very slow progress through the city. The levitation tanks were blasting away and the remaining ASV was keeping the hordes away from the APCs. A few of the Pod jumped on the APCs only to be flung off the moving vehicle or picked off by the machine gun on the ASV. The Pod seemed to recognise this, with Tyson picking up a sense of urgency from the Pod to attack the ASV. Although he couldn't understand all the words as his magics were still attuning to the language barrier, it was enough to understand the Pods' plan.

Sure enough, at a narrow part of the road, six Pod jumped on the ASV in front of Group One's vehicle and after a brief fight the ASV skewed sideways, blocking the path of the other vehicles.

'Out everyone,' Kabel shouted, 'we are sitting ducks if we stay in these vehicles, if we go down, then we go down fighting.' With that, Kabel released the lock on the vehicle and the back doors were flung open and he leapt out with the remaining soldiers followed by his companions. Tyson jumped onto the back of the APC and pulled his photon blaster out and activated one of his seckles. He coolly used both to good effect. One Pod jumped and whilst in mid-air Tyson shot him, causing the body to leap back in the air from the force of the shot, and then another came from behind him but his force-field, thankfully, did its job as the blow bounced off him. He brought his seckle into the fight, ripping into the muscled stomach region that was less hairy then the rest of the animal. He then threw the creature off the APC as, with a look of disbelieve and pain, it held the open wound in its hands.

Tyson was shocked; the fear he felt emanating from the beasts was overwhelming. It was driving them on insanely in their attack. *Why are they so scared?* he thought.

Good question, Tyson, I feel it as well, Kabel echoed in his mind as his two seckles cut deeply into a Pod in front of him.

And I, thought Belina.

Now was not the time for deliberation. Kabel joined his brother, along with Amelia and Gemma. Bronstorm and Hechkle went to help the civilians in Groups Four and Five, who had lost the majority of their troopers. The roofs of the buildings were full of the beasts. Tyson saw in the disappearing light that there was a sea of blue in every direction. Sweat ran down his face as the intensity of battle increased.

'General Corder, Sir, what should I do?' said Lieutenant Michaels. The messages for support came thick and fast, yet General Corder still hesitated. The crew listened with horror to the cries for help, casting angry glances at their commander. It was only when Admiral Koshkov burst into the Command and Control Centre with a face like thunder that he acted.

'Launch ten Cobras, Lieutenant, immediately,' General Corder ordered, his uncertainty gone. Koshkov glared at Corder but did not say anything; there would be time for that later.

Gemma and Belina were using every martial art move they could muster. Tyson marvelled on how Gemma, who reached only to Belina's shoulder, took on the beasts that dwarfed her. She didn't flinch and her face was full of concentration as she spun round and used a roundhouse kick to propel one of the creatures off the top of the APC.

On the ground, Walter Moore had picked up a photon shotgun and with a wild look of fear in his eyes blasted anything that came into his radius.

'Well, bro, at least you have seen your home planet,' said Tyson, standing back to back with Kabel. His brother could only grunt as the exertion of the defence was taking its toll.

Gemma disposed of another attacker below him, at the side of the APC that caught Tyson's eye. *God, you look sexy*, he said telepathically, shading his thought from Kabel.

You are only human, well sort of, she retorted, with barely a smile. This was no time to inform him that she had moved on. The interplay was then disrupted as both dispatched another two attackers.

Neither saw that Amelia had caught the glance as she fired unerringly at the mass of creatures before her. Her stomach churned with jealousy and drove her to defend with increased vigour, driven by her rage. Tyson picked up the increased intensity of her emotions and her less than pleasant thoughts of Gemma. He decided to ignore them and focused on the task at hand, knowing he had to sort out his feelings for the two girls' once and for all.

Kabel was worried. They had lost one of the levitation tanks at the back of the convoy when a number of the Pod had collapsed a building onto the top of it, crushing and burying the men.

Amelia was at the side of the APC and was so intent in picking off any Pod approaching her that she didn't notice that she had become separated from Gemma. A sixth sense made her turn round and it was only then that she realised that she was alone on this side of the APC, with Gemma moving to the front of the vehicle. Her second mistake was in taking her attention away from the Pod. A claw crashed into her gun and it fell to the ground smashed to bits. The giant male Pod then grabbed her arm and pulled her into an alleyway.

'Tyson, help me,' she cried. Tyson saw Amelia being dragged off and with a leap jumped of the APC, closing the distance between them. With a flash of his seckle he cut through the hairy blue arm holding her and the limp remainder of the arm lost its grip and fell away from

Amelia. The Pod gave a great squeal of pain. Tyson put the creature out of its misery.

'Run back to the vehicle,' he said, monitoring closely the other creatures converging on them. Amelia didn't need to be asked twice. She set off and ran with her head down. Tyson began working his way with backward steps down the alleyway, picking off any Pod with his blaster.

At that moment, when all hope was disappearing, suddenly explosions on either side of the convoy cleared their nearest attackers. Kabel looked up and saw *Elanda*'s fixed wing aircraft. Wave after wave of Cobras launched a devastating non-nuclear payload from their propulsion cones, followed by deathly rounds from their photon machine guns. All around the survivors of the expedition there were cries of fear from the Pod and many died. Huge explosions blew the buildings around the alleyway which Tyson was desperately trying to exit.

'Run, Tyson, run!' shouted Kabel. Amelia turned around and looked down the alleyway. Tyson, with his bright blue shield flaring, was running towards the entrance of the alley. The buildings either side of him shook with the explosions and then came tumbling down on top of Tyson, burying him.

'Tyson!' Amelia cried at the top of her lungs and started to run back but Bailey grabbed her and held her. Amelia fought against Bailey's grip, to no avail. The explosions continued throwing up sheets of dust and shrapnel.

'Amelia, into the vehicle, it's too dangerous,' said Bailey, as Hechkle came across to help him bundle the struggling girl into safety. Bronstorm was not far behind, panting from the fighting. He peered into the gloom and saw a mountain of debris where Tyson had stood. He looked up at Kabel and shook his head. Kabel swore.

The Pod retreated, disappearing with their injured, just

as quickly as they had appeared. Soon the only sound was the crackle of fires ignited by the bombing and the cries of the injured convoy personnel.

It took them sometime to move the AVS out of the way and unblock the rubble strewn road. Reinforcements were sent from the *Elanda* by General Corder, to provide cover. They again checked the area where Tyson had been standing and the amount of rubble made it impossible for them to find him. Reluctantly, Kabel gave the order for the remaining vehicles, three levitation tanks and four remaining APCs, to limp into the safety of the perimeter as the deep gloom of night descended. The friends were all distressed and Kabel vowed they would go back in the morning with heavy lifting equipment to see if they could retrieve Tyson's body. He was in no mood to lose another brother.

Of the seventy-two members of the expedition, forty three survived. Shattered and with heavy hearts the remaining members sought the security of their quarters. Amelia had ignored all attempts by the rest of the group to comfort her and left those looking after her, soulfully making her way to her room.

Later, there was a knock on her door. Amelia ignored it. She didn't feel like talking to anyone. Tyson was gone. He had given his life for hers. She could never forgive herself. The knocking on the door was persistent and anger flared up within her. She pulled herself from the bed, wiped her tears away on her sleeve and stormed to the door, ready to give whoever was there a mouthful. The door slid back.

Any angry remark was struck from her vocabulary. Standing in front of her was an equally distraught Bailey. His eyes were rimmed red where the tears had come thick and fast. Amelia stepped back and he shuffled in and simply stood in the middle of the room with a hopeless look. She stepped forward and wrapped her arms around him and with a glazed look he slowly placed his arms around her. They didn't know how long they stood there before Bailey left, for each was wrapped up in their own memories of a person whom they loved deeply.

Chapter 11: Olive Branch

Tate stumbled back down the shaft where they had entered Reinan. This was their main secret entry point from the Aeria Cavern, which provided a secure way to salvage any materials or stores in the hastily abandoned capital city. The entrance was purposely made to look like one of the Pod entrance points when they invaded the city all those years ago. Tate had been a young boy when the city was attacked by the Pod. That night had left him scarred. His father had woken him from a deep sleep in the Malacca Royal Palace and they and the rest of his family had fled to the basement where their escape hatch to the Aeria Cavern was. As they rushed into the room the Pod crashed through the impressive front door, cutting through the few troops left to guard the building, with the majority sent to fight a rear guard retreat outside the city, some two termins away but the speed of the fall back had come as a shock to both the soldiers and the Reinan population. The blaring alarm telling them all was lost. Those who were not wealthy and did not have their own escape hatch were forced to make their way to the Transportation or Royal Council buildings through the dangerous streets. Many did not make it... men, women and children cut down by the creatures, hell bent on annihilation. Tate still remembered the screams of the guards and from those unfortunate enough to be outside as his family made it through their escape hatch…he didn't stop shaking for days after and it was then he vowed, if he became a soldier, he would look after every man, woman and child irrespective of wealth.

He turned his attention back to the tunnel. After the strategically placed foot and hand holds dug into the soil of the hole, further down there was a steel hatch requiring a passcode to enter. The steel hatch was the beginning of a long chute-like tunnel with rungs inside attached to ultra-thick zinithium strengthened steel. The chute entered the main tunnel near the South Gate entrance. The rest of the party of six climbed down with their plunder and dropped into the tunnel.

Tate was still in shock. The others had already begun descending when the noise outside stopped them, they were caught in two minds, not wanting to be out in the dark with the roaming Pod to deal with but intrigued by the noise. They had heard the vehicles and all could not resist taking a look out of the broken windows. They were initially shocked at seeing the heavily armoured invaders. This was how they viewed the convoy, as invaders, which is what they thought they were at first. It was only when they saw the troops and civilians approach the Royal Council building that they realised that this pre-conception was not altogether right.

'Look, that is a Blackstone,' said Kron, pointing to the tall figure at the front of the soldiers.

'Yes, and Fathom and Malacca troops as well,' said Tate, 'but who are they?' He pointed to some of the figures that didn't tally with the usual characteristics of the five clans. His eyes fastened on two young women who were chatting with one of the men who seemed to be related to the girl with spiky black hair. He then saw her.

Belina was checking her shotgun with her gaze focused downwards. She then looked at and laughed with the man who was standing with the other two females. Tate could see that they were close. It was when her head turned and looked at the Grand Zein Central Transportation hub that Tate had seen her face clearly: it was one of the most beautiful faces he had ever seen. He carefully retreated slightly to prevent her from spotting him peering from the cracks in the broken windows.

When the invaders decided to shift their attention to the building he was in, Tate decided that it was time to go. He saw the light diminishing and hoped that these strangers knew the risk they were taking. No one stayed out after dusk if they wanted to stay alive. They were just in the process of exiting the building when Tate was spotted by one of the men, an unusual man. He saw the tell-tale Blackstone blue eyes but this was no Blackstone. His magics smelt danger, conflicting magics within the blood of this man. He was young but there was an edge to him. Tate had seen many things in the last few years, fought many battles, faced incredible odds, yet he felt the hairs on the back of his head and on his arms stand up. He felt fear.

He hurriedly climbed down the shaft and joined the team in the tunnel. 'Kron, call an emergency session of the Inner Council,' he commanded as he hurried along the tunnel. Kron saluted and ran ahead to do his master's bidding. Tate removed his pack and outer armour when he reached the Inner Council building. He poured himself a glass of water and thought what the arrival of the invaders meant. It was obvious that this must be the returning Expeditionary Force as he had seen Zeinonians, but who were the strange race with them? They looked very similar to Zeinonians but there was enough difference for him to identify that they were an alien race.

Members of the Inner Council were beginning to arrive. He could see the puzzlement on their faces over a request for a meeting with such short notice. He had sworn his squad to remain tight lipped on what they had seen. They were his most experienced men and he could trust them. Safah Blackstone arrived with Eben Southgate, both whispering conspiratorially. No Jaida Blackstone and no Taio Southgate. Both had volunteered to accompany Myolon to the Pod breeding grounds and the placement of the deadly serum into the underground reservoir. The group was fifteen strong, any larger and it would be difficult to move without detection. They all carried personal cloaking devices which hid them from easy detection but this would matter not if the Pod were near to their position. The rest of the group was made up of two soldiers from each clan and the Changelings. Jaida had been placed in charge.

Quinlan walked in with his daughter, Brisis. After the performance by Kingsley, in the last Inner Council, Quinlan was erring on the side of caution. Brisis was a strong woman of some thirty years, plain but honest and hardworking. Tate liked her. As they took their seats there was a gasp.

Heathlon, High Priestess of Zein, and the Changelings had just entered the room.

It was rare to see her at this forum and only Tate and Safah had access to her quarters. Others were strictly kept away. People tried to guess what age she was but it was so difficult to gauge the age of a changeling. Some said she was nearly one thousand years old. Her face, although lined, was surprisingly still relatively young looking, however, the Changelings were the experts in camouflage.

A hush fell on the room as she sat down in Myolon's seat. Surrounding her were six unyielding warriors, eyes flicking around the room to identify any threat to the woman they called "Mother of Life".

Tate cleared his throat, uncharacteristically nervous. Heathlon's eyes stared at him without blinking, seemingly measuring his courage and wisdom. 'Greetings, your Excellency.' Tate bowed to Heathlon, who raised her delicate right hand and acknowledged the recognition. 'And to you your worshipful Elders,' he concluded his salutation to the rest of the clans. 'First I would like to thank you for attending this emergency Inner Council meeting at such short notice.'

'No proper notice and you drag us here at this late hour, ridiculous,' Eben fumed, he was grumpy from being woken up from his much needed late afternoon sleep. Even Safah raised her eyebrows in frustration at her peer. It looked like the grandfather had replaced the grandson's stupidity.

'Eben, that's why it's called an *emergency* meeting,' said Brisis, sarcastically. Tate laughed inwardly as Eben squirmed under the steely gaze of the Tyther princess.

'Quite so,' said Tate, earning a glare from the old Lord Southgate. Tate again cleared his throat as he felt the displeasure seeping out of every pore of Heathlon; she hadn't come here to watch minor bickering. Heathlon had sensed a change within Zein's balance of power. She could detect subtle changes in the shift of the magics and the power they brought. This afternoon that shift had not been subtle but more like a sledgehammer, a tool which at the moment, she would gladly ask one of her guards to take to Eben's head.

'This afternoon we saw invaders in our capital city,' said Tate, calculating what would be the reaction around the room. He was not disappointed. There was fear, wonder and then questions began to rain in, tumbling over each other. Tate held up his hand and the noise subsided. 'Please, one question at a time.'

'Who are they?' said Quinlan, before anyone else could get in the obvious question. Tate steadied himself ahead of his next words; this was going to have a major impact.

'I am pretty certain it was the Zein Inter-Galactic Expeditionary Force returning. They were accompanied by an alien race we have not seen before, similar to us but apart from one individual, no magics,' said Tate. He may have well set off a bomb. Everyone was on their feet. Questions came thick and fast. *So much for one question at a time,* he thought.

How many of them?

Are they here to save us?

Will the aliens attack us?

Tate held his hand up and called for calm but it was the regal voice of Heathlon that cut through the babble.

'Fellow Zeinonians, I for one would like to hear everything that Lord Malacca saw, wouldn't you?' The noise subsided,

The members of the Inner Council sat down and waited for Tate to speak. He told them what he had witnessed; the convoy, the mixture of clans and alien race and the sophisticated weaponry. It was when he started to explain and describe the individuals, especially the tall Blackstone man and the alien he had seen last, that he saw Safah and Eben learn forward with their interest truly engaged. Tate finished his briefing and leaned back into the throne.

'They obviously do not know about the Pods' nocturnal habits or they would have left well within daylight,' said Quinlan, stroking his chin in thought.

'If it is true that a royal from the Blackstone clan has returned, will they not have the sole right to your throne?'

said Eben, pointing out the basis of Zein Law. Safah had forfeited her right three years ago when the Blackstones transgressed by storing zinithium in their enclave. Up to that point Safah had been a reluctant Lady Chancellor after her husband, Ricken Blackstone, had died in a Pod attack. Jaida had abdicated her right. She had no interest in holding such a responsible position.

'Why you…' said Kron, stepping forward menacingly.

'Hold it Kron, Eben is right that if they are part of the royal bloodline then I will relinquish this throne to their care,' replied Tate.

'Now don't you be too quick, Lord Chancellor,' said Heathlon, as she stood up and moved onto the council floor, 'We need to be careful. Even if these are our kin they have already shown a lack of knowledge of our ways.' The other council members listened astounded. For many meetings the Changelings had sat quietly, not becoming involved; now not only had Myolon forced his own agenda but now the High Priestess herself was taking centre stage. She continued, 'We should send a delegation to the newcomers and seek talks, but let's not relinquish our safety and the safety of many Zeinonians until we are comfortable that the Pod have been exterminated from this planet.' The last words were said with fire in her eyes.

Studying the reactions in the room, Tate, knew that they now could not stop the chain of events. The liquidation group sent to the Pod breeding grounds had gone and would carry out their task. Until then he vowed he would not relinquish his position unless it benefited Zein.

The delegation was decided with relative ease. Surprisingly, the Changelings opted not to attend, so when the suns rose in the morning a delegation led by Tate and including Kron, Quinlan, Safah and Eben headed for the surface. They were supported by fifty of the toughest soldiers from all the clans. Today history was to be made.

ᗡᗡᗡ

The moulded hard rock that made her impressive throne rested easily against her back. The throne arched up to the ceiling of the deep cavern. It started narrow and then curved outwards until it touched the surrounding two walls. The walls themselves held basins which tar burned in to provide light, although they needed little light. They had grown as a species used to the solitude of the darkness over centuries. They were an old tribe, born when the planet was born, at one with the earth and elements. Theirs had been a simple life once; now those days had passed.

Festilion, the Queen of the Pod, High Priestess of Zein, leaned forward to take the report of her oldest son. She had many sons and daughters as she was the queen who gave birth to the many and not the few. Her brood in turn gave birth, albeit not as readily as she did. She had many suitors, brave warriors who fathered her children. It was this way that saved them from the evil before. Evolution at its best.

She observed her son move slowly across the room. *You are carrying a wound, my son?* She passed her thought silently, carefully blocking it from the others assembled in the Great Hall. He gave a lopsided grin, his incisors looping down his face at one side, blood from the ripped throat of a terrified Blackstone trooper still clinging to the ends, *I moved too slowly my Queen.*

Dominion, I hope you did not enter into the foolishness of your son? she admonished him. He hung his head, the shame of his son trying to communicate with that evil Zein leader of the Aeria Cavern! The Queen saw that her trusted eldest son was not as naïve as her grandson and decided she needed to know more.

'Please provide your report,' she ordered as her Head Royal Proctor, Redulon, handed her some cool water to sip. Dominion spoke slowly and clearly, ignoring the pain of his wound, starting on how his look outs had spotted movement within the Aeria Cavern and he had sent a small patrol to track the movements of the Defilers, the name they gave to the people who sheltered the hated Malefic. It was then that they had seen the great ships on the plains and the dust of vehicles travelling into the cursed city. He told her of the attack and that they had suffered greatly. Festilion knew this. She had felt the pain and fear of her brethren as they fought to rid their planet of the invaders.

'Their weapons are too powerful for us. Much more powerful than those in the Aeria Cavern,' said Dominion, transferring his weight to his left leg due to the throbbing pain from a wound on his right leg. 'The ship they came in is the one they left in all those years ago. They have returned to strip us of our land,' he said with considerable anger.

'What about this alien who was not Zeinonian but exhibited the evil of our enemy?' Festilion asked.

'We captured him,' said Dominion, his chest expanding, showing his pride. 'He is in the dark caverns in a deep sleep, guarded by my son, your Highness.' There was a babble of voices in the room. A prisoner. An alien in their hands. The High Priestess stood up, she was pleased.

'I am glad my, son. Bring him to me when he is awake. I have many questions for him.' She dismissed him and walked from the chamber.

Chapter 12: Truths

Tyson gradually awoke. He remembered the explosion ringing in his ears. He had seen the building collapsing on him and seen a hole in one of the buildings beside him. He had flung his body through, ensuring he switched on his protective shield, but not before some of the falling debris had hit him hard, winding him. That is all he remembered as he blacked out.

He blinked and glanced round his surroundings. He was in a cool, dark cave. The walls were smooth, all the rock had been carefully either chiselled or machined away. He was lying on a hard slab of rock. There was no door to what he was guessing was a cell of some kind. He ran his hands carefully over his body and apart from some small cuts and abrasions he didn't appear injured. He stood up gingerly and casually walked to the open door. A figure moved to block his exit in front of him.

He found he was staring at a Pod. The Pod was male, extremely tall and muscular. He held no weapon apart from his claws. He had simple coverings across his waist for modesty but other than that he was covered in dark blue hair, apart from his chest area. Tyson concentrated and focused on his magics to blast the guard away so he could escape.

He thinks he can use the accursed magics here. He is going to be upset - they are no use down here.

Tyson straightened up. It was the same guttural language he had heard during the battle but now he could translate it. *They are so puny. Take away their little toys and magics and they are nothing.* Tyson raised his head and caught the creature glaring at him balefully. His internal magics must be enabling him to form the language he had just heard.

What is your name? The guard stepped back in amazement. No outsider had ever been able to converse with anyone in the Pod before. The alien repeated the question.

What is your name? My name is Tyson.

'Wernion,' said the tall figure aloud, surprised at the voice within his head. 'My name is Wernion.'

'I am from Earth, a distant planet,' said Tyson.

'Earth? I have never heard of the place. Are you here to hurt us as well?' said Wernion, a half threatening and half fearful look on his face.

'No, no. You attacked us and we were just defending ourselves. We are here to seek those my friends left many years ago,' said Tyson, placating the towering creature. He noticed the poultice of leaves on the shoulder, held by long palm tree type leaves wrapped round the top of his shoulder. There was another wound to his waist.

'You have injuries,' said Tyson, pointing to the wounds.

'They will heal.'

Tyson was not to be put off. 'Were you in the attack on the convoy?'

Wernion shook his head in answer. 'We attacked the Defilers some two suns ago, we broke into their supposedly impenetrable tunnel,' said Wernion, proudly.

'What tunnel?' said Tyson, backing away from his jailor and sitting down on the stone bunk.

'Where the Defilers and Malefic hide from us.'

'What do you mean, who are these people?' asked Tyson, growing intrigued by this formidable creature's ability to hold a meaningful conversation. Wernion studied the alien. He noticed the slightly different features when compared with the Defilers but he still had those hated blue eyes, a sign that he had been turned by the Malefics. However, he seemed different, calm, and almost normal. How could that be? For years the people who converted the magics had transformed their idyllic life into death, destruction and endless fighting. The sickness that the Malefic had exported invaded the very land in which his ancestors had lived free and without pain for centuries.

'Please, I want to learn,' said Tyson, as he saw the indecision within.

'The Defilers are like you,' started Wernion. 'They were given the power of the magics by the Malefics, who in return wanted land and favours.'

'I don't understand, who are the Malefics?' asked Tyson, something nagging him as he tracked the movement of the hulking presence blocking his escape. Though to be true he was now more interested in learning about what was actually happening on Zein. Wernion rested his body against the door frame and the flickering light of the burning tar caught the eyes of the creature. Tyson then realised where he had seen the same black flecked amber eyes.

Zebulon! This creature had the same eyes as the Changeling! Then he remembered that Zebulon had fought as a Pod in some of the battles on Earth. The Changelings are the Pod. The Pod are the Malefics. The Malefics are the Changelings, completing the circle! He remembered the hologram in the library on the Pod; how they were part of the planets evolution and were the true indigenous race. They were held back by their primitiveness and lack of technological advancement. It was thought that this was by choice rather than by lack of ambition.

Tyson wanted to know more and it appeared the creature was willing to tell him when heavy footsteps were heard outside. Wernion sprang back from the door concerned that he may be seen to be too friendly towards the alien. It was his father.

'Is the alien awake?' his father asked. In answer Wernion stepped to one side and Dominion could see the alien was wide awake and seated. He frowned and looked back at Wernion, his expression conveying that he wanted to understand why his son had not informed him. Wernion shrugged indifferently.

'Bring him,' said Dominion, directing the two warriors behind him to enter the cell. Tyson, who heard and understood every word, stood up much to Dominion's amazement. The two warriors each took one of his arms and Dominion placed a funny looking rope made of some kind of hemp around his wrists to bind them. Tyson guessed that this cave may prevent use of the magics but outside it was this rope which would prevent such use; like the red manacles used by the Zeinonians. Wernion followed them.

They marched him along a number of tunnels with torches lighting the way. He saw communities living off the tunnels in mini caverns which held cooking areas and sleeping quarters with many animal pelts lining the floor. He saw young baby Pod suckling and older children playing. He caught the relaxed and comfortable thoughts they had as they enjoyed the family atmosphere. Family, yes that was what he felt, an overwhelming bond of love and security. These were so different from the threatening creatures he had battled in Reinan. They passed a group of female Pod cooking what looked like a thick soup in a boiling cauldron over a roaring fire. One of the females stood up and waved at Wernion and he tried very hard to ignore her, worried that his father would see him.

Who is that? asked Tyson

My female mate, Hersion, responded a morose looking Wernion.

Are you not pleased to see her?

Yes, but in our culture, when you are on duty there is no contact, she should not have waved to me, explained Wernion.

Tyson looked back at the disappearing Hersion and saw the disappointment on her face as she returned to stirring the cooking pot. 'She obviously does not follow the cultural aspects of this relationship, weird, just weird,' he said under his breath and attracted a cuff from one of the other guards. Wernion chuckled, amused at the alien's humour.

He was taken into a large cavern with a spectacular stone throne. The cavern was empty, except for a tall female Pod wearing a crown of sorts and a few guards. The crown was made of gnarled twigs that were weaved intricately to create an understated regal statement. He was marched forward until he was before the throne. She, like Hersion, wore an additional brief garment across her chest

Dominion pushed him to his knees and then stood to one side with Wernion on the other. The other two warriors stood behind him. Festilion was fascinated. She noticed the strange alien features, different from the Defilers', but like Wernion, noticed the existence of magics by the blue eyes and her own sensitiveness to the condition.

'Is this the one you said showed the strong magic?' she asked Dominion. Before he could answer, Tyson thought it was time to announce his capability to hear the strange language, in what was presumably a royal court.

'Direct your questions at me and you may receive the answers you require?' said Tyson. Festilion stepped back in surprise and Dominion's mouth fell open and the back of his hand snapped back to install some manners in the prisoner. When the hand swept down, Tyson easily dodged the blow, much to the anger of the Pod.

'Why you…,' said an angry Dominion but Festilion held up a hand to stop him giving retribution for the inferred slight of the outsider's boldness.

'You speak our language?' said Festilion, still reeling from the surprise.

'Yes, it must be the curse of these magics inside me,' said Tyson, bitterly.

'Curse you say, do you not revel in the magics?' she asked, surprised to hear the bitterness of the tone.

'I was born with these magics but I never wanted them. They have just brought me violence, uncertainty and pushed my friends away from me.'

Festilion, exchanged glances with Dominion. This was becoming interesting. 'Normally I would have you killed. You are an abomination of Zein, created from the magics that our own kind and others have used to defile our world,' Festilion said without a hint of rancour. To her this was something she had lived with for many years.

'But you won't, will you?' said Tyson, reading her thoughts, 'You want to know who I am and what our plans are?' Festilion smiled and returned to her throne. Once seated she raised one of her hands and Dominion pulled Tyson up off his knees.

'You are correct, I want to know where you are from and what is your story,' said Festilion, waving forward one of the warriors. 'You must be hungry and thirsty. Redulon, please arrange to bring…,' she hesitated.

'Tyson, my name is Tyson.'

Festilion studied him, impressed with his courage and his abilities. 'Bring some fruit and water for Tyson,'

ordered Festilion. Redulon, hid his surprise at the gesture.
Prisoners were usually questioned and then killed without
delay. He did not say anything, not wanting to feel the
wrath of Festilion and hurried off to do her bidding.
'My name is Festilion, Queen of the Pod, the true High
Priestess of Zein and not the one who commands the
Malefics. You are in my Ceremony Hall.' She waved her
hand around the cavern. 'Now talk.'

Tyson told her of Earth and his upbringing of meeting
his half-brother and of the pursuit of the group by Zylar.
He kept from her the extent of his magics but told of the
kidnap of his mother and the final battle. He could see in
Festilion's eyes her sympathy for the plight of his mother.
The Pod were very much about family and trust, caring
deeply for their family unit. The guard, who Redulon had
instructed, returned and Tyson was given some fruit and
water, which he quickly demolished. When sated he found
his audience keen on further information.

'Tell me about your ships?' she requested.

Tyson told her of the journey, the attack of the Xonian
ships and the landing near Reinan. He saw her eyes widen
at the mention of the Xonians.

She is afraid of them.

'Why come back?' said Festilion, shaken about the
mention of the Xonians. More invaders.

'To find any survivors,' said Tyson, simply.

'Not to find methir?' She saw Tyson's confused look.
'Our sacred mineral which you misuse.'

'Zinithium, we call it zinithium,' said Tyson, putting
two and two together. He didn't expect the flash of anger
in the High Priestess's eyes.

'You give it a name that means nothing,' she shouted,
'Methir is in our air, water and food, yet you Defilers take
it and abuse it for your own pleasure.' Tyson cowered from

the anger he felt not just from the figure on the throne but also from those beside and behind him.

'Sorry, I have no idea why it is so bad to mention the mineral,' said Tyson, timidly. Festilion saw that he was confused and that he didn't understand.

She stood up and walked across to a bowl on the side. She raised the bowl to her lips and had a long drink and then began pacing.

'Methir is in everything you see around you,' said Festilion, gesturing to the ceilings, walls and the water she had just drunk, 'Some of our kind wanted more than the simple life we lead and they started transforming the use of the methir.' Tyson remembered his thoughts in the cell on seeing Wernion's eyes.

'The creature we know as Changeling?'

'Your insight serves you well. We do not call them Changelings but Malefic, which to us is translated as evil transformers,' Tyson thought of how often Zebulon had transformed and saved their lives. He did not see the evil this priestess was referring to.

'By the time we had uncovered their coven it was too late,' said Festilion, angrily, 'their numbers were great and they killed their own kin to escape.'

'Why is it so bad to develop the magics?' said Tyson. Festilion stopped pacing and looked deeply into what felt like his very soul.

'How do you feel with the magics?' she asked softly, and on seeing the turmoil in his look, 'Precisely. The magics twist you, changing your very essence. Before they mastered the magics a few went mad and killed whole families.'

Tyson swallowed hard, knowing the darkness that enveloped him at times. 'But don't they simply allow you to change shape or protect yourself?'

Festilion shook her head, 'The very act of changing shape disturbs the circle of life. The body has to change how it thinks, works and manages during the change. This can lead to changes in bodily functions and natural ageing.'

'Why is that bad?'

'The Malefic have very few young and live for many, many years. This increased life span creates its own uncertainty and almost greed to improve life and power. This in turn can infect other races, which can result in them attacking their own flesh and blood,' said Festilion, sadly.

'You mean the magics naturally create conflict?'

'Yes, when I found out, they fled and sold their way of life to the Defilers, as if it was a simple barter for food,' said Festilion, her face stricken with deep memories, 'Magics for the promise to kill all the Brethren.' A tear ran down her face.

'I still remember the death. Male, female and children dying as they poisoned the very air we breathe. I escaped but many of my people didn't. The horror still lingers today and drives us to rid this planet of all Defilers and Malefics once and for all.'

Tyson felt her pain. Deep within him the magics stirred in empathy, which now he knew stemmed from the latent magic within these beasts.

'Now don't you see we can't let them live as they will have us all killed. They can't allow us to survive. That is why I order so many attacks on where they live. It is either them or us,' Festilion finished and seemingly tired by the emotion of the discussion, sat down on the throne. She looked tired and less threatening to Tyson. Then a thought struck him.

'You attack to reach the Malefics and not the Defilers, don't you?' he asked quietly, using the names she recognised.

Festilion fastened onto his face; this creature had insight. 'Yes, we are not happy with the transfer of the magics but it is the threat of the Malefics that we most fear. The Defilers stand in our way and they need to be dealt with first.'

'That's is why I and my brother felt the fear during the attack rather than hatred,' said Tyson turning his gaze to Dominion, 'because you don't know whether we will support the Malefic in their aim to kill your entire species.'

Dominion didn't answer. He didn't need to; the downcast look to the floor told the story. Tyson made a decision.

'I will help you if you let me?' he said.

Festilion's face was scornful. 'How can you help us? You are not really a Defiler but an alien to our planet,' she said.

'I am brother to Lord Blackstone, and he would help if he knew the facts?'

'The Blackstones were the worst. They accepted deeper magics in return for a solution to kill us,' she said, angrily standing up and squaring up to Tyson. Tyson didn't back down.

'I am my own man. My brother is different from the Blackstones you have experience of and we will help you,' he said, keeping his eyes locked with hers. Festilion calmed down, it had been an exhausting day. She turned her back on Tyson and returned to her seat.

'Dominion, take our guest away, feed and water him but do not allow him out of the cell,' Festilion ordered.

She waved him away and when the warriors took hold of his arms he knew the audience was at an end.

Chapter 13: Old Bonds

No one noticed the small bird fly through the Outer Perimeter Barrier when the convoy left for Reinan. Zebulon watched the convoy enter the city village and with regret turned left towards the mountains to the north-west of Reinan. He couldn't believe how ruined the city was and how far the conflict had gone. He thought time was a healer and a truce would have occurred. He had been wrong.

He decided he wanted to feel the grass between his feet and returned to the precious Zein land, transforming into his favoured wolf shape. The usual uneasy feeling he experienced when he transferred happened but his body grew used to it over the hundreds of years he had lived. There was nothing he could do. His father and Myolon made that choice for him, so many years ago.

Zebulon bounded across the ornamental park, with its beautiful falls cascading down the three sides of the cliff. The water crashed onto the rocks below in a spectacular display of noise and mist. He knew the way. Memories never faded and he remembered better times when this park had been full of smiling and happy Zeinonians playing and picnicking.

In truth he had missed Zein; the Earth Colony was a good alternative but when compared to this place of his ancestors and where he was born there was no competition. He had grown fond of Kabel and the other companions, they had been through a lot but now that he was home he had unfinished business and they would have to take a back seat

He ran out of the park into the grasslands and then the mountains beyond. He hoped the entrance he had created so many years ago still remained or he would be in trouble. He didn't need to worry. He found it. The entrance was small and at the foot of a particular high cliff face, surrounded by boulders. He transformed into a buzza fly: an animal so small it would make a mosquito look like a giant. He flew through the stone gap which widened into a steel lined tunnel he had prepared. He then returned to his wolf shape and twisted and turned through the tunnels until he came within close proximately of the main South Gate entrance.

There he waited patiently in his secret hiding place and was rewarded when a returning group of soldiers emerged from the steel tunnel. Taking advantage of the opportunity he changed into a butterfly and flew into the main tunnel where the recon party had come from. He fluttered above their heads as the steel barricade creaked and made way for the young Zeinonian in his battered red armour and his companions.

Then the weak Inner Perimeter Barrier was turned off behind the main entrance. Zebulon flew into the Aeria Cavern without anyone noticing a thing. Good. That was what he wanted.

Zebulon observed the group and heard the leader call for a meeting and on the spur of the moment decided that he would follow this young man and watch the proceedings of this emergency meeting. He watched the members of the Inner Council enter and caught his breath; there she was, not changed for almost one hundred years. He heard her speech to the Inner Council and was shocked; he had arrived home just in time.

The Inner Council meeting ended and Zebulon followed the Changelings back to their enclave. The Changelings lived in a generous, almost presidential area of the city. There were parks and impressive residential houses.

I did a good job, he thought, impressed his work had lasted through the years.

Heathlon, walked into her quarters. She felt uneasy. Her magics were strong and they were disturbed by a presence, something she had not felt for a long time. 'Are you going to show yourself or skulk in a corner?' she said, removing the cloak from her shoulders.

'I see you still have the skills,' said Zebulon. Heathlon let out a gasp of shock. Her hand flew to her mouth as she spun round to face the newcomer.

'Greetings, Mother, I hope I find you well?' said Zebulon, in his newly transformed shape that mirrored the way the Changelings on Zein liked to be seen.

'Zebulon, you are alive,' Heathlon exclaimed.

'Yes Mother, I came in with the task force.'

Heathlon's surprise was total. She had thought he was lost to her and seeing him now had answered many prayers. He approached her and she reached out to him. They embraced.

'I thought I would never see you again,' she said, releasing the embrace and taking a seat.

'Mother, I am glad to be back, but in the Inner Council you talked of a quest to extinguish the Pod,' said Zebulon. 'How can you make that mistake again?'

'You don't understand my son, the Pod are growing more powerful and I think they are turning to the magics.' Heathlon dropped her head in shame, conveying that she doubted her own words.

'And if they did, does that make them any worse than us?' said Zebulon, 'Do you want mass murder on our hands again?'

Heathlon shook her head. Zebulon sat next to her, seeing that her advanced years were masked by the youthful façade. He took her hands. 'I have struggled to live with what we did,' he said quietly, 'I have wandered for many years waiting for this very moment. I am here to put right what was wrong.'

He lifted her chin. 'I am so pleased to see you and be back home. I have made new friends who have accepted me as I am – no questions asked.'

'It's too late, Zebulon. Your brother set out two termins days ago and is on his way to the breeding grounds to launch the serum.'

He patted her hands, 'One thing which these humans have taught me is never give up,' he said firmly. 'How is my dear brother?' Heathlon's face told the story. 'So he is still reckless then?' said Zebulon.

'Yes you know your brother, he has made us isolated, where once we were integrated,' said Heathlon, 'He wants to rid Zein of the Pod once and for all and forced me to speak at the Inner Council, knowing no one would stand against me.'

'Isolated?'

'We stay in our enclaves and do not mix with the other clans. We have a sickness and he will not seek help.' She took hold of his hand, 'Son we are dying, we have very few children and there is an illness the magics bring. We need help.'

Zebulon shook his head. It was the reason he had taken up the request by the young Lord Chancellor Morgan Blackstone to support the Zein Expeditionary Force all those years ago. He and twenty of his personal pack had agreed to support the quest. He had lost most of his brethren during the journey. They had landed on a planet they thought would be hospitable to the Zeinonians; however, they were attacked by monstrous beasts that required the Changelings to protect the Lord Chancellor. Many died. Others died during asteroid and mercenary attacks. The few who survived perished in Zylar's attacks on the quadrants until he was the only one left. He had given up, voluntary becoming an attraction at the Federation Fair until he had seen Morgan's grandson strolling across the fairground.

'I have seen death and destruction from hatred and greed. My father and your husband recognised that when he absorbed and controlled the magics there was no return.' Zebulon became pensive as he remembered the events that happened a long time ago.

'We were wrong. We shouldn't have corrupted the scriptures and remained one with Zein, like our brethren.' He shook his head. 'To try and wipe our own kin off the face of this planet, not just once but twice, when they were in the right all along, is a travesty.'

Zebulon slumped into one of the large chairs in the room. He placed his hand over his eyes.

'But our magics helped us defeat the Xonians,' said his mother, defending history.

'Maybe, maybe or we may have bonded with the Defilers and defeated the Xonians, who knows.' Zebulon was tired. He had lived for over three hundred years, seen many things, and fought many battles.

'I think my father knew this when I volunteered for the expedition. He knew that I needed to escape Zein and seek out a new world were this sickness does not invade the body.'

'Did you find it on this Earth?'

Zebulon, bit his lip in concentration 'Not fully. They have their own share of misery, evil and greed but conversely I see something in them which exudes hope and peace.'

'So what do we do now, my son?'

'I am not sure, but Mother, I have returned to put right what I feel is wrong. Things will change, I promise you that,' said Zebulon with an evangelical look on his face. For the first time in many years Heathlon felt there was a future for them.

Chapter 14:
The Morning After

Slowly the companions woke up as the daily activities on the ship began. Kabel untangled himself from the still sleeping Gemma. He swung his legs out of the bed and placed his head into his hands. His dream last night had switched from an angry Tyson sat in a cell, to an underground lake. He knew it was on this planet due to seeing Pod all around him. But they weren't attacking, they were dying. Fear all across their faces as both child and adult died by the thousand. The dream ended with a strange human like person with a spiteful look upon his face. The eyes, the eyes reminded him of someone.

There was a groan behind him as Gemma stretched. She sensed his pain. Her hand touched his heavily muscled shoulder and brushed along the ridges.

'Another dream?' she said quietly. He gestured that it was. 'Was it about Tyson again?' she asked.

'Not all of it,' said Kabel, 'though I do think he is still alive.' Gemma felt relieved, worrying most of the night on whether Tyson had survived or not.

Kabel stood up and moved athletically to the table where a jug of water rested. Gemma stared at the curve of his back and the magnificence of his nakedness.

'Tell me about the dream,' Gemma coaxed, as she patted the side of the bed. He sat down and told her everything. Gemma was a good listener and he wanted to share as much of his dream with her as he could remember.

'That sounds awful,' said a horrified Gemma, after he described the mountain of bodies littering the underground caverns, 'how did they die?'

'Well, not all my dreams come true.' He hesitated, not sure how to put it. 'They are flashes of what could be or will be and I have a chance to alter them.'

'Those creatures are frightening; maybe it is good that they are destroyed?' said Gemma, shuddering with the memory of the attack yesterday. Kabel reached across and lightly touched her face with his fingertips. She kissed the end of his fingers when they touched her lips.

'It was strange yesterday, I know they were attacking but it wasn't out of hate but fear,' said Kabel, telling her about the swirl of feelings that came from the seven foot creatures, which was also felt by Belina and Tyson.

Much to her disappointment he stood back up. 'I am going for a shower,' he said purposely, 'we need to find out what's the plan for today.' He saw the disappointment on her face and realised that after the shock of yesterday, she was seeking comfort. 'Of course, there is room for two in the shower,' he said over his shoulder as he strutted towards the shower cubicle. Gemma wasn't far behind him.

Later, suitably refreshed, they went to the Command and Control Centre. Another heated argument between General Corder and Admiral Koshkov was underway.

'We should have had air support faster yesterday,' said Admiral Koshkov, furious with the hesitancy he had witnessed yesterday and not satisfied by the explanations given. His shock at what he thought was a dereliction of duty, further underlined that the commander of the Expeditionary Force had ulterior motives.

'The convoy had sufficient firepower, Admiral,' General Corder replied calmly. His second-in-command was just going to retort when Walter Moore interrupted.

'I think our focus should be on what we do next and not on what went wrong,' he reasoned.

It was Kabel who stepped forward. He was tired and filled with the horror of the battle the day before. On the way to see General Corder, Kabel had sought out Bailey and the others to tell them details of his dream, minus the element concerning the Pod, and that he thought Tyson was still alive. Both Amelia and Bailey, especially, were relieved but all their concern did not evaporate and wouldn't until they saw Tyson alive and kicking.

'I need to be debriefed,' he said to the warring officers. He had their attention. Admiral Koshkov pursed his lips to prevent his anger spiralling out of control but that didn't mean this argument was over, just postponed. 'In private,' Kabel said pointedly.

They all funnelled into the main conference room for that deck. The only one of the companions not there, apart from Tyson, was the Changeling. Kabel could not find Zebulon anywhere and even though he asked for a broadcast over the ships intercom for him to meet in the Command and Control Centre, he still did not appear. In truth no one had seen him since they had left for their ill-fated trip into Reinan.

Walter Moore and the latter's personal assistant, a woman called Grace Connor, whose job was to record the session, made up the remaining members of the meeting.

Kabel brought the others up-to-date on his dream involving Tyson. Both Walter and Admiral Koshkov where pleased, General Corder less so. Koshkov, glared triumphantly at the American guessing this was not part of his plan. Kabel ignored their reactions and pressed on to cover the sequence of events once they had left the Outer Perimeter. Walter Moore outlined what he and his companions had learned from the hologram programmes in the library. It was Hechkle who began to explain the retreat and the attack of the Pod, when Kabel held up his hand to stop proceedings. Hechkle stopped his report and waited.

'Tyson saw someone before the attack and conveyed that image to me,' said Kabel, looking across at the team.

'Why didn't you tell me?' said Gemma, hurt that he hadn't mentioned that this morning. Kabel ignored the question and pressed on. Gemma threw a filthy look at him.

'He was youngish and had red armour on which had seen better days,' he described.

'Malacca clan?' said Bronstorm.

'Yes, I think so.'

'Did he say anything or do anything?' General Corder asked, intrigued.

'No, he looked surprised and then they disappeared into a hole in the ground,' Kabel explained, 'Tyson was going to follow but then the Pod attacked.'

'So there are Zeinonians alive,' said Hechkle, 'we must find them.'

'Agreed Hechkle, but we need to make sure we do not place the expedition at risk,' said Admiral Koshkov, carefully. Kabel and General Corder agreed.

Kabel sought Gemma's attention, not sure whether he should share the rest of his dream with the committee. Gemma initial petulance at Kabel for not telling her about what Tyson had seen had evaporated, intrigued by the discussion and she nodded her head encouragingly.

'I have something else I need to share with you,' said Kabel, and then outlined key details of his dream. The rest listened in horror when he described the gut wrenching death of thousands of the creatures.

'I have not had this dream,' Belina challenged. Her dreams had started back on Earth as the magics built up inside her. She saw in Kabel's shared memory what he had seen but was not sure what the vision meant.

Kabel lifted his hands in resignation, 'Sorry, dear sister, but I did as you now know, and I found it disturbing.'

Bronstorm had been quiet in the exchange and then brought up what they had all felt during the attack. 'We all felt that the Pod were attacking out of fear and not hatred.' He waited for Kabel and Belina to support his view.' They did. 'Why would they risk such a loss of life out of fear is the question we should be trying to answer.' Bronstorm stated. 'Maybe it is this vision which Kabel had. They fear death from an illness?'

'Fair question Bronstorm, but I don't tend to dwell on why someone or something is trying to kill me when I am protecting my life,' Hechkle's gruff voice spoke up. It was reinforced by similar views from both Gemma and Amelia, both of whom had felt immensely frightened yesterday.

'So what are we going to do?' Walter asked, having listened quietly to the views around the table.

It was Kabel who suggested a recon party, firstly to search for Tyson, just in case his dream was misleading and then to seek the hole the men, who Tyson had seen, disappear into. They agreed the size and participants of the party required and then ended the meeting.

As they exited the conference room, the warning klaxon sounded. As one they all rushed into the Command and Control Centre.

Lieutenant Lavelle, the Communications Officer on the *Elanda*, had a picture up on the forward screen. It focused on a position near the Outer Perimeter Barrier. Standing there, silently, were a group of people, numbering between forty and fifty. In front of the group was a Zeinonian clad in battered red armour.

'Ladies and Gentlemen,' said General Corder, drawing in his cheeks as he bit on his inside cheek, 'looks like we don't need to go looking for them.

Chapter 15: Simple Life

Cronje was working his homestead in the Eastern Quadrant. He still supported the Inner Council meetings on Earth but had placed his right hand man, Reddash, in charge of the remaining Malacca troops. He was tired of fighting and when Kabel had asked him to be Vice-Chancellor he readily accepted but was also worried as he was not a political animal. If you placed him into a battle, against the odds, no problem; place him in a war of words and he became tongue-tied. Kabel gave him assurance that Lords Fathom and Southgate would cover that and he should be there to provide the necessary advice and support.

He had met a woman named Marcy, who had two teenage children, a thirteen year old boy called Tredegar, or Tred as Cronje called him, and a fifteen year old girl, called Sasha. Marcy's husband had died in the recent fighting and Cronje had met up with her to make sure she was coping. They both were hurting and hit it off. Marcy was a timid, petite woman whom Cronje immediately felt protective towards. He had moved into this tiny homestead some four months ago and spent his days ploughing the lush field and updating the buildings of the little farm.

He saw them coming down the road. The two teenage children were with Marcy's aunt in the nearby city village of Emula and Marcy was in the kitchen cooking the evening meal for just the two of them. He made out the bulky figure of Reddash and ten other soldiers as they sped towards him on their hover bikes.

Cronje shut off the sophisticated ploughing conveyor and hopped off. He purposely made his way back to the homestead. Reddash would not have come out this far unless something was wrong.

As Cronje jogged back into the driveway the hover bikes, with a screech of brakes, came to a stop before him. Reddash and the soldiers jumped off the bikes, resting them on their hover brake, a light emanating from the bottom of the machine which created a mini force-field that prevented any movement of the bikes unless the operator restarted the machine.

'What's the matter, Reddash?' Cronje asked.

'Can we go inside, Sir?' answered a breathless Reddash. In answer Cronje gestured for all the soldiers to come in for refreshments. Marcy had already begun preparation of the cold refreshing drinks, as she heard and saw the soldiers pull up outside the house.

After the soldiers had all taken in refreshments, Cronje took Reddash to one side. 'Tell me, what is going on?'

Reddash placed his iced sweet tea down. 'They are disbanding the Malacca Clan Eastern Army,' said Reddash, handing Cronje an order paper, 'by order of the Joint Inner Council,' he finished bitterly. Cronje read the order.

'Why?'

'There has been a lot of trouble. Since those two hitchhikers were beaten, we have had many more humans travelling to the Eastern Quadrant,' said Reddash, as he took a sip of his tea. 'Most of them have been fine, causing no problems but a growing minority are causing fights, drinking too much as Emula is now seen as something called a stag destination.'

Cronje grimaced; Emula was the Eastern Quadrant's capital city and was a beautiful, quiet place with many beer establishments. Now it appeared the human illness of too much alcoholic indulgence had spread to his quadrant.

'Surely we can manage this trouble?' Cronje asked. He knew the Malacca army, which in the old days numbered in excess of seventy-five thousand men and women, was significantly smaller now but shouldn't a few troublemakers be dealt with comfortably?

'Sir, you don't understand, with the conscription law repealed our numbers on Earth have dropped below twenty thousand men and women. Our best soldiers are with the Expeditionary Force,' Reddash explained. Cronje disagreed, he did understand that despite the repeal of the conscription laws the Malacca clan still had a professional fighting unit, although, he also knew that with twenty thousand of his best troops with the expedition, they had an experience gap. But this was just a few drunken revellers.

'Where are our soldiers now?' Cronje asked as he pulled on his uniform; the farm would have to wait.

'Two thousand are in the Core supporting the US Army and Russian troops and the rapid expansion of the settlement. Eight thousand in the Eastern Quadrant and the rest scattered around the other quadrants.'

'How many troops from Earth are there in the Core?'

'At last count, about ten thousand,' said Reddash.

'Why so many?'

'The Core has nearly doubled in size and now holds nearly one hundred and sixty thousand Zeinonians and humans,' said Reddash. He saw Cronje's surprise. 'They are mining vast parts of the zinithium fields and with the *Freedom of Movement Act 2014*; no one can prevent immigration rights across Earth.

'Madness! What are Lords Southgate and Fathom's views of this?' Cronje demanded, cursing that he took such a back seat. Reddash just shrugged.

'I know that Lord Southgate has challenged the decision on behalf of Zein but I have not heard from Lord Fathom in over a month.'

'That's disturbing. Anyway, why disband our army?' said Cronje. Reddash went red with embarrassment.

Cronje paused, pulling on his tunic. 'What's happened?'

Reddash fidgeted and the other soldiers who had overheard some of the conversation also looked anywhere except at their Commander-In-Chief.

'Spit it out, man,' said Cronje, expecting the worse.

'A few nights ago there were ten fights in different parts of Emula and the local militia were overrun. The fights didn't seem connected but then they seemed to join up and bars were destroyed, local villagers were attacked so I sent in the garrison.' Reddash couldn't look Cronje in the eye. Cronje didn't give him any respite as he bent forward and locked his penetrative glare at his second-in-command. 'We had no choice, they were wrecking the bars and the Royal Council building,' Reddash pleaded.

'What did you do?' Cronje had a hard knot in the pit of his stomach.

'Some of the rookie soldiers panicked and opened fire.' Was the hushed response. Cronje felt ill. He knew the humans well enough that, whatever the provocation was, live rounds on an unarmed crowd was strictly off limits.

'How many injured?'

'Thirty, with five deaths,' said an ashamed Reddash.

Cronje threw a fist at the wall, making an indentation in the plaster. He then calmly turned to Marcy informing her he would be away for some time. He finished dressing and pulled out his seckle and photon blaster from their hiding place and strapped the blaster on. He went to collect his bike from the barn.

'Let's go,' he ordered Reddash and his troops, once safely sitting astride the impressive machine. Before long they were moving at incredible speed across the wilderness of the Eastern Quadrant towards the city village of Emula. When they were half a mile from the village border they saw the checkpoints. Cronje raised his hand to halt the procession. When he saw the unmistakable markings of the US and Chinese armies, he called forward one of his men. He knew that nothing good lay ahead.

'I want you to go back to the homestead and take Marcy to the safe house in the mountains.' The soldier saluted and roared away. Cronje then called forward another soldier.

'When we are through the checkpoints I want you to collect Marcy's children and take them also to the safe house,' said Cronje. He then turned to Reddash and the remaining soldiers, 'Whatever happens from now on, don't react just accept what is to happen, that's an order,' he commanded. They all acknowledged the order.

They set off to the checkpoint. There were six soldiers at the checkpoint. The senior US officer stepped forward and asked for papers. Since the unification all Zeinonians had been provided with a licence stating name, clan, date of birth, village of birth and number. The original purpose was to enable free movement around Earth; now it was being used to control Zeinonian identification.

The US Army officer looked at all the soldiers' identification, when he came to Reddash's licence he motioned for the soldiers at the checkpoint, including two Chinese soldiers, to arrest him. Before they could move, Cronje acted. He grabbed hold of the officer and placed his seckle against his throat.

'Drop the weapons, now,' he said. The humans hesitated but then followed the order.

'No action you said?' Reddash raised a quizzical eye at Cronje.

'That was for you, didn't apply to me,' retorted Cronje, pleasantly. Reddash groaned.

Cronje directed his troops to tie them up. They then carefully approached the city village, placing their bikes against one of the houses. Dusk had fallen so they went in slowly and not by the main exit. The streets were quiet. The soldier who he had commanded to collect the two children left them.

'We need to get a message to Lord Southgate,' said Cronje to Reddash. 'I will do that; you need to find the barracks and pull together the Veterans.' The Veterans or Vets as they were more fondly referred to, made up the core of the remaining Malacca Clan Eastern Army. Their expertise was gained in the hard fought border wars, the invasions of the other quadrants and the battle at the Southern Quadrant Palace with the Ilsid. Everyone knew not to mess with them.

They decided the best approach would be to split up into two groups, one travelling at street level, the other clambering over the roof line. Cronje was at the street level and Reddash took the other troops across the buildings.

Cronje cautiously crept along the street with the three troopers with him. He heard the clump, clump of feet and the group merged in with their surroundings. Around the corner came twenty soldiers of the Chinese People's Liberation Army Ground Force. Their marching was synchronised expertly. They waited until they went past.

Cronje felt the anger rising within him. Foreign soldiers had never been on Eastern Quadrant soil and if he had his way they would not be staying.

They carried on with their journey to the Transportation building in the centre of Emula. They dodged a number of patrols, which Cronje noticed contained no one from the Malacca clan. They approached the inner circle with the main buildings in front of them. Cronje took in that all the bars with their cascade of brightly covered chairs, which used to provide a cheerful and pleasant atmosphere around the circle, were closed. He saw the damage to some of the windows which were now boarded up.

Outside the Transportation building there were two US Army soldiers standing guard. Cronje motioned for one of the troopers to loop round and then make a disturbance. He and the remaining two troopers worked their way round until they were close to the two soldiers standing guard.

There was a shout across the circle and the US Marines immediately were on their communication links. One of the soldiers left his position and raced across to investigate. Cronje moved swiftly. He crept up on the remaining soldier and knocked him unconscious. They then entered the building dragging the inert form with him.

They made their way to the transportation room which was locked. Cronje removed his card and swiped it across the lock. The satisfying noise of the locks unfurling could be heard. He pushed the door open.

'Vice-Chancellor Cronje, good to see you,' said a colonel of the US Marines. Behind him there were another ten soldiers with automatic rifles at the ready. 'What brings you here on such a fine night?' Behind Cronje and his soldiers another squad of American soldiers arrived.

'Just taking a gentle stroll,' said Cronje.

'Fine, I have been ordered to escort you to the Core,' said the soldier, 'After you have placed your weapons into our safe-keeping.'

'Who are you and who sent you?'

'I am Colonel Travers and I am here under orders of the Inner Council.'

Cronje weighed up the odds and decided he needed to play this one out. With his step-children safely spirited away, he could bide his time.

'Colonel Travers, let's go,' said Cronje as he pulled out his weapons and passed them to the nearest guard.

They entered the transportation field and teleported to the Core.

Chapter 16: Skegus

Zylar strode confidently down the ship's walkway surrounded by twenty of his Ilsid. Beside him was Leila.

Since that fateful night when she had given herself to him, Zylar, if it was at all possible, appeared to be smitten by her. His requests for the young women in his captivity reduced and Leila was a regular in his quarters.

Leila hid her disgust at what she was doing but she now enjoyed considerably more freedom round the ship. He had appointed the big, lumbering, young Malacca soldier who had guarded the medical bay with the sallow faced man, as her permanent guard. Leila found out that his name was Clancy and apart from a slowness of mind, he was quite sweet. He held doors open for her and was more protective than threatening.

She walked dutifully beside Zylar, keeping her head down and her gaze averted from him. Even with this precaution, when she saw the wonder of the Skegus city of Quentine open up in front of her, she could not stop her mouth from flopping open in amazement.

In front of her was a city so beautiful that it defied the logic that cities were large conurbations with dirt, noise and energy. Not here. There were buildings of wonder reaching so high in the sky that some of the tips disappeared into the cloud. Their sheer sides of black glass shone with the reflected sunshine. In contrast, surrounding some of the largest buildings, were exquisite structures of every type of material and construction. It was a rich patchwork quilt of colour and style that gave an overwhelming feel of a sophisticated civilisation.

The wonder did not stay long. In front of them was a welcome committee that made Leila extremely fearful, causing heart palpitations in her nervous body. Ahead was a contingent of what could only be called reptiles in armour; their blue scaly skin secreted a loathsome fluid which kept it moist. Leila felt repelled and fought against any outward sign of her disgust…something which she was finding hard to do.

There appeared to be a variety of types of alien, with the tall ones in front, whom Zylar greeted with a low bow, representing what must be the senior leadership and then there were the aliens that were nearly half the size just behind them. They made up the bulk of the guard but it was the gruesome beasts that a number of the soldiers were holding by reins that made her really shiver. The creatures reminded her of extremely large crocodiles with legs twice the size of those on earth. Snouts dripped saliva onto the ground as they sniffed and pawed at the ground in front of her. She could see the strain on their handlers' forearms of the power which these animals had. One creature yawned making Leila swallow hard as a vicious array of teeth, embedded inside the yawning maw of the creature, was displayed.

She felt all the reptiles eyes scan over her and she had the passing feeling that they were weighing her up for lunch, rather than welcome. She nervously pulled the cloak around her and dropped her head again, staring at the floor, knowing that the eyes remained on her.

Zylar paid little attention to the supporting cast and concentrated with many grunts and guttural sounds in conversing with the tall, more senior reptiles. Leila didn't understand a word. If Zylar noticed the interest the human had triggered with the Xonians, he ignored it. He had brought Leila to show them what was on offer, to back up what he had said during talks with them from the safety of his ship.

'The creature smells delightful,' said Yisli, his forked tongue sliding over his blue scaled lips. His report from his initial meeting with Zylar had caused great excitement and greed. He was the commander of all two hundred thousand troops in Sector Four, which covered five galaxies, including the Capulus Novus System where he could call on half of that force if required. He only had Zein left to conquer and was only delayed by a rebellion in one of the other galaxies, which his army was crushing at this very moment.

'Remember, there are over six billion of these creatures on one planet in a galaxy with no other life,' said Zylar, waiting for the reaction from the remaining Xonians. He guessed that greed would overtake any caution and he was not disappointed. 'Now my reckoning is that would feed the Xonian Empire for decades.'

Yisli turned to his second-in-command, Maeli, and gave a horrific smile, before turning back to Zylar.

'I can only agree to your safety here, all decisions need to be sanctioned by Our Exalted Prince Jernli,' he said, spitting out the words in distaste. Even Leila could read the disgusted look on the tall warrior's face, which communicated an intense dislike for whoever Prince Jernli was.

'You didn't mention this in our other discussions,' said Zylar, disappointed that he needed to convince another of his plan.

'Believe me when I say that I thought there would be little issue but this Prince is weak,' said Yisli, not even attempting to hide his disdain. 'I would have conquered Zein many termins ago but the Exalted One feels we need to consolidate our bases here and on Oneerio before invading Zein.'

Zylar grunted his agreement; Zein should not be difficult to conquer and it did seem to be very conservative with such a massive army to call upon.

'In that case take me to Prince Jernli so we can discuss the strategy,' said Zylar, and then as an afterthought, 'I would like to move my concubines to more comfortable quarters near me and have your promise that they will be unharmed?' Yisli confirmed that this would be the case.

'This is my principal concubine,' said Zylar, pointing to Leila, 'she is the only one who will be able to leave my quarters.' Again Yisli bowed his head in acknowledgment.

'Your concubine is welcome in the city. A word of caution, I would advise the alien female that it would not be wise to travel too far without protection,' said Yisli, oily. 'My troops may mistake her for dinner.' He flashed his eyes hungrily in her direction.

Leila saw the exchange and delight on Zylar's face at the last comment. She felt the bile rising up within her.

The party moved off the presentation platform and entered the city. Leila looked around her in awe. The well-tended gardens that broke up the thousands of magnificent buildings gave the city a life and colour that simply took your breath away. They walked past a new building under construction near what seemed to be an external barracks. Massive photon guns as large as a truck were being winched into the fortifications that surrounded the city.

It was not the guns that caught her attention. Working on the fortifications were a people of such gentle features you could see every grimace as the whips of the overseers unrelentingly crashed down onto their half-naked golden backs. The majority were at least eight feet tall with arms that reached the ground. Each of the arms ended in eight long digits that wrapped around the pulleys and stone with ease. There were also fellow creatures who were half the size working with them. One of the smaller creatures lost his grip on the pulley and the gun lurched to the ground, but the tall male figure next to him caught the pulley in flight and his huge muscles flexed and took the weight. He then hauled it back to its position, where another of the creatures set it in place.

The overseer raised his whip and before it came down on the back of the smaller male, the huge hand of the tall male shot across to grip the overseer's hand, preventing the downward application of the whip. The Xonians all around screamed at the creature and they raised their whips to tame this insubordination. The figure straightened up and stared bravely at the smaller figures and his fellow prisoners went to his side. Around the building site there were others of the same race, going by on their own graceful, subdued errands. They all stopped and began to move to where the prisoners were. Hundreds of bystanders swarmed to the site.

Yisli, who had been studying the altercation with amusement, saw the impact on the wider community. He acted swiftly. He issued a series of commands. The overseers dropped their whips and backed off. He spoke to the tall commanding but gentle looking figure in front of him.

In reaction to the shouted commands the tall male figure spoke. Leila marvelled at the musical tone of the voice. It travelled on the breeze and immediately calmed you.

'It is all right my people, please go on your way,' he calmly said. Leila was surprised that she could understand him.

The fellow creatures converging on the site stopped and then carried on their way, their heads bowed again. The figure turned his attention to Leila. Interest flickered across his face, before he moved onto Zylar. Leila was sure he saw him recoil.

'That is Yi, the King of Oneerio and Skegus, Leila,' whispered Zylar.

'What did the Xonian say to him?'

'Just warned him that if this aggression continues, then everyone around him, including his son,' Zylar pointed to the young male who had let go of the pulley, 'would be put to death.'

'That's barbaric.'

'That's Xonian Law, and that is why they reign over a hundred galaxies,' said Zylar, admiringly. Not for the first time Leila couldn't look at the monster who stood next to her. She watched King Yi return to his work after patting his son on his head.

Now that peace was restored the party carried on with their journey. They approached a stylish building that had a castle-like appearance for the first ten floors with battlements ringing the building. Guarding the walls, which had numerous murder holes, were a large number of Xonians in full battle dress. Behind the battlements the rest of the sleek black glass façade reached high into the sky. It shouldn't have worked as a building but it did, maintaining an almost medieval wrapper around an ultra-modern inner building. Zylar saw her take in the building.

'They do go in for the dramatic don't they, Leila?' Leila ignored him and he shrugged his shoulders at the lack of interest in her response. They entered a tower like entrance and it was here that Leila was separated from Zylar and led away by her escort with Clancy trailing.

They travelled in a lift, which was a mini teleport, up to a much higher floor.

The room she was placed in was beautifully furnished with a separate seating area, a large bedroom and ensuite bathroom to the side. Clancy was positioned outside the door of the room and before he left her, Leila asked him to notify her when the other women were brought to the building. Tired, she rested on the bed and soon fell into a restless sleep.

It was a couple of hours later that a knock on the door woke her. Groggily she raised herself from the bed, and went to the door and on opening it was faced with Clancy standing there respectfully, clutching his hands in front of him and struggling to look her in the eye.

'The women have all been transferred,' he said, nervously wringing his hands as he noticed Leila had just a vest top and pants on which accented her curves. He was ten years younger than the human but over the months on the ship he had wrestled with his emotions. A simple man, who was always given the boring and easy roles, he was a sensitive giant. His size stopped some of the hurtful barbs of how slow he was but Leila had treated him with kindness. Recently he had fought other, deeper feelings. He hated how Zylar treated her and marvelled at how caring she continued to be even when subjected to the humiliation heaped on her by his leader.

Leila was no fool and noticed the wringing of the hands, the blush on his cheeks.

He likes me. That may prove useful.

When they entered the room of the other prisoners, Leila was swamped with hugs and questions. Delilah was so pleased to see her and as she hugged her, Leila thought back across the last six months, noticing how she had changed from a shy teenager, into a tough and vibrant young woman. Leila had protected her from Zylar and other guards' attentions. It was not particularly difficult, as Zylar was focusing on the humans rather than Zeinonians.

The three children were lying down in a corner.

The two girls, Hanna and Adira, gurgled happily as their eyes followed the handmade shiny animal mobile dangled above them. Megan and Devra, the two mothers respectively, had accepted that their children may have been born from forced relations but they were just as much theirs as Zylar's. The latter was a quiet Jewish girl, snatched from a small kibbutz outside Jerusalem. The boy, Cian, was the oldest, crawling away from his Irish mother, Shannon, his shock of dark, curly hair already growing thick and fast. They were all pleased to see Leila.

Leila patiently told them what had happened and that she had a plan. When she left the room there was hope in the air. Everyone needed hope and now she just needed to deliver on her promises.

Chapter 17: New Alliances

That morning it was decided that a good sized advance force would follow Tate Malacca back to the Aeria Cavern to demonstrate solidarity with the people of Zein. The force numbered thousands with more following later that day with some armour.

Of the initial force over half would be a mixture of the Malacca and Blackstone clan supported by a brigade of US Fighting First troops. Others making up the numbers included the companions, Walter and his main senior science team. The troops coming later would be mainly from the Malacca clan and US Marine Core.

Prior to this a small group, led by Kabel, went to search for Tyson with one of the diggers. The digger made short work of the rubble where Tyson had been seen last. Much to the relief of the companions, especially Amelia and Bailey, they found no sign of him. They returned to the *Elanda* with a spring in their step, upbeat that Kabel's dream that Tyson was alive could be true.

When they marched into the Aeria Cavern, all the clans came out to greet them. This was the day of their dreams; the Inter-Galactic Expeditionary Force was back and with help.

There was a heady excitement as they entered through the main South Gate. Gemma felt the thrill of the occasion. Leading the troops were the two Lord Chancellors, Kabel and Tate, who were initially cagey around each other, the former due to memories of the Eastern Quadrant on Earth, the latter with his distrust of the Blackstone clan.

One person, who couldn't keep the smile off her face, was Safah. *A Blackstone Chancellor! Now we will see who is in charge.* Kabel caught the triumphalism of his distant relative and didn't like what he had heard. He decided that she was one to watch.

The soldiers marched in orderly ranks through the cheering crowds. Kabel noticed the ramshackle but tall and strong barricade and the decay apparent within the perimeter. He saw the fear and relief in people's eyes and how thin and malnourished they were and was thankful that he had thought ahead and asked for stores to be brought from the provisions on ship.

'Why do you have the barricades outside the Outer Perimeter Barrier?' he asked Tate.

'Our zinithium stocks are so low and the shield we have is weak. If we allowed the Pod to attack it they would weaken it so much that it would collapse.'

'So you take the brunt of the force and thereby retain a semblance of protection?' Tate confirmed that this was the correct interpretation.

Kabel assessed the inner defences behind the Outer Perimeter Barrier and he was shocked, as the wall was only roughly twice the height of him, with a raised platform behind it for those defending. With any kind of athletic scaling or ladder, you would easily breach it. He made this point to Tate, who didn't disagree.

'We don't know whether it will work or not, no Pod has ever breached the barricades,' said Tate, with a slight shrug of his shoulders. 'It was built as an afterthought and I do agree with you that it may prove ineffective.'

Kabel grunted and ran his eye around the inner wall as far as he could see. At least there were no breaks in the wall except for the iron gates at each watch tower which guarded the approach to the main gates.

'You may be better pulling back and giving your superior weapons more of a field of fire.'

'You mean give away a line of defence?' said Tate, surprised at the suggestion.

'If your enemy climbs over that,' said Kabel looking at the high barricades, 'then a wall that size is not going to stop them. You may be better using it to break up the attack and then picking off the attackers with their momentum broken.'

'Hmmm, you may have a point,' said Tate, as a young girl ran forward and handed him some small flowers. Tate smiled and took the flowers after ruffling the little girl's shock of red hair. The little girl smiled and then ran back to an older girl with the same coloured hair.

Bailey, who was strolling in with Hechkle and Bronstorm, stopped in mid stride as he caught the flash of red hair and his eyes were drawn to the older girl. It was like seeing a ghost. Both his friends followed his glance and their faces expressed the same surprise…if they hadn't known better there stood Evelyn, younger yes, but the same fierce and passionate look. The girl must have been only around fourteen but already was wearing full body armour.

Bailey stepped closer to Tate and tapped him on the shoulder. 'Who is that girl?' Tate looked towards the girl Bailey pointed out and smiled.

'That's Eva and the small girl is Mia, they are the daughters of the late Lord Fathom.'

'Who looks after them?' Hechkle asked, as he peered at the two girls as they ran off to watch the parade. In answer Tate pointed to a youngish woman and it was easy to see she was a Fathom, her hair making any argument pointless.

'And she is…?'

'Cadence Southgate, married to Prince Taio,' replied Tate, struggling to hide his disgust for the prince; something which was not lost on Hechkle.

'Once we have settled in can you please introduce us?' asked Hechkle. He felt protective towards the girls and seeing Eva brought all the memories back of Princess Evelyn.

They moved onto a large road that was busy with cheering crowds. He spotted two massive doors ahead to the left, regal looking and closed which appeared to lead to a walled-in settlement.

'What's behind those doors?'

'That is where the Changelings reside. Those doors are rarely open.'

'Why, surely they have to come out for food and water?'

'They are self-sufficient and eat and drink very little.'

'Hate to tell you, Lord Malacca, but I think those doors are not staying closed now,' said Kabel, just as the heavy doors started to open. He was immediately amused and interested to see who and what was behind the opening gates - would it be a pack of wolfhounds like Zebulon? The large wooden gates opened slowly. Tate and Kabel brought the soldiers to a halt. The cheering stuttered and then stopped with all eyes drawn to what was going to come out of those gates.

The gates fully extended outwards and all those waiting saw a wondrous sight. Fifty Changelings ran out and formed a decorative honour guard, twenty five each side. They held large swords with which they saluted the following Changelings, who in full regalia marched out of the compound. Kabel noted that the soldiers also held three-pronged weapons, which could only be called tridents, and they marched in rows of ten abreast. Their golden tunics and blue trousers provided a colourful yet surprising picture.

'Who the...?' said Tate. His gaze rested on the two people leading the column. There was a woman in a breath-taking and sumptuous jewel encrusted dress, walking with immense pride and dignity, but it was the person beside her that caught his eye and the other inhabitants. The man's demeanour was of royalty, a fact reinforced by the Changelings who had run out from the gates to provide the salute, snapping their heels together and bringing their swords to their noses. They then bowed and pushed the sword away from their bodies in an arc which itself was a token of respect. The broad shouldered Changeling continued on his path, heading for them, not looking left or right, his eyes adjusting to the welcoming committee in front of him. Kabel could see that Tate was confused.

He doesn't know who this is, strange.

There was something familiar in the stride of the Changeling, the way he carried himself and as he drew nearer, Kabel took in his countenance and then looked into his amber speckled eyes.

Zebulon! It was the missing Changeling.

As the realisation hit him the party reached them.

'Hello, Kabel, Lord Chancellor,' Zebulon addressed his friend first and then Tate.

'Zebulon, is that you?' said Amelia, before Kabel and anyone else could say the words.

'Yes, I am Zebulon the Great, son of Heathlon and Keeper of the Zein Star.'

'Holder of what?' said an incredulous Bailey, as his eyes drank in the sight in front of his disbelieving eyes.

'It means that he is the keeper of the magics and that makes him the most revered of his kind and of all people on Zein,' answered Tate, slightly in awe.

'Wow, and there was I thinking he made a good pussy cat,' said Bailey, not able to resist a witticism.

Zebulon ignored him. Bailey was not surprised.

'My people will no longer hide behind gates but stand with all Zeinonians against any invaders to fight for our planet.' The rest of the remaining Inner Council cast their eye over what appeared to be approximately five hundred heavily armed Changelings who had marched after the two majestic individuals before them and now stood silently. They were all the same height and very similar in looks. In their silence they projected a menacing air that made the hair on your arms stand up.

Our planet? The way he said that it was if this was his planet, puzzled Tate.

Kabel stepped forward and offered his hand to Zebulon in welcome. Zebulon took his hand with a firm grip. Tate, gave the more formal Zein salute, which Zebulon mirrored back. 'We have a seat available for the emergency Inner Council meeting to discuss the Pod threat,' said Tate, 'do you want to join us?'

Zebulon agreed and directed his guards to remain where they were. As the senior members of the Expedition Force and the Inner Council all moved to the Royal Council building, Bailey sidled up to the imperious Changeling.

'Like your new look Zeb.'

'Feels a little strange, if I were to be honest,' said Zebulon, not falling for Bailey's grinning barb.

'Y-you prefer to be a dog?' stuttered the surprised human.

'Got you,' said a smiling Zebulon, causing Hechkle to start laughing at Bailey's confused face. Bailey, seeing that he had fallen for the line, grimaced. It wasn't every day he was suckered in but he couldn't resist a smile at how the tables had been turned on him.

They entered the Royal Council building and took their places in the Inner Council with the Expeditionary Force represented by General Corder, Kabel and Belina. The others remained outside. Due to the extraordinary events, Tate had decided that the meeting was to be a public and open meeting and speakers were turned on for the benefit for the inhabitants of the community. It was something which was done a few times a mano, to broker unity. Tate Malacca stood up to address the council and the people of the Aeria Cavern.

Belina noticed his huge, strong, coarse hands that gripped the lectern in front of him. She could not help herself and found her eyes wandering up his body, taking in its strength and poise. She felt the immediate attraction to the brooding figure, taking in the battle weariness around his eyes, a hint of sadness but also strength. Belina had spent many of her joyless early years experiencing Malacca warriors' macho posturing, which they had made an art form. The man in front of her was no bragger, no need for unnecessary fits of temper to impress his will on others – you could see that from his bearing and the haunted look in his eyes he had nothing to prove, either to himself or others. Kabel straightened up next to her as he caught the turbulent thoughts in his sister. He held back his disapproval but with his protective nature couldn't help narrowing his eyes at Tate in warning.

Tate for his part noticed the change in the magics and struggled to pin point where it was coming from, until his eyes fixed on Belina and was instantly captivated, *the girl from Reinan,* then he felt a presence just behind him.

'Are you all right Lord Chancellor?' It was Kron.

Tate became acutely aware that he had stood and allowed the change in the magics' flow to disrupt his opening speech. He glanced around and saw the questioning glances as they waited for him to speak. *Pull it together man,* he admonished himself.

He cleared his throat.

'Greetings, your worshipful Elders and honoured guests, after so many years of hope we have been blessed with the return of the Zein Inter-Galactic Expeditionary Force. We welcome you and our new allies.' With that he bowed to General Corder, who hesitantly, not sure what to do, returned the bow awkwardly.

'As Lord Chancellor...,' said Tate, and then stopped. Safah had stood up requesting the floor of the Council. Tate hid his annoyance and waved her forward to make her point. *What does the old battle-axe want now?*

'Point of order, Lord Malacca, I would like to make a recommendation to the Inner Council,' said Safah, in a condescending tone that communicated that she was far superior to him and the words requesting to speak, were just a nicety.

Lord Malacca rather than Lord Chancellor.

Tate sensed Kron tensing next to him and hidden by the lectern, he pushed the palm of his hand repeatedly down, in an attempt to calm his second-in-command.

'According to Zein Law, Lord Blackstone should be the Lord Chancellor, though I would like to say for the record what a good job Lord Malacca has done for the community as an able deputy.'

Her insincere words grated on Tate. With all the battles he had won, family lost and sacrifices he had made, then to be cast aside as a "deputy", was galling. He had no idea how he maintained his passive face.

There was no way on Zein that Kron would let this go.

Sure enough the fierce warrior next to him pushed aside all protocol. 'How can you say that? If it was not for the Lord *Chancellor* Malacca you would all be dead,' Kron shouted, emphasising the missing element of the title as provided by Safah. She didn't flinch.

'Lord Malacca, can you keep your pet under control in the Inner Council or have him removed,' she said coldly.

'There is no need for that Lady Blackstone.'

Tate turned to Kron and attempted to placate him. Kron's eyes shot daggers in the direction of the patronising Blackstone and even Safah's egotistical swagger retreated somewhat. Tate sent a warning glance at Kron and the intimidating warrior simmered quietly. When he saw Kron had accepted, albeit reluctantly, the request he returned to his address to the Inner Council.

'Lady Blackstone and honoured members of the Inner Council, I am fully aware of Zein Law and protocol. This will be the last Inner Council I will chair and I will ask Lord Blackstone to accept his rightful position, as one of the agenda items today.' Safah's triumphant look grated on Tate but he ignored it.

'What is more pressing is that the attack in Reinan yesterday was an escalation of Pod activity. Our scouts have said that movement in the Pod breeding grounds is unprecedented and we must prepare for an imminent attack.'

'We need the Expeditionary Force to protect us,' said Eben, licking his lips nervously at the prospect of another overwhelming attack. He had nothing left, the fight extinguished from his slight frame, burned out by the constant battles and family loss.

'I agree we need their assistance but we need to decide how that can be provided effectively,' said Tate, looking across at Corder, Kabel and Belina.

General Corder cleared his throat and spoke first. 'We of course would like to help. Has this Inner Council considered an offensive action rather than just defending your position?'

Tate replied. 'A unit is on its way to neutralise the Pod as we speak.'

'What do you mean, neutralise?' Kabel spoke for the first time. Tate explained the quest. Some of the Inner Council looked uncomfortable as the plan was outlined. Even in the light of the aggression the Pod had shown it seemed a harsh decision, females and their children to be slaughtered as well as the males. Outside there was an excited buzz which filtered through to the room at this latest news.

Zebulon stood up and there were audible gasps around the chamber. When Heathlon had spoken at the previous meeting that had been a first but now to have a Changeling stranger address the Inner Council was unique. Everyone's eyes were on Heathlon; was not she the spokeswoman of the Changelings? Heathlon didn't move and made no attempt to prevent the impressive Zebulon from speaking. The expectant silence hung heavy in the council chamber.

'I have to warn you that I cannot let your attempt to eradicate the Pod continue.' The buzz outside turned into heckles as the general population expressed their displeasure.

'What! How dare you tell us what to do?' shouted Eben, echoed by other clan members, with Safah incandescent with rage. Kabel gasped with amazement at Zebulon's statement. It was only Tate who remained calm, Belina noticing how still he was. She could see he was rocked by the latest statement but she also could see that he was computing the why and what behind the comment.

'What is your authority to make such a statement to the Inner Council and people of Zein?' said Tate carefully, not forgetting the public broadcast. Shouts of approval for the challenging question came from all directions, including outside. Belina smiled, impressed, he was still the one they followed.

Zebulon didn't answer the question immediately. He was considering whether to hold back or not. He looked around the room at the expectant faces and then his eyes rested on his mother's. She gave him a barely perceptible nod.

Zebulon, where is this going? asked Kabel

A long, long way from when you met me at the Federation Fair, my friend.

Zebulon drew himself up and stripped away the years of camouflage he had layered on his physical appearance. Everyone in the room for the first time saw the true majesty of the person in front of them. He radiated the essence of power, not to hurt or cripple but to care for, improve and develop the very environment they all lived in. Those in the room did not fear him but felt comfort and awe in his presence.

'I am Zebulon the Great, Son of Riolon and Heathlon, Keeper of the Zein Star and King of all life on Zein,' said Zebulon, providing his full title to the astonished Inner Council members and those listening outside. Before anyone could interrupt him, 'My father gave you the power over the magics many, many years ago and I have the power to take those magics away for future generations.' The last statement caused uproar to all who heard, Kabel was bewildered, and Tate struggled to bring order. Cries from Safah and Eben amongst others demanded Zebulon to be arrested and placed in the community prison.

Through all this commotion, Zebulon stood motionless. Safah shouted an instruction to her two supporting soldiers to arrest him. The soldiers flanked and closed in on him, whipping out some of the manacles that Kabel and Belina recognised from their previous confinement on Earth. Just as they were in touching distance of him, Zebulon raised his hand and a violet force-field surrounded his body, pulsing with such intensity that everyone had to avert their eyes. Tentacles of energy came from his fingers and wrapped the two soldiers in bindings that slammed their arms against the sides so that they couldn't move. The intense shield spread to cover all the Changelings in his group.

The doors of the Inner Council were flung open, the Changelings had overpowered the guards outside and Bailey and the remaining companions were penned back away from the door. Zebulon stepped into the centre of the chamber, the force-field effortlessly following him.

Scared and troubled eyes followed him now, with their previous angry protests silenced. There were only four people in the room who kept their cool, Tate and Kron, Kabel and Belina. The latter due to their past relationship and how Zebulon had saved their lives many times, the former simply demonstrating the strength of character that they had shown defending the Aeria Cavern over all the years.

'I didn't want to resort to this yet you force my hand; you need to understand your own history.' His voice was quiet but every word could be heard clearly and distinctly.

Crowds outside had seen the Changelings, who had stood silently, suddenly move into action. They secured the approach and entrance to the Royal Council and the Zeinonians had at first backed off and now were crowding against the protective wall which the Changelings' bodies had created around the building. The crowds felt intimidated by the chain of events and nervously studied the Changelings and what was unfolding before their very eyes.

'My father, Riolon the All Powerful, granted you the magics that you enjoy today. Our people wanted a new life and had taken that decision to throw off the remnants of the old way we used to live.' Outside, his voice echoed powerfully across the cavern; no one stirred, all entranced. 'We embraced the magics within Zein's core and shared them with you. You need to understand what can be given can be taken away.'

Shocks of surprise and fear ripped through the crowds. Safah shrank back from the majesty in front of her eyes. Zebulon slowly turned his gaze onto her.

'The Blackstones convinced us that if we shared the magics then we would walk as one, and we did for a time. However, the royal clans always wanted more and I saw on Earth what that could lead to.'

'But we are not all like Zylar, he is a monster,' said Belina, unable to hold back her resentment at the broad comparison of all Zeinonians to her previous guardian. She had good cause and history: Zylar had lied to her, played the part of a benevolent uncle whilst at the same time killing and following his own twisted path.

'I know, but now I have a choice to make. In this choice I want you to understand one thing: I can't let you destroy the Pod.' Outside the Zeinonians, who had only just been informed of the quest, muttered angrily, deeply resentful of the loved ones they had lost to the vicious Pod. They had lived in this dark, dank place for many years and wanted it to all to end. Reason had gone, to be replaced by an all-encompassing hatred for the creatures that made their life a misery.

'Why, they attack us with only one aim, to destroy us?' said Eben, overcoming his fear of the sudden turn of events.

'They attack you to get to us,' said Zebulon sadly. Puzzled looks swept across the Inner Council and outside, where they could only hear Zebulon's voice. But that was sufficient for them to realise the enormity of what was happening to everything they had held true.

'All those years ago we devised the annihilation of our own race. My brother forced my father's hand. Myolon and others took the magic to new unacceptable limits and my family had to follow him to save our lives. Once free we found that we had the power of the magics but nowhere to live. My father devised a pact to share the magics with you in return for sanctuary.' He let that sink in and all in the room could see the distress his memories brought. 'Yes, we are the Pod and the Pod are us.'

Stunned silence met this statement and then shouting, pushing outside took over.

'Silence!' Zebulon's voice became more forceful and the tone of his demand hurt people's ears, so much they had to grab their heads before they could recover.

'I will lead a team to prevent my brother instigating the same mistake we made all those years ago. I will seek peace with the Pod and find a way to restore a way of life for everyone on Zein.'

'Is this the Prophecy?' whispered Belina to Kabel. He didn't answer, enthralled by the events in front of him. 'Is Zebulon the Prophecy, and not Tyson,' she asked again, amazed. Zebulon turned to her. She remembered the Prophecy that Zylar had taught her that 'One will come from another world to lead all races. Zein will be free once more.' Zebulon had come from another world and now he wanted to bring the Pod, Changelings and Zeinonians together!

'I wish I was, my child, the Prophecy was created by my father at the first Royal Inner Council all those years ago. It is and has always been a destiny that I am a part of the Prophecy but not the instigator, although, I did not realise it fully until I was back on Zein.' With that he swept out of the chamber into the street. His soldiers created a guard of honour back to their enclave. The Inner Council members watched him go, still surrounded by his pulsating force-field.

The crowd had heard his last statement in awe. Would Zebulon bring the Prophecy to its conclusion? It started slowly; the people nearest him dropped to one knee and placed their arms across their chest, others followed. As Zebulon made his way to the enclave more people dropped to one knee and gave the sign of fealty, like a light wind wafting across a field of grass and the grass bending in submission to the more powerful force.

Zebulon saw the reaction of the crowd and hid his surprise and pride. He had waited many years to fulfil his promise that his father had bestowed on him when he was a mere child. Even though he knew he was irreplaceably entwined in the Prophecy, like Kabel, he had not known that he would only be supporting someone else in delivering the fabled quest. As the Changeling enclave doors opened up in front of him, he knew that there was still an awful lot more to do.

Tate called the stunned Elders back to the Inner Council and they duly completed the agenda of making Kabel, Lord Chancellor. When Tate removed his collar of position and ceremonially placed it around Kabel's neck, he felt the pressure he had been under for many years evaporate and when he strolled out of the chamber he felt free of the heavy burdens he had carried over the last few years. Next to him strode Belina and briefly their hands touched. For both, it was like being hit by a photon shot. The glance they gave each other sealed the Joining. Belina battled against her feelings for Bailey but this was life changing and she knew in her heart that Tate was her mate for life. Bailey was confused when Belina half-heartedly greeted him when she came out and her face had an apologetic look.

'What's the matter?' he asked her.

'Nothing, but we need to talk,' said Belina struggling to make eye contact with Bailey. She felt bad. He didn't deserve this but when a Zeinonian fell for a mate it was difficult to ignore. Some sixth sense told Bailey he had lost her. He could see that she had eyes for only Tate and he didn't feel anger, just rejection. He steeled himself as they trudged off to talk in private.

Kabel was not happy at the interplay, his lips thinned, anger flaring. The idea of his sister with a Malacca made him angry. There would be no Joining if he had his way; however, for the moment, more important matters needed his attention, including a genocide to stop. He fired off orders and directed the strategy that he thought was their only choice. Within an hour, a team was pulled together with Zebulon leading a small group of Changelings and Amelia. The rest of the companions would stay in the Aeria Cavern supporting the defence of the city. Bailey argued that he should go but Zebulon was adamant. This was a Changeling expedition to repay past wrongs and the reason for Amelia's participation was if Tyson couldn't control his magics. There was only one person who could calm him down.

General Corder left with a small squad to hasten the arrival of more troops before dusk and to bring a handful of levitation tanks down to guard each of the four entrances. Walter and his team began to study how they could boost the zinithium powered Inner Perimeter Barrier, fully knowing it would take a number of days to achieve full protection.

The Changelings were ordered by Zebulon not to support a defence of the Aeria Cavern if the Pod attacked, unless their families were threatened. They were one and the same as the Pod and the Zeinonians had to defend themselves and no Changeling would again, willingly, kill their own kind. Tate and Kabel had argued long and hard for Zebulon to change his mind, that his people could be slaughtered and that they should defend themselves by allying with them…but to no avail, he was adamant.

Amelia sat on the step of the Royal Council, flicking pebbles onto the road, distracted and distant from the bustle going on around her. Hechkle was overseeing a group of Southgates carrying a large iron fence panel to reinforce the front barricade. He saw Amelia with her head in her hands and peeled off after providing some further orders and sat down next to her, removing a bottle of water from his bag. He didn't talk straight away but studied the hive of activity in front of them.

'I have never met anyone like Tyson,' said Hechkle. He bit his lip nervously, unused to talking to a girl, or a girl as pretty as this girl. Amelia turned her head to look at the hulking Fathom soldier, still resting her head on her palms. 'Now don't get me wrong, pretty sure most people have never seen a person with his magic, but I wasn't referring to that.' He had her attention now.

'You can see he is wrestling with something that is contained within his body and he is frightened.' Hechkle had dropped his voice, wonder in every syllable. 'Yet in the Core and in the battles we have fought together, he always did the right thing, the brave action to protect us all.' Hechkle for the first time turned his head to look at Amelia. She could see the respect reflected in the warrior's eyes.

'You can't extinguish that goodness, that inbuilt reaction to do the right thing,' said Hechkle, emotion creeping into his voice. 'I, you and many people owe our lives to Tyson, and we will find him.' Amelia smiled and wrapped her arms around his and rubbed his shoulder, thanking him for the kind words. A faint blush spread on Hechkle's cheeks but he didn't pull away. They sat like that for a while; each with their own thoughts, knowing that over the next few days' events would test them to the full, taking comfort in the presence of each other.

Chapter 18: The Magics

Tyson sat quietly in his cell. A few hours had passed with plenty of food and water on supply, curing his hunger pains. Wernion stood guard facing the open door not engaging with Tyson's attempts to talk with him. The power of the young human's magics was eroded by his surroundings, but his ability to enter people's thoughts was undiminished. He concentrated hard and allowed his mind to reach out and connect with all living things in his immediate radius.

He first encountered Wernion who was playing back what he had heard in the Ceremony Hall and he saw that his guard was confused about what he believed in. Then Tyson picked up thoughts from other brethren, feeling the fear and apprehension and realising that some great event was occurring which was sending shockwaves through the community.

Tyson listened hard and found mainly older female and children's voices. Very few older males. He experienced fear and trepidation, a mother soothing a crying child who called for her father, only to receive no reply.

Odd, what was happening?

He searched for senior brethren but there were none. He tried the Queen but Festilion was impenetrable, surrounded by a curtain of seeming invisibility, which not even Zylar exuded. Tyson had never experienced so much power in anyone he had met so far in his travels.

It was during this wide search for information that on the outskirts of his ability he sensed a different mind-set. Some thoughts resembled those of the Pod but were different. He sensed the strong magics within them. Tyson then picked up Zeinonians' thoughts who were accompanying a small force, similar to…yes the Changeling…like Zebulon.

He pushed his mind hard and picked up their leader, who was similar to Zebulon and on the same wavelength, same strength of purpose but subtly different. A hatred. A hatred that was so intense it hurt Tyson. He let out a stifled grunt as the strong personality pushed back on him. He rocked back and forward in his seated position.

'What's the matter?' said Wernion, jumping into the cell. He saw Tyson with his head in his hands. His face was creased up in pain. Tyson didn't answer. He was busy extracting his mind from the powerful grip of the leader of the group.

'You are all in danger.' It had been a painful experience but it yielded a disturbing piece of information.

Wernion felt the worry emanating from Tyson. He tasted it, all his body sensitive to the surroundings around him.

Tyson's body tightened. 'You have the magics?'

'We all have the magics. We are the magics,' said Wernion.

'No, you have taken it further. You have already changed,' said Tyson carefully as he probed the tall Pod's mind. Wernion wore an uncomfortable look on his face.

'You can tell me?' cajoled Tyson. He licked his lips as the taste of the magics cascaded over him from the young Pod as he released his secret he had kept from his father.

'I wanted to know what it felt like,' said Wernion, scuffing his bare foot against the ground as a naughty child would when found doing something they shouldn't.

'What felt like?'

'The magics of course, letting it, and allowing it to live with you, inside,' Wernion said quietly and with an element of regret.

'You didn't like what you found, did you?'

Wernion shook his head.

'Instead of you controlling it, it is controlling you?'

'Yes, I thought I could but I feel it growing inside me. Stretching and magnifying everything around me,' said Wernion, uncomfortably as he rubbed his stomach.

'I know the feeling, Wernion,' said Tyson, seeing his gaoler for the first time in a new light, now understanding what had attracted him to this tall creature. They were kin, of sorts.

'You have to let me go.' Tyson stood up and Wernion, who had inched into the cell, suddenly realised his surroundings and his duty.

'No, I can't, my father would never forgive me.' Wernion stood in his way, blocking his escape, hopping from one foot to another, clearly agitated and fighting inner conflicts of his role guarding the prisoner clashing against his liking of this strange alien in front of him. His confusion flooded across his features. Tyson repressed his impatience, knowing instinctively that he needed this creatures support. You didn't win support by force; well, not the kind he needed now.

'Something is happening, Wernion, there is a group of Changelings and Zeinonians approaching your brethren. They mean to poison the water and kill you all.' He had his attention now.

'They can't do that!'

'Why not? Your kind has attacked the Zeinonians' sites with impunity,' said Tyson, challenging the young Pod's defence.

'We only did that to protect ourselves.'

Tyson decided he needed to share what he was hearing with Wernion to provide the necessary wakeup call. Decision made, Tyson deflected the horrific thoughts of the leader of the group now making its way closer and closer to its final destination. The thoughts hit Wernion like a runaway train and if he could go pale then now was the time. His hands shook as he heard of the plan from the thoughts collated by Tyson.

'Let me go? I can stop them.'

'No, no, I can't,' Wernion refused but the unpleasant thoughts he was passed by Tyson's nimble brain, hurt him, cut him deep – threats to his family and friends in an organised genocide. In despair he gave his acquiescence to the request.

'Good, you have done the right thing,' said Tyson as he stood up and moved to the front of the cell. As he approached the front entrance, Wernion stood in his way forcing Tyson to stop in his tracks. Tyson let out a frustrated yell.

'Move out of my way, Wernion.'

'I am going with you.' It was a statement not a request.

'Your father wouldn't forgive you,' said Tyson, looking up at the fearsome creature.

'Too late anyway, I can't hide my magics anymore. The Queen will pick it up and I will be executed in accordance with our law,' Wernion replied. 'At least allow me to save my family and friends?'

Tyson thought for a moment and then agreed. It would be useful to have someone with him who knew the tunnels. He told Wernion the direction from which he had heard the voice. The young Pod predicted roughly where the strike-force were; it would not be long before they reached the reservoir. They set off down the adjoining corridor until they reached the main interlinked Pod grid. Wernion leaned into a closet built into the rock. He pulled out two large coats, like raincoats. Tyson was puzzled.

'We have to pass through the Mygolwich to intercept them.'

'What's that?'

'Mygolwich in our tongue means "Provider of Life".' When Wernion saw the confused look still on his new companion's face he elaborated. 'It is where the liquid that sustains us collects. It comes from the winter and what you call the reflection period, channelling down into ancient deep pools.' Tyson now understood, what he was describing was the reservoir. At that point they emerged into a huge cavern that stretched for miles. The silent, still, expressionless water lay as far as the eye could see. High above the water the huge stalactites hung menacingly from the rock ceiling, each one the size of an inverted electricity pylon, yet still they seemed well into the distance, such was the cavernous height of the natural ceiling. Moisture dripped into the lake, causing small ripples where it entered into the embrace of its fellow droplets. The water lapped up gently onto a shore strewn with fine black sand. The whole picture was breath-taking and Tyson stood at the entrance of one of what were many tunnels into this great hall of nature.

Suddenly, Wernion grabbed Tyson by the collar of his raincoat and pulled him back into the tunnel and thrust him into an alcove. Tyson's anger flared and then he saw a patrol materialise out of the murkiness. Twelve strong, no weapons except the vicious claws that Tyson had come to respect. The patrol moved with easy strides as they swept the end of the cavern for any threat.

'The patrols are weak tonight,' said Wernion, watching his brethren undertake a task that he had completed many times in the past. They moved past them and then disappeared down one of the other tunnels. He saw the puzzlement on Tyson's face from his comment. 'I thought you could read minds!'

'Usually, but the closeness of this ore and water seem to be suppressing it,' said Tyson, ruefully.

Wernion didn't answer immediately as he scanned the nearest reaches of the cavern for any other patrols. Assessing it was relatively safe to assume that there were no other patrols in close proximately, he explained his point.

'They are massing to attack the Aeria Cavern tonight,' said Wernion, quietly, still concerned that they may run into a patrol.

'I need to get back. My friends are there.'

'Many of my friends will die tonight, but we need to halt these people coming to kill my people,' Wernion's eyes flashed. Tyson knew he was right.

'Where next, alien?' Wernion growled.

Tyson ignored the barbed comment and looked at the different corridors. He fed his magic out. It licked the floor, walls and the rocks as it tried to penetrate the suffocating stillness.

The ore was overpowering. It combatted, fought against his magics. It seemed to resent his power. Tyson was rebuffed, once, twice and then he subtly shifted his mind and began to merge with the ore. He felt it enter his mind, getting used to his alien DNA. He began to realise that the ore was not a mineral but a living organism.

He gasped.

'What?' Wernion had seen the strange expression form on Tyson's face.

'It, it's alive…,' Tyson spluttered. Wernion smiled, his fangs poking out across his bottom lip.

'Took you long enough, alien.'

Tyson swallowed hard.

'Don't you get it?' said a now serious Wernion, 'Why do we fight against the magics? Why do we fear the Malefics?' Tyson shook his head, still taking in the recent information.

'The ore is the first indigenous race of Zein – we evolved after and you are all aliens here and it resents that,' said Wernion. 'When the Malefics immersed themselves in the ore magics they became the host, living long and not having their own identity.'

Tyson recognised the truth of this feeling. He felt the magics gnawing away at his very soul but somehow his body fought back.

'But we have this same ore on our planet which we never knew about. Are you saying that we are aliens on our own planet? We evolved there, it has been proven.'

Wernion shook his head. 'Probably not,' he admitted. 'We evolved on Zein in close proximity to methir. We became one with our surroundings and accepted methir for what it was; a powerful living organism. It sounds like you grew and changed with the planet with very little contact with the mineral you call "zinithium". That's different.' He then paused as if countering his first thought. 'Mind you ask yourself the question who evolved first?'

Tyson was quiet for a moment. 'If we choose to, though, we could leverage the magics this ore or organism produces?' Wernion shrugged, not altogether interested in what may or may not happen on a distant planet. For Tyson it was a momentous issue. If the humans understood the great magics they could tap into, would they reject the chance of power due to the side effects? He knew the answer, magics first, worry about anything else second.

Wernion tugged his arm. He switched back to his study of what was around them. He picked up the Changelings and Zeinonians and pointed to a corridor off the great reservoir. Carefully they made their way to the entrance, keeping a wary eye out for any patrols. Tyson's coat dragged on the floor but he ignored it. The coat worked, keeping the condensation and constant drops of water from soaking him to the skin.

The corridor was flanked by rough granite rock with flaming torches in holders lighting the way. They had travelled around half a mile in the dull spectre of the poorly illuminating torches until they stumbled into a break in the corridor where four tunnels met. They could hear voices emitting from a tunnel to the left of their tunnel, sound echoing against the bleak rock walls that glistened with water from the natural coldness of the stone. Wernion reached across Tyson's chest and pushed him into the wall. Their position enabled them to see into the converging intersection and the three separate entrances. It was the one with the sound growing louder and louder that drew their attention and they saw the flickering light from a torch expand as the semi-darkness was consumed.

Tyson waited as he felt a strong surge of power in the magics and a quick glance at Wernion confirmed that he had felt it as well. It was menacing, not as dark from what Tyson had felt from Zylar but twisted, unrelenting and with a stone cold certainty to it. Tyson felt intimidated for the first time since he had experienced the magics affecting him. He wanted to run away but the strong arm of Wernion held him in place. Tyson felt the flare of the magics grow in him and his hands began to emit the comforting blue glow. The force-field wrapped around his arms and lazily travelled up his forearms. Wernion's arm was beginning to struggle to hold the power in his grasp. Tyson felt Wernion's fear at the strength of the magics inside his human companion.

The raiding party stepped into the cross section. Tyson heard Wernion gasp and he followed his gaze to the strange creature that stood regally at the front of the small group. He was a man but not like any other Tyson had seen. The flickering light of the torches caught his unusually coloured eyes, which shone in the semi-darkness.

Tyson drew in a deep breath as he remembered the Fathom clan members in the Core and their blank white eyes. His dread dissipated quickly. This was different. He felt an attraction, caused by the magics, to this powerful figure and the magics were also present in the other, similar creatures, he was with. He noted the different coloured tunics of the soldiers and there was a beautiful young woman talking in whispers to a vain, sallow looking man. A couple of the soldiers carried rucksacks that clinked with whatever was within them.

It was not Tyson that gave up their pitiful hiding place. Wernion suddenly pushed Tyson away and charged towards the commanding figure at the head of the raiding party. Tyson picked up what Wernion must have felt that this creature had come to destroy the Pod; the magics could not hide the drive and ambition of mass death which flooded the pores of this creature.

The Changeling, though initially shocked raised his trident and used it to blunt the attack and force away the charging Wernion, flinging the creature away from him onto the floor. Wernion was swiftly back up on his feet, the previous injuries forgotten; before he could charge again the sallow faced Blackstone attacked him with two extremely long seckle type weapons. He was ably supported by the beautiful young woman.

Tyson knew Wernion would not survive a double attack for long. He threw his body into the space between the girl and Wernion and used his now activated seckle as a block.

The girl's eyes widened in surprise and Tyson used this element of surprise to throw her to the ground. Behind him, the man was trying to bring his weapons to bear but Wernion was fast and he came in close to the Blackstone man, nullifying the threat. His claw caught the man on the shoulder, ripping into his skin, the force causing one of the weapons to fall from his hand. Wernion was not interested in the Blackstones and he rushed towards the Changeling.

Jaida lay breathless on the floor with the shock of the power from the man supporting the Pod.

He is a Blackstone!

Shrugging aside her surprise, if he was a friend of the Pod then he was no friend of hers. She struggled to kneel up and before she could re-join the fight, an enraged Taio leapt at the strange man with his one surviving weapon.

Tyson tracked the move in slow motion and knew his magics were formulating. He confidently saw the attack and anticipated the blow. He didn't want to hurt the man so he ducked the offending blow and used a quick spurt of power from his hand to send him clattering into the wall. Then the girl was upon him and she was quick. He blocked blow after blow, keeping in the corner of his eye that Wernion was now wrestling with one of the Changelings. Eventually he was able to make enough room to send a force-field shock that knocked her own force-field out of commission and allowed him to thrust her hard against the wall, where she crumpled to the ground, dazed.

Taio saw the woman he loved collapse of the floor and rage took over. He swung his seckle viciously at Tyson but it bounced off the force-field easily.

Wernion charged Myolon, who changed into a colossal reptile with a mouth full of razor-sharp teeth, a Xonian!

He caught the young Pod by its scale covered muscular arms and in one fluid motion he threw Wernion into one of the walls were he lay unmoving, Myolon then moved in for the kill.

'Myolon!' The voice rang out with power and command. Myolon, with spittle spilling from his reptilian mouth, stopped in his tracks and smoothly turned to face his new opponent.

The rescue group had made good time with a transport dropping them close to another of Zebulon's secret entrances. Once he had gained entry they had moved swiftly, guided by the majesty of Zebulon. As they had entered the intersection, Amelia had gasped as she saw Tyson. *He is alive!* Her heart jumped in excitement and it was only the restraining arm of one of Zebulon's guards that stopped her running into the midst of the fight happening before her.

'Zebulon, so nice to see you,' said Myolon, his harsh rasp escaping his Xonian snout. Myolon saw the rest of the party and his eyes ran over the companions as he changed back to his Changeling form and reached out to one of his followers for his trident which he had dropped and one of his guards had retrieved.

'Tyson,' shouted Amelia and, pushing away her guard with surprising strength which even took the experienced warrior by surprise, ran to Tyson's side, throwing her arms around his neck as his force-field dimmed. Tyson was pleased to see her and returned the hug before gently disentangling her from him as he became acutely aware of the power building in the room between the two Changelings.

'Well, dear brother, long time no see,' smirked Myolon as he twirled the sinister looking trident, 'What do I owe this pleasure to?'

'I am here to stop you releasing that liquid,' said Zebulon, pointing to the rucksacks that the cowering Blackstone troops held.

'Why so caring for the Pod, Zebulon? I remember a time when you embraced their extermination. You have gone soft!'

'I came to my senses, brother. We were wrong all those years ago and you are wrong now. I will take the serum and destroy it safely,' said Zebulon, seeking the residue of any goodness left in his sibling.

'I can't let you do that, Zebulon,' said Myolon, as he squared up to his older brother, 'I am no longer in your shadow, you left our people just when they needed you, now I am going to put right what you got wrong!'

'If you release that into the Mygolwich the entire Pod will die. I can't let that happen.'

'You could try to stop me but I am too strong for you.'

'We will see about that Myolon.' Zebulon pulled his cloak off and the fine clothes under the cloak were impressive.

'You dress well, Zebulon. Like your new tailor.'

There were shouts down the corridors with the Pod patrols, hearing the commotion, making their way through the tunnels to the disturbance. The two parties eyed each other distrustfully but also glanced down the four main corridors of the intersection nervously. This was not a place you wanted to fight a pitched battle in.

Pounding footsteps materialised into squads of the Pod defence patrols in each tunnel. The soldiers and Changelings put aside their distrust and took up position at each entrance.

Zebulon just smiled and with an outstretched hand sent a beam of blue light to two of the entrances. Myolon glowered at his brother, and not to be outdone he did the same to the other two entrances with the beams of energy slowly working down the entrance until a force-field was formed. The Pod ran into the force-field, which, with a flash, threw them back. The angry creatures hung back away from the painful light and shuffled back and forward, waiting for their opportunity.

'So, brother, your powers are fully developed, I notice,' said Zebulon. He saw Tyson and then looked across to the winded Wernion and tasted the vortex of magic in the air.

'Met my human friend, I see?'

'Yes, so much raw power but I sense an uneasiness in its use…you are becoming sloppy…I thought you would have tamed this creature a little more?' said a mocking Myolon.

'I can't let you release that liquid,' said Zebulon, turning his attention to the matter at hand and reiterating his position.

Myolon leapt at his brother swinging his trident viciously at his opponent's head and Zebulon effortlessly shimmered and moved his body away from the blow whilst at the same time drawing his short sword from its scabbard. He swung the sword and caught his opponent's trident in mid-air. There was an almighty clash of steel, forcing Myolon to tighten his grip to prevent losing control of his weapon. Zebulon then leveraged his sword so he was pinning Myolon's trident to the floor using the strength of his massive shoulders. He then released the trident and thrust the sword at Myolon's head. Myolon saw the attack and rolled away and the sword blade hit the floor rather than the flesh. Myolon sprang up, sweat pouring from his pores at the exercise, and he brought his trident up in front of his body.

'Nice try, brother, but you are still soft,' said Myolon with a grin which slowly disappeared, turning into a gritty and daggered look. 'Now that is going to get you killed.'

The two brothers breathing hard stood transfixed, they knew this was a fight to the death. The rest of the group stood in silence, mere bystanders to an epic contest.

Tyson regulated his breathing as Amelia held him close, both stunned by the fight evolving in front of them. Something told them that the future of Zein rested on the outcome of this battle.

Chapter 19: Defence

'I am going to be Joined with him,' snapped an angry Belina.

Since she had broken the news to Bailey, who had disappeared to lick his wounds, the relationship between Belina and Tate had swept the populace of the Aeria Cavern. Tate was their saviour, their hero and now one of the strangers was laying claim to his heart.

'A Blackstone has never Joined with a Malacca in the history of our people,' said Kabel, visibly angry that his twin was now causing an issue he hadn't expected.

'Do you not think, Kabel, that if there had been more Joinings between our two clans, we may have prevented the Quadrant Wars?'

'Rubbish, Zylar just used that as an excuse and you know it!'

Belina slowed her breathing as she felt her magics trigger through the emotion she was feeling. She walked to a table that had a jug of water resting upon it and poured out a glassful.

Kabel was still pacing back and forth. She saw the additional stress lines on his face that had developed with his new responsibility as Lord Chancellor for the Aeria Cavern. In the last couple of days Kabel was everywhere, meeting all the senior royals of the clans, the people on the street, and reviewing the defences with Tate and General Corder. He looked tired and Belina regretted that she had added to his worries. However, she was clear in her own mind that the feelings she had for Tate were special. She sipped her water and sat down on the comfortable chair that was placed near the table.

'Kabel, I am sorry to bring this worry to you, but I cannot ignore my feelings just as much as you can't ignore your feelings for Gemma.'

Kabel paused in his pacing and sighed. 'Maybe you're right Belina and it is me who is wrong. Everything is so mixed up and I have to admit my experience with the Malacca clan is not a good one,' Kabel conceded. 'Can we agree to discuss matters once we have finished the review of the defences?'

Belina smiled and placing her drink back on the table gave her brother a quick hug before leaving the room. Kabel walked to the balcony and looked out upon the bustling settlement. From his advantage point he could see the West, South and North Gates in the distance, the large gates reaching up high until they met the ramparts. The gates, ramparts and barricades bristled with new weaponry brought from the ships, with thousands of men and women manning the gates. Outside the gates the captains were setting up three rows of troops, first rank on the floor with rifles propped against their cheeks, second row kneeling and the final row standing.

Inside each gate ranks of troops were put through their paces. Numbering approximately two thousand per gate these would be the next line of defence if the gates and other defences were breached. They would stand behind the weak Outer Perimeter Barrier which glimmered behind the main gates and also the Inner Defence Wall a further short distance behind the Outer Perimeter Barrier. Everyone knew the sheer numbers of attackers would break though both these defences without much delay. What Kabel decided to do was prepare a workable fall back defensive position.

The soldiers were broken into columns, taking the lead from Napoleon's approach to battle as his French columns used the tactic to smash through the enemy. Kabel had studied hard in his history lessons, now he was putting it into practice. He saw Kron line up the troops in the columns behind the South Gate and other defences. The four columns would be five abreast and one hundred deep, marching side by side with enough gap for the enemy to be sucked in down the sides. Behind the columns would be another hundred troops dispatching any of the enemy that made it past the heavily armed troops. Further troops were strategically placed to support an orderly retreat, if required.

The general population, who were not manning the entrances, were moving to the central area and into the Central Zein Transportation and Royal Council buildings. They carried cherished belongings and worried young children. Remembering how the Pod scampered over the buildings, every building had troops behind makeshift bunkers to blunt any attack and Kabel had also impressed Tate by setting a ring of steel and bullets around the central area, to act as the final defensive position. If the Pod breached that then the city was lost.

All in all they had nearly seventy thousand troops across the settlement. Kabel crossed his arms and shuddered, the picture of the Pod swarming over the buildings still haunting him. Seventy thousand or not he still felt threatened.

Near the South Gate, Kron was barking orders. 'Keep your columns tight, if those in front of your fall walk over them; think of a hammer blow that is what you are doing. This is an offensive not defensive approach,' said Kron and then pointing to his head, 'Think, and keep your nerve.'

The gates were open and Tate was with the troops outside. Hechkle and Bronstorm were near him chatting with Gemma.

'Where's Bailey?' asked Hechkle.

'At the North Gate, he didn't want to be near Belina and Tate,' said Gemma, taking in the preparations.

'Poor lad,' said Hechkle, gruffly. He exchanged glances with Bronstorm, who understood immediately. They both knew that Joining was hard to resist but they felt for Bailey.

'Be careful, Gemma, stay inside the gates with the troop columns and Kron,' said Hechkle and then he rubbed his chin, 'Apart from Remo and Cronje, I don't think I have seen a harder man than Kron.' Their eyes followed Kron, as did the troops, fear and respect in their expressions.

'Where are you going?' asked Gemma.

'Off to the North Gate,' said Bronstorm. Gemma smiled and said a silent thank you.

'We will look after him, no worries,' said Hechkle, with the emotion catching him unawares. As they moved off, Belina walked past them to Tate and Gemma couldn't hide a little resentment at the woman who had broken her brother's heart. If Belina's magics read the thought, then she did not display it on her face.

Not long after Belina passed by, Kabel went to find Gemma. He and Tate had agreed that Tate and General Corder would command the external forces, and Kabel with Kron, those inside the settlement.

'Everything all right?' asked Kabel, as his eyes swept the area.

'If you mean everyone is running round looking both important and terrified, then yes,' said Gemma, as she checked her blaster for power. Kabel smiled grimly and walked out of the gate. Gemma found that she was still confused about her feelings for him and was left wondering whether Zebulon had found Tyson. Did she love Kabel?

General Corder climbed out of his jeep. Behind him one of the levitation tanks swivelled its turret as it took up its pre-planned position at the side of one of the pill-boxes. He waved on the other three tanks sending them to the other gates. Each tank was supported by three thousand troops, split evenly by US and Malacca forces. He had wanted more tanks but Koshkov had argued that in such a confined space they would be a hindrance and he could ready a fast reaction force in the case of attack. Corder had seen the sense of the discussion and relented. The troops were the first additional contingent and more were to follow in the morning. The soldiers disappeared down their respective tunnels to the other gates following in the wake of the tanks.

He turned his attention to the South Gate defences. The Expeditionary Force soldiers were already patrolling in front of the gate and up the tunnel. He and Kabel had positioned soldiers on the ramp-way to provide an early warning of any attack. All those in the Aeria Cavern lapsed into a strained silence as the day wore on and night descended.

Lieutenant Morrison was at the entrance to the surface and marvelling at the stillness of the evening, when he heard thunder.

'What the…?' The sound grew and the soldiers around him became uneasy, the noise grew to a crescendo and then over the hill hundreds of amber lights could be seen in the blackness of the night. The amber lights were bouncing up and down and the hundreds, turned into thousands. Morrison gasped in disbelief, his stomach churning with fear with the realisation that the amber lights were eyes and those eyes were attached to the most ferocious animals he had ever seen.

He grabbed the nearest radio man and picked up the transmitter.

'Come in Base 1, Scouting Group A here, Come in Base 1,' said Morrison, trying to keep his nerves intact. The enemy was still a mile away but closing fast. The radio crackled into life.

'Base 1 here, Scouting Group A, what is your report?'

'Tell the General they are here and shut the gates, all of them.' Morrison shoved the radio back and waved his arms for the soldiers to move back. They had no cover or chance to disrupt this charge. The signal was relayed to General Corder, Tate and Kabel.

'Shut the gates,' said General Corder and the message was hastily relayed to all the gates via one of the soldiers who carried another radio backpack. Each gate had two of these specialists assigned to them.

Kabel and Kron took up their positions with the rearguard and waited. Outside the gates, General Corder climbed into the tank where he could keep communications open to the ships and the other gates and Tate stood next to the troops in the first line of defence. The first thing they saw were the troops falling back, leapfrogging each other, one group providing covering fire and the other group running back. Lieutenant Morrison was shouting the orders. The noise was deafening and the defenders waited nervously. The soldiers made it back to the partial safety of the armed ranks lined up in front of the South Gate.

'Morrison, how many,' Tate asked as the US Marine made a beeline towards him. Tate drew his sword and pulled his blaster from his holster.

'Too many,' said Morrison, though his face was resolute.

The Pod burst out of the large tunnel.

'Oh my God,' said Gemma, looking through the barricades. There were thousands of them, their rage bouncing of the walls. Kabel's throat constricted as he held his panic in check.

Tate waited for Morrison's troops to pull behind his now ready and waiting trio of ranks and then he lifted a loudhailer to his mouth as the noise drowned out his normal voice.

'Wait for it, wait for it.' The mass of creatures was only two hundred yards away and the professional soldiers from the United States, United Kingdom and China felt their hearts pump with the fear they felt. Mouths dry but hands steady.

One hundred and fifty yards.

'Front rank, fire.' The shots rang out and the front row of the attackers jerked as if manipulated by a puppeteer as the shots crashed into them.

'Second rank, fire.' The troops kneeling fired and the puppeteer continued as arms and legs jerked with the smash of the bullets. The Pod surge didn't even break stride. Thousands followed those that fell.

'Third rank, fire.' As the next rain of bullets slammed into the Pod there was a slight pause in the attack.

Good. We can stop them, thought Tate and then as the Pod wavered he saw the pressure of those entering the main tunnel push the momentum forward.

No! How can they take such losses? Tate was at a loss as he activated his seckle?

'Fire at will,' he shouted and then flung away his loudhailer as the Pod launched their bodies at the troops. Vicious toe-to-toe fighting took over. Tate ducked under a fist the size of a football and his hands moved fast as he cut the beast open and delivered the killing blow.

There was no time to rest as another creature swiped at him, bouncing off his force-field and he used his seckle defensively. Another blow and then another. He felt his force-field under threat so he attacked and as his seckle and sword found the soft flesh of the creatures in front of him he lost himself in the violence of the moment.

General Corder was directing the tank's firepower as fast as his men could load as the first line of defence bravely pushed back the first wave, clubbing with their guns and firing when there was space to do so. Morrison was beside Tate, fighting hard but even his size was dwarfed by these brutish creatures.

'They are not going to last long,' said Kabel to Belina, surveying the battle from his vantage point above the gate. He had left Gemma with Kron in charge of the fourth line of defence, if the outer and inner gates didn't hold. The troops on the ramparts were shooting and throwing anything they could at the mass of bodies in front of them. It was making little difference.

'Sir,' said a strained voice behind him and when he turned he recognised one of the Southgates.

'Yes, what is it lad?' asked Kabel but he could see the answer in the young boy's eyes.

'Lords Southgate and Tyther have asked me to convey to you that they don't think they can hold their gates.'

Kabel felt the bottom of his stomach churn with fear. Below him he saw a near manic Tate fighting for survival and the buckling line of their initial defence. He had to act quickly to bring the survivors back within the gates. Before he answered the breathless runner he turned to Belina.

'Tell Kron to open the small gate and try to get as many of our troops back within the main gate without compromising our defence.' Belina took in the request and then ran down the steps to inform Kron.

He turned back to face the wide-eyed young runner. 'Why did they send you and not send the message via the radio packs?'

'They are all dead sir, radios smashed.' The teenager wore a terrified look on his face. Kabel, made up his mind.

'Right, here is what you need to pass on to Lords' Tyther and Southgate and also check with Lady Blackstone as well,' said Kabel and then proceeded to give the young man the necessary orders. The boy's eyes widened with shock at the orders but bravely saluted the Lord Chancellor and ran off to complete his duty.

Down below the survivors were funnelling through the open door under the sustained supporting cover from those on the ramparts and barricades. Kabel raced down the steps to join the force at the gate.

They found an exhausted Tate and an injured General Corder, the latter with an imperfect sling holding a clearly broken left arm he had incurred when exiting the tank that had used up all its charge.

'General, you need to get that seen to,' said Belina, noting the pain on the soldiers face. Additionally Lieutenant Morrison was helping him support an injured leg.

'I am okay, Belina, I am going nowhere,' was the defiant response of the proud soldier.

Kabel wasn't listening, his attention was on the gates. They had managed to pull most of the troops back behind the outer gate and the Inner Defensive Wall but now the Pod were climbing up the barricades, irrespective of the weaponry, providing a horrific killing field. He looked through an inspection hatch and saw that they had hardly scratched the forces against them.

'Brace the gates,' he shouted to a team of fifty men who held wooden pikes that could be pressed against the gate to provided more stability. The soldiers efficiently went about their task.

Tate joined him, still gasping for air. Kabel noticed the tear in his uniform on his chest and the blood seeping from a cut. If Tate's force-field was failing then they would be hard pressed to keep the Pod out.

'You injured?'

'Just a scratch.'

'I have sent a runner to the other gates to consider Plan B at a set time,' said Kabel, as he dodged the falling body of a Malacca soldier, thrown from the rampart. He looked up and saw desperate fighting as the Pod began to swarm over the enormous barricade.

'Good thinking,' said Tate, as he saw Belina walk back to stand near him after making General Corder go back to the central area to have his wounds seen to. The old soldier had carried on arguing but even Kron had been against him and loss of blood made him accept the inevitable.

Kabel couldn't help but notice that Tate and Belina seem to radiate off each other. He could not ignore the strength of feeling which due to his magics he could feel. Maybe he was wrong and Belina and Tate may be the recipe to prevent the infighting, which had happened for too many years between the two clans. Other thoughts for this union were pushed to the side when the gates buckled under the weight of the rage driven opponents.

He looked up following Tate's gaze; the ramparts were all but lost. The hundreds of soldiers that had looked so intimidating a mere fifteen minutes ago had either been slain or were retreating. If they didn't act quickly and fall back, there would be no inner defence. The Outer Perimeter Barrier was gone.

The gates strained inwards from the pressure of the Pod attackers, which in turn was pushed back by the wooden and steel supports held by perspiring soldiers fighting for their lives but the pressure of bodies from the outside was immense. The gates buckled one last time and then burst open.

'Fall back behind the Inner Perimeter Barrier and Inner Defensive Wall now,' shouted Tate and Kabel together. Those not fighting ran back. From the thousands of troops that manned the first two defences only a third survived. The shield was switched off for a short period of time and the bedraggled defenders ran behind both the zinithium barrier and the Inner Defensive Wall where the formidable columns of fierce and determined soldiers waited. Kron and Morrison had taken up their positions to command them with Kabel, Tate and Belina joining Gemma with the skirmishers. The zinithium powered barrier was switched back on and the faint glimmering barrier stood before them. They waited with dread in their hearts.

The other gates were experiencing a similar situation. At the North Gate, Bailey wiped away the sweat trickling down his face. In his hands he held firmly his favoured photon shotgun, his grip rocking back and forth as his adrenalin built up in anticipation of the next phase of the fight. Beside him were the equally determined Hechkle and Bronstorm, who had fought gallantly in front and, on top of and behind the North Gate and ramparts. They knew Eben Southgate was dead, and that on the West Gate Quinlan Tyther was seriously injured, the latter bravely saving his son from two Pod. Losing two senior Lords had shaken the defenders and it looked like the two gates would be lost.

Then the Blackstone troops arrived, thousands of them. Quinlan had sent a runner to Safah, not expecting any help as the Blackstones were holding the East Gate near their enclave, with the Tyther clan relocated to the West. He had not reckoned on that fact that Safah had the blood of the Blackstones coursing through her veins and without hesitation split her forces. Retaining half her force on the East Gate under the command of her most senior officer, she brought ten thousand troops across to the West and North Gates. When she arrived she had sent a guard to protect Lord Tyther and launched counter attacks first on the West Gate and then when the Pod were pushed back, on the North Gate. Without her command they would have been lost.

Safah joined Hechkle, Bronstorm and Bailey accompanied by fifty tough and capable soldiers and a young runner called Bertrand.

'Thanks you, Lady Blackstone,' said Hechkle, bowing to the previous haughty and disapproving royal. Now, seemingly fired up by the plight of the Aeria Cavern, her Blackstone instincts for command had overridden her political games. She stood proudly with a battle-axe in her hand and surrounded by a throbbing force-field like a present day Boadicea. Automatically all the soldiers of the clans flocked to her banner and regal authority. A striking horn made from a weinder beast tusk hung from her belt. It had many marks upon it from heavy use.

Safah took in the state of the North Gate; she knew the East Gate was at the moment the most secure as the Pod had thrown their might at the other three gates. At that moment a breathless Southgate runner ran to her and gave her a written message. She read hastily, biting her lip at the contents before deciding on the next course of action. The Southgate runner was exhausted so she called upon one of her men.

'Bertrand, go to the West and East Gates and when they hear my horn they are to fall back to the Inner Defence

Wall as one. No delay. Do you understand?' Bertrand saluted and ran to pass on the command.

'Lady Blackstone, are we falling back?' asked Bronstorm, who had led the small contingent of Fathom soldiers courageously.

'The South Gate is nearly fallen and if we are to provide any chance for our people we need to fall back together,' said Safah, wishing she had Jaida beside her. The North Gate buckled under the pressure from outside and the Pod were overpowering those on the ramparts.

Safah carried on directing the forces to fight for every inch of ground and when an exhausted Bertrand ran back to her, breathing hard and saluting her, and informed her the East and West Gates were ready, she didn't hesitate and swung her horn from her hips to her pursed lips and blew a loud, deep blow. The sound echoed around the Aeria Cavern, as it bounced off the ceilings and walls. The effect was immediate, with no panic the gates were left and the soldiers hastily retreated behind the deactivated Inner Perimeter Barrier and Inner Defence Wall. The forces previously holding the gates, many injured and maimed, were ordered to fall back to the last line of defence where the people of the Aeria Cavern huddled fearfully. Their retreat was met by a howl of triumph from the Pod and the gates were ripped apart and even Safah had to draw in her breath when the hordes burst through.

How can they defeat such a driven enemy?

As the Pod approached the columns of men and women, the Inner Perimeter Barrier was switched on. The Pod threw their bodies at the barrier and initially the force-field pushed them back, enraging them in the process. Hundreds of bodies charged the shield, again and again, only to be rebuffed.

Bailey licked his lips, dry with fear, comforted that he had the columns of soldiers beside him, commanded by senior officers including Hechkle and Bronstorm.

*Tell me, Bailey, why am I here? Next time someone says, 'Let's go millions of light years away from home and family to another planet with unknown dangers,' just say no...*he thought.

The shield faltered under the unrelenting assault, flickering and spluttering with the effort to stay active. Then it went out and even the Pod were initially surprised and their attack halted briefly before continuing with their advance, swarming over the inadequate Inner Defence Wall.

The wall did its job, providing a break in the momentum of the Pod and reduced the numbers in the front ranks whilst they waited for their chance to scale the obstacle in front of them. Safah knew that this was the time for attack. Lifting her horn to her lips she blew three short, sharp blows and the columns began marching.

They were impressive, just like Napoleon's French grenadiers; they marched directly into the enemy hordes, punching great holes in the lines of their attackers. Many of the soldiers in the front row were instantly killed as the Pod pulled them away, ripping off arms and heads in glee, but behind them others filled the holes and the motto was "don't stop going forward".

Safah continued her surveillance behind the columns as the five tightly wedged columns drove the bulk of the attackers back to the Inner Defence Wall. Those that made it through the gaps were caught by a line of skirmishers held back for such a job. Bailey was one of them. They mercilessly gunned or struck down any Pod that made it through.

Behind the South Gate, Tate stood with Kabel in the skirmishing line accomplishing the same. Side by side they gave the troops the morale to keep fighting. Tate swinging his sword with great effect made a fearful sight, Kabel holding a blaster and a seckle striking down any enemy near him. Both supported by Belina and Kron, not losing an inch of ground. A great roar went up as they began to back the Pod back to the ruined Inner Defence Wall. The Pod lay two or three deep in places, they had taken enormous losses, yet still they streamed through the outer gate.

'How many of these creatures are there?' Kabel gasped.

'We have never seen the like before,' said Tate, slicing through the leg of a Pod with his sword, before using his shield to throw another back.

'I hope Zebulon is right that stopping Myolon is the secret to peace,' said Kabel, shooting a Pod as he closed down on Gemma, who grimly smiled a quick thank you before defending another attack.

'If he is not I am not sure how long we can last,' replied Tate.

'Look,' said Kabel. They both watched as the front of the columns that had made great inroads on the Pod began to be torn apart by sheer numbers and hatred. The columns began to stop as fear began to take a grip.

'Call them back, now or they will be annihilated,' said Tate to Kron, who was covered in blood, not his, but still covered. Kron pulled out a similar horn to that Safah had but without the crest and gold flecks upon it. He placed the horn to his lips and blew one long blow and at the same time two more long blows sounded, clearly heard from two of the other gates.

Tate and Kabel shared a look. The gate, barrier and wall had fallen and their fourth line of defence had been swept aside in quick measure.

The columns stopped and then began their organised retreat. The soldiers on the roofs gave covering fire as the remnants of the defenders steadily moved back to the central hub and last defence of the Aeria Cavern.

On the North Gate, Safah was overseeing a similar retreat and her messages to the East and West Gates meant that they were now retreating in some sense of order. It was at this time that Safah showed her lineage greatness. The political and haughty woman was gone... replaced by a leader and general. All the clans looked up to her as she masterminded one of the greatest retreats in Zein history. Without her intelligence and strategy many more thousands would have perished. Beside her strode the giants of the 'Battle of the North Gate', the herculean Hechkle, the quicksilver Bronstorm and the never-say-die alien called Bailey. All figures would be remembered in the years to come.

The preconceived plan for the soldiers on the rooftops to provide cover worked. The defenders were well armed and all had an escape plan to fall back across the rooftops if they feared their position would be taken or when the last of the survivors have passed their position. By doing this they gave an element of protection to those on the ground and in flanking the retreating masses, protected them from the Pod hordes. The survivors made their way to the daunting and impressive last line of defence around the Royal Council and Transportation buildings. There they found the rest of the population, crammed into every available nook and cranny, scared, fearful, yet defiant. The soldiers on the rooftops began to retreat in a well-rehearsed orderly manner once the bulk of their colleagues had safely passed them, until they settled into the ring of steel around the remaining population created by their colleagues.

Kabel and Tate burst through the entrance of the hastily erected but impressive final barricade and surveyed the wreckage of their defence teams. Many injured were lying on the floor being looked after by the overworked medics. Children could be heard screaming in fear from the Transportation building, where most were housed.

The whole population now rested in a circle at the centre of the Aeria Cavern that covered five streets deep of the main hub; they included the Changeling enclave who stood ready for the onslaught.

Every space was taken up as they looked up to the roof of the massive cave and prayed for their respective Gods' help. As the last survivors tumbled in, the last person in was Safah, holding her weinder beast horn and seckle, the latter which dripped many a Pod's blood. As she approached Kabel and Tate, many of the soldiers, including Hechkle and Bronstorm bowed in respect.

'North, West and East gates have fallen Lord Chancellor,' said Safah, with little emotion. Kabel thanked her, marvelling at the transformation in front of them but not surprised. Now, there were no clans or different races, just a people facing extinction from a rabid enemy that was hell bent on destroying them. At that point Kabel knew that Zebulon had spoken the truth and all hopes now rested on him.

Around the desperate men and women of the Aeria Cavern the Pod stopped and massed. A terrifying noise began to sound, echoing and driving fear through the defenders' hearts. Hundreds of thousands of the creatures began to beat their chests and roar. The noise was like a battering ram smashing through a flimsy door. The noise increased so much that the defenders had to place their hands over their ears in protection.

'What are they doing?' said Kabel

'It is an ancient message from many years ago,' said Safah, having to shout above the din.

'What message?'

Safah paused, deliberating whether to reply or not and then, shrugging her shoulders, relented. Kabel felt the prickles of fear and desperation climb over him and ensnare his hope as he read her mind before she could speak the words.

'It is your time to die.'

Chapter 20: Siblings

Myolon grinned wickedly, enjoying the moment. Zebulon was watchful, suspicious of his brother and remembering all the malicious tricks he used to play against him when they were younger.

'You pulled me into the magics younger brother?' said Zebulon.

'I didn't see you resist too much.'

'I once remembered when our family was happy and contented and you changed all that.'

'What, to be one of the Pod, when all the magics are at the touch of your hand?' said Myolon, his face twisted in a grimace. The Pod who were behind the magically created barriers heard the words and roared their disapproval. Silent and standing behind the force-field at the head of her royal guard was the High Priestess, watching, waiting.

'You could have said no,' said Myolon as his hand sneaked behind his waistband where he had hidden a wickedly sharp short dagger in a concealed pocket which now he could manoeuver into his free left hand. The blade was dark and gleamed red, tainted by something unwholesome.

'You left us no choice: if our parents and I had not joined you the law states we all would have lost our lives anyway, to prevent the cancer of the magics within the family circle,' said Zebulon, anger fuelling him, disturbing his concentration and his personal internal shield.

That's what Myolon was looking for.

He launched his trident and Zebulon blocked with his sword, his body turning with the thrust, and as he did Myolon swept in holding his left hand low.

'Zebulon, blade!' shouted Tyson.

The powerful changeling reacted quickly, but not quickly enough and Myolon's arm swung back and then thrust forward with considerable force. The dagger cut into the side of Zebulon, who let out a groan of pain. The grin was back on Myolon's face as he pushed deeper. Zebulon's face registered the shock of the blow. His sword dropped from his grasp, bouncing on the stone floor a couple of times, until finally resting forlornly on its side.

'Die, dear brother.' Zebulon looked down at the knife, which Myolon removed. He then looked back up to his brother whose face was impassive.

'You…that knife…'

'Coated in methir and then dipped in the Mygolwich and then forged with the magics,' said Myolon.

Zebulon dropped to one knee, clutching his side. Tyson went to him with Amelia as Myolon stepped to one side and his troops readied for the onslaught from the waiting Pod.

'What's just happened?' said Tyson as he saw an unhealthy greyness spread over Zebulon's face.

'The…the blade…is…poisoned to overcome my magics,' gasped Zebulon. Amelia caught him as he fell to his left struggling for air.

'Is there anything to stop the poison?' said Tyson.

'Need to…to get…to the Mygolwich.'

'Pick up those bags,' said Myolon to his soldiers as he turned away from his mortally wounded brother, picking up his trident. He glanced at the High Priestess and her guard and was just considering which barrier he would remove when…

'You are not going anywhere with those bags.' The voice was chilling and said with a finality that stopped Myolon in his tracks. He turned slowly and his eyes rested on the alien figure.

Tyson instinctively knew that he had to stop this Changeling. The magics maybe attacking his very core within him but his human empathy with Zebulon and the knowledge that Myolon carried the destruction of many caused him to rally against the cancer within him.

'Well, well, the alien speaks. You want to dance, pretty boy?' Myolon goaded, still holding the lethal knife in his left hand.

Tyson was still, motionless, holding no weapon but inside his magics began to crank up to an explosion that felt like a dam ready to burst.

Myolon's smile disappeared and he flung his body at Tyson, thrusting the trident forward and holding the knife ready for the deadly end. Instead he met a wall of blue light that arrested his speed of light attack. He unleashed all the magics he had built up within his body and a tainted brown hued light sprang from him, initially holding the brilliance of the blue light, that was so bright all had to shield their eyes.

Myolon let out a cry of joyous glee as he burrowed deep inside his soul and threw all he had at Tyson. His face registered shock and horror as Tyson's magics swallowed up the powerful magics and then surged to encase the Changeling within a prism of energy. Myolon twisted and fought against the power emitting from Tyson's hands and when he looked into his opponent's eyes he felt a fear that he had never experienced.

Amelia was also looking at Tyson's eyes, which were a burning blue light of energy in a pale and emotionless face. Her heart leapt with worry and concern and she was going to go to him when Zebulon's hand grabbed her and kept her close to him.

'Leave him, girl, he has to finish this himself,' said Zebulon, struggling to catch his breath as the poison worked through his body.

'W-w-h-hatt do-do you mean?' stammered Amelia, resisting the hold on her hand.

'Tyson is the Prophecy, always was. He has to finish this once and for all,' said Zebulon, the pain beginning to overtake him. Jaida and Taio who were near the fallen Changeling heard the words and looked at Tyson in a new light. They had grown up with the same Prophecy and like many others had consigned it to the back of their minds as meaningless superstition; now the perpetrator of their survival was a mere few feet away.

Myolon began to emit a painful screech as his brown tinged force-field, which unusually for a Changeling emanated from his body was fading as the shining blue magic hammered at his defences. Then the blue light found a weakness and it streaked into the Changeling whose scream grew as the pain increased until Myolon threw out his arms as the hybrid magic tore him apart.

Abruptly the blue light stopped and the lifeless remnants of Myolon's body slumped to the floor. Tyson let out a cry and fell to his knees, holding his heart and his head.

'Go to him now, Amelia, he needs you,' said Zebulon, falling back onto the stony ground. Amelia rushed to Tyson's side and enveloped him in a loving embrace as

Zebulon and the rest of the group saw the magic induced force-fields, holding back the Pod from the four entrances, disappear. They nervously prepared for the attack. Jaida and Taio pulled out their seckles and the soldiers readied their photon shotguns and rifles. But the attack never came.

The High Priestess walked towards the group and, sending a curious look at Tyson who had leaned into Amelia's embrace, went to the side of Zebulon and crouched down.

'Zebulon, is that really you?' she asked.

'Yes, Festilion,' responded Zebulon, and then remembering the etiquette, 'Yes, High Priestess.'

Festilion laughed. 'I don't remember you being that formal when we were playing those many years ago.'

Zebulon smiled, the memories all but gone but wisps of a simple life still remained. She placed a gentle hand on his forehead and waved Redulon, to her side.

'Take Lord Zebulon, to the Mygolwich and immerse his whole body into the waters. Then take him to our healers.'

'But, High Priestess, he is one of the skin-changers, a Malefic. Our law is clear, he has to die.' There was a murmur of agreement from the rest of the Pod. The remaining Changelings readied to defend themselves and glanced nervously around the cavern.

Festilion stood proudly. 'The time for killing to end has come; we need to find a way to live together.' Redulon began to interrupt but she put up her hand to stop him and he lapsed into silence.

'Follow my command, Redulon and also send messengers to Dominion to pull back from the Zeinonian settlement.' He bowed to her and gestured for four of the Pod to hoist Zebulon onto their shoulders to take him to the Mygolwich.

As they picked up Zebulon, who was beginning to look extremely ill, he motioned for Festilion to approach him, which she did.

'You will be too late, a message has to be sent another way, by telepathy,' gasped the poisoned Changeling.

'There is no other way, I don't have that kind of power to reach my army,' said Festilion, dismissively.

'But he does…' said Zebulon, pointing to Tyson who was recovering and now listening to the conversation.

Festilion frowned and then walked across to Tyson and bade him to stand up. Tyson did, with Amelia holding him steady.

'Zebulon says you can reach my army to prevent further blood being shed, is that true?'

'Not sure, I think I can but I'm not sure how I do it sometimes,' said Tyson, simply, as he wrestled with the changes in his body from the recent battle.

Zebulon, who was now resting on the four Pod shoulders as they waited to take him away, looked down at Tyson. 'Look inside you, Tyson, see the Aeria Cavern, the rock, the buildings and then reach out to all the inhabitants and all those within the city limits. Feel the magics, be one with the "Provider of Life" and let it sweep through you.'

Tyson shook his head, still shaken from his battle with Myolon. Zebulon took a knowing look at Amelia, who understood the importance of the request.

She took Tyson's hand and looked lovingly into his face. 'Tyson, you can do this, it is not like a fight and the magics used for destruction, but instead you will be using them to save lives,' said Amelia, brushing her fingertips on his cheek, 'I believe in you.' Festilion waited, unsure what to expect but holding back sending the messengers. Wernion who had been stunned by the initial fight, groaned as he came to. Tyson's gaze rested on him as the large creature he had befriended rubbed his head where a large lump now protruded. He then saw the High Priestess and the crumpled body of Myolon and his eyes gave a questioning glance at Tyson.

Yes that was me.

Wernion gave an impressed shrug. Festilion listened to the interchange.

What is this alien capable of?

Tyson let go of Amelia and gingerly sat back down and crossed his legs as if mediating. He emptied his mind, very much like he did in the Core when connecting with the infected Fathom soldiers. Everyone's eyes were on him and he firstly picked up their thoughts.

He saw the questions in the High Priestess thoughts and of the disbelieving Pod. He then found there was wonder in the soldiers and apprehension in the remaining Changelings. Utter belief was in Amelia's thoughts and that pleased him; he knew then how much he loved her and that Gemma was simply an unwanted temptation.

Once he had encountered the thoughts of those around him, he stretched out his mind to the caves and picked out the fear and trepidation of the Pod who had not gone to battle. They worried about loved ones and their own future. He then went into the open; he crossed the Great Plains and felt the simple thoughts of the weinder beasts and other animals on the surface. He entered the minds of the birds gracefully sweeping across the blue sky and the inhabitants of the forests and rivers. His mind wandered through the barren streets of the deserted villages and roamed around the gardens and waterfalls until he came to the entrance of the Aeria Cavern.

It was here that he felt the first pain. His face creased in concern and as Amelia made to comfort him, the High Priestess waved her back. This remarkable alien was accomplishing a feat that had never been done before and any disturbance could disrupt the trance. The pleading look she gave made Amelia back off.

He felt the pain of those wounded, human, Pod and Zeinonian alike. He felt the ferociousness of the Pod as they attacked and instinctively reached out to all their minds and understood that their hatred was based on fear for their future. He went through the thousands of combatants until he came to Dominion, who was leading the attack and had just decapitated a young soldier from the Blackstone clan, near the Transportation building. He weaved through Dominion's self-consciousness, making the impressive figure pause in his next attack, confused as to what was happening to him.

Tyson then pushed into the minds of the defenders. He found a people fighting for their very lives, with Kabel standing shoulder to shoulder with Tate and Belina pushing back the hordes. Bailey, holding an injured arm and Hechkle with a nasty looking bandage around his head. He initially met resistance from the Changelings, who were intent on protecting their enclave from the Pod, until even they succumbed to the powerful telepathic force. He saw Safah, with multiple wounds, lying on the floor with her men trying to protect her as she lay stricken.

Tyson's face was agonised, feeling the pain, and he let out a groan. Quickly, Amelia went to his side, ignoring Festilion's desperate attempts to stop her. Tyson didn't come out of his trance but seemed to radiate warmth from Amelia's presence. He continued to wrap around the minds of the rest of the defenders including the crying children and the other Zeinonians hiding within the buildings. When he had entered all their minds he settled his own mind to what he needed to tell them.

The message when it came caused all in the cavern to collapse to the floor in pain. Those holding Zebulon had to lower him to the floor so they could place their hands over their ears. The animals on the plain began to run round in circles as they fled the insertion into their minds, birds flew to the ground and staggered bewildered.

Stop, put down you weapons, no more killing.

Tyson repeated the words, which echoed round the planet. In the Aeria Cavern, the Pod stopped in their tracks; they dropped their homemade weapons and dropped to the ground, trying to defend against the message reverberating in their heads.

Kabel deactivated his seckle and with his magic was able to control the power of the message inserted to a reasonable level. The Pod stopped their attack, shocked and stunned by what was happening and Kabel ordered his men to lower their weapons; the majority already had as their more basic or non-existent magics did not provide them with the ability to resist the telepathic message.

*Tyson. There is hope…*thought Kabel

Tyson found Dominion and isolated the separate message he wanted to share and the picture of him and Wernion working together. He then sent a message to Kabel explaining what had happened.

Dominion straightened up and then realised he was facing Kabel, the person who Tyson had said to trust. Tate astutely recognised the commander of the Pod forces and informed Kabel.

Tyson fell forward in the cave, his energy spent. Amelia poured some water from her flask and soaked a cloth taken from her bag to wipe his face.

In the Aeria Cavern, Dominion, his breast heaving and his fur matted with blood, held up his arm with red stained talons gleaming in the artificial light and with one last look at Tate and Kabel, motioned for his soldiers to retreat. The brethren retreated slowly at first and then when they realised no attack was going to come, they quickened their retreat. Soon an eerie calm descended on the battlefront.

Back in the cave, the injured Zebulon raised his body from the floor and stood up and then painfully approached the exhausted Tyson, who had climbed to his feet with the help of Amelia. Jaida and Taio were speechless at the turn of events.

'You are very brave, human,' said the deep bass voice of Zebulon. 'My people owe their lives to you, as do all others of Zein. For that I swear today, that I and all my people will serve you.' Then Zebulon surprised everyone by dropping to one knee and bowing his head to Tyson. The other Changelings in the group did the same, followed by the remaining Zeinonians. And after a brief nod from Festilion, the Pod did as well. The Prophecy was fulfilled.

'Please stand, this is all very embarrassing,' said Tyson. They all stood except the injured Changeling and one look into Zebulon's eyes and he knew that there was no joke behind the act. Tyson now had his own army. University and his relaxed lifestyle seemed a world away. He laughed at the absurdity of what was happening...the others, if surprised by the laughter didn't show it. Festilion beckoned her soldiers to support Zebulon and assist him to the waters of Mygolwich. The others followed.

On the shore of the great cavern the Pod bearers carrying Zebulon on their shoulders, walked into the lake. A low hum emitted from Festilion and the other Pod brethren, young and old, came from the variety of entrances, carrying small torches, all emitting a similar hum as the High Priestess. Zebulon was immersed in the lake and the noise grew to a crescendo with Festilion raising her hands to the cavern ceiling. Zebulon was lifted from the lake and Tyson saw a ruddy brown unwholesome fluid seep from his wound into the lake. The noise became quieter and the group from the Aeria Cavern could not help but feel a little fearful as now the once empty shore was packed with the Pod. But they didn't attack and simply continued their humming. Zebulon was laid down onto the shore and suddenly he convulsed once, twice and then lay still. The noise stopped and the Pod began to move away.

Festilion walked past Tyson. She stopped when she was beside him. 'He will be fine now, the poison has been flushed out of him and he just needs rest. My carers will look after him.' He thanked her and as the cavern emptied his thoughts turned to his mother and his despair returned.

Chapter 21: Hope

Leila's eyes flicked open. She lay in the bed as the morning light streamed through the sides of the blinds that covered the impressive all-window wall that enabled you to look out across the high-tech city.

Voices could be heard drifting through the entrance to the bedroom. Zylar was no longer in the bed they shared and Leila couldn't suppress the cold shiver that crept up her spine and her neck, as she pondered what she was putting herself through; he left her cold. This was their third week in Quentine and every waking minute she wanted to run away, escape this planet, the Xonians and never set eyes on Zylar again. Leila knew patience was the key. Watch, listen and then act she told herself, over and over again.

She climbed out of the bed and pulled a robe on, tightening the belt to secure the garment around her. Making sure that any noise was kept to the minimum, she crept to the partially opened door and peeked out.

Zylar was fully dressed. Facing him was Prince Jernli, the more moderate ruler from Xonia, if you compared him with the forbidding figure of Yisli, Marshall of the Capulus Novus System. Her eyes were drawn to the repulsive Yisli, who stood quietly behind his master's back. He took in every word Zylar uttered and Leila could see the contempt he had for his prince. She listened hard to what they were talking about; struggling with the harsh guttural sounds the Xonians made as they talked though their voice synthesizers.

'My scouts have confirmed that the joint human and Zein Expeditionary Force have landed on Zein,' said Zylar, patiently. He needed the support of Prince Jernli; he couldn't win this war with the meagre troops he had. Leila's heart almost burst with happiness, she just knew that her son was with them.

'Why is this news to me? They are simply an annoying buzzing fly that is a mere irritation to the Xonian Empire,' Prince Jernli retorted, dismissively.

'They have great firepower and defeated your ships on their journey, do you not remember, your Excellency?'

'That was just a small scout group. Do I need to remind you I have thousands of those fighters?' said Prince Jernli, seemingly bored with the conversation. Zylar knew better.

He is trying to negotiate with me.

'If we defeat this army then we will have destroyed their most powerful weapons, leaving six billion people defenceless against our forces.' Prince Jernli could not hide the gleam of greed from his face at Zylar's words and even Leila, some distance away, could see the naked desire in his facial expression.

*Got him…*Zylar thought.

'So what do you suggest we do?' asked the Xonian royal, hooked by the mouth-watering prospect of such a bountiful prize. His father would at last recognise he was the one to inherit the throne.

Zylar sat back in his chair, carefully masking his triumph. 'We must ensure that they only attack with the two destroyers and hold back with the main ship, *Elanda*.'

Prince Jernli edged towards the front of the chair eager to listen to the plan.

Fool, Zylar thought as he wrapped his victim in his half-truths to fulfil his own selfish needs.

'Why not destroy all the ships?'

'Because, Your Highness their combined firepower is too much for our defences, especially if they land their forces on the Skegus Plain.' Zylar was referring to the vast plain which led up to the city. It stretched as far as the eye could see and before it stood an inadequate outer wall which had no discernible protection.

'We must engage the *Elanda* whilst still in orbit,' said Zylar. He wished he was dealing with the scowling Yisli, who was still standing behind his master, but they both knew where they stood.

'I understand. So you want my ships to engage the *Elanda* and you will battle the two destroyers in front of the city?' said a now very-pleased-for-himself, Prince Jernli.

'Yes, then we have a chance,' said Zylar.

'Your Highness, you should be made aware that we have only one battleship in orbit, the rest of the fleet is not due for another week,' said Yisli.

'What, where are my star cruisers?' said an exasperated Prince Jernli. It took a few minutes for Yisli to explain that due to a rebellion in the outer reaches of this galaxy, the star cruiser and three other destroyers had left over a week ago to quash any insurrection.

'How can we defeat these invaders then?' pressed Prince Jernli.

'The *Elanda* is slow and they will not be expecting an attack if we have just one battleship. If we can cripple the *Elanda* and use our superior forces on the ground we will blunt the initial attack and leave them vulnerable,' said

Zylar, confidently. 'Blunt the ships and my Ilsid and your Xonian troops will tear their infantry apart.'

Yisli looked up and across to the door causing Leila to jerk her head back and in doing so bumped into the table near the door. One of her bracelets shot across the top of the table and fell onto the plush carpeted floor. The noise on the table seemed to be incredibly loud to Leila, who took off her robe and jumped back into bed as she heard the chair creak and footsteps walking towards the bedroom.

Zylar poked his head into the room and looked at the seemingly still asleep figure on the bed. Leila peered out of her half closed eyes and saw him shake his head with puzzlement, and then he remembered that his guests were still in the room and returned to the lounge, closing the door behind him, unaware that Leila was frantically trying to hold her breath to stop her panting out aloud from the exertion. She heard the guests leave and waited for Zylar to go on his usual daily tours. Leila knew then that she had to get a message to her son and to Zein.

The day went slowly and Leila ensured she visited the girls and the three, fast growing toddlers. When Leila entered the room the children were crawling across the floor with Clancy chasing after them. His face, happy but bright red with the exercise.

'Wow, the kids are really coming along,' said an impressed Leila. It was true the children were progressing very fast with their hand and eye co-ordination incredible for such a young age.

Megan beamed a proud smile, 'That's my girl,' when Hanna picked up a square block and slotted it through the right hole, rapidly followed by a triangle through another hole. Leila was impressed. *Their advancement is a marvel and a little disturbing.*

'Clancy, can I have a word with you?' asked Leila. The big lumbering Malacca man slowly climbed to his feet and stumbled after the retreating back of the lady he had come to admire. When they were a safe distance away from the rest of the imprisoned girls, Leila leaned closer to Clancy on purpose, who immediately felt a little flustered at the closeness. He struggled to hide his feelings; used to the females in the Eastern Quadrant on Earth shunning him.

'You like us don't you, Clancy?'

Clancy looked back at the women and the three little children and a lopsided smile formed on his face. That was a sufficient answer for Leila.

'Would you help us escape?' Leila held her breath. She was taking a massive risk and knew it as the Malacca man was scared of Zylar; like many others that fear had made him do unspeakable things to other prisoners in the Eastern Quadrant. Her concerns seemed to be real when Clancy's face immediately displayed the concern of going against his master. Leila reached up with her hand and stroked his cheek. The hulking figure of a man almost sighed with pleasure at the unusual sensation and his fear seemed to ebb away.

'You know I am fond of you and the girls are as well,' said Leila, coaxing away his barriers as she continued to touch him with light and almost sensual touches. Clancy could not resist, confirming he would help them.

Good, now for the next part of the plan.

'Can you take me to where they are keeping King Yi?' Leila knew that the King and his son were brought back, into the Royal Palace at the end of each working day.

'Yes.' Clancy didn't hesitate motioning for Leila to follow him and, after carefully locking the door behind them; they made their way down a number of floors until they came to a door guarded by two Ilsid. Clancy told

Leila to remain where she was and then walked up to the guards. After a quick few words from Clancy, the two Ilsid left their posts and he waved Leila forward.

'What did you say?' Clancy just shrugged his shoulders.

'They need to eat, programmed to keep their strength but I just gave them some encouragement that Zylar had ordered them to…they know I am his personal guard so they didn't hesitate,' said a smug Clancy. Leila gave him a "well-done" smile and walked through the now opened door.

She found a luxurious apartment and a surprised King Yi and his son, Yian, who had both stood up for the unexpected visitors. Leila needed to act quickly, knowing that the Ilsid wouldn't be long.

Taking a number of steps to bring her closer to King Yi, she bowed, which he returned, his regal face displaying puzzlement at seeing this strange lady again.

'Your Majesty, I overheard this morning that my people and the Zeinonians have returned after travelling far from my home planet and are now currently on Zein,' said Leila, pleased to see the intrigued expression on Yi's face. He gestured to a seat and then sat down himself just as an elegant lady walked in from the bedroom. Now it is said that the male Oneerion is gentle, skilled and creative beyond any other race and it was also true that the female Oneerion was just as beautiful and graceful in equal measure. Leila, of course, had seen female Oneerions as they shopped in the market stalls outside; however, she was now looking at the most beautiful person she had ever seen.

'This is my concubine, Gi,' said Yi, gracefully. When he said concubine it was not with disdain or for control, he was simply following the Oneerions own culture to call their partner by the age old term. The way he said it was full of love and pride, which told Leila everything she needed to understand about the strength of their relationship.

They exchanged pleasantries and all settled down with Yi casting concerned eyes at the hulking figure of Clancy. Leila didn't miss the inference of the look.

'Clancy is here to help us, you can trust him,' said Leila, allaying his fears, giving the awestruck Malacca man a dazzling smile of encouragement.

Yi was hungry to learn all about Leila's world. She told him of the land and the sea, the great cities, the many people. When she was describing the different cultures she started off with her own country and the very thought made her tearful and she had to stop briefly. Yi was patient, seeing the pain and love in the alien's demeanour. Leila then went on to the many other varied cultures of Earth. Both Yi and Gi were captivated by both the description and the emotion they saw.

Leila then told Yi what she had heard this morning and her plan to free the human hostages and bring the human and Zeinonian army to Skegus to free the Oneerions. Yi listened closely, neither confirming nor challenging Leila's thoughts. When she finished with her escape plan, he languidly stood up and made his way to the large spectacular window that overlooked the bustling city. He saw the Xonian patrols augmented by the Ilsid moving between the sparse crowds. The gun placements at each intersection swivelled their barrels every few minutes, conveying the threat to the Oneerions and other races that lived in this luxurious city. He glanced over his shoulder and looked at Gi, who inclined her head as if she knew what he was thinking.

She probably does.

He turned to face Leila and Clancy. 'My people are a gentle race, we do not go to war, which makes us vulnerable to those more aggressive than us,' said Yi, collecting his thoughts. 'How do I know that your race is any different from the Xonians? I want to help but I do not want to replace one conquering race with another.'

Leila could see his point; why trust her? 'We have our faults but I can only say we have the best intentions,' said Leila, slightly unconvincingly. It was Gi who stepped in to support.

'Love of my life,' Gi started with, Yi half-smiled, already acutely aware he was going to lose this discussion. 'The Xonians have no mercy in their blood, and see what they have done to our people. I say we take our chance with the humans.' Gi bowed as she finished her pitch.

'My wife is not only beautiful, succinct but correct,' said Yi, addressing Leila. 'You have our support. When do you want to execute the plan?'

'Tonight, Zylar has requested that I do not stay with him tonight,' said Leila, inwardly shuddering for the poor girl who would take her place in his bed. 'Clancy will free me from the dormitory we are kept in and if you can smuggle me into the communication post then I can contact Zein.'

'It has been many years since we have contacted the Aeria Cavern settlement, they may not be monitoring incoming messages,' said Yi.

'I will take the chance, if not for me, for my fellow prisoners.' The tall Oneerion stared hard at the determined woman in front of him.

Maybe we have chosen the right people to align with, was his final thought before his guests gave their thanks and left the room.

He felt a warm arm on his shoulder. Gi had wrapped one of her beautifully tattooed arms around his massive golden skinned shoulders. 'She is an impressive female, my love,' she said, with a slight edge to her voice. He reached up and stroked her arm. 'Yes, very impressive,' said Yi, grinning, until he felt the arm tighten around him as GI's jealousy overcame her. He smoothly stood up to face his concubine. 'My love, she pales next to your beauty and body art,' he said, running his hand up the golden decorative arm.

'Oh gross, do you have to do that?' said Yian, in disgust as he stomped off to his bedroom, leaving his parents laughing and hugging. Their smiles quickly evaporated as they discussed the previous conversation.

'Do you trust them?' asked Yi.

'I trust her.' Was the pointed and simple response, whether I trust the rest of her race, I am not so sure. 'I have heard the reports from the Sagone Sector and we need to do something,' Gi said. The rumours had indicated that the Xonians had exterminated a race called the Pipers, for daring to fight back. Every male, female and child they could find had been rounded up and placed in one of the cities, until there was no space left. The Xonians had then teleported to their ship and bombed the city, intending to leave no one alive. Once the story rippled out from the few survivors who had managed to hide in underground makeshift warrens, other rebellions faded due to the fear of retribution.

Yi was concerned like her that one whole quadrant of the busy city had been cleared of all residents and they had seen prison transport ships flood in over a short period of time, the tell-tale sign of the crossed bar insignia on the side of the large ships indicating the slave cargo.

Yi's spies, scattered amongst those retained to clean out the homes and office blocks in the quadrant, fed back on the wide range of species from every planet conquered by the Xonians who spilled out of the cargo hold. They talked about the stench of the hold, which they were made to clean, and what distressed them the most was the bodies they had to bury, who had died in the cramped and appalling conditions; some still chained to their position on the hull floor.

For a race like the Oneerions, the callous disregard of life the Xonians had demonstrated by this slaver mentality shook them to the core. Yi was a kindly man, and on hearing these stories he had sought out Prince Jernli to protest. It had changed nothing, except place him and his son on menial work adding to the city defences as punishment for his insubordination.

He felt the arms of Gi encircle his waist. Yes if the Xonians were to be defeated, belief and trust in this new race from across the stars was needed. They stared across the city as the sun fell in the sky until the planet was plunged into an uneasy darkness.

□□□

Zylar cautiously stepped forward to review his latest recruits. Since his arrival he had worked tirelessly in building his new Ilsid army. When he had arrived the Xonians had shown why they had conquered over one hundred galaxies. Their organisation, ruthlessness and readiness to follow commands had delivered over seventy-five thousand new recruits to his zombie-like army.

He surveyed the floor of the skyscraper with its many cubicles containing the thrashing bodies of the prisoners they had presented to him as part of the deal. This was the tenth and last floor today for conversion. The subjects were still struggling with the drug which was the first stage of the conversion to an Ilsid warrior.

Zylar moved to the first cubicle and the Xonian medical staff pulled back the dome cover. He found himself staring at a humanoid figure, similar to a human except that there was no nose or ears. He had been clear in his instructions that he needed two legged, relatively tall and strong males or females of adult size who were fit or strong. The Xonians had scanned their vast prisoner ranks from conquered worlds that had never known what had hit them when the dominant armies of Xonia invaded. Surprisingly they had found many species that fitted the specifications. Without any thought of the safety for the prisoners, they shipped them out toe to toe in disgusting conditions on the basis, if they were weak they would die and the strong ones would live. Zylar laughed out loud, making the staff around him jump…he had to give it to them, they were the lowest type of scum he had ever seen. You just had to admire them.

He looked on the thrashing body in front of him, noticing the good muscle tone. He reached forward and place his hands either side of the creature's head and concentrated. His magics flowed from his fingertips into the skull of the prisoner as he built the connection to his subject. The intensity increased until the body slowly stopped thrashing and lay still. He readied himself for the first rush of thoughts, which was a natural part of the "change". Old memories, loved ones and details of a life that had once been calm and full of hope. Even now Zylar felt the pangs of regret as he wiped the creature's memories from his brain…the little good inside him rebelling against the magics that had taken his soul away many, many years ago. The brief rebellion was quelled immediately, any pity was ruthlessly extinguished. The creature became a silent shadow of what it had been, its thoughts now a simple vessel for Zylar's commands.

'Death do us part,' Zylar said, humourlessly, before he moved to the next victim and repeated the same process.

ロロロ

The day went slowly as Leila waited for the early morning of the next day. She tried to pass the time playing with the children but time still dragged. She slept in the early evening as Rosanna was taken to Zylar's room. Rosanna was Italian and a very beautiful girl from Milan. She was fortunate that Zylar paid her little attention as he seemed to prefer lighter haired girls, but tonight her fate was one with which Leila would not wish upon anyone. She gave her a quick hug, told her to be brave and she would see her in the morning. As Rosanna left, Leila vowed that she was going to free all of them as soon as she could.

She again drifted off, warmed by the heat in the room and came to only when Clancy shook her awake. Leila looked at her watch and saw that it was early morning and groggily pulled her body from the chair she had dozed in.

They made their way carefully through the corridors. They were on the tenth floor of the building and the communications room was on the fifteenth. The plan that Yi had devised was for one of the cleaners to set off a fire alarm so the room would be evacuated and the whole floor cleared. A door would be propped open allowing Leila to gain access to the room and Yi had provided one of his operators, a young Oneerion called Kian, to patch her into the communication link connected to the Aeria Cavern on Zein.

She remembered his parting words as she left. 'We can make the link but you need to understand there may be no one on the other side to take the message. It has been years since we sent any messages – Zein became lost to us.' Leila had heard the words but struggled to take them in; with all this danger the prospect she may fail with the message was something she just could not accept.

The corridors were quiet due to the time of the night. The few Xonians they did pass had grown used to her presence and since there was the intimidating figure of Clancy with her, the patrols had more pressing matters to progress. Leila noticed that a number of Ilsid were appearing more frequently as part of the patrols causing her forehead to wrinkle with concern. The training must be increasing at speed – yet another part of the critical message she needed to send.

They entered a darkly lit corridor and at the end was a locked door with one of Clancy's colleagues guarding it. What had happened to the fire alarm? Leila turned to Kian with a questioning look, who in return shook his head in confusion, he could only guess that the soldiers had prevented the cleaners entering the room and curtailed the ruse.

'Stay here,' Clancy ordered, taking charge. He sauntered up to the Malacca man, an unsavoury type with a sullen look about him whom Leila remembered as one the guards she had sent to tell Zylar of the birth of Hanna. They conversed briefly before the man stood to one side. As he walked past Leila and Kian, his eyes lingered over her, not hiding his desire or intention. Leila glared back at him and he simply smirked. She hurried past as Clancy opened the door.

'What did you say to him? How can you trust that he will not go straight to Zylar?' Leila whispered worriedly, still rattled by the loathsome look the soldier had given her.

'We go back many years, joining the army at the same time. Believe me he has no love for authority and Zylar scares the living daylights out of him,' said Clancy, leading them into the communication room.

There were three people in the room, one operator and two more soldiers, all Malacca men. Clancy shook their hands, clapping them on their shoulders and gave them a knowing wink. All three laughed and left their positions, going into a room at the back which Leila glimpsed was a kitchen of some sorts.

Clancy came back to his companions. 'What are they doing?' asked a confused Leila. Clancy looked a little embarrassed, which made Leila press her question.

'I hope you don't mind, my lady, but I had to say something to give us a little time here. They are taking a little break.' His face blushed red.

'What did you say?' said Leila.

'I said that I was on a promise, of eh…some fun, if I could have the room for a few minutes, and that I had an operator just in case a message came in,' said the squirming Malacca man. Leila then surprised him by laughing, which the guards and operator heard as the door was closing on them – they let out some raucous laughter. When the door was shut, Leila stopped laughing and became business like again. She tapped him on his tree trunk like forearms.

'You did well, just thought I would give you some bragging rights later.'

Clancy beamed his delight.

Glancing at the closed door, with the laughter echoing from the kitchen still, Leila beckoned Kian to the controls. Kian moved fast. He took out the recorded message that Leila had given him and which he had converted to the necessary authentication security algorithm, allowing it to pass through the security firewall to the external connectivity drives that fed the Universe-recognised messaging services. His hands flew over the controls, pressing the many holograms of information. His two watchers behind his back, kept their attention on the main door and the door to the rest area. They didn't have much time for her message to be uploaded.

The soldiers' rough tones and language echoed through the thin door to the rest area and it was apparent that they had waited long enough. Kian made his final inputs and then stood up abruptly and moved away from the main control and stood silently with his head bowed. Leila leaned her body into Clancy and wrapped her arms around him. Clancy, surprised and a little slow on the uptake, left his arms at the side of his body. Leila grabbed one of his arms and placed it around her.

The returning soldiers took it all in as the couple came into their sight. They let out whoops and more bad language. Leila pushed away from Clancy with a suitable innocent look and Clancy, well Clancy just stood like a lump of wood, not sure what to do.

The Malacca operator joined in the jocular puns and sat down at his console. His hands darted across the dials and he frowned slightly and turned his head to look at Kian who kept his head down, refusing any eye contact. The operator kept his gaze on the top of Kian's golden forehead and then shrugged his shoulders and returned to his work.

'Clancy, can we go back now…I would like to show you my appreciation of seeing such a great room,' said Leila, shyly. The inevitable hoots followed and the two sentries again gave Clancy many pointers. Clancy decided enough was enough and he hurried Leila and Kian out of the room. The guard on the door gave another lecherous look at Leila, which she ignored. They hurried through the corridors with Kian, peeling off to go to his own quarters, only after Leila gave her thanks for his help. He bowed deeply on their parting.

Back at the female quarters, Clancy took up his position on the door outside and Leila tired and worried that her message had not got through, fell onto her bed and into a restless sleep.

ם ם ם

The console cranked into life under the layer of thick dust. The room, a darkened bunker deep under the transportation room in the Aeria Cavern, was an unremarkable room, empty of furniture except for a large chair in front of a sleek black desk with four main screens, which until a moment ago, had remained dormant for many years.

A wave of red dots flashed across one screen, the other screens began to emit a green code as the old system began to receive its first message for a long time. The noise increased until the room was filled with a whole range of whirrs and clicks. Then, as suddenly as the noise had started, the console switched off. Message received. The room returned to its quiet state, the console still covered in dust and no one the wiser for the noise. High above the room the Pod were scaling the barricades…the message lost within the unused console.

Chapter 22: Rebellion

Cronje blinked as the transportation from the Eastern Quadrant to the Core was completed. Although he and his team had been stripped of all their weapons they had not been shackled. When they were split up, with Cronje separated from his men, Reddash made to resist the move, and then caught his commander's small shake of the head and he capitulated to his captors. Reddash joined the other men and was marched away. Cronje was taken down a few corridors when Colonel Travers turned into a room, the men escorting Cronje pushing the Malacca man in after him. It took the entire experienced soldier's self-control not to kill them both.

'Greetings, Vice-Chancellor, how are you?' In front of him were Lord Fathom and Lord Southgate. Lord Fathom looked ill, paler than usual; he sat listlessly on a comfortable chair. Colonel Travers saluted Lord Southgate and left the room.

'Drink?' asked Lord Southgate, an offer that brought an icy look from Cronje. This was no time to drink.

'What's going on, Lord Southgate?'

He didn't answer but continued to pour the wine into his cup. Cronje noticed the flushness in his face and slurred speech indicating that this was not his first glass.

By Tucan, what the hell was going on!

Cronje maintained his inscrutable look, not sure what else to say, at least until he knew more.

'Shocking turn of events in Emula, hey Cronje, what were your men thinking of?' said Lord Southgate. Cronje didn't answer. Lord Southgate waved away the lack of response. 'Don't worry, I spoke with the Inner Council and pointed out you could not have had anything to do with that madness,' he reassured the army man.

Cronje kept his own counsel. He was fine with the Blackstone brothers but he was more suspicious and less patient with the likes of Lords Fathom and Southgate, due to their longer relationship with what had happened within the quadrants. He had made his peace with Lord Fathom somewhat after Evelyn's, his late daughter, bravery in fighting Zylar but he had very little to do with Lord Southgate. He was waiting for where this was all going.

'They want blood though, Cronje, yes blood,' said Lord Southgate, bringing his drink to his lips. His expression was one of regret and reluctance.

*Here it comes…*thought Cronje.

'The Inner Council would only agree to dropping the matter if we, I mean myself and you as members of the Council, agree to three proposals.'

'And they are…?' asked Cronje, finding his voice, trying to hide the sinking feeling in his stomach. *This was not going to be good.* He looked past Lord Southgate at the pale and ill looking Lord Fathom who was steadfastly ignoring the conversation.

'What is the matter with Lord Fathom…Sir?' said Cronje, belatedly adding the respectful title, the delay not missed by the wily politician.

'We are not sure. He was fine up to two weeks ago and then became sicker and sicker. My only guess is that he is missing his daughter.' Cronje could see that Lord Southgate generally cared for his fellow Lord's health and Lord Fathom appeared to take little notice of their conversation.

Cronje returned to the matter at hand. 'So, Lord Southgate what did the Inner Council ask us to sign up to?'

Lord Southgate pulled aside a chair to sit down. 'The three things are that the Malacca army is stood down, weapons handed in and their duties undertaken by units of the human army, secondly that the officer in charge is taken into custody and finally that they instigate an act of martial law across the colonies.'

'They are not having Reddash,' said Cronje with feeling. Lord Southgate, expecting the pushback from the experienced soldier didn't respond immediately but poured another glass and handed it to Cronje, who initially declined and then relented...a drink would do no harm. Lord Southgate relaxed slightly and swirled his wine round his glass as he considered the best way to proceed with this tough and capable man.

'Reddash would have plenty of time to state his case and the Inner Council will make the judgment – which for his protection includes both you and I. Pretty sure we can play the politics correctly to make it a misdemeanour charge, or do you feel he is completely innocent?'

Cronje averted his eyes. He knew from reading Reddash's response when he gave his report that some fault should be proportioned to him. That didn't mean he wanted him hung out to dry and he would fight that. Now with Lord Southgate's help they had considerable influence in the Inner Council. The by-laws of the Inner Council meant that if the two nominated Zeinonian individuals voted together they could overrule a change in law over the quadrants. It was a safeguard negotiated by Lord Southgate and the Lord Chancellor in return for insight into the use of zinithium, a powerful lever in the negotiations.

'What about the army standing down and martial law, don't we open ourselves to becoming prisoners?'

Lord Southgate stroked the top of his hair and paced across to the window where you could look across Lower Town.

'Not sure we have much option, Cronje – if we don't then we lose their trust and if we do then we lose our freedom of movement,' said Lord Southgate. 'I like neither of them too much.' He turned back to face Cronje. 'I will back you on what you feel is the right move. I think we have to accept Reddash has to face questioning for his part in this mess but I am with you, we can't allow for the Malacca army standing down and I completely feel the implementation of martial law is over the top.'

Cronje felt an element of relief, he hated these political games. 'When is the next Inner Council meeting?'

'In two days' time and we are expected to attend and support the amendments.'

'I don't like how this is playing out Lord Southgate,' said Cronje, frustration clear to see. 'How do we ensure Reddash obtains a fair trial?' Cronje remembered all the difficult times they had faced and he owed his life a number of times to the big Malacca man.

Lord Southgate shrugged and held out his hands. 'They need us to mine the zinithium and more importantly make use of it,' he reasoned, 'They will not jeopardise that!'

The conversation continued in a similar vein until Cronje threw up his arms and agreed there was no way round it. He was free to go, all the soldiers were free to move freely around the Core, except, of course, Reddash who was placed in one of the Fathom's Palace dungeons.

Cronje decided to take a walk down to the Lower Town. In the Fathom Palace there were a few Fathom guards and Southgate militia amongst the heavy presence of the United States and British armies. On the levels down to the Lower Town, the care for the lawns continued but he saw the fearful looks of the Fathom population under the human forces. He marvelled at the extension to the original Core with the Outer Perimeter Barrier now set well back from the Fathom Palace and with the new buildings under construction nearly doubling the size of the community. The streets were bustling with street hawkers selling their wares amongst the heavy patrols. The humans were taking no chances. He was walking through one particular market and stopped to buy an orange. He hadn't eaten since he had left his homestead.

'Don't turn around my friend, you are being followed,' said a deep voice, which was kept artificially low. Cronje continued to look at the fruit, picking up an orange and tossing it up in the air and catching it easily on its downward journey. He half turned to reach for a bunch of bananas and out of his peripheral vision he saw another man buying fruit.

Remo.

Cronje was pleased to see and hear from a trustworthy friend; matters were becoming extremely weird.

Remo walked off indicating to Cronje to follow him. They both entered an adjacent alleyway. Remo glanced left then right, his face worn by strain and stress.

'What happened in Emula?'

Cronje told him the full story, including the proposals to be voted upon by the Inner Council. He shouldn't share such confidences but he was worried and he needed to share what he thought was an out of control situation. Remo listened quietly and when Cronje had subsided into silence he shook his head.

'It is what I feared.'

'What?' Cronje's fears had just multiplied as he monitored the wave of expressions on Remo's face, which was usually so resolute.

'Over the last month they have moved a considerable number of troops down here, nothing noticeable in any one movement but the aggregate number is a concern.'

'What are they doing?' asked Cronje. There was a noise from the street and they peered out to the main street and a Fathom man was arrested by two US Marines and hauled off.

'That's what has been happening,' said Remo, with a grim expression. 'They make arrests for public order or terrorist offences at will. It looks like it is not coordinated but each arrest focuses on Fathom clan members who have extensive knowledge of our systems, zinithium usage or our history.'

'What do Lord Fathom and Lord Southgate do?'

'Lord Southgate is rarely here and I spoke with Lord Fathom only a week ago but it didn't seem to register, he looked ill,' said Remo.

'Yes, just seen him, looks like Princess Evelyn's death has hit him hard.' They both fell silent as they remembered the fateful battle when she was killed by Zylar. Then, realising they were suspiciously hanging around in the alleyway, Remo carried on with his assessment.

'They closely guard the shifts down to Base Station Zero,' said Remo, mentioning the main mining cave below their feet. 'The zinithium is not kept here but shipped somewhere else. I tried to find the coordinates but they are wiped clean from the memory.'

'So someone is stockpiling,' mused Cronje, 'but why, what is their plan?'

'It's not clear but the people down here are scared, and today they reduced the number of Zeinonians who could travel.'

'Are there others we can trust down here?'

'There are the remainder of the Fathom Royal Guard but they number less than one hundred and fifty. There are some of your Malacca Vets hanging around.'

'How many?'

'Probably another two hundred and a scattering of Tyther and Blackstone would double that number.'

'What about the Southgates?'

'Staying close to Lord Southgate and will not make a move without his say so,' said Remo glancing over his shoulder. They needed to move. Cronje picked up the urgency.

'Remo, I will track down some of the Vets and tell them to make their way towards the Palace without drawing attention, you talk with the rest,' said Cronje. 'The Vets will need weapons.' He looked enquiring at Remo.

Remo was already ahead of him. 'I know where they keep the guns; I will just need to convince Lord Fathom to give me the pass.' With a plan forming they shook hands and first Remo stepped out of the alleyway and then walked away with his long loping stride. Cronje followed soon after and made his way to one of the many bars on the main street. He had a good idea that he would find his men scattered within these buildings.

ㅁㅁㅁ

The Speaker waited for all the members of the Cabal to call in with their predefined code. When the last woman joined, a powerful political figure in the US who came from old money and to whom the new President of the United Sates was beholden for the positive campaign she had coordinated behind the scenes, the Speaker brought them all up-to-date, concluding with an assessment of the potential loss of life as they neared the final stages of the takeover.

There was an audible gasp from some when the scale of some of the civilian injuries and losses that were expected were announced.

'I thought we were not going to do this on the back of a high body count, Speaker?' said a Germanic voice. The Speaker was amused; the man came from one of the most powerful families in Germany that controlled one of the largest global multi-national companies.

Pretty sure his father was not saying that when the Nazis were flexing their muscles…thought the Speaker.

'It is regrettable of course but need I remind you that we are building a dynasty that will have the power to step out into the Universe and be a force,' said the Speaker. There were a few grunts of acknowledgment on the phone. 'Let's not forget that the amount of zinithium we are collecting has never been collated by any one nation, from what our contacts in the quadrants say.' *True*, the Speaker thought, with such an amount of the most powerful raw material known to any living being in this group's grasp, untold power and wealth was theirs for the taking.

As expected the greed and avarice of the Cabal members cancelled out some of the more squeamish of the group. The Speaker had no such issues of course – soon the Cabal and the role of the Speaker would be shared with the rest of the world, but by then Earth and the quadrants would be under their full control.

Chapter 23: Memories

Bailey stood up and wiped the sweat forming on his forehead. He was helping clear the debris from Reinan as the Zeinonians began the small steps to a new life without fear of the Pod.

The meetings between Kabel, Zebulon and Festilion had initially started cautiously and then developed more positively. It became acutely apparent that it was not only the Zeinonians who were sick of war but also that the Pod had reached their outer limits of patience with the death and destruction. They were driven by fear. Fear of the Changelings, fear of what the Zeinonians had done to their breeding grounds. After many sessions of talks it was finally agreed that the old breeding grounds which hosted one of the main villages, would not be rebuilt but remain Pod land, along with whole swaths of mountainous land which sat above the Pods main settlements. Heathlon, had relinquished her title to Festilion, content to enjoy the remainder of her days away from the pressure of office: the duplicated roles only served to present confusion. The line of authority was now via Zebulon, for the Changelings and Festilion, for the Pod, simplifying matters greatly. They now could live in peace and in return, Festilion had asked only one further request.

Bailey knew of the request and he waited patiently, searching the airstrip where one of the transporters would return Tyson from his recent trip to see the wider planet. Festilion wanted to speak to Tyson, once again, a request that Bailey knew his friend would have no problem accepting when he arrived back. The two had previously met on a number of occasions and each time Tyson's knowledge of the magics grew. Bailey knew he was hungry for more information on the magics, however, it also unsettled his friend and they hadn't caught up after the last discussion between Tyson and the High Priestess and he would not settle until he saw his friend back, safe and sound.

'What are you stopping for Englishman, hard work too much for you?' said Sean Lambert, heaving a ripped and useless settee onto an increasingly high pile of rubbish that would be burned later in the day.

'I am not soft like you northern guys,' Bailey retorted to the Scot, with no malice in his voice. He bent down and picked up a couple of broken shutters and then stopped. Tate and Belina were walking up the street, hand in hand. Tate was directing the clean-up and the men and women around him were happily following his demands, respect for what he had done for them over the last few years still present, even with the growing recognition that it was now a Blackstone who reigned as Lord Chancellor, echoing the mastery of the olden days.

Bailey had accepted the position that Tate and Belina were inexplicably drawn to each other but that didn't help dull his memories and how he felt. Some of the other girls within the human civilians had made moves to attract him but he wasn't interested. The old saying, "once bitten twice shy" was a true one for him. He shook his head and muttered, 'My, my Bailey, you have gone soft in your head.'

'What's that?' Sean was at his shoulder. The soldier followed his friend's gaze and placed a hand on Bailey's shoulder. 'That was a hard thing to take, laddy, and I know you are hurting now but someone else will come into your life, when the time is right.'

'Maybe, maybe,' said Bailey, as Belina caught his looks and smiled at him. Tate saw the exchange and didn't seem in any way perturbed; he knew the bond they had was now unbreakable.

There was suddenly a roar as a transporter came into land. Bailey threw the broken shutters onto the pile of rubbish and ran to the temporary landing strip near the ships. Kabel and Zebulon came out first, closely followed by a thoughtful looking Tyson and Amelia who had hooked her arm through his. Bailey pushed past the guards waiting to escort Kabel and made his way to his friend.

'How did it go?' Bailey asked the pair.

'We were shown around the whole planet, it is vast,' said Amelia, glancing at the pensive looking Tyson.

'Give me a few minutes with Bailey would you please, Amelia,' said Tyson. Amelia supressed her surprise and gave him a quick peck on the cheek and went to look round the clearing up of the city.

'What's up, mate?' asked Bailey as Tyson walked away from the hustle and bustle. No answer was forthcoming so Bailey traipsed after him, until they were on the edge of the Falls. Tyson sat down on the grass picking at the flowers in the meadow. Bailey joined him.

'It is beautiful?' said Tyson, knowledgeably. 'You really have no idea how much effort has gone into making this place?' His hand swept across the Falls and then Reinan. Bailey shook his head. 'Centuries…' He drifted off, unfinished, concern littered across his face.

'So?' Bailey said, not following.

'The so is, Bailey, that the magics unpicked this idyllic life, led to thousands dying and took a race of people a fraction from annihilation. All due to the magics!' said Tyson, more vehemently than he wanted to. Bailey was taken back but began to understand his friend's concern. He reverted to his favoured protection and remained quiet, waiting for the full story. He didn't need to wait long.

'Before I left, Festilion told me the stories that led them to fear the Changelings,' said Tyson, stopping to make sure his friend was listening. He was. 'The likes of Zebulon were the success stories but for every Zebulon who wanted to become a skin changer there were many where it did not work well.' He stopped again seeing Bailey's confusion, 'That's the translation for Malefics, the name the Pod gave to the Changelings.'

'Got it,' said Bailey, knowing this was leading up to Tyson's underlying worry.

'Remember also, Zebulon was somewhat forced to convert by the actions of his younger brother and then his parents in the interests of saving the family unit; great motivator to make it work.' Bailey was in listening mode, soaking up all this new knowledge. 'She told me the horrible deaths some of the Pod or Changelings went through, people she knew from a child. The magics twisted them and hollowed them out, until they were just shells of their former selves.'

'You're worried that may happen to you, aren't you?'

Tyson's face seemed to age and Bailey held himself back from comforting his friend, the usual man to man reservation, which was a very natural occurrence between men. If Tyson minded his friend's aloofness he didn't show it, they had known each other since young boys and been through adventures not many friends would ever experience. Now he just wanted a friend to listen.

'It is hard to describe, I feel this incredible anger inside me that, when I release it, I feel powerful and nothing can stand in my way. When it recedes I just feel empty and if it was not for Amelia I would struggle to hold it together,' said Tyson.

'What did this High Priestess say, and Zebulon for that matter?'

Tyson shrugged. 'They said they had never seen such a powerful distortion of the magics and thought my control was astounding.' He tailed off.

'I feel there is a "but" in there, mate,' said Bailey, reading his friend's expression well...he should do after so many years.

'The High Priestess said that irrespective of the control I would lose myself to the magics. There was a sense she picked up of my human genes fighting against the magics and by doing so increasing the power.' Bailey was engrossed and was hungry for more news.

'What does that all mean, surely the magics are not all bad, they helped us end the fight before?' he reasoned. Tyson leaned down and picked a white flower.

'Do you know that this is the hanish flower which makes their strong beer? They take these flowers, crush them, add water and place it through a zinithium powered press and then let it stand for over twelve months, before distilling – the flower then disintegrates. That's why it is so strong,' Tyson explained to his now increasingly confused friend. He gave a lopsided smile. 'What I am trying to say, my friend, is that this flower is no longer a flower and changes completely over time, so much that it does not exist in its previous form.' Bailey began to comprehend what Tyson was trying to get across.

'So you are worried that sometime in the future, you would cease to be and become someone who looks like you, talks like you but is not you?' said Bailey and Tyson nodded sadly. 'What you going to do then?'

'Zebulon will look after me and he has promised that he will remove the magics before the point of no return.'

'He can do that? How can you or he assess what the point of no return is?'

'I don't know, I just have to trust him.'

Bailey was still bewildered, something he was becoming used to in this topsy-turvy world he was within. 'How can Kabel and the other Zeinonians deal with the magics? Won't they also have a tipping point?'

Tyson smiled wearily. 'It's different for them, their ancestors were exposed so often to the raw power of the planet that when the Changelings imparted their so called gift they were able to place an element of control on the spread of the magics...unless...'

'...unless you are Zylar craving it all?' Bailey finished.

'Yep,' said Tyson watching a galloping mantelope across the meadow.

Bailey stood up and offering his hand to his friend said, 'Enough lazing around for you, time to get stuck in with the others.'

Tyson smiled and accepted the proffered hand and then using Bailey's counterweight sprang up from the blue grass. His then free hand clasped Bailey's other forearm causing Bailey to look quizzically at his friend.

Tyson smiled warmly. 'Bailey, please don't change,' he said, slightly choking on the words as he conveyed the years of friendship in a simple grasp and a few words.

Bailey grinned. 'Never, one freak around here is enough for anybody!'

They both laughed and went to re-join the clean-up work, when there was an almighty shout. Both whirled around to see the fleeting figure of Eva speeding towards them carrying what looked like a beef sandwich. Tyson reached out and caught the teenager by her arm.

'Let go of me,' Eva shouted, wriggling this way and that way.

'What have you been up to, Eva?' Since Tyson had seen her on that first day, he went out of his way to talk to her. The girl was trouble, with a capital T, but when he started talking to this wonderful Fathom princess who fought like a whirlwind, he was drawn to her, like a brother. A panting Hechkle joined them, slightly red-faced and pursued by an equally bemused Bronstorm.

'Thanks, Tyson, she pinched my lunch,' he said with a pained face.

'You are too fat for this,' said Eva, brandishing the large sandwich, much to Bailey's and Bronstorm's amusement.

'Now, Eva, that is not a nice thing to say, is it?' said Tyson, holding back the smile that wanted to break out on his face. Eva's face was sullen, half hidden by a mass of ringlets and scrunched up red hair.

'Hechkle needs his food; otherwise he will not have the energy to chase you, will he?' he admonished. Eva grinned wickedly and the look she gave Tyson, took his breath away - it was Evelyn, bottled up in this tightly coiled spring of a girl. His face gave the game away and Hechkle's face softened. He knew.

'Please give Hechkle his sandwich back and I will make sure someone makes a similar sandwich for you?' said Tyson.

Eva bristled at the request. 'What's the fun in that?' she snapped.

'Eva...' warned Tyson.

'Who wants his stupid sandwich anyway,' said the petulant teenager and thrust the sandwich at Hechkle, who took it, made to backhand her across the cheek and when she flinched, leaned back and laughed, earning another glare.

Bronstorm stepped forward and made an extravagant bow. 'Come on, Princess Eva, may I escort you to the Royal Sandwich Maker?'

Eva giggled, all of a sudden her rebellious streak disappearing, she had a soft spot for the quicksilver Fathom soldier and curtsying back with a now radiant smile on her face, 'Well thank you, kind gentleman, at last someone treats me how I should be treated,' she said loftily. Hechkle scowled, which caused everyone to laugh. Bronstorm offered his arm which the young girl took and they strolled away as if nothing mattered, followed by a grumbling Hechkle.

'They would do anything for that girl, wouldn't they?' said Bailey.

'Yes, as I would do.' said Tyson, his laughter dying away as old memories came back.

Bailey placed a hand on his friend's shoulder. 'Come on, why don't we grab one of those lovely sandwiches?' Tyson smiled his agreement and they set off after the disappearing tree of a man called Hechkle.

ooo

Amelia's attention was taken by Tyson and Bailey holding their deep conversation wondering what they were talking about.

'Anything the matter?' said Gemma, who was enjoying the company of the older Jaida, who had shown a mischievous side to her personality as she provided joking assessments of all key members of the Aeria Cavern. Gemma was intrigued to hear about her on and off relationship with Tate and surmised that Jaida knew exactly how to get her man.

'No, not really, they just wanted to talk,' said Amelia, knowing full well something wasn't right with Tyson…but there again that was not anything new.

'Really glad you two have got together,' said Gemma, hiding her small resentment that Tyson had not even attempted to flirt with her since their kiss on the ship… *now was not the time to be petty.*

'Thanks,' replied Amelia, not picking up the slight undertone in Gemma's voice.

Her friend studied her. Amelia was a classic beauty, an understated model, a girl who when she walked down the street all male eyes, of whatever age, would follow. *I suppose in Greek times, the phrase, "Her beauty launched a thousand ships," would apply,* Gemma supressed the irritation she was feeling, linking her friend to the mythological Greek figure Helen of Troy.

Over the years in school, Gemma always played second fiddle to Amelia for boys' attention. On Valentine's day, all the way back to when they were ten years old, Amelia would have five or six cards or chocolates left on her desk, Gemma nothing. Before the Proms, in secondary school, the boys would be nearly fighting over whom was taking her; no one asked Gemma. To protect herself from the upset of losing the attention of boys she liked to the unwitting Amelia and always pushed to the side lines, she had altered her dress sense, had tattoos, piercings, and dyed her hair.

I am the alter ego of Amelia, Gemma said to herself, half-smiling, half grimacing, and now Amelia had Tyson, hook, line and sinker, the one boy who had chased Gemma all these years and she had ignored his easy to see attempts to woo her. *I suppose I always thought I could have him anytime,* thought Gemma, as Amelia turned to Jaida to ask questions about Reinan.

Gemma knew that even with this resentment swirling round her head, she loved Amelia; you could not but love Amelia. Gemma fought against her jealousy and when looking across at Tyson, who wore a cheerful smile as he stood up and clasped the arm of her brother, she quelled her feelings for him. She was very fond off Kabel and he treated her right, *time to move on girl,* reaffirming her earlier conviction. With that definitive thought she broke into her own smile and joined the conversation of the two other girls, who were discussing how the city village had fallen those many years ago.

'So do you have any memories of what happened here?' asked Amelia, taking in her surroundings, noticing the debris slowly being removed, revealing some of the previous hidden grandeur of the city.

Jaida pulled an orange from her pocket. She had taken an instant liking to this unusual fruit which had been frozen during the journey and now introduced to the Zeinonians. She peeled the orange and rather than remove any segments, simply bit into the whole orange causing juice to run down her chin which she absently wiped away.

'I was only a child, so my memory of events is a little murky,' said Jaida, after swallowing her first bite of the juicy fruit. 'I was in the Blackstone Royal Palace asleep when I was woken by my father.' Jaida's voice trailed off just as Gemma joined the conversation. Still today, the emotion of that day when her father was severely wounded, a wound that he never really recovered from, was never far from the surface.

'Go on,' coaxed Amelia, recognising the raw emotion on the tall woman's face.

'You see it wasn't a major surprise and I guess others have told you their stories?' They all agreed it was a common topic amongst the Expeditionary Force. 'Well, as you know we had been under attack for a number of days and had retreated within the city, evacuating the outer reaches,' said Jaida, pausing as she took another bite of the orange. The others waited patiently as she chewed and then swallowed the sweet fruit.

'The Elders had already started evacuating and had used the transportation portal to send waves of inhabitants to the Aeria Cavern for safety.' Jaida appeared to drift off, letting the memory wash over her and then as if realising that she had an audience, resumed, 'The sheer numbers teleported through the portal drained the meagre amounts of zinithium and when the Pod surprised the city's defences, we were overrun. The Pod burst into our home cutting us off from our own escape tunnel and we fled, like everybody else, to the Royal Council where my father opened up the main emergency passage way leading directly to the Aeria Cavern. It was madness so many people to evacuate, scared, crying, locked in the last safe haven. Anybody outside lost to the slaughter. My father led the last stand in the Royal Council with the remaining Blackstone troops and threw back the Pod time after time.' Gemma found she was holding her breath, captivated by this beautiful young Zeinonian's story.

'Just Blackstone Troops?' asked Gemma. In answer, Jaida's pretty face twisted with hate.

'Some of the other clans yes but no Malacca soldiers – the cowards ran away to safety.' Jaida spat out. Gemma began to understand why there was so much friction between the two principal clans.

Jaida continued her story. 'We thought the last of the rear guard would escape, and then the Pod burst through the floor, tunnelling into the library. My father scooped me up and managed to make it into the passage away and I still remember the screams of the troops left behind as the Pod tore them apart.' There were tears glistening around her eyes as the memories proved too much.

Gemma placed an arm round Jaida's shoulders to comfort her.

'What's the matter?' It was Kabel, who had stood his guard down to obtain a little more freedom of movement. Not that it worked, his guard moved just another few paces away…no one was coming near their Lord Chancellor.

'Nothing,' said Gemma. Jaida wiped away the tears and angry at letting the humans see her upset, brushed aside Gemma's arm and stormed off.

'If that is nothing, hate to see what "something" is,' said an amused Kabel. Gemma proceeded to tell him the story and Kabel was unsurprised.

'There has always been resentment between our two clans. Tate explained that on that night it was the main Malacca regiment holding the line away from the city and they were surprised, surrounded and majority were killed. He was lucky to escape, thanks to his quick thinking father,' Kabel explained. 'It is time our two clans moved closer and maybe just maybe we can prevent these mistakes occurring again.'

He was interrupted by a US Marine, 'Lord Chancellor, you and Tyson are requested to attend an urgent meeting in the *Elanda*,' said the soldier, catching his breath. *Whatever it was something major was happening*, thought Kabel. He turned away from Gemma and headed off to the *Elanda* as the soldier headed off to search for Tyson. Gemma watched him go, before deciding to go and look for Jaida to see if she could do anything for her.

As Kabel strolled up the ramp leading up into the belly of the *Elanda*, relatively relaxed and if the cares of the world had been removed, he didn't know that events would move fast, events that would be hard to predict and lead the companions into danger that surpassed any they had previously encountered.

Chapter 24: Planning

Tyson was shown into the briefing room off to the side of the Command and Control Centre. He was met by a cross section of individuals who were the principal members of the new force. *Crikey, someone means business,* was the only thought it could muster. Facing him, along with Kabel, the Zeinonians were represented by the injured Safah and Quinlan, both now rested after the battle, the human contingent by General Corder, Admiral Koshkov and Walter, the Pod by Dominion and his son Wernion, and the silent figure of Zebulon stood to one side with a curious looking being. He was amused by the dazed looks on both Safah and Quinlan's faces who were stunned that they were in the spaceship that formed the basis of almost their religion. Quinlan's injury was the worst of both, a nasty cut on his forehead, now safely bandaged up. But if their expressions made him smile the looks on the Pod representatives trumped it. They were terrified and desperately trying not to show it. From their simple subterranean life in the depths of the planet they found themselves, on the orders of the High Priestess, on a dazzling spaceship, which was, until recently, part of their nightmares.

'Glad you could join us Mr Mountford,' said General Corder, laced with heavy sarcasm. He was still recovering from his injuries from the battle but that didn't deter him from baiting the troublesome boy wonder. His broken arm was in a cast that was folded across his chest and supported by a sling.

'No need for that tone, General,' said Kabel, witnessing Tyson bristle with the challenge; they still didn't see eye to eye after their disagreement on the *Elanda*. Kabel didn't see Admiral Koshkov stroke his goatee beard thoughtfully during the interplay; the Russian still had a suspicion that the American was not aligned with the objectives of the expedition.

'So what is the panic stations for?' Tyson felt belligerent, his previous calm mood, set by the presence of his friend and the influence of Eva's sparkling personality, evaporated into the abyss of life events.

'Please take a seat, Tyson,' said Kabel, the others in the room wary of triggering the volcanic nature of Tyson's rage.

'I'll stand,' was the blunt reply and Kabel didn't want to push it further. He indicated to Walter to take over the briefing and Tyson's eyes switched like a trident missile from one person to the next, his magics flaring up as he read the undercurrents and scattered thoughts in the room.

How will he react?

Why is everyone so scared of him?

Will he act first or listen?

'What is this all about?' he demanded and then the other thoughts hit him and he knew.

'My Mum, what about my Mum?' Tyson began to pulsate with his magics, those in the room stepped back. Wernion stepped forward wanting to help his new friend but his father grabbed his arm and held him back, shaking his head to deter him.

'Continue Walter?' said Kabel, as he indicated Zebulon to move closer to Tyson. Tyson saw the move and turned to Zebulon. His new protector sent messages to him telepathically to manage his breathing, retract his anger. By this time Tyson's body was nearly shaking with power and Safah and Quinlan needed to turn their heads away to shield their eyes. Then the soothing words worked and Tyson began to stabilise, until the force-field resided in just his hands. Zebulon noiselessly congratulated him on his control. All in the room breathed a sigh of relief.

Walter cleared his throat and flicked on the overhead screen, which was deployed.

'During the battle for the Aeria Cavern, Lieutenant Lavelle, picked up a signal transmitted from Skegus to Zein,' he started, nervously as usual. 'The message was sent in code so we recorded it and after the battle had ended, no little thank you to you, of course,' said Walter, pointing to Tyson proudly, who in turn ignored the compliment, gripped by the unfolding reason for the briefing.

'My mother, Walter!' said Tyson, through gritted teeth.

'With the help of Tian, from Skegus,' Walter, quickly continued, pointing to the tall golden skinned figure, who bowed. Tyson bowed back briefly, still fixing his stare on Walter, who gulped nervously. He clicked the remote he was holding in his hand.

The voice filled the room. Tyson shook as he heard his mother's voice, the desperation behind the message, and the horror of what she was witnessing. Others in the room diverted their eyes as they felt the full range of emotions play across Tyson. He didn't hear the door open or see Amelia slip in. Kabel had sent for her as soon as he had heard the tape. He knew that Tyson needed the emotional support of the one he loved. The message finished and there was an uncomfortable silence, no one wishing to say the first words.

'I want a ship.' The statement was said with no room for negotiation but General Corder took the bait.

Not a good move, thought Kabel.

'I know it is your mother, Mr Mountford, but you will not be going off on some hair-brained rescue mission, as long as I am in control of this Expeditionary Force,' said General Corder, squaring up to Tyson, across the table, still smarting at the trouble he had caused on the journey to Zein. Tyson didn't reply but leapt over the table, too fast for the guards or anyone else in the room to react, to land in front of General Corder with his face an inch away from the soldier's face.

'I can rectify that,' Tyson snarled.

It was Zebulon who intervened. Moving just a fraction slower than Tyson he was there beside them and he inserted his frame in front of Tyson, again sending calming messages to him, then Amelia was there, grabbing hold of his hand, soothing away the anger. General Corder, stepped back, pale, uncertain and a little afraid.

'You are a liability to this task force, Mr Mountford, I will have you removed to the cells.' His injuries weakened him and he cursed the fact Tyson had made him uneasy.

'Try it,' snarled back Tyson. No one was backing down.

'Gentlemen, we need to sit down, take the heat out of this discussion and think calmly how we can free Skegus, defeat Zylar and the Xonians and free any prisoners,' said Admiral Koshkov, calmly. 'Mr Mountford, we will get your mother back but we need to decide how we can do that without jeopardising hundreds, if not thousands, of lives.'

Tyson, with one last hard glance at the general, reluctantly agreed and took a seat at the table. The others in the room did the same with General Corder sitting well away from the instigator of the tension in the room. Amelia and Zebulon sat protectively next to Tyson, more to keep an eye on their friend, than to safeguard Tyson from others in the room.

Admiral Koshkov was all business, this was his strong point and he knew it. 'Is what Mr Mountford's mother is saying true about the plains, the frontal defences?'

It was the Oneerion who spoke, in a halting dreamy voice. 'We never needed to have strong defences, relying on the support of Zein for protection,' Tian said. If he was nervous no one could tell. 'They have added to the fortifications, though they are still relatively weak.'

'How many troops do they have?' This was a question from General Corder, attempting to gain back respect from those in the room. He failed. The Oneerion was just going to reply, when Kabel stepped in. 'Before you answer can you tell us how the Xonian manage the relationship between Oneerio and Skegus?'

Tian cocked his head to one side as if he were contemplating whether to answer or not, then he spoke. He spoke about the first day they came, the unnecessary killing, how they rounded up their women and children and began to execute them until all the secrets of the mining operation were provided, and then they continued anyway until even they grew tired of the screaming and stench of death. He told them how many of his friends were taken away to be experimented on, never to be seen again. There was no sound in the room as the horrors unfolded. The humans in the room feared for the six billion on Earth and what would happen to them if the Xonians defeated their armies.

Tian continued as he lay out the defences which faced them. The Xonians treated the Oneerions as slave workers in the mines of Oneerio and there were nearly fifty thousand troops guarding them with two destroyers in orbit. On Skegus their numbers were nearer one hundred thousand and in orbit there was a space cruiser that held over eighty fixed wing spacecraft.

'Can the ships in orbit of Oneerio reach Skegus in time?' asked Admiral Koshkov.

'It would take them a few days to reach an attack position on Skegus,' Tian said, 'The Xonians are an experienced warrior race and would not leave their mining operations undefended, irrespective of an attack on another outpost.'

'If we go for a full frontal attack, will that not place the hostages in danger?' said Tyson. 'Couldn't we teleport in following my mum's DNA signal, like we did at the Southern Palace?'

Tian shook his head. 'We have security protocols that prevent any teleporting outside official routes within the metro limits.'

Tyson jumped up and brought his fist down on the table. 'We can't just attack and hope they don't use the hostages as shooting practice.'

It was Kabel who calmed matters down, saying, facing Tyson, 'Tian says there is a way for us to enter the city but it is dangerous.'

'What is it?'

It was Lieutenant Morrison who replied. 'I discussed this earlier with Tian. If we climb up the mountain which overlooks the city and prevents any attack from the back, we can freefall using our specialist parachutes to land on the tallest building in the city.'

'We are not all special forces you know,' challenged Tyson. Morrison held his hand up in acknowledgment.

'Yes, I am aware and that we can deal with. Tian here says there is a secret passage that goes through the mountain into the Oneerion Royal Palace.'

'What about their Xonian space cruiser?' asked Quinlan.

'We attack the cruiser first with the *Elanda*, the *Manhattan* and the *Brooklyn* will support the initial landing on the ground with the *Elanda* joining them, after dealing with the cruiser, to off load the levitation tanks,' said Admiral Koshkov, he looked across at Quinlan. 'The Tyther clan, I believe are specialists in the technology arena?'

Quinlan's chest puffed out with pride, 'We are, although the Fathoms have always wanted our crown on that one.'

'Good, we will need scaffolding and tools to help our troops breach the outer barricades of Quentine.'

'On it.' Quinlan stood up and left the room.

'Then the only remaining business is to decide on the insertion team,' said Kabel. That discussion took some while, until they decided on a team of thirty, their task to locate the main prisoners, escort them to the Quentine transportation portal and send them to the *Elanda* portal room, before or during the main attack if possible.

Chapter 25: Uncertainty

Hechkle pushed the weights harder and harder. He felt lost, unusual for someone who rarely showed any weakness, yet recently, with the death of Princess Evelyn, doubts had crept into his thoughts. He was relatively young – still in his forties – and a strong man with yet much to do in his life, but he realised he faced an uncertain future. His doubts stemmed from how Evelyn had lost her life to Zylar post her abuse at the hands of Manek Malacca. Both Bronstorm and he had failed in their designated role, to protect the royal household. He found that the nightmares still happened every night – Evelyn's pained face clear to him. He cranked up the speed on the weights.

'Hey, take it easy Hechkle.'

Hechkle was brutally torn away from his self-pity by the beautiful voice of the girl he harboured a strong liking for. Amelia stood over him, dressed in lycra and having just finished an intense workout herself. He found he was tongue-tied. Even when she wore no make-up and was hot and sweaty from her running he could not but like her. He would never show his liking for her, as he could see she was head over heels in love with Tyson, young love, and that is how it should be.

'You look like you were trying to double your muscles and I can tell you if you do that, you will need a whole new wardrobe!' said Amelia, giggling and Hechkle laughed with her as he sat up placing the weights down safely.

Amelia was comfortable in his presence, though she wasn't so naïve not to realise he may find her physically attractive as year after year it was a natural response she grew to recognise, allowing her to steer male attention away without hurting their feelings. With Hechkle she felt an affinity, here was someone with whom she had stood back to back and fought many battles, each had saved each other's life a number of times and Amelia knew that Hechkle would protect her if it was necessary.

'You look troubled?' said Amelia, taking a swig of water from her bottle, before offering it to Hechkle, who took a long drink. 'Hope you don't mind me asking, you probably guess you are not the only one I see with that concern across their face,' she said with a wry smile. Hechkle smiled, it would be good to talk.

'I sometimes think I could have helped Evelyn more,' said Hechkle, struggling to find the words and also seeing Bronstorm, who was pounding a boxing pad, taking an interest in their discussion.

'Ahhh, yes, something which Tyson plays back and forward in his mind, until it drives him mad,' said Amelia, before sighing resignedly and taking hold of the strongly muscled hand, startling him. 'Evelyn had a destiny, and that destiny was to free her people, which she did. You played your part and how many times did you save her in Base Station Zero?'

Hechkle shrugged. 'I don't see it as saving her life, just doing my duty.'

'Well, you did save her life and ours and when you released us from our imprisonment we were able to use our freedom as a spur to defeat the Malacca clan and then Zylar.'

'I suppose you're right,' said Hechkle, seeing Bronstorm swagger across to them. Amelia followed his gaze and squeezed his hand.

'I know how much I need you and Bronstorm beside me, you both make me feel safe,' said Amelia, as she backed off and threw a pleasant smile to Bronstorm, who went the same colour as his t-shirt...red. Hechkle made a vow there and then to be there for Amelia at whatever cost.

Amelia gave Bronstorm a quick hug and then went off to the showers. Bronstorm sat next to his friend.

'That is some woman,' he said.

'Agreed,' replied Hechkle, dropping his head in thought. He then lifted his head to look at his friend and pointed at the retreating back of Amelia. 'Will you promise me that if either of us is injured or killed the other will protect that girl?'

Bronstorm grinned and held his hand out in the human way they had readily adopted.

'Sure.' They then both lapsed into silence and departed to continue their exercise, wondering at how their lives were now inexplicably tied to that of an eighteen year old girl from an alien race.

□□□

In the Captain's Quarters on *Elanda*, Prescott Corder poured himself a generous portion of Talisker's twelve year old malt whisky and made to pour another one.

'No thank you General, I never drink on the eve of an operation.'

'Very sensible, Lieutenant Morrison,' said General Corder. He twirled the spirit around in the glass before raising the glass for a sip. The liquid reacted with the back of his throat, its strong taste and alcohol content soothing his slightly sore throat, the drop of water he placed in the glass making sure that the aromas impacted the back of his throat taste buds, rather than the front of his mouth.

'What did you find out?' General Corder was referring to his request for Lieutenant Morrison to check who the American contingent could rely upon in the event of any future disagreements.

'The bulk of the civilians will stand with us as their main objective is safety and since our force is the largest that makes sense, although saying that, the Russian civilian contingent will side with Koshkov and I see his soldiers as the main threat.'

'What about the Chinese, British troops and the clans?'

'The Chinese are relatively small in number and they have no distinct relationships, the British troops are mainly English and are fans of Tyson, seeing him almost as an old fashioned hero,' said Morrison, chuckling.

'The English are always the ones easily led by fools,' said General Corder, as he took another sip. 'What about the clans?'

'There are deep divisions between the human and Zeinonian ranks and, anyway, they see Kabel and Tate as their saviours and Kron simply as a force of nature,' said Morrison, with a respectful tone, giving away his liking for the enforcer in the Malacca army.

'Now, Lieutenant, don't go liking these damn aliens too much, you know our orders.' General Corder's eyes narrowed, he could not have his American forces second-in-command going soft. No longer smiling Morrison met the rebuke impassively and with a terse agreement.

'Right, that means we can only really rely on our own troops and personnel, not something I did not anticipate.' He thought for a while and then taking a swig from his drink. 'Make sure Nicolai's troops are heavily used in the attack with the main Zeinonian army and those frightful creatures of theirs.'

'You mean the Pod?' said Morrison, trying to show no reaction to his commanding officer's disdain for his allies. He was there to take orders and put them into the action.

'Yes, never did I think I would see the day that the US Army would side with animals,' said General Corder, shaking his head. Morrison bit his tongue on retorting back and rose to leave. It was at the point of opening the door when General Corder spoke again.

'Lieutenant, if you were to return without that bastardisation of an English boy that would help us considerably,' he said, taking another a sip of his whisky, ignoring the shocked reaction of his second-in-command. Lieutenant Morrison saluted. The bile at the back of his throat captured what he felt about that last order: orders were orders but that didn't mean you needed to like them. He opened the door and went to brief his team for the insertion into Quentine.

Chapter 26: The Cabal

Cronje arranged to meet both Charles Hamilton and Victoria Kirk prior to the Inner Council meeting. Cronje had a good working relationship with both as they developed the understanding between the two races and trusted their judgement. Victoria thought it was important to discuss tactics ahead of the critical vote around the implementation of martial law in the colonies and disbanding the Malacca Clan Army. Cronje and Lord Southgate had already made the unilateral decision for Reddash to stand trial on the basis he would receive a full hearing of the events leading up to the fateful decision. Cronje was more comfortable as Lord Southgate would be on the court martial panel providing a Zeinonian balance to the proceedings.

Cronje sought time with Lord Southgate but he had not arrived from the Core. Entering the exclusive hotel that they had all agreed to meet in, he spotted Charles reading a paper in the lobby. Walking up to the table he was acutely aware of the mixture of stares, some hostile, others more appraising, interested in the confident attitude of the Zeinonian. Once seated, they were joined briefly by Victoria who then left them to discuss their wider concerns after pledging her support. She assured Cronje that they would make time to cover off their strategy prior to the vote later that day.

Charles poured a cup of coffee and then dropped in a couple of sugar cubes and then realising his companion did not have a drink. 'Coffee?'

'Yes, that would be good,' answered Cronje. Charles poured a cup for the Malacca man.

'How is Lord Southgate?' he asked. Cronje didn't want to share his disquiet over his last trip to the Core. On his travels around the bars and talking to a number of the Vets, he was pleased by the level of support pledged. Remo should be arming them now and if they could take control of the Core then the people of Earth would have to listen.

'He is fine, though Lord Fathom did not look well last time I saw him,' said Cronje and then went on to say how pale and disconnected from recent events he was. Charles expressed his concern; he liked the big hearted lord of the Fathom clan.

'Are you and Lord Southgate ready for the Council meeting this afternoon?'

'Yes, we cannot support martial law across the quadrants or the disbanding of the Malacca Clan Army, the trouble was overblown,' said Cronje as he sipped the scorching hot coffee, slightly burning his lips.

'The British government will stand with you but there are detractors who will stand against us.' Charles saw the hostility coming from some of the other tables, the news of the deaths in the Eastern Quadrant was front page news all around the world, and it conveniently did not cover the problems caused by the human elements, just the actions of the Zeinonians.

'We can prevent the motion coming into reality if you, casting Lord Blackstone's vote and Lord Southgate act together and with the British and American votes then even if the French, Russians and Chinese vote against, we can prevent the motion being carried.

Cronje and Charles both knew instinctively that they were against something much more powerful than a few misplaced riots. Charles hid his growing fear from the Malacca man, if it was not for Victoria, his own government would have forced his hand against the Zeinonians.

'I hope so Charles, I hope so.' With those words Cronje finished his coffee, shook Charles's hand and headed back to his hotel with a United States Secret Service armed guard.

The Inner Council session came quickly. Cronje met with a subdued Lord Southgate briefly and he took in the red rimmed eyes of the once irrepressible Lord. Not much was said and Cronje felt the uncertainty building up within him. Charles gave him a reassuring smile as they filtered into the room for the closed session. Cronje and Lord Southgate with a personal guard of the Southgate's clan Palace Guard. All took their place and for the next hour, cases were made for both sides of the argument. Cronje saw shock on the face of the French President when the full extent of the riots in the Eastern Quadrant was made known. The French President's demeanour seemed to cool almost immediately. Cronje saw an almost imperceptible shake of the man's head to one of his entourage; that meant one vote lost.

It came to the vote. France joined Russia and China who both predictably backed the martial law and the disbanding of the Malacca Clan Army, the Americans and British voted against the motions, leaving the two remaining votes from the Zeinonians. Cronje voted against, leaving Lord Southgate. The old wise man of Zein stood. Cronje was shocked, there was no need for speeches, they were finished – this was a straight vote.

'My esteemed colleagues, it is with a heavy heart that I stand here before you on this important vote,' began Lord Southgate. Cronje could see Charles's complete confusion. 'It has come to my attention that there are elements within the good people of Zein who are working against the ideals we set out some time ago.' Cronje felt two of the Southgate guards move behind him; he tensed, his battle-hardened antenna anticipating trouble.

'Yesterday we intercepted members of the Veteran Malacca Army, who had been approached and received orders to take over the Core.' Gasps of shock echoed around the room. Cronje's stomach dropped alarmingly, he made to move but his arms were grabbed by the two soldiers behind him. He wore no weapons; it would be futile to resist.

Voices shouted out asking for the ring leaders to be named. Lord Southgate appeared happy to accommodate.

'I am afraid the order came from one of my most trusted associates.' He turned to face Cronje, and the rest didn't hear the whisper, 'I am sorry, Cronje, they have Lucinda.' Cronje bit down on his lip trying to retain his anger. His expression softened at the old man's predicament.

'I therefore cast my vote to support the motion and in the interests of the sanctity of this chamber, I have this letter of consent, from none other than Lord Fathom, to also support it.' Lord Southgate waved the paper above his head. 'We need protection from both internal and external forces and the application of martial law and the disbanding of the Malacca Clan Army is the only way.'

Charles was stunned. It didn't feel right that his friend, such a firm believer in the Zein way, would agree to the lock down across the quadrants. He shook his head and vowed to find out what was behind this incredible decision.

Cronje was shackled and taken to the transportation portal from where he was sent back to the Core. There he was taken down to Base Station Zero, where he was shocked to see a new prison complex built and a large number of faces he knew from both the Vets and the Fathom clan. He searched for Remo but he was not there. Hope remained as long as Remo stayed free.

□□□

The Speaker made the connection for the conference call, after checking all the security protocols. One by one the members joined the call.

'Ladies and gentlemen, stage two is complete and stage three has started,' said the Speaker, 'all unruly elements are now being rounded up and incarcerated and anyone with royal magics is receiving special attention.'

'How many will die?' asked the cultured voice of an English aristocrat. The Speaker knew that any dissent needed to be dealt with quickly.

'Only those who resist will face any danger. In any war there are collateral losses. You all know me and that if anyone is to know this then my family and I are the ones.' There was no retort; they knew the Speaker's family history in conquering countries across the globe.

'My colleagues, from today, all aliens will have to wear a symbol on their clothes to ensure they are distinguishable from humans,' the Speaker spelt out. 'If any alien does not wear the symbol of the hanish flower then the punishment will be severe. Whole families of anyone connected with any misguided attempts to challenge this authority will be locked up. The martial law also allows for extreme force to be used to protect the innocent. Of course we will decide who is innocent.'

'What happens when the Expeditionary Force returns?' Someone was already thinking of the longer game. Good.

'We have that covered and that is all I want to say on that matter,' the Speaker replied. The questioner grunted in response.

'I think that concludes this call.' Victoria Kirk terminated the call with the Cabal pleased that they were in one of the strongest positions they could hope for, with hers and their forefathers probably very proud of their achievements, if they could be alive today. She picked up a glass of the finest red wine and took a sip. Shortly it would be the time to take greater control of Earth and the United Nations. Soon no one on Earth could stand against them. She raised the glass to her father, a domineering figure in a crisp uniform peering down at her from the painting above the fireplace.

'Today the United Nations, tomorrow the Earth and then the Universe,' she said triumphantly.

Chapter 27: Liberation

Tyson found Amelia struggling with her body armour, the fastenings just didn't want to wrap round her to enable her to connect the shoulder protector to the main body armour.

'Nervous?' said Tyson with a big smile on his face.

'Yes, a little.'

'Are you saying you have never dodged radar on a clandestine mission on an unknown planet in the black of night and walked down a winding tunnel after climbing a steep mountain into a hostile city?'

Amelia laughed out loud. She was pleased to see a smile on Tyson's face, realising it was the anticipation of rescuing his mother that was behind it. He helped her with her body armour and then gave her a quick kiss.

'Ugggh, please get a room you two,' said Bailey, putting on a jokey disgusted face. Just to wind him up more Tyson kissed her again.

'Hey, you two, I have not eaten yet – please,' shouted Hechkle, joining in the fun as he barged Bronstorm out of the way as they selected weapons to strap on around their waists.

Lieutenant Morrison stood back and took it all in. He knew they were simply diffusing the tension they felt but he couldn't but be impressed with the group's attitude. His disquiet of General Corder's attitude towards the group was eating away at him, through recent events they had clearly demonstrated what the combined force could provide once self-interest was pushed to one side.

Going with the group was Amelia with Gemma staying behind with Kabel. Both he guessed had never experienced real combat training. Knowing this he was even more impressed after he saw them practising their accuracy and fitness, especially Gemma with the support of her martial arts background. He knew Hechkle and Bronstorm were well trained and seasoned fighters; they even bettered some of the Navy SEAL officers in the duals, no small comparison; SEAL soldiers represented soldiers at the top of their game who could operate in any environment across sea, air or land, from which the acronym was derived from. Tyson and Bailey, you could see were the best of friends and when Tyson wasn't causing issues at strategic meetings with his out of control temper, he came across as a straightforward guy. No Morrison's concern was the statuesque Changelings. Zebulon did not take part in any training and simply stood to one side along with four of his men. They made him nervous and he just could not read them.

He looked across at his men, half SEALs and the rest US Marines, all tough and used to action with him countless times. In total, the party numbered thirty. He wasn't a fan of taking civilians on such a difficult mission but General Corder was adamant. Morrison knew he just wanted Tyson away from the main action.

Kabel came by with Tate and Belina, partially to see Gemma. He didn't want her to fight but Gemma was beginning to feel left out of things. Ever since the battle for the Aeria Cavern she was not party to the strategy meetings and due to the request of Tate and Zebulon, found she was pushed to one side. Kabel, to his credit, didn't treat her any differently and Gemma found she was looking for him more and more through the busy days. Gemma had fully moved on from her feelings for Tyson. She could see how much he loved Amelia and she knew acceptance of the situation was the only healthy course.

Kabel and Tate spoke to everyone, wishing them luck. Belina went to talk to Bailey.

'Hey, be careful out there,' said Belina.

'I will, what are you planning?'

'We are going to knock hard on the front door.'

Bailey laughed. 'You keep safe,' he said, reaching up and brushing a loose strand of hair from her face. Belina welcomed the gesture, pleased that Bailey accepted the situation with her and Tate. They parted and went their separate ways.

Kabel approached Tyson and held out his hand, his eyes riveting him to the floor. Tyson smiled and took the hand, at which point much to Tyson's surprise, Kabel pulled him so his face was just inches away. The others paused in their goodbyes and Bailey went to separate them but was stopped by Zebulon, by placing a hand across his chest.

'Leave them,' said Zebulon, interested in what was going to happen.

Bailey stopped, ready to jump in if needed.

'Brother, I didn't know you cared?' said Tyson, amused by the action. 'Glad you brushed your teeth.'

Kabel didn't smile. 'Bring back my Delilah, kill anyone who gets in the way,' he said through gritted teeth, the leader's civilised veneer evaporating. Tyson stopped smiling. He knew this feeling.

'I will Kabel, I will.'

Kabel struggled to hold back his anger and it was Tyson who, with his other hand, clasped his brother's arm.

'Kabel, don't worry, no one is going to get in the way of getting my mother and your sister, and if they do then they will regret it.' Tyson matched Kabel's steely determined look.

'Good,' said Kabel and using the same hand that grasped Tyson to him the first time, he pushed his brother away from him. As he turned away from Tyson his smile returned and the others only saw the commanding presence of their Lord Chancellor. No one was fooled for an instant that what they had witnessed was naked aggression. Irrespective to what they had just seen, they fully supported Kabel.

'Bring the prisoners back to me at all costs,' said Kabel, to the wider group, 'I have all my faith in you that you will.'

Wernion observed the interchange and caught Tyson's eye. They swapped good luck messages. Wernion would be leading the Pod contingent with his father, Dominion, on the attack of the front gates. Since the events on Zein, Tyson had spent considerable time in the gentle giant's company. Zebulon had also taken the young Pod to one side and provided some guidance on how to prevent the magics taking hold of him and convincing him that he was best keeping to his present body rather than turning into a Changeling. Wernion had agreed not to develop his magics further, much to his father's relief.

Soon the group for the insertion was safely on board a transporter that would travel to the other side of the mountain in the deep of the night. They would fly under the Xonian radar and the transporter would drop them half way up the steep climb on a natural plateau of which Tian was providing the coordinates for.

The transporter lifted off and the powerful zinithium engines made short work of what would be a much longer journey for any shuttle from Earth over a similar distance. They approached from the north of Quentine, hidden behind the imposing mountain behind the wondrous city.

The coordinates guided the pilot to the plateau where it landing safely. The insertion team exited the transporter, which in turn set off for its return trip, leaving the members watching the departing ship with just a little trepidation.

Morrison organised the scouts to go ahead of the main group and they headed off on the still steep climb. The air was cold and biting, they needed to move fast as the main attack was to be launched at dawn, when the sun would be in the defenders eyes, adding to the advantage of the attacking army.

Tian set off with the scouts looking for the entrance to a tunnel, which his ancestors had built to act as a doorway to the top of the mountain in the time where they had made animal sacrifices to their gods. The entrance led to a set of stairs that wound down the mountain. It was no longer used and only senior members of the royal household knew of its existence. The majority of the group would use this entrance to enter the Oneerion Royal Palace, secure the prisoners when the main attack commenced on the Skegus Plain and then escape via the attached Transportation building.

Morrison with four SEALS would skydive onto the top of the tall building, following the instructions of the message left by Leila, directing them to the communications room which needed to be disabled to prevent any outside chance of Xonian reinforcements from Oneerio. They would then meet up with the rest of the force.

Tian and the scouts made quick work of the climb and it wasn't long before they reached a smaller plateau which had a stone altar in the centre, once part of an important tradition where the great and good of Oneerion society would pay homage to the gods, but now covered in thick moss with cracks tapering up the sides. Tian ignored the altar and went straight to a pair of doors hewn into the cliff face, his long fingers feeling carefully around the centre of the doors. They found barely-there finger holds and he pressed hard with all his fingers and the stone block doors rumbled open just as the rest of the group made the second plateau.

Tyson, who was leading the following group, keen to get to his mother and Delilah, took one look and without hesitation made for the door.

'Tyson wait,' said Morrison, but Tyson wasn't listening. He brushed past the two soldiers with Tian and started down the winding steps. Amelia and Bailey didn't wait either and hurried past the protesting man mountain of a US Marine, followed by Hechkle and Bronstorm. Zebulon and the four Changelings brought up the rear.

Morrison, frustrated told his remaining men to follow them. He and his four men prepared for the sky dive onto the Oneerion Palace. He left two men on the door as he didn't want the only manner of escape to be lost and once the fight was over they would be radioed to join them in the city.

Tyson was running energetically down the steps, which were many and seemed to go on for ever, curving this way and that, so that even the fittest of the soldiers found they were breathing hard. It was not so much the steps but the lack of fresh air, the limited air coming from ancient pipes hammered into the sides of the mountain. The light was poor with only flickering neon lights that had seen better days providing a hazy atmosphere.

Just when they thought it would never end the steps and wall hewn out of the stone turned into smooth marble.

The stairs also turned into a more manageable width; they were entering the section of the tunnel that was part of the Oneerion Royal Palace.

Tyson saw a pair of doors ahead of them and he reached out to pull one of the handles, when the big hand of Tian stopped him.

'No my friend. Just in case our enemies found this passageway only a member of the royal household can open these doors. If anyone else tries to open the doors they are programmed to bring the roof tumbling down on you.' He pointed to the roof and Tyson saw the beams holding back what must be a ton of boulders. He grinned ruefully and extravagantly waved the Oneerion ahead of him. Amelia smiled despite the tension she was feeling.

Tian's hands ran across a panel near the door and a number of lights came on and then faded, He then reached out to one of the handles and opened carefully. Those that had heard about the booby-trap, kept their gaze on the boulders above their heads. No movement. You could hear some sighs of relief.

The room they entered was dark and their footsteps echoed on the floor, as they all filed into the room. Tian left them and walked across to the far wall. He switched on the lights and all were taken aback by what they saw. They were in what must have been the store room, but what a store room. They were standing on a white marble floor that matched the walls and high ceilings. On each wall there were floor to ceiling racks of food of every conceivable type. Hechkle took charge.

'We stay here until the attack commences like we agreed,' said Hechkle, directing the comments to Tyson who was pacing, glancing at the door that would take them up into the main palace, and to the main floors where they could rescue the prisoners.

Tyson glared at Hechkle but he had agreed to the plan, seeing the sense of drawing away troops from the Oneerion Royal Palace to meet the threat from the Skegus Plain. That didn't make it easier because somewhere above him was his mother.

ㅁㅁㅁ

General Corder barked orders as *Elanda* came out of its hyper-drive. First the release of the transporter to Skegus and second, attend to the enemy.

They were in sight of the large Xonian battleship and even as his orders were given the enemy was launching its fighters…but they were ready.

The Cobras, led by Kabel and Lambert, fought with skill and precision as multiple dog-fights between opposite fighters erupted. Soon space was full of a choreography of explosions and colour as missiles found their targets. Kabel was calm and collected as he found the weakness at the base of the enemy fighters, which all the pilots, now found with impunity.

Enjoying yourself? he asked Gemma as his zinithium guided missiles tore apart the plane in front of him, the screams of the occupants echoing in his mind.

Yep very therapeutic, was Gemma's reply as she manned one of the guns on the top deck of the *Elanda*, targeting a fighter that had broken through the Cobras.

General Corder leaned across the command desk, glad to be in the thick of the fighting, his disagreements with Admiral Koshkov pushed to the back of his mind. 'Hit the main ship with two missiles,' he ordered the young gunner. Two bright blue missiles screamed towards the hull of the large battleship, crashing into the force-field. The enemy force-field did its job but the power behind the missiles was immense and the field flickered with protest.

On the Xonian battleship, Prince Jernli, who had left Yisli in charge of the city defence, a decision which he was now regretting was flung across the Commander's control tower, the Commander a particularly large Xonian was himself, unceremoniously dumped on his backside.

'Get me out of here now!' yelled Prince Jernli.

'But your Royal Highness, we will lose all our fighters,' protested the commander of the ship.

'Leave them; just get me out of here!' Prince Jernli's face was an angry purple, the blue scales turning an unhealthy colour. The commander knew when to cut his losses, it had taken him many termins to obtain this post and to throw it all away was not in his career plan. He had not anticipated such a ferocious attack.

He shouted orders at his helmsman and the coordinates for a hyper-jump were made. The Venings on-board computers picked up the signal and panic ensued. Some fighters near the main battleship made it back but the vast majority were too busy escaping the wrath of the Cobras or were too far away from the docking bays. When the battleship sped away, the remaining fighters were either blown away or transmitted surrender signals. In total, ten of the enemy aircraft were captured by the Elanda and their crews imprisoned. The others were all destroyed.

General Corder sat back in his chair, satisfied. They had lost two fighters, no damage and the battleship had fled. 'Over to you, Nicolai,' he said to no one in particular, watching the two destroyers entering the atmosphere to pave the way for the ground attack. The plan was for the destroyers to knock out the main guns on the battlements and soften up the front defences and then the *Elanda* would land on the plain.

The had listened hard to Leila's intelligence and that had led to the attack on the battleship first before upsetting the odds by not just using the destroyers but landing the *Elanda* on the plain, thereby enabling them to use the levitation tanks to support the infantry. From what Leila was saying this would be a surprise to their hosts.

General Corder was content and full of confidence. His plan was challenged of course by the more careful Nicolai: however, the rest of the War Committee had agreed with the plan and the veteran Russian admiral had walked away muttering under his breath.

Admiral Koshkov was on the bridge of the *Manhattan* as they burst through the atmosphere of the planet. He may have disagreed with the plan, but that would not prevent him from carrying out his duties.

'Corporal, ready our guns, remember to only fix on the outside battlements and not inside,' he ordered. The corporal, a member of the Red Army, flicked his hands over the controls and switched on the main missile and photon machine guns at the front of the destroyer. The destroyer did not have the large Bofor type guns across its spine and protecting its flanks, relying on the plentiful photon machine guns embedded in the front of the ship. This gave it much more speed and agility but made it rely on its defensive shields.

The two destroyers flew out of the sky with the sun at their back dazzling the enemy in the early sunrise. They both released their loads at preconceived programmed targets provide by Tian. When they hit, the sky was lit up like the humans' Bonfire Night. Another order was given and a second round of explosives was launched. The impact was immense. Plumes of stones and battlements were thrown into the air. Bodies of Xonian troops lay scattered across the front of the city.

Admiral Koshkov monitored the screens in front of him and gave a satisfied grunt. 'Inform General Corder he can bring in the *Elanda* to offload the tanks.' General Corder received the news well and he readied the crew for the entry of the huge ship into the planet's atmosphere.'

The *Elanda* swooped down, more like an albatross than a hawk, its sheer size making any quick manoeuvres difficult. The two destroyers defended the perimeter by squeezing off photon machine guns further punishing the front battlements bringing much death.

When the *Elanda* landed, Kabel was on the Embankment Floor with Gemma, Tate and Belina preparing the tank crews so that they were ready for the invasion and capture of Quentine. Spirits were high. The twenty-five tanks would be supported by thirty thousand land troops, mainly Russian, US and Malacca troops. The Pod had contributed two thousand male warriors to the attack in a display of solidarity. The tanks would be split into five columns with five tanks in each column each supported by six thousand troops, with the Pod part of the last column, as they were better suited to the close urban, street-by-street fighting within the city's walls.

Kabel was entranced when the tanks were unloading down the huge ramp, marvelling at how they glided across the floor, with the blue tinge of the zinithium power crystals faintly reflecting back off the surface. Sean strutted past him with his confident gait, flashing a "what do I care" smile, he was going to drive one of the tanks in the front column.

'Hey Sean, don't get too far ahead of the other columns,' said Kabel, in warning. The other columns would stagger their attack to reduce targets for the remaining Xonian gunners. They may have destroyed most of the fixed gun towers but you could not right off a Xonian army which had conquered most of the Universe.

'Stop worrying Kabel, when have I ever been overly ambitious?' was the Scot's underplayed response, making Kabel laugh.

'What are you two smirking about?' It was Gemma, who wrapped one of her arms around Kabel, still thrilled by the fight they had just been part of.

'Oh, nothing, just your beloved acting like some over worried parent,' said Sean.

'He does have that tendency,' said Gemma, landing a playful punch on Kabel's shoulder.

Sean gave a quick wave and then climbed into the lead tank. Soon his column was on the move with the other columns setting off at two minute intervals. They had landed some two miles away but that distance was quickly eaten up by the levitation tanks, noiseless except for the slight hum of the zinithium crystals and the crunch of the marching boots of the soldiers. In Sean's columns there were elements of the Scots Guards including a few pipers playing their battle song and the Russian Federation Army.

General Corder gave his orders. He told his support team to bring up the front of the city on his screen and he saw the destruction the four missiles and the photon machine gunfire had brought.

'Admiral Koshkov, any signs of a counterattack from the Xonians?'

'No, General Corder, small arms fire has been seen with a small element of mobile photon machine guns, nothing which our forces can't handle.'

'Good, good.' General Corder again sat back in his command seat and waited.

Kabel and Gemma were in the second column and Tate and Belina in the third. Kabel was looking through his view finder as they approached the city, keeping watch for any trouble.

Then column one disappeared, all five tanks and the six thousand support soldiers. They disappeared into a massive collapsing pit, as if by magic, but in fact controlled by the grinning Yisli in a reinforced part of the city wall, the wall which Leila had stopped to watch the Oneerions working on.

Kabel didn't hesitate, appalled by the loss of life. 'Retreat, all retreat, it's a trap!' he yelled into his intercom. His driver flung his tank around, just as Yisli set the next booby-trap off. Hugh sheets of explosive ripped the second column apart, three of the tanks behind Kabel exploded, but somehow the quick action of his driver had saved them. Soldiers lay screaming where the hideous explosive mines that flung out lethal shards of metal had exploded, sending a wall of death scything through the soldier ranks.

On the *Elanda*, General Corder looked at the scenes in horror. He was just weighing up his options when an audible gasp came from Corporal Batten.

'Sir the radar has picked up five ships.'

'What do you mean…why didn't you pick them up before?' said an exasperated General Corder.

'I-I-don't know, Sir, the ships must have used the planet to shield the ships from our radar,' said the equally confused soldier.

'Lift off now.'

'But, Sir, the men on the ground.'

'Number one priority is to safeguard this ship, Corporal, now get us out of here and place us on battle stations,' said General Corder.

'Aye, aye, Sir.' Corporal Batten pressed the necessary controls and switched on the battle stations. The ramp that had enabled the offloading of the levitation tanks slowly closed as maintenance men ran quickly back on board. Not all made it. The commanding hulk of the *Elanda* rose slowly into the sky.

We are sitting ducks, thought General Corder. 'Patch me into Admiral Koshkov and Colonel Jeffries,' he said. Colonel Jeffries was the high ranking senior office in command of the *Brooklyn*. This took mere seconds. The two officers filled the second and third screen, the nightmare of the massacre on the Skegus Plain on the first screen. The admiral's face, though resolute, showed the strain of seeing his men, which made up the bulk of the force, at the mercy of booby-traps and the remaining guns of the Xonians. He hated being right.

'Admiral Koshkov and Colonel Jeffries, we have five ships on our radar, take both destroyers and engage. You need to give us time to reach orbit before we can use our main weapon,' said General Corder, causing those in Command and Control Centre to look round in shock. They knew what this meant. The three commanders stared silently at each other for a matter of seconds but these where seasoned soldiers, sometimes you made decisions which were unpalatable, though necessary.

'We will be leaving the soldiers on the ground with no air cover?' said Admiral Koshkov.

'Once we are in orbit I will send Cobras to support them, Admiral,' replied General Corder. His Russian counterpart, inclined his head to acknowledge the promise and order. Without further hesitation he and Colonel Jeffries, wheeled the *Manhattan* and *Brooklyn* around and being more agile than the *Elanda* and already in flight, they shot off to meet the incoming surprise attack.

On the ground the slaughter continued.

Chapter 28: Prisoners

Morrison and his men glided down to land on the top of the impressive Oneerion Royal Palace. The sun was just beginning to sweep across the plain and as Morrison skilfully manoeuvred his sky diving parachute, he scanned the targeted building.

The Oneerion Royal Palace was one of the tallest, most striking buildings you could ever see with its gold leaf finish catching the early morning light easily, almost caressing it in the wind. The team landed and efficiently detached themselves from the state of the art parachutes, moving swiftly to the access door and silently making their way down to the communication room. There was one guard on the door and he was quickly dealt with and when they burst into the room the enemy soldiers stood little chance. They placed charges all around the key terminals as outlined by Tian, setting the timers to go off to synchronise with the attack. A pleased Morrison then took his team down to the floor where the prisoners should be and waited. It was now just a matter of patience.

□□□

Leila woke up to find that Zylar was already awake and up, in fact she had noticed that the amount of time he slept was becoming shorter and shorter, it was as if he no longer needed the rest that sleep brought to function. She slipped on a dressing robe and walked into the main lounge, where she was surprised to see two Ilsid by the door.

'Good morning, my dear.' Zylar's voice still made her shudder. Flat. Emotionless. Haunting. Leila knew that she needed to keep him on her side and went to him, slipping an arm through his arm as he gazed out of the window at the dazzling sun rise.

Then she saw it. A ship, a monstrous ship with two smaller ships hovering over it, like over-worried parents witnessing their child taking its first steps. She sneaked a quick glance at Zylar's face as a thrill spread through her body. They had received the message!

'Looks like your friends have arrived and…,' he sniffed the air as if he smelt an exotic perfume, '…and I feel the presence of strong magics.' Again her heart gave a leap.

Tyson…Tyson is here.

Hi, Mum. Leila nearly stopped breathing; quickly glancing up at the impassive Zylar who showed no indication he heard her son's words. She was assailed with multiple feelings. Fear and hope all in one thought, Zylar must not know he is here.

In the Oneerion Royal Palace basement Tyson had sent out tendrils of his magic searching for his mother. The strength of feeling surging through Leila when she saw the ships had made the connection easier, although he would have found her soon anyway.

Son, it is so nice to hear your voice. Leila tried to keep it together but was struggling.

Are you okay? Are you injured?

I am fine, don't worry, I am with Zylar on the eighteenth floor.

I am coming to get you.

Leila struggled with her emotions and then in front of the gates on the Skegus Plain she saw the ground collapse beneath the soldiers and tanks and then the explosions rip apart another column. She gasped in shock and raised her hand to her mouth. Her eyes watched the large ship as it began to lift off and in the distance specks of other ships could be seen.

'Thank you for inviting the Blackstones into my trap,' said Zylar coldly.

'W-w-what?' said Leila.

'You don't think I fell for that seduction game, do you?' said a sneering Zylar. Leila's heart dropped. She had been led into setting a trap that her rescuers had conveniently triggered.

'The Skegus Plan is mined and booby-trapped and soon the Xonian armada will be destroying the once mighty *Elanda*, all because you thought you could play me.' The sneer had gone, replaced by the cold heartlessness that she was used to.

'By the way, if you are hoping that lumbering ox of a Malacca man is going to help you, think again. I had him served up at the Xonian's dinner table last night,' said Zylar, with some misplaced amusement. 'They found him more than enough to satisfy their appetite.'

Leila wrenched her arm from his grip and gulped strongly to keep down the vomit that she felt rising through her stomach and up into her throat.

'If you think you are going to be rescued, don't bank on it.' I have eighty thousand Ilsid warriors from all the races and the Xonians have also provided me ten of their destroyers to travel to Earth and lay the groundwork for the invasion.'

Leila was numb with shock.

'Yes, my dear, thanks for warming my bed but you have just signed the death warrant of over six billion people. I couldn't have asked for more.'

That was enough, Leila ran through the bedroom and into the bathroom to retch into the toilet.

What had she done?

Tyson in the basement monitored the horror of what was happening from others' thoughts and the blue force-field sprang into life, the rage rising in his body, his face a cold mask but hiding every unpleasant emotion he could suppress. Amelia immediately saw the change, as did Bailey.

'What has happened Tyson?'

'Enough waiting, we are going, the attack was a trap and our forces are being killed for fun.' There was increased determination on the seasoned soldiers' faces; they had many friends in the ranks of the attacking forces.

'What do we do?' It was Bronstorm, his face white from the picture that Tyson had painted, shaking him. Tyson knew that meant nothing, Bronstorm would not hold back.

'We follow our plan and rescue the human prisoners,' said Tyson. There were no dissenters, with Zebulon rising from where he had rested, along with his personal guard.

Tyson led the team from the basement, and onto the ground floor. There were not many guards, with the majority on the front battlements. The few which were on guard, Tyson killed with precision.

'Take us to the prisoners, Tian,' he asked. Tian pointed to a door off the main impressive hallway, which was studded with some of the rarest jewels in the Universe and had the most exquisite floor and ceiling structure.

They headed for the door to the passage when a patrol of Xonian warriors halted their progress.

'We will handle them, Tyson, just go,' said Hechkle, gruffly. Bronstorm moved to the warrior's side and a number of the other soldiers peeled off to support. Tyson acknowledged the gesture and the rest of the group continued on their way.

The patrol swelled as other Xonian soldiers seemed to materialise from the other rooms. Hechkle and Bronstorm did what their training taught them, they charged, taking the Xonians by surprise. Soon, with the small number of US Marines, they were deep in a struggle for survival.

The rest of the group made their way to a lift via a discreet doorway, though it didn't look like a lift, simply a platform that was on the outside of the building, covered by a glass front. Tyson thought the lift would send them hurtling up but nothing like that happened. Tian entered some numbers and the usual teleporting pull experience engulfed them. Before they knew it they were on the eighteenth floor.

Tyson launched himself out of the lift, straight into four Xonians. Before any could react, two were dead, then the other two were taken out by Bailey and Amelia.

There she was!

Leila, now dressed, was under the escort of two Ilsid soldiers. Zylar was in front of her when Tyson came hurtling around the corner.

'You,' Zylar snarled.

Tyson didn't reply, sending his razor-sharp seckle directly at Zylar's head. He easily ducked and fired a number of shots, two which caught the soldiers flanking Tyson. Both fell to the floor dead.

Bailey let go two shots, which the two Ilsid fended off. Zylar ordered them forward and he grabbed Leila's wrist and dragged her to one of the lifts – similar to the one they had travelled up in.

Zylar pulled her onto the platform, leaving the two Ilsid to defend, closed the door and set the co-ordinates to match with the floor where you could access the Transportation building.

Tyson ran forward, raising his right hand seckle to block an attack by one of his adversaries and then plunged his second seckle into the Ilsid's side, killing him. No sooner had he completed this move, his right seckle had cut the throat of the second Ilsid.

The rage was bubbling within him and he let out a great roar when, having flung the lift door open, he found his mother and Zylar gone.

He turned to Tian. 'Do you know the coordinates to where they have just gone?'

'They can only go to the floors programmed in the lift. You can track the last floor where the teleport occurred.' The Oneerion didn't wait for the order; he knew it would come and looked at the readings, 'Its level two, which takes you onto the connecting corridor to the Transportation building.'

'Right, we need to go after them,' said an increasingly angry Tyson.

'Tyson, what about the prisoners and the Oneerion royal family? We have to rescue them?' said Amelia, holding Tyson back. His mind was not on the other prisoners or royal family.

'Tyson, you promised Kabel…Delilah?' was Amelia's questioning approach. The soft play of her words breached the fog of anger and he remembered back to his promise to Kabel. He made a split second decision.

'Okay. Bailey and Amelia you go with the rest of the troops and free the prisoners and take them to the level two floor. Zebulon, you and your guard come with me. Tian, can you key in the coordinates to the floor attached to the Transportation building?'

'Yes, I can also collect and take King Yi and his family to a safe haven, once I send the prisoners down to the level two floor,' said Tian. 'He is unlikely to be guarded but I may need a weapon,' he asked. One of the soldiers passed him a spare gun.

'We shouldn't split, Tyson,' Amelia pleaded.

'I am going with you, mate,' said Bailey.

Tyson shook his head as he climbed into the lift with the Changelings. 'Look after my girl, Bailey,' said Tyson, firmly and Bailey relented, remembering his vow to his friend. Within seconds Tyson had teleported to the coordinates Tian had programmed. The rest of the group, led by Bailey, made their way to the floor above.

Bailey climbed up the stairs with two of the remaining soldiers beside him, and as they turned the second corner they came face to face with a gun. The shock was only fleeting as the resolute features of Lieutenant Morrison were behind the gun, which dropped to his side once he saw who it was. His eyes scanned the group.

'Where is Tyson?' Bailey brought him up-to-date with what was happening with the attack. Morrison shook his head at the news, and then quickly made up his own mind.

'We continue as planned. There are only two men guarding the human prisoners, with another six soldiers down the hall in the guardroom.' He split the team up, with Bailey and Amelia attacking the two men guarding the prisoner quarters and Morrison leading the attack on the guardroom.

'Go,' he directed. They went round the last corner at a run. Bailey took aim and took one of the guards out immediately, the other managed to return fire, before one of the SEALs caught him with a fatal shot. Morrison went pelting past the door and crashed into the guards piling out of the room at the end of the corridor. He took two men down and then the rest of soldiers were on top of him and he reverted to his knife, which he used to good effect.

Bailey blasted the prison door open and raced in, only to be met with a wall of screams that stopped him in his tracks. There were many women in the room and he noticed children. *Children? What?*

'Delilah, is Delilah here?' said Amelia, who stepped from behind Bailey into the room and dropped her weapon to her side, Bailey did the same.

'Bailey, Amelia, is that you,' said Delilah. Both Bailey and Amelia were dumbstruck. They had not seen Delilah since the battle at the Southern Palace but the change in just under a year was amazing. They faced a beautiful young woman, her face framed in silky black hair, a face so open, vulnerable and pure that Amelia was initially stunned. She heard Bailey suck in his breath; it seemed it just wasn't her who was struck by the change in Delilah who ran to her and gave her a big hug. Amelia returned the hug and then gently pushed her away.

'Hi, Delilah, we are here to take you to Kabel.' The young woman's face lit up at Kabel's name and Bailey found a little jealously creep into him, until he realised it was more a sisterly fondness that he saw.

'Kabel? Where is he? Is he alright?' said Delilah.

'Yes, looking forward to seeing you again. Now can you all pack up, we need to get out of here as soon as possible.'

The prisoners didn't need to be asked twice. There was a mad scramble as they packed a few clothes and items. Amelia noticed the three young toddlers and like Bailey was surprised. Delilah saw the look and shook her head, making Amelia hold asking the questions she wanted and not make any comments. There would be a time to catch up later.

'I'll take that,' said Bailey, removing the bag from Delilah's hand. Delilah gave him a winning shy smile and Amelia, watching the exchange, missed nothing.

They all exited the room. Morrison and the other soldiers joined them after overpowering all the other guards and Tian took the group to the nearest lift to teleport them down in two groups. Tian waited until all had teleported safely before pulling out the unfamiliar gun from his waistband and travelling down to where his King and family were locked away.

Chapter 29:
Mass Destruction

The photon missiles crashed into the *Manhattan* sending Admiral Koshkov crashing into one of the consoles. The battleship, like the *Brooklyn*, was buffeted by the intense firepower of the new ships, still some distance away and still issuing lethal payloads.

Trap. How could they be so gullible?

'Return fire,' he ordered.

'Sir, we will weaken the force-field, not sure the ship can take the hits,' said the soldier manning the controls in front of him. Admiral Koshkov steadied his body that swayed with the multiple hits, he knew it was the strong zinithium barrier that had saved them.

'Soldier, if we don't attack at some point, the force-field will fail. We attack.' The soldier saluted and returned to his controls just as another two missiles slammed into the ship.

'Patch me into the *Brooklyn* and *Elanda*.' He was joined by Colonel Jeffries and General Corder, their faces on the split screen.

'We need to attack or they will pummel us to death,' said Admiral Koshkov.

'I have a plan,' said General Corder and then hesitated knowing what the reaction would be to his crew on the deck before continuing, 'We need to use the atomics.'

The cautious Admiral Koshkov sucked in his checks and the usual unflappable Jefferies paled, although they were expecting the order. The crew on the three Command and Control decks held their breath.

'We have not tested since injecting the zinithium to the bombs,' said Admiral Koshkov. Those near General Corder carried on their tasks to take the *Elanda* into orbit to face the incoming threat, with one ear on the conversation. General Corder knew this and he also knew his office meant that he had to make the hard calls.

'We have no choice. When those ships close in on our position they will have the strategic advantage.'

Admiral Koshkov, even after their recent disagreements, couldn't help but admire the American and helped him make a swift decision.

'We will make you some time.' The conversation was at an end and the two officers signed off, gave the necessary orders and the *Manhattan* and *Brooklyn* closed in on a headlong collision with the enemy attack. General Corder ordered ten of the Cobras to launch to protect the troops left behind.

On the ground, Kabel had made contact with Tate in the column behind them. Out of the twenty five levitation tanks, only twelve remained, with the Venings sent from the Xonian star cruiser, strafing the troops and tanks creating a field of death.

Kabel calculated that before the trap had been sprung they were in range of the heavily damaged city wall which meant that with a concerted push they could threaten the city and nullify the Venings' attack. They would not fire into their own troops surely?

'Kabel, the gates!' It was Tate over the communication link. Kabel twisted his head to look out of the tank vision field and saw streaming out of the gates, around twenty thousand Xonians, with the objective to crush the remnants of the force sent to defeat them.

'Tate, pull together the troops, we need to head on a direct collision.'

'That's suicide, we can't fight off the Venings and defeat this army,' said a disbelieving Tate. Beside him Belina was shaking her head also in disbelief. Kabel hurriedly explained his idea and Tate reluctantly saw the logic. They fed the commands through the remaining officers of the depleted troops and soon the twelve remaining tanks and the soldiers raced towards the advancing Xonians, skirting the hell holes that had consumed their fellow soldiers.

The Venings continued their attacks and the Expeditionary Force fought back. They had lost nearly three full columns but these were all battle hardened veterans and they pressed on with grim determination as the high velocity bullets from the Venings tore into them.

Kabel's tank took a massive hit and slewed to one side, crashing into the ground. Kabel and Gemma were thrown against their cockpit strappings. The driver in front of them smashed his face against the console, stunning him instantly. The soldier behind them, loading the gun, had his neck broken when his body was flung to one side.

Smoke filled the tank; the turret had all but been blown off. Kabel's head was spinning, then he felt an arm around him, releasing the straps, and, half aware stood up, still dizzy.

'Careful now Lord Chancellor, take it easy,' said Kron, his good arm wrapped round Kabel. Kron pulled him out of the tank where other members of the Malacca clan where on hand to help.

'Gemma?' said Kabel, his voice barely audible.

'We got her, she is fine and we have the driver as well,' said Kron.

'The Venings?' said Kabel, finding his voice.

'No worry, Lord Chancellor, the *Elanda* has sent help,' reassured Kron, his face covered in blood from a nasty cut on his forehead.

Kabel looked up into the sky and saw a squadron of Cobras engaging the enemy ships. The Venings had pulled away from targeting the troops on the ground and were busy protecting their own lives…and losing.

'Right, Kron, get the troops ready to engage the enemy,' said Kabel, the buzz in his head receding.

'Ready, Sir,' said Kron, with a look that made Kabel glad he was on his side. Kabel looked around him and the surviving American, Russian and Malacca troops were all positioned ready to fire a devastating round into the advancing Xonians who seeing their ships blasted apart, were slowing down their advance.

Too late.

The thousands of Expeditionary Force soldiers sent a wall of steel and photon bullets into the defending ranks, slicing through the approaching troops like a knife through butter. The alien ranks stuttered and then, when the next round tore into them and they saw the Cobras turn their machine guns onto them, began to flee back to the city. The Pod were only lightly scathed as the enemy had targeted the weaponised element of the attack. Dominion was now in full battle cry and his troops charged after the retreating backs of the defenders.

Above them there were almighty flashes, that had all the soldiers and residents of the city look into the sky. The two expeditionary battleships were in heavy engagement, taking huge hits. The *Elanda* was behind them and suddenly the two destroyers parted, allowing the *Elanda* to launch its deadly cargo.

The nuclear bombs sped from the photon missile tubes in the *Elanda*, already fifty times more powerful than those launched against Nagasaki and Hiroshima, now enhanced by zinithium injected into the core, to make them another hundred times more powerful. Corder, in the *Elanda*, knew that even one of these bombs could demolish a small planet by destroying its whole environmental system.

On the Xonian star cruiser, Prince Jernli, who had agreed to the previous false retreat to set up the trap thought out by Zylar, was just considering what demands he could make of his father after such a victory. He had initially been annoyed when he found the whole meeting in Zylar's room was a ruse to snare some human into unwittingly helping them spring the trap. He calmed down when they told him that it needed to be as believable as possible if the girl was going to fall for the entrapment.

'Your Highness, two missiles locked on,' shouted one of his officers manning the radar.

'Let them try, we will swat them away and destroy every one of them,' said Prince Jernli.

The missiles hit the shields. The shields had no answer to the power of the missiles and evaporated on impact, the rolling thunder of the blast ripping into the side of the star cruiser…Prince Jernli did not have time for last thoughts as he, his men and his ship imploded in a powerful flash and ceased to be.

The other destroyers saw the destruction of their command ship and fled, leaving the crews in the damaged *Manhattan* and *Brooklyn* cheering madly.

On the ground the troops, who had to turn their heads to one side at the intensity of the flash, raised a throaty cheer, still smarting from the recent battle.

'That was some show,' said Tate, walking up to Kabel and Kron with Belina.

Kabel agreed, watching in awe the events in the sky. He then adjusted his gun at the side of his armour and hauled Gemma to her feet. Gemma was a little bruised but he saw the toughness in her and when they locked eyes they both knew they loved each other, all doubts gone.

Kron cleared his throat and Kabel flicked his eyes to him and saw the expectation in his gaze. Tate and Belina pulled their seckles from their belts and activated them. They were ready.

Kabel saw the remaining men look across to him for the next order. He may have been Lord Chancellor by name before but now he had earned the title by his actions. He pulled his seckle and activated both the seckle and his body shield as the charging Pod fighters tore into the retreating Xonians. His chest swelled with emotion and pride; they fought as one.

'Time to take this city. Remember the Oneerions are our allies but hunt the Xonians down, every last one of them,' Kabel yelled at the top of his voice. Kron smiled his wolfish smile and with Kabel leading them they charged towards the city across the remainder of the Skegus Plain with the sole purpose of victory.

Chapter 30: Fury

Tyson burst out of the lift, straight into a waiting squad of Ilsid, sent by Zylar to stop him. Tyson's energy was strongly coursing through him, he brought his seckle to block an attack by the nearest Ilsid and then he spun around and sank his seckle into the back of the soldier, killing him instantly.

Zebulon was not slow either, as he thrust his trident into one of the Ilsid and then clicked a switch and a wicked blade slid out of the bottom. He retracted the trident from the now dying Ilsid and stepped to one side to miss the falling body and then swung the trident so the sharp blade cut the arm off another soldier. One of his guards then finished the attack by driving his trident deep inside the body of the injured creature.

The fighting was intense and one of the Changelings took a fatal blow much to the anger of Zebulon and though Tyson was in a world of his own, he still had to marvel at the strength and skill of the Changeling.

'Tyson, over here.' It was Hechkle who was carrying an injured Bronstorm clutching his side. Only one of the US Marines had survived the ferocious fighting on the first floor and he was providing much needed cover for the pair.

Tyson ran across, forcing his temper down, almost swallowing it in his effort to control what was building up inside him. He grabbed the other arm of Bronstorm, and they helped him into the wide tunnel to the Transportation building, just at the time another squad of Ilsid entered the tunnel, blocking their way. Tyson could not see Zylar in the group facing him. That didn't matter. No one was going to stop him reaching his mother, whoever it was.

'Patch me up,' said Bronstorm to his friend. Hechkle hesitated initially. 'Do it, man, give me a Medicare pack.' His inaction over, Hechkle pulled one from one of his compartments in his armour and Bronstorm took it from him, tearing the cover off and then stuffing it down inside his armour where the wound was. Hechkle then helped him up.

Zebulon and the three remaining Changelings and the US Marine, whose name for the life of him Hechkle could not remember, dispatched the remaining first group of Ilsid. The tunnel was now littered with many bodies. The Ilsid at the far tunnel started to fire on them. The group crouched behind some marble garden tubs that had contained what had been flowing sycamore-like trees – now blasted to smithereens.

The lift opened and Morrison with the first load of prisoners piled out into the body-strewn corridor, immediately ordering the women with him to crouch as the lethal photon shots bounced off the walls. Morrison crawled to where the others were after sending some men to scan the corridors either side of the lift. He didn't want any surprises.

'We have all the prisoners, what is happening here?'

'Zylar escaped with my Mum and we will need to get though those soldiers in front of us,' said Tyson. Morrison accepted the position on the proviso they wait for the remaining prisoners. Tyson kicked the floor in frustration. It wasn't long before the second group exited the lift and immediately took defensive positions. Amelia waved to Tyson and received no response. Her boyfriend was focused on the obstruction preventing him rescuing his mother. Fear rose up inside her. She knew what that meant.

'Tyson! No,' said Amelia, just as Tyson's eyes went a bright blue and his face a cold pale grey. He stood up and advanced on the remaining Ilsid. They increased their fire but it simply bounced off Tyson's force-field. The cold fury took over. He had placed one of his seckles back into his armour and he stretched out his hand, almost in a dreamlike state.

'Everyone, avert your eyes,' shouted Bailey, knowing, like Amelia, what was to come.

Pure blue power pulsated from his fingertips, cascading into the Ilsid who all died horribly. The power sent windows and beams crashing to the floor. All the time Tyson stepped forward relentlessly. He dropped his hands and advanced on the twisted metal and bodies at the end of the corridor.

The final group of prisoners offloaded with the children taking advantage of the latest lull in fighting...the lull didn't last long.

'Watch out,' said Bailey, as Xonians entered one of the corridors to the left of the lift. The two SEALs there fought back.

'Quickly, into the tunnel,' shouted Bailey, grabbing hold of Delilah's arm and launching her into the tunnel, which now was their only escape.

The prisoners all ran and the remaining soldiers laid on the covering fire. Hechkle was the first to reach the end of the tunnel, just as Tyson stepped through into the Transportation building. There was a loud creak as one of the metal beams began to give away. Hechkle reached up and using all his considerable strength he braced his body against the beam.

Bronstorm saw the danger and hurried the survivors through the gap remaining as Hechkle took the strain. Morrison brought up the rear with the two remaining SEALs, most of his other men dead or dying. One of the men keeled over when a Xonian caught him with a shot.

Morrison went to help Hechkle, but the Fathom soldier shook his head, the strain showing on his face. The remaining SEAL was killed and Morrison realising the Xonians were streaming into the end of the corridor that they had just moved from, stepped through the gap.

Bronstorm was on the other side beckoning Hechkle to run.

'No, my friend, if this comes down the whole tunnel collapses. Get out of here now,' Hechkle pleaded with Bronstorm, just as a photon shot slammed into him, then another. Hechkle didn't utter a word, just grunted as the shots hit him and he gritted his teeth, as blood spread from his wounds. 'I didn't pull you out of that well to die here, remember your promise to look after Amelia,' he said, gasping for breath.

Bronstorm was beside himself, realising at this very moment how much he truly loved this man mountain. 'I will, I will, but...,' he said.

'Go.' Heckle cut him off. It was the last thing Bronstorm heard from his guardian and friend. Morrison grabbed hold of the protesting Bronstorm and pulled them both to safety as the steel girders crashed down onto Hechkle, sealing the tunnel and ending the life of the Fathom soldier.

Bronstorm was yelling for Hechkle and Morrison and one of the few remaining soldiers grabbed hold of him and half carried, half pulled him into the transportation room. There they were greeted by a sobering sight.

In the large transportation field there were the remnants of Zylar's force, probably around fifty men he had kept back, with no intention of leaving his hard-earned army ready to defend Quentine. A few moments ago the Ilsid were just about to be teleported when Tyson rushed in from the tunnel, followed by the rest of the group. Zylar grabbed Leila and was now ordering his men to attack, whilst holding Leila around her waist, with his other hand holding a seckle to her neck, a think pinprick of blood welling up beneath the point of the seckle where it cut into the soft and yielding flesh.

The Ilsid poured over the ramp and charged Tyson who stood there like a rock. There was an almighty explosion and the doors of the Transportation building from the street were blown open. There was intense fighting outside on the streets but Bailey saw Kabel, Tate, Belina and Kron at the forefront of the reinforcements. Half the Ilsid immediately peeled off to engage with this new threat, the others attacked Tyson.

In the main entrance from the street, Kron brought his barbed mace attached to his stump down on the arm of one of the Ilsid, smashing it in the process, and swung his favoured machete to sever the soldier's neck. He then launched his body into the midst of the attackers, ably supported by Tate and Belina. Gemma held back. When the main doors burst open she had seen that Zylar held Leila and was edging towards the console near the teleport. By skirting around the room hugging the walls she could approach Zylar from behind. He had not seen her, with his attention fixed on the explosive Tyson, who was swatting the Ilsid out of his way; the power building in him so much that Gemma had to shield her eyes from the brightness.

Zylar was fuming. He saw his children and prisoners in the hands of the humans and saw his vision of a master race slipping by. Tyson was closing the distance between them and the Ilsid who were unfortunate to be in his way suffered horrible deaths from the power emitting from the hybrid's body. Zylar saw a young woman run to Tyson's side with someone he also recognised from the battle at the Southern Palace. It was his human friend carrying a photon shotgun.

Zylar shifted his weight, slinging Leila to one side so as to free his gun arm. He didn't notice Gemma to his side until he realised someone was grabbing hold of Leila, wrenching her away from him.

He slashed downwards with the arm holding the seckle aiming for the young woman. Gemma saw the blow but was too slow and the seckle caught a glancing blow on her side of her head making her let go of Leila's arm. Leila was at the same time pulling away from Zylar, taking advantage of the loosened grip as his other hand was firing his photon gun at the mixture of Malacca and human troops.

Kabel saw Gemma take the hit from Zylar. With a roar he sliced through an Ilsid's chest and pushed him away from him as he raced towards Zylar, throwing his seckle at the head of his uncle. Leila had nearly freed herself from the grip of Zylar and for a minute he relaxed his grip further as his attention focused on the wickedly spinning seckle sent from Kabel. Zylar leaned back and the seckle spun past his neck and on its return to Kabel crashed into the chest of Bailey, cutting it deeply, before returning to its owner's grip. Bailey let out a scream of pain. Zylar shoved his seckle back under his armour and grabbed the wriggling Leila again, hauling her back from freedom.

When those that survived the battle looked back later no one really knew what happened. People remembered there was an almighty beam of energy emanating from

Tyson, causing Amelia and the injured Bailey to be thrown away from him like rag dolls. Amelia catapulted some fifty yards into the marble wall of the room before sliding down in a heap, motionless. Bailey was flung the opposite way, crashing into the US Marines streaming into the hanger. He laid stunned, blood seeping from his wound, barely conscious. The only one left standing within close distance of Tyson was Zebulon. His natural shield was active and he had pushed it outwards so everyone could see the low eerie light.

Zylar was also blasted backwards. Gemma, only momentarily dazed by the seckle, was on the floor and kept her head down when the blast came. While everyone was stumbling around dazed Gemma took her opportunity by grabbing the half conscious Leila and dragging her away from the console.

'Lie here, Leila, you will be safe, I have to see how Amelia is,' whispered Gemma to the near unconscious Leila, glancing across the room at the inert figure of her best friend. Leila half mumbled, half shook her head in answer. Gemma left her position and was running past the console next to the transportation portal when a hand snaked out and grabbed her ankle, causing her to fall awkwardly. Zylar hauled his body up and realising it was Kabel's sweetheart grabbed the winded young woman, who immediately fought back.

'What is it with you humans, do you not know when to stop fighting?' he said, before slamming his pistol onto her head. Gemma blacked out. He pressed the final coordinates and hauled Gemma's inert body into the force-field and the zinithium crystals flared up and in a moment he had gone.

Tyson was out of control, his body pulsating with power, those not injured by his blast kept back by the raw power. Zebulon wrapped one of his arms around his waist and

Tyson fought back, sending beams of light into Zebulon, who remarkably, took everything that Tyson could send at him. He spread the fingers of his other hand over the head of Tyson and the power began to pulsate into Zebulon. It was like the Changeling was sucking in the magics.

Indeed, this was what he was doing; the energy entered into Zebulon, mixing with the innate magics he had. He both revelled in was repulsed by the magic but held on. The power dulled and then was extinguished from Tyson, who fell to the ground, his body ravaged. With his eyes half closed he saw Zebulon join with the other surviving Changelings and share the dangerous magics as they tried to eject it from their bodies, something they eventually did.

Tyson's vision was blurred and his memory poor. He saw the damaged body of Amelia, crushed against the wall and the medics trying to revive Bailey. He didn't know whether his mother was saved or if his other friends had survived. He fell into an uneasy unconsciousness.

Chapter 31: Real Life

Tyson's eyes flickered open and straight away he was staring into a pair of eyes set in a familiar face. A gentle hand was pushing a flannel across his face. He opened his eyes fully.

'Hi Tyson, son, you are on the *Elanda*,' said Leila and Tyson couldn't hold back his delight at seeing his mother. His body may hurt and his insides felt all churned up but to see his mother safe and well was worth it. He reached up and they hugged.

'Where is Amelia?' he asked. He saw the answer in her face and feared the worse.

'When you,' Leila searched for the right words, 'exploded she took a bad knock. She is still alive,' she hastily added as the alarm spread across her son's face. 'She is in a medically induced coma to see if she will recover with rest.'

Tyson grimaced. It was entirely his fault, if only he could master the magics.

He remembered something else, 'Bailey?' Leila shook her head and then seeing the crestfallen look on his face realised that she had given the wrong message to her son.

'He is in intensive care; he lost an awful amount of blood.' Tyson still looked worried and she reassured him he would be fine with rest.

'What happened?' Tyson remembered feeling the magics build up inside him and remembered the anger bursting forward. Then all other memories of the battle were gone.

Leila took him through the events, how Zebulon had acted when he saw the magics consuming him and had used his ability to remove the magics to stabilise Tyson. She told him that a man called Hechkle had died saving them. Tyson closed his eyes in grief and then asked after Bronstorm knowing the man would also be distraught. Leila confirmed he had struggled to come to terms with it but the others had rallied around him.

Tyson thought back to Hechkle, remembering the big man fondly and Leila let him absorb the news, knowing other questions would be coming…and there it was. She saw Tyson's eyes widen as he realised what she had said initially about the magics.

'So I have no magics now?' said a relieved Tyson.

'Not quite,' said another voice in the room. Tyson looked across the room and saw the cat curled up on a chair. The cat jumped off the seat and metamorphosed into Zebulon.

Leila stepped away and Zebulon walked to the side of the bed.

'I have removed the magics as best I could but I have never seen or felt anything like it, the power was incredible,' said Zebulon, shaking his head in wonderment. 'You should have no abilities left but I cannot be certain.

'How did you do that?' asked Tyson, searching for the magics within him and finding nothing. He felt just stone cold relief.

'I can absorb magics and it does not harm me but flows out of my body into the surrounding environment,' said Zebulon, still shaking his head. 'But I have never seen so much power in one individual. It was wrapped around your body like a coiled spring.'

Tyson tried to get up but he was too weak and after protesting slumped back into bed. His thoughts drifted to Amelia and Bailey, guilt assaulting him. Leila moved back to the side of his bed as Zebulon left, knowing she needed to be there. She would stay with him for a little longer before checking on the women and children rescued. They were now placed in a number of rooms on the tenth floor of the ship, with good food, bedding and medical treatment. Leila had popped in earlier and it was good to see them laugh and experience freedom. They had grown close to her. They also knew that for now her attention must be on Tyson.

Kabel remained on Skegus with General Corder to meet with King Yi and agree new trade agreements with Zein and Earth. It was agreed that the Expeditionary Force would help with the retaking of Oneerio post the completion of any repairs. Once Tate heard the negotiations were complete and Kabel had returned from Skegus, he went to find him. Tate found him on one of the observation decks of the *Elanda* gazing morosely out of the window at the rapid rebuilding of Reinan.

'Zylar has Gemma then?' said Tate, just as Belina joined them from one of her many hours seeing to the injured. She ignored Tate, walking right up to the pensive looking Kabel and placing her arm around her brother, who in turn appreciated the comfort.

'Yes, but we have managed to find out where he has gone,' said Kabel. They had tracked the coordinates to a landing pad outside Quentine that had held the destroyers provided by the Xonians. They had rapidly left the Capulus Novus System and Kabel was informed that an analysis of their trajectory and direction of travel gave a good indication of where they were heading.

'He has gone back to your Earth?' guessed Tate. He had heard many stories about this land and he was intrigued by a planet that could have over six billion people living upon it.

'Yes, he has my Gemma and he has to die and I will do it. Not Tyson, not you but I will see the life ebb out of his eyes for what he has done.' said Kabel, his anger flashing in his eyes. Both Tate and Belina did not doubt him. The Lord Chancellor cast a formidable figure as he gazed out of the window, his back ramrod straight and at that point Belina struggled to tell him apart from Tyson. They were truly brothers, driven by a destiny written for them with no clear ending. She could only do what a sister could do and stand silently with him as his thoughts drifted to another planet and an uncle whom he would hunt down to his very last breath.

Chapter 32: Epilogue

It took a few days for Tyson to be sufficiently well enough to drag his complaining body out of the Medicare bed. The first thing he did was to seek out Amelia. She was in a room close to his and when he first saw her motionless body lying on a similar bed he had been lying upon, his stomach lurched and he felt sick. A nurse was taking some tests and on seeing Tyson enter, quietly placed the vials of a blood test on a tray and carried them out of the room. He caught a glimpse of his face in his mirrored reflection on one of the side cabinets and was surprised to see brown eyes staring back at him.

He sat down and took her arm, which was warm to his touch, taking in the array of tubes and monitors connected to the girl he loved and nearly killed. Amelia's peaceful face looked back up at him and he rationalised that she was one girl who would look beautiful whatever condition she was in. He bowed his head, tears welling inside him, the guilt too much to take. He sat there for some time with his cheek against her arm and in the warmth of the room he must have dozed and slipped into one of his many dreams.

He was in his home town, a cold day with a morning mist, walking arm in arm with Amelia, in the company of Kabel and Gemma, across an empty municipal golf course. They were laughing and larking around and then the laughter ended and darkness seemed to descend. The group tensed, peering through the mist. It was Tyson who saw him.

Zylar was there almost like a ghost, gloating, and Tyson expected the rage to come from Kabel or him, but instead it came from Gemma. Tyson was holding her back, struggling, then they all fell in a tumble of arms and legs as Zylar's dark shadow cast its net over them.

Tyson woke up and frantically looked round as if he expected Zylar to be in the room with him. He saw that he was still holding Amelia's hand. The vision had shaken him, why was he back in his home town, what was Zylar doing there? His eyes flashed across the still body of Amelia. Did that mean Amelia would pull out of this coma? He knew that some of his visions were nothing but wishful thinking.

He felt useless, impotent. His grip on Amelia's hand tightened and he closed his eyes, the anger at how she had been hurt by his magics hitting him hard, his emotions in overdrive…he did not hear the slight crackle or see the small spark as a bright blue tendril emitted from his fingers.

The End

Appendix:
Clans and Key Figures

Blackstone Clan

The Blackstone clan led the Zeinonians away from slavery. This ensured the enshrinement in Zein Law that they would have the right to appoint a Lord or Lady Chancellor from their royal ranks. They brokered the deal for the use of "magics" from the Changelings under the suspicion from other clans that they obtained greater powers. The Prophecy is thought to be the destiny of one with Blackstone royal blood. Their principal magics are the ability to see in the future, telepathy and great speed, the latter enabling them to watch others movements in slow motion enabling them to act swiftly. Key figures and others:

Earth Colony

- Lord Logan Blackstone: Lord Chancellor of the Zein Earth Colony prior to attack by Zylar on the Southern Quadrant. Husband of Melissa Blackstone and father of Kabel and Belina Blackstone. Died from poisoned wounds from an Ilsid attack.
- Lady Melissa Blackstone: wife of Logan Blackstone and mother of Kabel and Belina Blackstone. Died when fleeing a Zylar attack in the Southern Quadrant. Former princess of the Southgate clan.

- Egan Blackstone (Zylar): brother of Logan Blackstone and uncle of Kabel and Belina Blackstone. Adopted the name Zylar, who wants to convert all clan magics to the "One Way" – which darkens the soul and unleashes power but also hate and madness.

- Kabel Blackstone: son of Logan and Melissa Blackstone rescued from certain death by General Malkin and raised by the Wheatstones in the Western Quadrant. Half-brother to Tyson Mountford. Hopes rest on him to lead the Zein people.

- Belina Blackstone: daughter of Logan Blackstone and sister of Kabel Blackstone. Taken as a baby by Egan Blackstone when he killed her mother, Melissa Blackstone, and raised in the Eastern Quadrant. Rescued by her brother and others during the attack on the communications mast.

- Morgan Blackstone: father to Logan Blackstone. Grandfather to Kabel and Belina Blackstone who led the Zein Expeditionary Force to Earth over 100 years ago.

- Prince Anton Blackstone: son of Egan Blackstone, nephew of Logan Blackstone, – killed by the Ilsid in the attack on the Southern Quarter Palace.

- General Malkin: Head of the Blackstone Royal Guard and named "Teacher" for Kabel Blackstone as he grew up in the Western Quadrant. Protector of the Royal Blackstones.

- Remo Shanks: Officer of the Gate (Southern Quadrant Palace). Senior officer in the Blackstone Royal Guard, tough, experienced and never say die attitude.

- General Jika Chad: served with Remo Shanks within the Blackstone Royal Guard. Mercenary who joined Zylar as his right hand man. Killed in the Eastern Quadrant Palace during the attack on the communication mast.

- Lieutenant Anders: young soldier killed whilst defending the attack on the Southern Quadrant Palace with Remo Shanks.
- Lieutenant Lavelle: Communication Officer on the *Elanda*
- Zachary Harris: Navigator on the *Elanda*.

Zein

- Lord Ricken Blackstone: previous Lord Chancellor and husband to Safah Blackstone. Father to Jaida Blackstone.
- Lady Safah Blackstone: wife of Ricken Blackstone. Mother of Jaida Blackstone who relinquished her right to be Lady Chancellor when her husband was killed in a Pod attack.
- Jaida Blackstone: sultry daughter of Safah Blackstone who has had relationships with both Taio Southgate and Tate Malacca. Skilled fighter.
- Bertrand Mallory: junior officer, communications runner in the famous Battle for the Aeria Cavern.
- Lady Cilan Blackstone: historical figure who led the Zeinonians from the repression of the Xonians and first colonised Zein.

Malacca Clan

They are a warrior clan, who provide one of the largest armies, along with the Blackstone clan. There is a long standing feud with the Blackstone clan due to their lower standing in history which influences them to side with renegade, Egan Blackstone (Zylar). Not overly prosperous, the riches of the Core are an attraction. There principal magics are the ability to feel or recognise strength of magics and can levitate their bodies. Key figures and others:

Earth Colony:
- Lord Barkley Malacca: father of Manek Malacca and working with Zylar. Vicious and has dreams of dominating Earth and Zein. Befriended and brutally killed the late Lord and Lady Tyther and their family. Killed in the Battle for the Core.
- Manek Malacca: son of Barkley Malacca and just as vicious as his father. Killed in the Battle for the Core.
- Cronje: Head of the Malacca Army who is a principled and experienced fighter who follows orders. Leads the defence of the Core against the Fathom Army and Tyson Blackstone. Becomes Vice-Chancellor to Lord Chancellor Kabel Blackstone in The Earth's Inner Council.
- Reddash: second-in-command in the Malacca Army and reports into Cronje.
- Milano: housemaid and long term friend to Belina Blackstone in The Eastern Quadrant Palace. Treacherous and is killed when she leads the friends into a trap.
- Chet: Eastern Quadrant soldier who guards the prisoners and is killed.
- Morgan: Eastern Quadrant soldier who guards the prisoners and is killed.
- Linus: Malacca soldier on the *Elanda*.

Zein
- Lord Lambert Malacca: Lord Chancellor of Zein killed in a Pod attack. Husband to Darya Malacca and father to Tate Malacca.

- Lady Darya Malacca: mother of Tate Malacca, strong reliable sensible.
- Lord Chancellor Tate Malacca: son of Lord Lambert and Darya Malacca who has stepped into the main role as protector of the Aeria Cavern. Skilled fighter.
- Captain Kron: seasoned fighter, used to follow Lord Lambert Malacca but now second-in-command to Tate Malacca. Has an injury to his arm and eye from the frequent Pod attacks.
- Clancy: soldier for Zylar who is appointed to guard Leila Mountford and the other human prisoners on Zylar's ship and also in Quentine.

Southgate Clan

Historically the Southgate clan are strong supporters of the Blackstone clan. Politically astute clan, who support their prosperity by utilising their ability for compromise and negotiation. They have formed militias rather than run a large army. They are the last quadrant conquered by Zylar and hold the protection of the young Blackstone royal blood in their hands. Their principal magic is the ability to leap great distances. Key figures and others:

Earth

- Lord Edgar Southgate: leader of the Southgate clan in the Western Quadrant and most senior lord after the Blackstone clan. Husband to Lucinda Southgate and father to Melissa Blackstone. Grandfather of Kabel and Belina Blackstone.
- Lady Lucinda Southgate: wife of Lord Southgate and mother to Melissa Blackstone. Grandmother of Kabel and Belina Blackstone.

- Hilal Wheatstone: guardian to Kabel Blackstone whilst he was growing up. Part of the Inner Council in the Western Quadrant and killed when Zylar invaded with his Ilsid.
- Maggia Wheatstone: guardian, mother to Kabel Blackstone whilst he was growing up – a healer.
- Philander Wheatstone: sister of Maggia Wheatstone. Aunt to Delilah and Drogan Wheatstone.
- Drogan Wheatstone: son of Hilal and Maggia Wheatstone. Bother to Delilah Wheatstone and adopted brother of Kabel Blackstone. Recorder for the Inner Council of the Western Quadrant. Killed when Zylar invaded with his Ilsid
- Delilah Wheatstone: daughter of Hilal and Maggia Wheatstone. Sister of Drogan Wheatstone. Adopted sister of Kabel Blackstone, kidnapped by Zylar to tempt Kabel to follow.
- Elder Vois: respected member of the Western Quadrant Inner Council who is killed during the invasion by Zylar and the Ilsid.
- Elder Barthelme: member of the Western Quadrant Inner Council and a supporter of Lord Malacca.

Zein

- Lord Eben Southgate: grandfather to Taio Southgate and influential member of the Aeria Cavern Inner Council.
- Taio Southgate: grandson of Eben Southgate, fiery and at odds with Tate Malacca. Husband of Cadence Southgate. Vain as much as he is fiery.
- Cadence Southgate: sister of Eva and Mia Fathom, wife of Taio Southgate, formerly a Fathom who married Taio Southgate when her father was killed in a Pod attack.

Tyther Clan

The Tyther clan are the designers and architects of the city villages and skilled users of the advanced technology. They pride themselves in being the best in the Universe, although the Oneerions would challenge that. Their senior ranks are made up of hard working and pragmatic men and women. They have a small ceremonial Royal Guard only. Their main magic is the ability to change their height which enables them to build and construct in different environments. Key figures and others:

Earth Colony

- Lord Benjamin Tyther: father to Gwen, Titus and Hector Tyther. Killed brutally by Barkley Malacca.
- Lady Sarah Tyther: mother to Gwen, Titus and Hector Tyther. Killed brutally by Barkley Malacca.
- Gwen Tyther: young daughter of Benjamin and Sarah Tyther. Suffered the same fate as her parents.
- Titus Tyther: young son of Benjamin and Sarah Tyther. Suffered the same fate as his parents.
- Hector Tyther: new arrival, baby of Benjamin and Sarah Tyther. Suffered the same fate as his parents.

Zein

- Lord Quinlan Tyther: senior Lord – Hard worker and engineer. Father to Kingsley and Brisis Tyther.
- Aaila Tyther: wife of Quinlan, killed in a Pod attack. Mother to Brisis and Kingsley Tyther.
- Kingsley Tyther: son of Quinlan Tyther - young, headstrong and wants to be a warrior rather than an engineer
- Brisis Tyther: older daughter of Lord Quinlan Tyther. Honest and hardworking.

Fathom Clan

The Fathom clan are the merchants and miners of Zein. They have considerable skill in mining zinithium and the use of the powerful raw material. They excel in business and are the richest clan. They have a very capable smaller professional army to protect them in the Core. Their principal magics are the ability to change their shape and also their fighting instincts. Key figures and others:

Earth Colony

- Lord Gregory Fathom: respected leader of the Fathom clan who rules over the mining colony in the Core. Father to Evelyn Fathom.
- Princess Evelyn Fathom: fiery young woman who is the daughter of Riley Fathom. She falls for Tyson before Zylar kills her in the Battle of the Southern Palace.
- Elder Elme Polter: member of the Fathom Inner Council and a respected Elder.
- Hechkle: warrior in the Fathom Royal Guard. Strong and fierce. Looks after the welfare of the younger warrior, Bronstorm.
- Bronstorm: warrior in the Fathom Royal Guard. Young, quick and a master of all weapons. Rescued by Hechkle as a boy and fiercely protective of the older man.
- Corporal Anders Riley: supports Hechkle and Bronstorm in the fight of the Lower Town in the Battle for the Core.
- Dante: Fathom clan soldier selected for attack on the Eastern Quadrant Palace. Dies in the ensuing battle.
- Grampian: Fathom clan soldier selected for attack on the Eastern Quadrant Palace. Dies in the ensuing battle.

- Stern: Corporal in the Fathom Royal Palace Guard who is part of the team who are successful in the retaking of Base Station Zebra and then falls at the hand of Manek Malacca.
- Dart: Private in the Fathom Royal Palace Guard who is killed in the battle in Base Station Zero.

Zein

- Eva Fathom: teenage sister of Cadence who looks after her. Fiery and similar to the late Evelyn Fathom on Earth Colony. Tyson and the Fathom soldiers, Bronstorm and Hechkle protect her.
- Mia Fathom: younger sister of Cadence and Eva.

Other Key Figures

Humans

- Tyson Mountford: son to Leila Mountford and Logan Blackstone making him a "half-breed". Troubled by the magics and is torn between Amelia Briggs and Gemma Carpenter. Half-brother to Kabel Blackstone.
- Bailey Carpenter: best friend of Tyson Mountford, strong, loyal and boyfriend to Belina Blackstone. Brother to Gemma Carpenter.
- Gemma Carpenter: sister to Bailey Carpenter and is attracted to both Kabel Blackstone and Tyson Mountford. Goth and rebellious teenager with martial arts skills. Best friends with Amelia Briggs.
- Amelia Briggs: daughter of rich and mainly absent parents. Attractive girl with fighting spirit who

Tyson Mountford falls in love with. Best friend to Gemma Carpenter and unaware of her friend's feelings for Tyson Mountford.

- Leila Mountford: mother to Tyson Mountford who had a relationship with Logan Blackstone. Kidnapped by Egan Blackstone in the Battle of the Southern Palace. Strong minded woman who looks after the other kidnapped humans.
- Michael Dunstable: United Kingdom Prime Minister who has strong professional relationship with Victoria Kirk. Married with two children and is killed by Egan Blackstone.
- Victoria Kirk: British Defence Minister and appointed Head of Zeinonian Support.
- Charles Hamilton: United Kingdom Deputy Prime Minister, intelligent man who builds a strong relationship with Edgar Southgate. Appointed United Kingdom Prime Minister after the death of Michael Dunstable.
- Walter Moore: scientist who recognises the Zein Earth Colony first and becomes the lead scientist for the Joint Expeditionary Force. Known as "Boff".
- Sean Lambert: Corporal in the Scots Guards and supports the attack on the Southern Quadrant Palace. He builds strong friendship with Kabel Blackstone and Tyson Mountford, skilful and experienced fighter.
- Xin: Corporal in the Chinese Army and expert in demolition and explosives.
- Sir Daniel Clifton: most senior British Army member of COBRA and Chief of Staff of all United Kingdom Armed Forces.
- Brigadier Michael Flintoff-Jones: Selected to lead the attack of the joint force on the Southern Quadrant Palace. He is killed in the battle.

- General Prescott Corder: leader of the Joint Expeditionary Task Force on the Elanda. He is an experienced, plain speaking American, who antagonises Kabel Blackstone and Tyson Mountford.
- Air Marshall General Nicolai Koshkov: second-in-command of the Joint Expeditionary Force on the *Elanda*. Hard-bitten veteran of the Russian Federation Black Sea Fleet who is at odds with General Corder and who is potentially an ally of the Zeinonians.
- Lieutenant Anton Morrison: General Corder's right hand man on the *Elanda*. A good fighter who is suspicious of the Zeinonians but develops his relationship fighting alongside them on Zein and Skegus.
- Colonel Jeffries: US Air force and commander of the *Brooklyn*.
- Henry Lampole: pompous Minister for Department of Energy and Climate Change.
- Yuri: Private in the Russian Federation who is stationed to guard the mobile nuclear weapons in the Ural Mountains in Russia.
- Captain Andropov: officer in charge of the mobile nuclear weapons in the Ural Mountains.
- Captain Chuck Grenoble: officer in charge of the nuclear submarine USS *Louisiana*.
- Lieutenant Chris Grayling: senior officer on the nuclear submarine USS *Louisiana*.
- Lieutenant Michaels: junior officer on the nuclear submarine USS *Louisiana* and the *Elanda*.
- Commander Waldo Peck: officer in charge of the nuclear submarine HMS *Vengeance*.
- Lieutenant Manning: Junior office on the nuclear Trident submarine HMS *Vengeance*.

- Colonel Travers: US Marine and senior officer of the Inner Council.
- Corporal Mike Batten: US Army radar specialist on the *Elanda*.
- Megan: British girl kidnapped by Zylar and mother to hybrid child called Hanna.
- Devra: Jewish girl kidnapped by Zylar and mother of hybrid child called Adira.
- Shannon: Irish girl kidnapped by Zylar and mother of hybrid child called Cian.
- Grace Connor: Administrative support on the *Elanda*.
- Josh Mulligan: Mid-twenties American man caught up in the attack on New York. Boyfriend of Amber.
- Amber: Mid-twenties American girl caught up on the attack on New York. Girlfriend of Josh Mulligan.

Pod

- Festilion: Queen of the Pod and High Priestess of Zein. Mother to Dominion.
- Redulon: Head Royal Protector of Festilion's personal guard and councillors.
- Dominion: warrior leader of Pod and father to Dominion. Festilion is his mother.
- Wernion: son of Dominion from Festilion who makes contact with Tyson during his incarnation with the Pod. Husband to Hersion.
- Hersion: Wife of Wernion.

Changelings

- Zebulon: The Great, Holder of the Zein Star and King of all life on Zein. Friend to Kabel and the companions, son of Heathlon and Riolon. Wants to bring peace to Zein. Older brother to Myolon.

- Heathlon: High Priestess of the Changelings and mother to Zebulon and mate to Riolon.
- Riolon: The All Powerful and father to Zebulon and Myolon and mate to Heathlon.
- Myolon: Brother of Zebulon, son of Heathlon and Riolon. Keen to eradicate the Pod from Zein.

Oneerions
- Yi: King of Oneerio, father of Yian and has concubine called Gi. Skilled in masonry and all crafts.
- Gi: concubine of Yi and mother to Yian.
- Yian: Prince of Oneerio, young son of Yi and Gi.
- Kian: trusted communications operator in Quentine supporting Leila Mountford.
- Tian: one of the few remaining Oneerions still on Zein who advises the Lord Chancellor.

Xonians
- Jernli: Prince of Xonia who is keen to demonstrate his value to the Xonian Empire.
- Yisli: Commander of Capulus Sector Xonian forces.
- Maeli: second-in-command to Yisli.

Lightning Source UK Ltd.
Milton Keynes UK
UKOW04f0622080715

254745UK00002B/24/P